A CINDERELLA RETELLING

ROOK DI GOO

THE WAR ON TARAS: BOOK 1

JENNI SAUER

ROOK DI GOO

© 2020 by Jenni Sauer

Published by Ivorypalacepress.com

Cover art by Ireen Chau at www.ireenchau.wixsite.com/website

Interior Design by Savannah Jezowski at www.dragonpenpress.com

ISBN: 978-1-7345096-1-8

Printed in the United States of America.

PRONUNCIATION GUIDE

CHARACTERS

ALARIC— al-uh-RICK

ANARA BELLATRIX—ah-NAR-uh BELL-uh-trix

BEHNAM—BEH-num

CALLINGER—CALL-in-juhr

CARRIGAN—CAIR-uh-gihn

DIZARA ANALI—diz-AR-uh AN-all-ee

ELISANDRA—el-ih-SAHN-druh

HALLAH—HOHL-uh

JARRETT—JAIR-et

LEIV—LAYV

MAREN—MAIR-uhn

URIAN—YUR-ee-un

Planets and Places

ADERYN—ad-uh-RIN

ALISETH—al-ih-SETH

ALVAR—al-VAHR

CYRENE—sah-REEN

ELASSI—uh-LASS-ee

ELIALECH—uh-LIE-uh-lech

LIOSA/LIOSI—LEE-oh-sah/LEE-oh-see

MAHSIRIAN—mah-SEER-ee-in

PHILOSANTHRON/PHILOSANTHRIAN—phil-oh-SAN-thrun/phil-oh-SAN-three-un

RESNA—RES-nuh

TARAS/TARISIAN—tair-IS/tuh-ree-SHUN

VERCENTII—ver-SEHN-tee

VERONIAN—vur-OH-nee-uhn

To all those who fight their own private wars,
each and every day.
You are strong and you are able
and you will get through even this.
And to those who are searching for their home.
Know that someday it will find you,
and it will be worth the wait.

ROOK
DI
GOO

JENNI SAUER

PART I

"Another lesson to be taken from [The Battle of Calphalite Falls] is that while courage, persistence, and unfettered tenacity are key in the winning of a battle, they mean nothing if not accompanied by an unwavering obedience to those over you. The disobeying of orders has shaped the course of many a battle and even a war, shown nowhere better than the battle in discussion here."

Excerpt from *Morals from the History of War* by
Seraphina Van Laar

CHAPTER 1

CADET ELIS NEEDED sleep.

As she stepped from the doctor's office onto the crowded street of Cyrene, she knew the wisest course of action would be to return to the barracks. After four long months of recovering from a gunshot wound, she'd finally been given a clean bill of health and had completed a mental assessment; she was officially cleared to return to duty.

Duty. She pushed back the images that came with that word, the things she'd done well beyond the call of it. Her chest grew tight as she drew in a shaky breath, pulling at the collar of the green jacket of her uniform.

She wouldn't actually receive her orders until tomorrow, but she knew what they would be.

Return to duty meant returning to Taras.

The street was filled with people, the buildings crowding in on each other seeming to draw all the closer as she sucked in a breath, but the air didn't want to reach her lungs. She sucked in another as she turned toward the direction of the barracks.

But even though she was tired, she knew she wouldn't actually sleep. Four months gave her a lot of time to think—too much—and all she did when she laid down was remember, the memories creeping up on her no matter how hard she tried to keep them at bay. Besides, going back to her cot had a finality about it that she wasn't quite ready to give in to.

She turned around, starting in the other direction. She needed to be back at the hospital before curfew but that was several hours away, giving her plenty of time for a walk. It was a good way to keep herself from thinking while also tiring herself out. The perfect combination these days.

As she walked, she took in the sights around her; familiar—the cramped buildings, the crowded street. The smells of spice and earth and musk were so like Liosa and yet so different, the scent a bittersweet reminder of what was not; the subdued colors, the muted browns and grays, unlike the lush greens and blues and oranges of home; the buildings of metal and wood made her miss the stone structures, the flat landscape so unlike the cliff sides and rainforests of her own planet.

The people were a mix of races—Cyrene was advertised as a melting pot, but most knew it to be a dumping ground. Natives, war refugees, soldiers, businessmen, and all manner of characters of shady intent had made the place their home or temporary stopping off place. The buildings were mostly shabbily thrown together—popup buildings put up in haste to serve their purpose in the moment, with no thought or care for whether they withstood in the future.

It had once been a thriving planet, the pictures predating the war filled with the beauty and pride of its people. It had since become nothing more than drab, muted photos used for war propaganda.

No. She didn't want to think about the war. She pushed back images that came of burning buildings, the fire so real she could smell it, accompanied by the helpless screams and pleading for mercy.

But she wasn't sure who had actually received the mercy begged for—those whose lives ended in that agony or those who'd survived only to face the horrors to come.

She picked up her pace, walking faster. She made it through the housing and business districts, moving to the docks without meaning to.

She found herself in front of the departure roster, the grimy screen flickering with ship names, departure times, and destinations. There were so many of them crammed onto the little screen, running on a rotation, that she was glad she wasn't the air control officer.

But it also meant there were so many ways off the planet. So many places to go. She could pick any destination and there was probably a ship headed for there sometime within the next twenty-four hours.

That was probably about how long she had until she shipped out again. Twenty-four hours and she'd be on her way to Taras.

Unless she left before that.

The thought was there in her head before she knew it, and she had no idea where it came from. She started to push it back, to shake it away, to bury it somewhere deep inside of her. What she was thinking about doing was treason.

She was a soldier. She'd made a vow to her planet, swearing it on her life—*rook di goo*. There was no room for anything else in her mind.

But it was a game, she told herself, just a fun game and nothing more. She'd indulge in the fantasy a moment before she came back to reality.

Obviously, she would want to go somewhere that didn't have an alliance with Liosa because that would mean there were extradition agreements. So that ruled out three planets.

The Federation seemed like the best choice, though their rulers were elected officials in a democracy rather than inheriting the title through a monarchy, and that seemed strange to her. But if that was the price she had to pay, so be it.

But which planet within the Federation was another matter altogether.

She didn't know much about some of the individual states, so she ruled those out completely. Of the others, she considered what she knew of them carefully.

Mulling over the scenery of each, she was displeased with what she knew of them—but then, would she ever find a place with enough trees to suit her? She also weighed out the military figures each planet had produced; though none could rival the genius of her own people, it would be nice to find a home among strong, fierce individuals.

But in the end, the planet that drew her attention most was Elialech. It was a mysterious planet, one that seemed easy to lose oneself in. It didn't have the damp humidity of Liosa but it had the trees and the lush greens and blues and sporadic pops of color from home. She thought she could trade a jungle for a forest, maybe not quite happily but close enough.

The decision had been made and she stood there a moment, not quite sure what to do with that notion. She had so easily decided to give up her planet for another, a good part of her ready to swap out the one for the other, as if Liosa weren't the very heart of her; as if the Liosi blood pumping through her veins was not, in fact, her very life.

She shook her head because no, she couldn't think like that. She couldn't actually consider any of that.

It was just a game, nothing more.

She turned, turned to go back the way she had come, back to reality and the responsibilities that lived there. She couldn't live on dreams and fantasy.

But resolving to return brought back the memories in a wave: razed buildings, fire—so much fire, the smell of smoke that clung to everything, an unnatural scent caused by the burning of things never meant to burn. And then there were the survivors.

There was war and there was what happened in Taras, and she knew the two to be very different things.

She couldn't go back. The very thought of returning, of being forced to do what she had done before, sent a rush of panic through her. The emotion—one she had never felt before she'd gone to Taras—had since become her constant companion.

Her legs wobbled under her as she turned to return to the barracks, refusing to take the steps that she commanded it to take. Even her own body had betrayed her.

Or had it? Perhaps it was simply more willing to admit what she was afraid to.

She told herself just a few minutes more on her walk, turning and heading further into the docking district. Past all the ships—in every state from new to falling apart and everything in between. Some of the fancier docking stations—like those on Philosanthron—had a screen beside each ship that announced the departure time and destination so you could see things like the pictures of the interior and read crew bios without actually having to talk to a crewmember.

But it wasn't a fancy docking station with that information provided and so El was left to wonder each one's story—where they were going and who was on them and when they were leaving and if they would ever return. Did they, too, have a place they called home that they wondered if they would ever see again? Did they see Cyrene as somewhere to miss or was it nothing more than a stopping off point in a much longer journey?

Where were they going? And were those places merely part of their wanderings, or did they have ones they loved waiting for them? Did they remain detached and uninterested in each place they went, or did they leave a piece of themselves behind whenever they left a place?

She continued to walk, pleased with her line of thought, as it was so much more pleasant than the things that had filled her mind for the last several months or more.

It was then that she came upon it—the *Aderyn*.

The name was painted on the side of the ship by the gangplank in a wilted, faded blue-gray. Made of gray metal, dingy and worn from obvious years of use, it was the sorriest looking ship the cadet had ever seen in her life. That didn't surprise her, given that the model hadn't been manufactured in the last twenty years. She guessed it might even be older than that, though she had little to base her guess on that wasn't mere speculation.

There was much she was schooled in, but the names and type of every ship in the galaxy wasn't one of them.

The gangplank was down, open and inviting, as if begging her to come inside. The thing was a bit rusty and rundown, but it looked sturdy and strong all the same. It reminded her of a bit of Liosa—obviously having been through a lot and showing clear signs of it, but still going strong with no chance of that changing any time soon.

But the Liosi were not ones to wander, preferring their own homes and people to experiencing others'.

"Did you need something?"

She jumped at the voice, realizing she had lost herself in thought for the second time today. She needed to stop before it became a habit.

Coming up behind her was a tall man, a scowl that looked as if perhaps it rested there permanently on his face. His complexion was not quite as dark as her own, tanned perhaps from the sun rather than heritage and history.

Besides the scowl, he wore a long beige jacket, like a Mahsirian—though his skin was darker than those of that race—as well as a shirt of deep red untucked from a pair of black trousers. Just the toes of his black boots stuck out from the hem, weathered and scuffed but shiny enough to show they had been polished somewhat recently. She had a lot of respect for a man who cared for his boots, even a pair as worn as these were.

His arms were folded across his chest as he continued to scowl at her expectantly, waiting for an answer. She opened her mouth to tell him she had just been admiring his ship but stopped herself short.

After a moment he sighed, understanding crossing his face. "You're the soldier they sent to assist us, aren't you?"

"I beg your pardon?"

He rolled his eyes like the entire conversation was beneath him. "I really need to get my ship off the ground so I'm only going to repeat this once. We're taking off now, so if your orders are to be on this ship, get on. Otherwise, get left behind, got it?"

She opened her mouth to tell him that he had her confused with someone else but stopped herself. He was looking for a soldier. A Liosi soldier.

And she was looking for a way to avoid going back to Taras.

She couldn't go back, couldn't face those demons again. Maybe she'd even learn to start sleeping through the night again.

It should have been harder to decide whether or not one was going to be a traitor, but she found herself saying the words before she could keep them back: "Yes, sir, I'm Cadet Elis reporting for duty."

She was grateful once again she had a title, a rank, rather than a name; she was grateful she didn't have to give him her name.

The man just rolled his eyes, like even what she had given him was more than he needed. "Great. Now get on board."

CHAPTER 2

EL FOLLOWED THE man up the gangplank, not sure what she was doing. It was as if her body moved of its own accord, and she didn't have the willpower to stop it.

Or perhaps that was simply what she told herself—that she had no control over her actions. Perhaps that made it easier to commit treason.

She cast a glance over her shoulder, sure she would see a flash of green and brass, a uniformed soldier come to stop her then and there.

There was only one penalty for desertion in Liosa.

The Captain would be really ticked then, she couldn't help thinking, given that it would delay his departure further. Plus then there would be blood on his gangplank.

"I'm Captain Behnam, by the way," he said as they stepped into the cargo bay.

Behnam. So he was Mahsirian after all. She supposed that would explain his ship, though not why he'd be working with a Liosi soldier. The Mahsirian were nomadic people with loyalty and allegiance to themselves only. They didn't get involved in the politics of the galaxy around them.

She didn't quite believe the tales of Mahsirian magic, she wasn't that superstitious. But it wouldn't hurt to be cautious.

He slammed down on a button at the side of the wide doorway and the room filled with a whirring sound, shaking as the gangplank began to draw itself up and seal them in. It was too loud for her to say anything in response to the Captain's introduction, though there honestly wasn't anything to say. She had already introduced herself, after all.

And she was supposed to already know why she was here. She'd gotten on the ship under the guise of an assignment, which would mean she'd been briefed. She honestly couldn't think of a reason why a back-alley ship would be assigned a Liosi soldier.

The door fell into place with a *thud* and there was a silence between them. Finally, El said, "How can I be of assistance, sir?"

"I don't know, what can you do?" he asked, a smile playing at the corner of his lips.

How was she supposed to reply to his question? Shouldn't he know what she was good at—or what whoever was supposed to be on the ship was good at—or was it some sort of a test?

But panic never solved anything. So no matter how fast her heart raced or how hard it became to breathe, she forced her words to come out calm, laced with far more confidence than she felt. "Aside from my combat training, I am a licensed navigator and trained in basic first aid and general mechanics. I also have a degree in communications."

"You're a communications liaison?" he said, his interest obviously piqued at that. That was good; no one liked working a comm system, and if he passed those duties along to her, she could control what messages came and went. She would know immediately if anyone sent anything out about her.

"Yes, sir."

He frowned, studying her a moment, as if making up his mind. Then he nodded once. "Why not? I'll take you up to the bridge and introduce you to our pilot. He can get you settled."

"Thank you, sir," she said, automatically. "I'm happy to be of service."

He had started walking away, though he turned, saying over his shoulder at her, "Most on this ship just call me Leiv or Captain. And you can drop the 'happy to be of service' bit."

"Aye, aye, Captain," she said, following him up the stairs at the far end of the cargo hold.

"What'd you say your name was?" he said as they reached the top and he moved down the corridor. He stepped on a squeaky patch and cringed, muttering something under his breath.

She ignored the last part—since she didn't actually hear what he said and didn't think it directed at her. "Cadet Elis." She barely managed to cut herself off at the last second before she called him 'sir' again.

That was going to be hard to get used to, what with the way she had been tacking it onto sentences for almost as long as she could remember.

He paused outside the doorway at the end of the corridor, turning to look at her with a questioning frown. "That's a mouthful. What do people usually call you?"

"Cadet Elis," she replied. "Or Elis. Or Cadet."

He turned back to the doorway, ducking to step through it, not saying anything but making it seem as if she had responded incorrectly or said something wrong.

"Hey, Trapp, I've got a surprise for you."

She followed him through the doorway. She stepped into the ship's control room and stopped just over the threshold until she was given precise instructions about where she was wanted.

Illuminated by a faint orange light from overhead, the cramped room had a set of locker-type cupboards to the right, which the Captain stood in front of, a panel of controls straight ahead with a chair in front that, who El presumed was, the pilot sat in front of, and to the left was a console with the oldest comm system El had ever seen—big and boxy—with a chair in front of it.

The pilot spun around in his chair and turned from the controls to face her. A mop of thick, dark hair covered by a red knit cap sat atop his head, his face graced with twinkling eyes and a lopsided grin; on either side were ears just slightly too large for the head they resided upon.

He looked her up and down with an appraising look. "You brought me an angry-looking military chick? *Ech*, that's certainly a surprise, yeah."

It was only then that she realized her crossed arms and scowl. It was a natural resting position for her and one she was going to have to keep in check. She wanted these people to like her and she would have to work harder to win them over. People who liked you weren't suspicious of you.

She relaxed, uncrossing her arms and letting them hang loose at her side, the action weird and unnatural. Her face relaxed too as she offered not quite a smile but certainly not a scowl either.

That was what Captain Behnam was looking for with his previous question. Making a split-second decision, she introduced herself with, "Cadet Elis. But you can call me El."

The Captain looked at her levelly but didn't say anything.

The pilot stood, offering her his hand in greeting, and El had to crane her neck to make eye contact as his frame rose higher. She came to about five-eight but he had to be over six foot. "Trapp Scully, good to meet you."

He wore a gray knit sweater, a longer tee-shirt of light gray sticking out beneath it. His black trousers were loose, tapering at the ankle where they were stuffed into a pair of scuffed boots.

As she shook his hand, a voice came from behind her, soft and sweet. "We have a new crewmember?"

El turned to find a petite redhead, a broad grin on her freckled face, standing behind her. As he retook his seat at the controls the pilot—Trapp—said, "And the welcome committee has arrived."

The young woman giggled at that, like an adolescent, though El guessed her to be twenty or so. Her hair was bobbed short, but the style suited her. She wore a pair of dark purple leggings and black flats. Her pale blue sweater was oversized and had sleeves that were a little too long and covered her hands.

"I'm Ginger," she said, holding out her hand for El to shake. "Ginger Nutbrown. I'm our resident medic."

Her nose was pierced, a small, subtle loop on her right nostril. It was something married Veronian women did, and there was a soft lilt to her accent that suggested she could be from there.

El took the hand offered her. Which of the men aboard the ship was the medic married to? She didn't share a surname with either.

"She's not a crewmember," Captain Behnam said, but there was something in the way he said it, like it was amusing to him, part of some private joke he shared only with himself. "She was assigned to us by His Majesty for the time being and so we're just getting a little extra use out of her."

Trapp shot him a questioning look, which he returned with a pointed expression. What did it mean? The pilot seemed satisfied with the reply, rolling his eyes and shaking his head as he turned his attention back to the controls.

It put El on edge; there was something suspicious going on aboard the ship.

Not that it was any of her business. If they wanted to get involved in things that were less than legal, that was on them. Though it would certainly be good for her if that were the case; people with their own secrets didn't go snooping around for other people's. And they were less likely to turn her into the law if they were not on good terms with the authorities themselves.

"So what exactly is she doing in my control room?" Trapp asked.

"She's a communications liaison," Captain Behnam explained. "So guess who is working our comm from now on."

"You're sure you're okay with that?" Trapp asked, giving the Captain a pointed look that said either Captain Behnam was really attached to the comm system himself or he was in the habit of sending out messages he might not want a cadet to see.

El guessed the latter of course since the man had been so eager to put her in charge of the comm in the first place; a man who loved the machine would not be so eager to hand over control of it.

But then the way Captain Behnam said, "I'm sure," made her think perhaps he had a secret comm system for such messages. Which meant it was still possible for him to send out inquiries about her without her knowledge. Doubtful, but still a threat. And one thing she had been taught was to neutralize threats.

She crossed to the comm system, taking a seat at the console, running her hand over the top and frowning at the outdated piece of equipment. "Is this the original comm that came with the ship? Or did someone have an even older model installed?"

Trapp snorted as he made eye contact with her, and she smirked in return. "See, Leiv, even the newbie thinks this ship's an outdated piece of junk."

"Takes one to know one," Captain Behnam shot back.

"What does that even mean?" Trapp demanded with a laugh.

"Don't mind him," Ginger said, her voice soft and light and entirely nicer than El was used to. She didn't know why but it warmed her and unnerved her all at the same time. "Leiv gets touchy when people speak against his baby."

Captain Behnam muttered something El couldn't quite make out.

"Is this the only comm on board?" she asked, shifting in the chair. *Victory*, it spun! She spun so that she looked at Ginger, then Captain Behnam, then Trapp.

"Why?" the Captain asked, frowning at her, his brows knit tightly together.

"When you're dealing with equipment this old, if there are other signals, it can interfere with the performance," she explained. She doubted any of that was true, but no one was questioning it, so she just kept going. "So I would like to know what I'm dealing with right off the bat."

"We have intercoms," Ginger told her. "They run the length of the ship."

"And we have a portable comm here," Trapp supplied, waving to the small box on his control station, looking as outdated as the device before her. "But it's connected to that one and all my messages run through there."

El offered them both a grateful smile. "The intercoms run on an entirely different system, and if the port comm runs through the main one, they shouldn't cause me any trouble. I mostly mean anything not connected to this central that's used for outgoing communications."

"We've got nothing like that," Captain Behnam said, looking at her steadily. It was almost a challenge. But she wasn't sure if she accepted or not because she wasn't entirely sure what he was challenging her about.

"Good to know."

Captain Behnam apparently found that an acceptable answer because he simply nodded once and then said, "Come on, Ginger, we've got work to do. Trapp, get us off the ground, would you? We're behind schedule as it is."

As they left, El turned her attention back to the comm itself, running her finger across the screen to bring it to life. The machine whirred, and she jumped at the sound, forgetting that older models were so noisy.

"Skittish?" Trapp asked, taking his eyes off the controls and looking at her over his shoulder.

"It's been a weird day," she admitted, offering him an easy smile. "And I haven't been off-world in a while."

If four months was a while. It felt like longer.

"Well strap yourself in, that's about to change."

She reached up, searching with her hand for the mentioned strap along the top of the chair, but she found none.

"Oh, sorry," Trapp said as he began flipping switches and pressing buttons, moving with rapid, dizzying precision. "That's just a saying. We don't actually have straps. Don't really need them. Take off's mostly pretty safe."

Mostly.

The comm had finally booted up at that point, its screen smiling brightly back at her. Too brightly, honestly, given how dim the room was. Except she didn't have time to figure out how to adjust the screen brightness. Not when it meant delaying the takeoff a few minutes—something the impatient Captain might throw her off the ship for.

As a means of venting that frustration, she said, "I can't do my job if you don't do yours. So please at least try not to get us killed."

"I like you," Trapp said, pushing a button and then pulling a lever, causing the entire ship to fill with a whirring sound. "You're going to fit in here."

"If I live long enough," she muttered as pressure filled the control room. Not too much that it was overpowering—El could have probably gotten up and walked around if she had wanted to. But was that wise? Perhaps safety belts might not be a bad idea after all.

"I'll see that you do, darling," Trapp said, a grin in his voice. But he was grinning at the controls as he guided the ship into the air, and somehow she thought the expression was directed more at the ship than her. There was pure joy radiating from his expression; was there anything in El's life that made her as happy as the takeoff was making the pilot?

She watched him for several moments before turning her attention back to the comm. The screen had gone dark once more and she ran a finger across it, bringing it back to life.

Of course, all she got was the loading screen, spinning around and around, a quiet, steady voice saying, "Please wait," every two seconds because the machine was an outdated piece of junk. Just like the rest of the ship. It needed an overhaul and she wasn't surprised that Trapp was so vocal about it. After all, as the pilot, he was the one who suffered the most from all of it—aside from the mechanic, he was the one who had to deal with the equipment the most.

After several moments, which she passed in frustrated silence as Trapp worked the controls, she let out a frustrated grunt as that sickeningly soft voice asked her once more to "Please wait."

"I am waiting, you low-tech hunk of junk," she muttered at it. "Now I see why everyone was so eager to give me command of this thing."

Trapp snickered at that. "Told you this ship was a worthless piece of scrap."

"Then why stay?" she asked in all earnestness. She had her reasons for being here, but she also didn't intend to stay. Especially not after seeing what equipment she would have to work with if she did. The pilot, on the other hand, clearly had a close relationship with the Captain, the kind that was only fostered over time. He must have been on the ship for a while.

Trapp shrugged easily, adjusting some of the controls as he replied, his attention on them and not her as he spoke. "It's not all bad. Give it a shot, and I think you'll fit in nicely."

She laughed at that because it wasn't that simple. If only he knew how not-that-simple it was. "I'm a soldier." It wasn't true, not anymore, but it was what he believed. "I'm not part of the crew."

He shrugged again, still not looking at her as he went about his job. "Just you wait—give it some time and before you know it, you will be."

CHAPTER 3

"EL, ARE YOU BUSY at the moment?" Ginger asked as she popped her head into the control room.

Takeoff had been a success—though the 'success' part was a little touch and go for a while—and El's job was all but done for the moment. But she wasn't sure what else she was supposed to be doing, so she'd started poking around the comm, trying not to lose her head completely at the insanely slow speed at which it moved.

Thankfully, she'd figured out how to turn off the annoying voice that asked her to wait every other second.

Grateful for a reason to turn her attention from the console, she spun in her chair to face the medic, enjoying the action more than she probably should have. "How might I be of service?"

"*Ech,* are you required to say that?" Trapp asked, spinning away from the controls to face them, brushing a dark curl from his forehead.

El nodded. "It's part of my training."

A grin spread across his face. "You should definitely keep it up and often; it'll drive Leiv crazy."

"Which is precisely why she shouldn't say it more than necessary," Ginger said, giving him a firm, pointed look.

They didn't interact like El imagined a married couple would, but then El didn't actually know much about married couples and how they interacted. So it was still possible Trapp was Ginger's husband, even if they didn't share a surname.

Ginger turned her attention from the man back to El. "If you're free, I thought I could show you around the ship a little bit."

El rose and followed her from the control room, entering the corridor she and Captain Behnam had come down earlier, illuminated by the light from the control room and the cargo bay ahead, but with no light of its own.

"These are our quarters," the medic said, motioning to the doors that lined the walls. "First on the right is mine, next to me is empty, and then Trapp is next to that. Then on the other side is you right across from me, then another empty one, and Leiv is on the end, across from Trapp. We'll get you settled in your room later." She frowned, a thoughtful look on her face. "Did you bring your things with you? I don't remember seeing them."

El waved her off dismissively. "It's fine."

She hadn't been expecting to go anywhere and so all her things were back at the hospital. Not that she had much, but she'd give anything for her few necessities right then.

Ginger frowned at her a moment then nodded, her red curls bouncing, like that was good enough for her. "Right, so then up here we have the cargo bay."

She started in that direction and El followed, back down the stairs until they were back in the room El had first come into, the entrance straight ahead.

"Cargo bay," Ginger said as she planted her feet firmly on the ground as if it weren't obvious. She moved toward the door under the stairs, which led into an open room, underneath where they had just come from.

There was a long table with benches around it, upon which Captain Behnam sat, head bent over a pile of papers and a serious frown on his face. He looked up when they entered, a question in his eyes.

"Just giving a tour, we'll be out of your hair in a minute," Ginger said, a soft smile on her face.

Framing the walls around the room were more benches, those padded and built more for leisure. Directly ahead was a partial wall and, from the glimpse El got, it looked like it led to a kitchen.

"Grubbery," Ginger said, waving her hand in that direction. She pointed to a door to the left. "Training room. And next to that is the med bay and the shower. There's a twelve-minute shower limit, so make sure you don't dawdle."

Like El needed more than twelve minutes. *Victory,* she could do what she needed in seven.

"Engine room's straight ahead," Ginger finished the tour. "But there's really nothing worth seeing there unless you're interested in machinery that's more patch job than engine." She frowned in Captain Behnam's direction, but the man didn't look up from his papers. She rolled her eyes.

Perhaps they were married after all but simply didn't share a last name. They certainly seemed to share some sort of a bond.

But then, Ginger had her own quarters; she didn't share with any of the other crewmembers. So maybe she wasn't married after all.

They headed back through the cargo bay, up the stairs to the corridor. They moved to the one that was to be El's, and Ginger opened the door. "Here's your room, feel free to get settled. Food won't be for another while."

Everything inside El froze as her heart raced at the thought of closing herself alone in that tiny room. She couldn't. She just couldn't. El had found that the smaller the space, the more room there was for her thoughts.

She realized then just how trapped she was, stuck in a tiny ball of metal, flying through space for who knew how long. And when they landed, who knew what would be waiting for her.

Or worse, who.

"El?" Ginger's voice was soft and soothing. "Are you all right?"

Her head was spinning but El couldn't tell Ginger that. She couldn't tell anyone about it. Her mind was her strength; if something happened to that, if people knew the truth, they'd never look at her the same again. She'd be useless.

"If it's all right, I think I'll familiarize myself with the comm," El said instead of replying. She couldn't do it, couldn't get settled in the room yet.

Ginger nodded, her concerned look still on her face. "Of course! Whatever is best for you. You know where my room is, and if I'm not there, I'm often in the med bay. Come find me if you ever need to talk about anything."

El thanked her but only to be polite; there wasn't anything to talk about.

Eventually, the rest of the ship went into night mode and El had to drag herself to bed. She could only sit at the comm for so long, and everyone else was getting settled.

Her quarters were small, consisting of a bed nestled along the far wall and a row of cupboards along the walls leading to it on either side. Below the row of cupboards on the right was a long board nailed to the wall serving as a makeshift desk or table. Upon further examination, she discovered that underneath there was a little stool that folded into the wall and could be pulled out.

The cupboards were empty—not that El expected them to have anything in them. She guessed the crew's were filled, no doubt with personal belongings and mementos.

What would it be like to be afforded the luxury of being able to collect such things?

Turning her attention to the bed, El noticed the white shirt and black pair of lounge pants sitting neatly folded on the end. On top was a note, written in a thin, confident hand.

In case you have need of these—Ginger

El wasn't entirely sure whose clothes they were—they were too big to fit Ginger—but she honestly didn't care. She only had her uniform and she needed to get out of it.

She reached down and unlaced her boots, a smile playing on her face at the familiarity of the laces and leather beneath her fingers. Slipping them off her feet, she shed her uniform and put on the shirt and lounge pants. Then she pulled the elastic bands from her bun, her dark hair falling about her shoulders, free.

She flopped onto the bed, then let out a sigh as she realized she'd left the light on. She didn't really need it out, did she? She could sleep with it on.

It only took about five seconds to realize that no, she could not, in fact, sleep with the light on. But then, she'd already known that; it was silly that she'd ever considered otherwise.

Dragging herself up, she crossed the room to press the button by the door, shutting off the light. She fell back into bed—literally—as she tripped over her boots in the dark.

She took a deep breath, letting her body relax. She was pretty tired after all.

Except that there was some sort of creaking noise. What was that?

She listened, trying to find the source of it, only for it to become quiet again. Fine, she didn't actually care what it was.

Another creaking started, coming from a different direction. Then a bang, followed by a low hiss.

That couldn't be good.

The creaking sound came again, followed by a moment of silence and then the second creak. Then *bang! Hiiisssss.*

Then silence again, but only long enough for El to take a breath before it all started up again.

But it was fine, she told herself. It was fine. She'd lived through war and a gunshot wound and the death of her mother and her father's distance from her. She'd lived through loss and separation and horrors most people couldn't even dream of.

She could fall asleep with a little noise.

Creeaakkk . . . It came again.

Silence.

Creeeaak . . .

Bang!

Hiiissss.

"NO!"

El jumped up with a start, tripping over her boots again, bashing her knee on the wall. She swore under her breath.

Turning on the light once more, everything seemed less serious. It was fine. Everything was fine.

She flopped back down on the bed once more as the cycle, of course, started again. And—was that music she heard? Who in the void was listening to music right then?

Then she saw it, there above her; just overhead was a fan. And fans generally drowned out other noise.

Standing on the bed, she inspected it to find it was, in fact, a fan with a switch that brought the thing to life instantly. She let out a happy sigh of relief.

She turned out the light once more and managed to avoid her boots on the way back to her bed, falling into it from exhaustion then. Closing her eyes, she took a deep breath again, unclenching her jaw, relaxing her shoulders—

Thud!

The noise was followed by the sickening sound of metal scraping against metal.

Then silence once more.

It was no big deal, El told herself. It happened. It happened. It was over.

Thud! Scraaaaap.

She suppressed the scream that threatened to spill forth, becoming instead a strangled cry of frustration.

Rising once more, she turned on the light and turned off the fan.

She wasn't sleeping tonight, that much was clear.

Slipping on her boots, she laced them up, a familiarity to them that grounded her. She took a deep breath, remembering that the ship had a training room, and if there was one thing that helped her fall asleep, it was wearing herself out completely.

The ship wasn't large, and El found the room without incident, grateful for the dim lights that hadn't been there earlier lining the walls of the ship and providing just enough to lead her way.

The training room lit up as she entered.

The floor of the room was covered in thin matting that squished under her feet as she walked to the punching bag in the middle of the room. The walls were lined with cupboards and drawers, but she had no reason to go rummaging through them. All she needed was the bag.

She began by warming up, slowly increasing the intensity of her workout until she lost herself completely. She had no way of knowing how much time passed; time ceased to exist. All thoughts flew from her head, her focus solely on the task at hand. There were only her and the bag.

Finally, she stopped, sweat pouring from her, her hands bruised, every muscle aching. She hadn't felt so alive in a long time.

She moved to the grubbery, looking through the cupboards until she found one that was filled with dishes rather than cans. She got herself a cup of water and downed it quickly, relishing the taste. She leaned back against the cupboard, eyes closed, a contented sigh escaping her.

Footsteps.

She straightened, cringing as the sound came closer. Had she made that much noise when she'd come down? She certainly hoped not.

Captain Behnam appeared in the doorway, his brow pulling in when he saw her. He crossed the room silently until he reached the grubbery. He reached around her to grab his own cup and fill it with water, taking a long drink before he said, "Snooping?"

"No, sir," she replied. "Utilizing the training room. I hope that's acceptable. I was led to believe I had permission."

He gave her a long, appraising look. "As long as you do your job and stay out of my business, I don't really care what you do."

He set his glass in the sink and walked away, leaving her alone to think of his words. It wasn't true; he would care if he knew the truth.

Her actions had branded her. If he knew the truth of them, he wouldn't speak to her so casually. He would look at her as everyone would when they found out: as a coward, as a traitor; untrustworthy and disloyal.

She was exhausted all of a sudden, weary and fatigued and unable to muster the strength even to drag herself to bed.

Setting her glass in the sink beside the Captain's, she made it as far as the dining area, her gaze falling upon the benches that framed the room, padded and, well, honestly simply there. Much, much closer than her bed, trapped in that room with all those endlessly annoying sounds.

Without a second thought, she curled up on the bench closest to her, closed her eyes, and fell asleep.

CHAPTER 4

EL WOKE SORE and far, far too soon.

She lay there on the bench a moment, letting out a sigh as she thought about how tired she was and how desperately she did not want to get up.

But those thoughts were instantly replaced with the realization that she was lying in a very public space, and it was clear she'd slept here. Any minute, someone would walk in and she'd be out of uniform and stuck explaining the situation.

That was enough to make her jump up and hurry back to her bunk to get back into uniform.

It took all of four minutes to get ready, the routine familiar, grounding. She realized that as she ran her fingers through her hair, pulling it back into a ponytail that she then twisted into its usual bun. It was how she'd done her hair for the last fifteen years, but she wouldn't have to do it for much longer.

As soon as she was out of her uniform for good, she could wear her hair however she wanted.

She froze, staring at herself in the mirror. How would she dress or do her hair once it was all over? Who was that woman outside of her uniform?

She looked down at her feet, secure in her standard-issue combat boots, a smile playing at her lips at the sight of her old friend and constant companion. She wouldn't have to give them up once it was over, would she? She didn't think she could do that.

With a quick shake of her head, she dispelled the thought; she'd worry about that later. Hair up, she was ready for the day.

Or, rather, as ready as she'd ever be.

She made it back down to the grubbery and found Ginger by the sink, filling a teakettle with water. The medic grinned as El entered, the smile warm and friendly. "Good morning. How did you sleep last night?"

"I slept fine," she replied. It wasn't strictly a lie, she'd slept; there was no need to tell where exactly she'd slept.

"Happy to hear it," Ginger said as she turned off the water and put the teakettle onto the stove. The stovetop clicked and then roared to life as Ginger turned her attention to the cupboards. "I hope you're not opposed to canned food. It's almost all we eat while we're in space." She pulled out three cans and set them on the little counter space by the sink. "Of course it's better than NETTLE bars."

Having eaten her share of NETTLE bars, El could attest to that; anything was better than eating NETTLE bars.

"Wait, is that canned hash?" El asked as she caught sight of the label. Of all the canned goods, canned hash was the best, no question.

"It is." Ginger eyed her quizzically. "Is that all right?"

El nodded, not wanting to seem too eager or excited. "Yeah, it's fine, that sounds great."

Ginger smiled at her. "Good."

Footsteps sounded behind them and El turned at the sound of them, recognizing them from the night before. But there was a second set with them.

Sure enough, a minute later, Captain Behnam appeared, Trapp not far behind. The pilot's face lit up as he entered the room, hurrying over to where they stood. "Is that hash?"

"You bet it is," Ginger said as she pulled out a pan, setting it on the stove, and clicked off the burner with the teakettle full of boiling water. "Could you open them for me?"

El moved to get out of his way as he moved to do as requested, finding herself standing next to Captain Behnam.

"Sleep all right?" he asked, not looking at her but instead watching Trapp and Ginger in the grubbery.

"It was adequate, thank you, sir," she replied, not sure why everyone was so interested in her sleeping habits.

He nodded once. "Good. I forgot the fan in your bunk was busted, so if you want to swap out, feel free to try a different one. Just, you'll have neighbors then, so make sure you keep it down."

"Yes, sir," she said. "Thank you, sir."

He looked at her then, one corner of his mouth wrinkled in a frown. "You can drop the 'sir.' Please. It's Leiv."

"That would be against protocol."

His lips curled upward, into something akin to a smile. Glancing around he said, "And this is all according to protocol?"

Since he'd brought it up . . .

"No, sir, it's not something that happens often," she replied honestly. "Why exactly am I here?"

He tilted his head as he studied her quizzingly. "Weren't you briefed on that?"

Right. Briefed. That was something a soldier who was supposed to be here would have been. "Yes, sir, you're right, of course. I just wasn't sure if there was anything more you wanted to add."

He frowned, thinking a minute before shaking his head. "No, I don't think so . . . "

Of course not.

"Breakfast!" Ginger called as Trapp carried the pan to the table. The medic followed behind with plates and forks, setting them down as everyone took a seat.

Everyone except El.

"Is there a problem?" Ginger asked.

There was, but El didn't know how to voice it.

The only available seat left El's back to the doorway to the cargo bay—vulnerable, exposed.

"Could I maybe . . . " How to say it? "Could I sit on that side?"

Ginger jumped up immediately, leaving open the seat El had requested and slipping into the other free one. "Absolutely."

All eyes were on El as she took her seat, and she kept her head down as they all stared.

"Did I tell you about the fellow I met in the bar the other night?" Trapp broke the silence.

And just like that, breakfast was served—canned hash and tea accompanied by a friendly camaraderie that made El ache. She didn't know what exactly it was she ached for—perhaps something that might have been, something she lost long ago before she'd ever actually had it.

Was that something one could ache for?

When it was over, Ginger cleared away the dishes, saying she'd wash them, and everyone else could get on with their important work.

"Is your work not important?" El questioned. As a medic, surely hers was a work to be valued.

Ginger smiled softly. "As long as you all stay in one piece, my services are blissfully unneeded. I can give you something for those knuckles though if you want."

El looked down and remembered the bruises on her hands, the ones from her workout the night before. She'd forgotten how it felt to have bruises on your hands, how alive it made her feel, that remembrance that she could feel something so deeply.

"Thanks, but I'm good," she said, offering the young woman a grateful smile. "Thanks for breakfast."

She hurried to catch up with the Captain, remembering then what she'd wanted to talk to him about.

"Sir!"

"Leiv," she heard him mutter under his breath as he came to a halt in the cargo bay. He turned to face her. "What do you need?"

"The comm, sir," she said, noticing the way he cringed visibly at that last word. She'd tried to hold it back, she really had, but it had just slipped out. "I noticed that it has every transmission and file still on it—they date back over twenty years. I was thinking, if we purged them, it might not do much, but it could really help a little bit in getting it to run at an almost normal speed."

"Purged them?" His eyebrow went up questioningly.

"Deleted them, sir," she clarified.

His face hardened, and she opened her mouth to apologize for the 'sir' when he said, "No. I need those. They've vital to . . . well, that's not important. But you can't delete them; that's an order."

An order? He was all but dying at her protocol and attention to the hierarchy, and he was ordering her about?

There was definitely something secret on that comm.

But whatever it was, if he didn't want it deleted, it wasn't El's business.

"Yes, sir," she replied. "I understand, sir."

He nodded once and then walked away, leaving El to make her own way to the control room. She knew it really was none of her business. It wasn't. If he had secrets to hide, she ought to respect that. She didn't want him poking about too deeply into her own life and lies.

But then he shouldn't have put her in charge of the comm in the first place if he had things he'd rather keep in the dark. And, if she were being honest, since it had been brought to her attention, she simply just wanted to know to satiate her curiosity.

He'd ordered her not to delete the files. But he hadn't said anything about her not being allowed to look through them.

And it wasn't like he'd given her anything else to do.

El started with the most recent messages, as those where the ones most likely to have any juicy tidbits about the ship's goings-on. But she discovered there were no outgoing calls, and no one contacted them over those few days. In fact, aside from the usual bulletin broadcasts that came through with news and 'Be on the Alert' info, the comm was virtually empty.

Which seemed odd, considering Captain Behnam had made it clear that his messages were very important. As far as she could tell, there wasn't anything of note.

Still, she felt weird going through them. She glanced over her shoulder to where Trapp was sitting at the controls, fiddling with a few of the buttons, his attention clearly not on her. What would he say if he knew what she was doing?

"How long have you known the Captain?"

Trapp looked up then, his easy grin spreading across his face. "We grew up together."

"Ah, so you're close then." It wasn't really a question, more a statement. More than anything, it answered her question; he was loyal to the Captain and probably wouldn't love it if he knew what she was doing.

Trapp made a sound that was somewhat non-committal by way of a reply, his focus on the board in front of him, a concerned frown on his face.

"Is something the matter?" El asked.

As if in response a *thud!* filled the cockpit as the lights went out. A second later, they powered back on as Captain Behnam's voice came through the intercom. "Trapp, what in the void was that?"

"Not me, Cap," Trapp replied as he spun in the chair, turning his attention to another part of the controls.

"What is going on?" Ginger's voice came through the intercom, gentle as ever but with a nervous edge to it. "The engine sounds angry down here."

She was in the med bay or the grubbery then.

"That would be what's going on," Captain Behnam said. El admired the calm edge to his tone. "Headed down there now. Trapp, do what you can?"

"Aye, aye, Captain," he replied, then added under his breath, "Not much I can do if the engine goes."

El rose.

"You're gonna want to stay put," Trapp said, not looking in her direction as he fiddled with a few more dials on the board in front of him. "This is going to get bumpy."

"I'm trained in basic mechanics," she told him. "And I'm not sure how much help I can be, but I figured . . . "

"Get out of here."

She hurried from the control room and made it to the steps down to the cargo hold before the second *thud!* sounded. El braced herself against the railing as the ship rocked, the lights flickering off before almost instantly powering up once more.

The ship somewhat stable again, El started once more, through the cargo hold and the grubbery, to where Ginger had indicated the engine room was located. It was easy to find because Ginger was indeed right—the engine did sound angry as the sickening crunch of metal on metal filled the air, a high-pitched shriek piercing over all of it.

Captain Behnam was already there, jacket off and sleeves rolled up, hands covered in grease though he'd only been there a few minutes. He looked over at her as she entered and gave her a glare. "If you need something, I'm a little busy right now."

He had to shout to be heard over the deafening sounds the engine made. Why were those the words he chose to use his energy on?

"I'm trained in basic mechanics," she yelled back. "I can help."

He shook his head, waving her away. "I've got it covered."

Another *thud!* sounded and the ship jolted. El stumbled forward, the anti-skid on her boots doing little to keep her in place. Her boot caught on a discarded part that lay on the floor, causing her to stumble further before she caught her balance.

"I've got this," Captain Behnam told her.

He didn't have it. By the looks of it, he had no idea what he was doing, and the engine room looked like it belonged as part of a museum tour more than a piece of equipment expected to keep thousands of pounds of metal hurtling through space.

Her training had been for newer, state of the art equipment, but on Taras that wasn't always what they'd encountered. And while she wasn't confident enough in her skills to call herself a mechanic, even a little experience was better than the alternative.

If the engine went, that was the end. They'd drift until they ran out of air.

El had imagined dying so many ways—it was a reality she had come to grips with a long time ago—but she didn't intend to go that way.

The ship rocked again, and El stumbled once more, trying to brace herself but doing so too late. She fell forward and crashed into the Captain's strong chest. He put his arms around her to keep her from falling further, steadying her a moment before releasing her.

A shock of electricity ran through her—not enough to hurt, but it sent a strange tingling sensation through her. What could possibly be wrong with the ship that she'd feel that?

"Thank you," she said before she realized he couldn't hear her over the sound the engine was making. Honestly, she was surprised his instinct hadn't been to push her off of him. But she didn't want to dwell on it any longer, especially not on the way it made her head spin; or maybe that was just the ship careening through space.

Right, that's what she needed to focus on.

Turning her attention back to what was in front of her, she found she had an even better vantage point and could see what the problem was. At least, she assumed that part wasn't supposed to be floating about like that, scraping against everything it touched.

"I don't suppose we can shut this off . . . " Maybe what she was looking at was the part of the engine that kept the lights on or something else relatively non-essential.

Captain Behnam just raised an eyebrow by way of a reply.

Okay, so it was essential then.

El watched the cycle of *thud!*, rock, lights out and then on again, keeping an eye on the moving part.

"Cap, situation down there?" Trapp's voice came over the intercom.

Captain Behnam replied by simply turning on the intercom speaker and letting him hear the engine's angry crunching noises.

"*Ech,* what're we doing about that?" Trapp asked.

"Just keep us—" The Captain was cut off by the cycle again.

By the time the cycle ended, El started to form an idea. She turned to Captain Behnam but realized she couldn't explain her plan to him over the sound. Her two options were to drag him out of the engine room to somewhere quieter—and she might be able to accomplish that, but he was bigger and stronger than her, so it would take some doing and she didn't know if she had the time—or to act and hope he wouldn't hate her too much for it.

But then, if she messed up, they'd all be dead, and he couldn't be mad at her in the afterlife.

Of course, he could be angry as they slowly suffocated.

The *thud!* filled the room again and the lights went out. In the split second before they whirled back to life, she shut the system off.

Victory, they were going to die.

And she was going to help them get there faster.

She heard Captain Behnam yelling behind her, demanding to know what in the void she was doing. But she didn't have time to process that or to reply. She reached in and retrieved the part.

His strong arms were around her waist and she felt another shock as he dragged her out of there. She reached to turn the system back on, but he was pulling her further than that, his words ringing out in the eerie silence that was left.

"Turn it back on before we burn in the void," she interrupted, wriggling out of his grasp. She got just free enough to smash down the switch, the system roaring back to life.

The Captain released her, looking at the engine running . . . not quite smoothly but decidedly better than before. It certainly wasn't shrieking or crunching any longer.

She turned to Captain Behnam, who was still standing there dumbfounded. She handed the piece over to him. "We should probably figure out where this broke off from, sir."

CHAPTER 5

I

T TOOK A good deal longer to figure out how to cobble the piece back into the engine while it was still running. But as it turned out, after Captain Behnam was done chewing her out, they actually made a decent team.

"You really do need a mechanic though," El said they left the engine room together. Maybe she'd actually sleep tonight instead of having to wear herself out before she passed out on a bench.

The grubbery smelled like tomatoes and rich, earthy spices as they entered. Ginger worked at the stove, cooking what looked like a pan of pasta and beans, while Trapp set dishes out on the table. He looked up at them and grinned.

"Is it going to hold together until we land?" he asked, nodding toward the engine room as if there might be some misunderstanding about what he was talking about.

Captain Behnam shrugged. "Hopefully."

"We need a mechanic, Leiv," Ginger said from where she stood at the stove. She punctuated her statement by waving her spoon in his direction, flinging a bean across the room, cringing at the unintentional side effect of her actions.

"I'm not going through that again," Trapp added, his task done; he closed the gap between them in a small step. "It almost sounded like the engine cut out there for a minute and if that'd been real—"

"Oh, no, it did," Captain Behnam said.

The room went silent, all eyes on the Captain, El casually trying to sink into the background before the attention turned to her.

Finally, Trapp said, "I'm sorry, what now?"

"El cut the engine," Captain Behnam explained and suddenly the attention she'd hoped to avoid was all on her.

She offered an apologetic smile. "I figured we were going to die either way so better take a risk to fix it?"

Trapp and Ginger looked to Captain Behnam, a question in their eyes, which the Captain shut down with the tiniest shake of his head. El wondered about what happened—about what had just been exchanged about her in such a way she couldn't even know if it were good or bad.

Ginger turned her attention back to the food on the stove, clicking the burner off and holding the pan triumphantly. "Well, I guess this calls for a victory feast then. Unfortunately, it's just pasta and beans."

"That sounds great," El said, moving around Trapp and Captain Behnam to grab the pan from Ginger and carry it to the table for her. As she turned, she found Captain Behnam directly behind her, so close she almost ran into him with the pan and had to jump back to avoid burning him. She realized he'd been moving to do the same thing, but she'd beaten him to it.

"Sorry." She mumbled the word, not sure why her heart pounded.

"My fault," he said, stepping back so she could get through.

She put the pan on the table and Captain Behnam dished up the food. For the next several minutes, the only sound that filled the grubbery was the normal hum of the engine and the din of four people grateful to be alive, inhaling their victory dinner of canned pasta and beans.

Ginger rose after the pan had been scraped clean and went to the kitchen area. "I'm making tea, and I'll be here if anyone wants to talk about what happened today."

Captain Behnam raised an eyebrow. "Pass?"

"That's fine," Ginger said. "But it's healthy to feel stressed about what happened today—"

"Because we almost died," Trapp interjected, as if he actually needed to clarify that for anyone.

"Right," Ginger said as she filled the teakettle. "Because we almost died. So if anyone needs help processing that or feels like the experience brought something up that they need to discuss, I'm here."

"Thanks," Captain Behnam said, rising. "I, uh, have to . . ." He waved his hand vaguely in the direction of the cargo bay. "I've got a thing."

He disappeared, leaving with very confident strides for someone who was all but running from having to discuss his feelings.

Not that El was keen to either.

Trapp took his leave next and El followed, offering Ginger an apologetic smile but hurrying off all the same.

El tried one of the other bunks but found it came with its own set of noises and bothers. After about fifteen minutes, she gave in to the fact that, even with everything that'd happened, she was going to have to wear herself out again.

She eased out of the bunk and slipped down to the cargo bay, intent on going to the training room but stopping short in the door to the grubbery.

Ginger sat at the table, a cup of tea in front of her, her head in her hands.

She looked up and met El's eyes. A smile played on her lips but there were tears in her eyes.

El froze. Maybe she should just go back to her bunk. But then, she wouldn't sleep, she couldn't. But it felt weird to go to the training room—right next to where Ginger sat—which only left one option.

A twinge of guilt filled her. Ginger had been so kind and open about being available if anyone needed to talk, and they'd all been so eager to avoid such a conversation that none of them had stopped to consider whether or not Ginger, herself, needed to talk.

With a resigned sigh, El took the few steps required to close the gap between herself and the table and took a seat across from the medic.

"Rough day?"

Ginger gave a sad smile, her gaze downcast as she looked at her tea, her fingers laced tightly around the mug. "You could say that."

"Do you want to talk about it?"

She looked up, hope in her eyes. "Do you want to?"

"No," El said, with a shake of her head. "But I'd love to listen if you wanted to talk about it."

That earned a smile something akin to real. "We almost died today, and I was completely useless. I just sat there in the med bay and listened to that horrible screeching and crunching and those angry, angry sounds, and I just wondered if that was going to be the end and if I was going to go out just sitting still."

El understood that feeling—it was why she moved so much, because at least then it felt like she was doing something useful. Even if she wasn't, at least she had the illusion of it.

"You're not useless," El told her. "Rook di goo, any medic worth their rations is the most valuable member of the team, anyone knows that. You keep us alive every day, we just get to return the favor from time to time."

There was silence between them. Had El said the wrong thing? It was likely. Ginger was soft, kindhearted, and entirely not the type of person El was used to talking to. She didn't know what to say, didn't know how to talk to someone like that. El's mother would have been much more useful in that situation; she had always been more the caring and comforting type. In fact, El thought her mother would have liked Ginger very much if they'd had a chance to meet. Ginger was the kind of girl a mother could be proud of.

"I have so much I wanted to do with my life," Ginger said, drawing El from her own thoughts and back to the conversation. "I never dreamed this would be where life took me. It wasn't supposed to be like this."

Didn't El know it? She'd never meant for life to turn out that way and there she was, hurtling through space on a broken ship, talking about feelings over tea with a medic she'd just met.

Except El didn't actually have tea. Would it be rude to get up and get herself some? Would that ruin what was happening?

Ginger sniffled and El turned her attention back to her; she couldn't make tea. It wouldn't be right.

"I just remembered how easy it is to die," she said. "We live in such a dangerous world and death is inevitable——I, of all people, should know that. Am I an idiot to keep hoping?"

El wasn't entirely sure what it was Ginger was hoping for, but she was crying for real and she had asked a question. "No?"

Ginger looked up then and shook her head. "I'm sorry," she sobbed out. "You don't even know what I'm talking about." She gave a small smile through the tears. "You should just go to bed."

El didn't know how to tell her that she'd come down here to exhaust herself in the training room and then crash on the grubbery bench. So instead she stood and said, "I was going to make myself some tea; do you want some more?"

"I don't know what I want," Ginger groaned, laying her forehead on the table. She lifted her head in an instant. "That's not true, I do know." Her forehead met the wood again. "I'm so stupid."

El didn't know Ginger well enough——and she had no idea what they were even talking about——to contradict her. So she crossed to the sink and filled the teakettle with water. Setting it on the stove, she turned her attention back to the woman still sitting at the table, head resting on the surface.

"When I get like this, it helps if I punch something," El said.

Ginger sat up, frowning at her skeptically. "I don't think that works for me."

"How do you process stuff?" El asked.

A light shone in the medic's eyes as understanding lit her face. "Organizing something helps."

"Great," El said, not admitting that sounded like a nightmare and really, really boring; they were talking about Ginger, not El. "So what kind of messes does this ship have?"

"Well, I can't fix the engine or the Captain," the medic said, smiling at that last part like she'd made some very clever joke. "Stars, I'm so tired. I should just go to sleep." She rested her forehead on the table again. "This is really uncomfortable."

She sat up then, all of a sudden, standing and grabbing her mug of tea. "I'm sorry. You came down here for a reason and I'm keeping you from it."

"I was just going to punch something," El told her honestly.

"Processing through today?" the medic asked with an understanding nod.

Processing through the last several thousand days was more accurate. Except it was more like avoiding processing through them. "Something like that. But I can stay if you want to talk more."

"No," Ginger said, waving her off. "I appreciate it. I really do. But I should get some sleep. Maybe journal a little bit. Thank you though."

She started to leave, reaching the door before she stopped, frozen a minute, before she turned around. "El?"

"Yeah?"

The medic offered her a soft smile. "I'm always here if you want to process a different way."

"Thanks," El told her honestly. She appreciated the gesture, even if she never would take her up on it.

El spent the next three days settling into a routine—meals and working the comm, and then a session in the training room each night before she fell asleep on a bench in the grubbery. She'd tried the other room but there was something about the bunks—she just couldn't sleep in them.

And she figured as long as she was careful and didn't get caught, it was fine.

That third day El spent almost all day poring over the comm until her head started spinning and she couldn't quite focus on the monotony of the routine messages in the back-logs anymore.

She got up to move with no destination in mind and ended up in the grubbery somehow. She heard singing—rather good singing too—coming from that direction, and, without think-ing, she followed the sound. It was a Mahsirian lullaby, and so El shouldn't have been surprised to find Captain Behnam there when she arrived.

She didn't expect him to be at the sink, elbows deep in dirty dishwater as he scrubbed the plates used at dinner.

She shrugged off her jacket and rolled up the sleeves of her button-up shirt. "Want some help?"

He looked up at her, startled, as if he hadn't heard her coming. His dark hair fell across his forehead. "You weren't joking when you said you did everything, were you?"

"No, sir," she said.

He scooched aside to make room beside him at the sink. "Well then, you might as well make yourself useful."

She stepped over beside him and picked up the spare sponge.

"I was going to come look for you after this," he said. "We're touching down on Alvar tomorrow evening. For a back-alley planet, they've got a rather sophisticated air control, so I'll need you to get us permission and whatever else is involved."

"Yes, sir."

He flinched at that but said nothing.

They worked in silence a moment before El said, "Don't you have someone else to pawn this off to? This isn't usually the Captain's job."

He gave her an easy shrug. "Ginger usually takes it upon herself to do them, but she had something to see to, and I have no idea where Trapp disappeared to."

"You do know you have an intercom system, right? You could just page him."

He snorted at that. "Yeah, that would work."

"With all due respect, sir, you don't seem to have the influence with your crew that a captain ought to have. They seem more like your younger siblings than subordinates."

As soon as she said the words, she knew she had said too much. "Forgive me, sir, I shouldn't have overstepped myself."

But Captain Behnam didn't respond to her apology as he scrubbed at a particularly crusty spot on the plate he washed. "So what if I can't get Trapp to do the dishes? He's loyal to a fault and I know he'll back me up without a moment's hesitation when it counts—and he has, far more than I deserve. We've been through a lot together."

He shook his head, a far-off smile on his face, like maybe he was thinking of those times. Then he continued, "And Ginger, well, it's good for her to stand up for herself and tell me if she needs a night off from time to time. When she first joined the crew, she was a little mousy thing, always doing what she was told. She's too serious, needs to let her hair down once in a while."

"Doing what you're told's a bad thing?" It seemed like a captain's dream to her.

"Only when it's a result of not being able to think for yourself. There was a time there when I wondered if she even had a brain inside her head. You've got to believe in the orders you're following—or at the very least, the one giving them—or it won't end well. You ought to know that, being in the military and all."

She ignored the ping his words gave her, focusing instead on the plate she was washing, scrubbing it a second time even though it had come clean the first.

"So you're telling me Ginger refusing to do the dishes is a sign she believes in you?" she pressed, partially because she wanted to understand, partially because she didn't know what else to say and the silence was maddening.

That got a smile out of him. "First of all, Ginger never refused. She politely asked if it was all right if she had some time to herself, and I agreed. If I had refused the request, she'd be here right now instead of us. And I was too proud of her for making the request in the first place to refuse. Besides, it's not my first time; I know my way around a dishpan and a sponge."

It was so sweet the way he said it, the far-off-smile coming back, as if he was smiling at Ginger in his mind. No one had ever smiled about El like that—not that she knew of. But then, she supposed they could have when she wasn't in the room, like Captain Behnam was doing then. Somehow she doubted it.

It made her heart ache just thinking about it.

"Can I ask about Ginger?" she asked after a minute, having wanted to ask for a while but not quite sure how to work it in. "I wasn't sure, with her piercing, if it symbolized . . . That is, she isn't married to anyone on board—I don't think?—and I was just curious . . . "

Captain Behnam pulled his hands out of the water with a small grimace just as El stuck hers back in, a small shock running through her as she did. It was just like when they'd fixed the engine, that same tiny shiver of electricity.

She shook her head and muttered, "You need to fix this ship."

"It's complicated," he said and El was about to tell him it wasn't really—he either hired a mechanic or they all died—when he continued, "He's missing, she's looking to find him; guess it's not that complicated after all."

Oh, they were still talking about Ginger and her husband.

"I see," El said, even though she didn't. "Are we sure he didn't . . . ?" She trailed off, realizing it wasn't her business to ask.

He stuck his hand back into the dishwater tentatively, as if he were testing something. "I wouldn't know. I never actually met the man."

Was that what Ginger had meant the other night when she'd said she'd wanted her life to go differently? And that must have been what she'd meant when she'd asked if she was a fool for hoping. El was glad that she hadn't known that before the conversation; she would have answered differently.

"I'm only telling you all this because she would if you asked," Captain Behnam said. "Even though it hurts her to talk about it. So I'd ask you didn't—"

"I won't say anything to her, *rook di goo,*" El hurried to promise. How would that conversation even go? She couldn't exactly tell the woman that, having been given more information, she was assuming her husband abandoned her, and that, yes, she was, in fact, perhaps a little foolish to hold out hope.

Especially because El was the last person who had a right to judge anyone about hope.

He nodded his appreciation. "Thanks."

There was silence, filled with nothing but the sound of swishing water, scrubbing, and clinking dishes.

"Why did you join the military?" Captain Behnam asked then, as if the question had just occurred to him and he thought it a good topic for casual conversation.

She looked at him, eyes wide, surprised. "Oh."

He put up his hands, almost defensively, flinging suds as he did so. "You know what, never mind. It's really none of my business."

"No, it's fine," she hurried to assure him, as she wiped suds off her face with her sleeve. "It just sort of happened. My father enrolled me in military school when I was young, and it just sort of stuck. There are really only two options for nobility on Liosa—become a soldier or join the court and become a diplomat. And, well, diplomacy isn't exactly my strong suit."

Much to her mother's disappointment, El was sure. She was glad the woman wasn't alive to see what she'd become.

He frowned at her, his brow furrowed. "I'm sorry if you felt like I was implying earlier that your career was doomed to fail. I didn't mean any offense."

But he had implied it. And honestly, she didn't want to think about how right he was. "No, it's fine. You didn't know."

He shrugged as he grabbed a towel and started drying the dishes they had washed. "Still, I really ought to think before I speak. So, your father was a career military then, all through your childhood?"

It seemed odd that he would ask that, given that it came right after him apologizing for saying too much. But she answered all the same. "He joined when I was eight, after my mother died." She ducked her head as she grabbed a towel and started drying as well. "He really gave himself to it. You could almost say he remarried his career."

He'd taken it so seriously, and somewhere along the way he'd forgotten he had a daughter; she'd become just another cadet who happened to share a name with him.

Captain Behnam nodded and there was a lull in the conversation.

"How'd you become a captain?" El asked since it seemed the best time to ask. He was more likely to answer since he had just asked her so many personal questions and seemed in a serious mood after her responses. He was maybe even feeling a bit remorseful about the whole thing. And if he was, he might jump on the chance to repay her by sharing some personal information about himself.

And she was in luck because that was exactly what he did, saying, "I inherited the ship from my parents. They used to fly her before I was born."

"And after you were born?" she asked.

He shrugged. "Their work wasn't exactly the safest and not conditions to raise a kid in. So they retired her. Then I brought her out of retirement several years ago."

"They worked on her together then?" she said, because she liked the sound of that. She had never worked with anyone like that, someone she wanted to be partners with. True, she'd worked with people in the military, but that was never a true partnership. Not like that. Far from that.

He looked at her and grinned. It unnerved her—she wasn't used to someone giving her so much undivided attention. "Yeah, they worked her together. You know, not many like referring to a pile of scraps as a 'her.' Trapp and Ginger even aren't ready to come around to that way of thinking."

She offered him a small smile in return for his grin. "Something with that much history deserves to be called something more than 'it.' I can see why you stand by her, even with her flaws."

He gave her a small shrug. "Eh. Perfect ships are overrated."

"So, why exactly are we touching down tomorrow?" she asked, realizing that was the question she should have asked first, rather than learning Captain Behnam's backstory. She should have asked him that when he was in the answering mood, willing to tell her anything. But then, even if she wasn't a crewmember, he ought to still be willing to share, given that he thought she was aboard by royal decree.

Or not. Her words shut him down, all ease and mirth leaving his expression. He pursed his lips a moment. Then he said, "None of your concern. Just some business."

Then he tossed the towel on the counter and left the grubbery, leaving El to finish the dishes on her own.

CHAPTER 6

THE *ADERYN* TOUCHED down on Alvar at exactly 19:07 local time the next evening.

El hadn't seen Captain Behnam most of the day, only at meals, where he did a good job of avoiding any conversation anyone tried to rope him into, preoccupied. And then later, when he popped his head into the control room when they were getting close to landing to tell her that as soon as she was finished doing her part with the landing, she was free for the evening—and implying she ought to make herself scarce.

Which is exactly what she intended to do. She knew the longer she stayed around, the more dangerous it got for her. She'd make it a lot farther if she moved from ship to ship, making no connections and not looking back.

Once the ship landed, El hurried from the control room to the gangplank to set out on her own adventures. Captain Behnam and Trapp had just headed out and she could see them as she got off the ship. As she had no idea where she was going, and she did not want to be accused of following them—nor was she interested in running into them—she decided to start in the opposite direction.

Except there was a man, dressed in nondescript jacket and trousers, his neck and face covered in tattoos, too preoccupied with the crew of the *Aderyn* to notice her. He was following them, that much was obvious, though he kept his distance, and she doubted his prey even knew he was there.

He had a look about him that put El on edge—shifty eyes, too many weapons, both carried openly and concealed on his person, clear bulges under the bulk of his clothing. He was well-built too, obviously trained in both combat and stealth. And the tattoos would suggest he was a Vercentii.

It didn't bode well for those he followed. And while she wasn't in their employ and them getting attacked would be the perfect diversion for her to slip away into oblivion, she was still a trained soldier. And she knew she could not leave those who had taken her into their care to die.

She'd always been loyal—a joke, coming from someone who had done what she had—but it was who she had always been. It was why she had stayed in the military as long as she did. It was why she changed her plans there on the streets of Alvar and followed them.

She could just see where it went and then slip away later. Captain Behnam had said their business would last a while, so she had time.

Gun in hand, she watched the stalker. Keeping back a good distance, she crept behind him as she hoped beyond hope that her own training in stealth did not fail her.

The task got harder as they moved into a more populated area. A bustling lane that El guessed to be the port's main street proved to be the bane of El's existence. Usually, she would be able to slip into the open here, to blend in with the crowds instead of cowering in the shadows, but she wore her Liosi uniform since it was the only outfit she owned—aside from the lounge pants and shirt El slept in and hadn't thought to wear as street clothes.

She would be easy to spot if the man glanced behind him, and if he did so more than once, it would be clear she was following him. But then a Liosi soldier slinking in the shadows was just as suspicious to the many ports-men who were all about her.

She could only hope that they were so busy with their own tasks that they didn't pay her any mind.

The crew turned down an alleyway and the stalker followed, El just a little further back. She breathed a sigh of relief to be out of the busy area. Though, being in such a secluded area proved to have its own set of challenges.

In fact, it was almost too secluded. A familiar wave of caution and anxiety washed over El. Something was off, and she knew from the churning in the pit of her stomach that it was not going to end well.

She flattened herself against the wall of the building, drawing her gun as the stalker fingered the handle of his own weapon strapped to his hip.

A man in the familiar fern green uniform of a security officer already waited in the alleyway. He was of average height and on the skinner side, with a muddy complexion and hair as unruly as hair ever was. It stuck up in all directions, thin and wispy, fluttering in the draft that blew through the alleyway.

She knew him instantly—Carrigan Gibbs, the son of her own commanding officer, though he'd chosen to become a security officer rather than follow in his father's footsteps. As such, he worked under El's own father, filling a role she'd never been able to fill. Though she couldn't imagine why he was here, in a back alley on such a tiny, insignificant planet.

He shook Captain Behnam's hand like they had intended to meet. If that was the secret Captain Behnam had been keeping, why keep it from a Liosi soldier?

Gibbs wasn't . . . disloyal, was he? She hadn't helped the crew get here so they could plot something dirty and underhanded against Liosa, had she?

She might have run, she might never be able to see her planet again, but that was because of what happened in Taras. That was the Philosanthrian war, Liosi just misguided allies in the fight.

No matter what they would say about her, she wasn't a traitor. Her heart beat true for her country; the blood of her ancestors—a fierce, proud people—pumped through her veins. She couldn't take part in something that would jeopardize her planet, her people, her heritage.

There was a doorway tucked in the corner of two buildings, an odd place for an opening really, and a woman came out to meet Captain Behnam and Trapp and Gibbs. She was sharply dressed in polished boots that came midway up her calf, fitted trousers, and a loose-fitting tank top. Her long curls were pulled loosely back, and her hand rested easily on the gun holstered on her thigh.

She spoke to those from the *Aderyn* but they were too far away for El to hear what was being said. El looked back to the stalker, who wasn't actually looking at those in conversation but to the rooftop above them. He was nodding to someone; a signal.

El glanced upward, all around the group in the alleyway, and found six or seven others, weapons drawn, aiming. Aimed straight at the son of her commanding officer. And suddenly all her doubts flew from her mind, her training kicking in and taking over.

"Gibbs, get down!" she screamed as she jumped to the ground, firing off a shot that downed the stalker in front of her. She didn't think, she couldn't. If she thought, she might freeze, and she couldn't do that. She could fight in her sleep, naturally, as long as her mind didn't get in the way.

She fired at the rooftop, though the other assailants had the sense to duck for cover in that time.

Trapp threw himself at Gibbs and dragged him toward a stack of barrels and crates in another corner of the alley. Captain Behnam drew his gun and fired at the rooftops, scrambling for cover of his own. The woman, too, had her gun out. But it wasn't the rooftop that she had it aimed it. In fact, it was aimed at—

El fired, hitting the woman, who staggered backward and dropped the gun she had aimed at Gibbs.

Captain Behnam glanced in her direction, offering her the swiftest of grins before rolling behind a barrel as a storm of bullets rained down on them. El went back to firing at will, managing to down at least one of those firing back at her.

A whistle to her right. She glanced in that direction, finding the Captain motioning to get her attention. He motioned to Trapp and Gibbs and then the door tucked in the far corner, the one the woman had come through.

She nodded, letting Captain Behnam know that she understood, and he grinned at her too easily for someone in the middle of a gunfight. Then he turned to give his instructions to Trapp and Gibbs.

She didn't like it. They had no way of knowing what was behind that door. And since one of their threats had come through it, there was a good chance there was nothing good beyond it. But then, retreating down the alleyway offered them little to no cover, and that seemed more of a risk.

There was a lull in the fight, a momentary ceasefire. El took the chance to reload. Trapp and Gibbs rose, getting ready to make a break for the door, Trapp in front with his gun drawn, the security officer behind. El awaited Captain Behnam's signal, and the assailants poked their heads up to see the reason for the ceasefire.

El and the Captain turned their full attention to the assailants as Trapp and Gibbs made a break for the door. Two more of the assailants, caught off-guard, fell while El and Captain Behnam fired on them.

When the pilot and the security officer made it safely through the doorway, Captain Behnam motioned for El to go next. She shook her head, frowning.

She was just another soldier and they could do without her. But the *Aderyn* needed their captain.

Not that she didn't want to make it out alive. But not at the cost of Captain Behnam's life.

An image flashed in her mind. A feeling, a thought, a face. Nothing concrete and too concrete all at the same time. They felt too real to ignore and yet they would not come into focus. Time warped as her mind raced.

She looked up and Captain Behnam was frowning at her. Of course he was disappointed in her. Everyone was. He motioned to her again, commanding.

He was the Captain. And she needed to follow his orders. That was how it worked; listen and obey or people die. But there were only two assailants left, if she had counted correctly, and it seemed silly to go off and leave Captain Behnam to fight them on his own.

And besides, he had made it rather clear that first day that he wasn't her captain.

An idea began to form in her head. She nodded to the Captain as if agreeing to his orders. Then she motioned to him that there was one assailant left, in front of him. He nodded in return, impatient, before motioning for her to get through the door.

She hoped beyond hope that he understood because otherwise, she would be dead in a minute.

She jumped up, scurried to the middle of the alleyway, and stopped, her gun held loosely in her hand as she held it above her head, as if she were trying to surrender.

"Elis, get down, you idiot!" Captain Behnam roared. She hoped beyond hope that he wasn't an idiot too.

She saw the second assailant, the last one. He was on the opposite side and to the left, poking his head up to see what was going on. His gun was trained on El.

She hit the dirt, twirling her gun into the firing position and getting off her shot before the man even had time to register what happened. As her own bullet found its mark, another shot rang out and she glanced to see the other assailant fall.

"You're an idiot, Elis," he said, but it wasn't so judgmental that time.

"Thank you, sir," she said, because it kept her grounded to the situation here and out of that alleyway in Taras. It had been she who had run into a building in the middle of the fight, likeness that of a comrade rather than an enemy.

She looked away from the body of the woman she had shot and toward Captain Behnam to focus on him and what he was saying. That memory belonged in Taras—it had no place in Alvar.

"Are you all right?" Captain Behnam asked, his voice deep with concern. She noted it—the difference between concern and pity. He didn't think any less of her—not yet—he just wanted to know if she was okay.

"I'm fine, sir," she said, even though her arm ached. Her old wound, healed but not happy with the way she'd fallen on it.

He frowned at her, hesitating a moment before nodding slowly, as if in agreement.

Trapp poked his head out of the doorway, gun drawn and ready. He gave her a questioning look and she nodded in return. They were safe.

Captain Behnam was still looking at her with his brows pulled together in concern. A warm sensation filled her, strange and unfamiliar. As the pilot and the security officer stepped into the alleyway she said, "We ought to keep moving, in case there are more."

That broke Captain Behnam's gaze and he looked to the rooftops, scanning for threats as he said, "Right, back to the ship then."

They made it back to the ship in less time than it took them to get to the alley in the first place.

Ginger came running down the gangplank to meet them, but her grin turned to a look of horror when she saw them. She fairly screeched, "Trapp, you're bleeding!"

Trapp rolled his eyes. "*Ech,* it's just a scratch."

"Did you get shot?" Captain Behnam demanded.

Ginger's eyes grew wider. "Why would he have gotten shot? Did you all get into a gunfight without telling me?"

The medic shook like maybe she would start crying at any second, and even El—who was not much of a physical touch person—felt the strange urge to hug the girl.

"You need to tell me these things ahead of time so I can be prepped for when you come back all shot up. Get inside this instant. I need to see to it before it gets infected."

"We didn't know it was going to end in a gunfight," Captain Behnam said. He shot a look at El with an intensity that she didn't much like. Was he mad that she was there? Upset that Trapp had been hurt? That wasn't her fault. Was it?

It was just a scratch, right? Trapp was going to be okay. He had to be okay.

Captain Behnam mounted the gangplank and entered the ship. The others followed. "I don't know why El was there since we told her to make herself scarce." He looked at her over his shoulder, appreciation written on his face. "But I'm glad she didn't listen to me because I'm fairly certain she saved our lives."

There was something about the words that made El feel something she'd never felt before. No one had ever spoken to or about her that way before. No one had ever looked at her that way before. She turned because she didn't like how giddy the look made her feel and—

Her gaze fell on Carrigan Gibbs.

A chill ran down her spine as their eyes met and the giddiness turned to dizziness. It was okay, she reminded herself. She was fine. Everything was fine.

Except she realized then that she wasn't supposed to have come back to the ship. She was supposed to have left and not looked back.

No loyalty, no attachments.

But then, if she'd done that, they'd be dead in an alleyway.

Glancing over her shoulder, she found the door had closed firmly into place, silent and unyielding. It was too late to leave.

She made a fist with her right hand, touching it to her shoulder as she bowed. "Cadet Elis reporting for duty. It is my honor to serve you."

"Ah, Security Head Elis' daughter," Gibbs said with a thin smile. "I should have known he'd send only the best to spy on me."

'Only the best.' Ha. If he only knew. Her father probably held more regard for the man standing before her than he ever had for his own daughter.

"I assure you I have no intention of spying on anyone." In fact, she would like to stay as far away from him as possible. "I'm here only to serve as needed."

She turned and found herself alone with him, Captain Behnam and Ginger no doubt having taken Trapp to the med bay.

Trapp.

She needed to make sure he was okay.

Fist to her shoulder, she bowed again. "Please excuse me."

Then, without waiting for an answer, she turned and hurried off in that direction to find the rest of the crew.

CHAPTER 7

WHEN EL GOT to the med bay, Trapp was seated on the table, overshirt off and wearing just a tee-shirt, the sleeve rolled up. Ginger patched him up with nimble fingers while Captain Behnam hovered nearby, a frown on his face as he flexed his fingers.

El stood in the doorway, feeling like an imposter. She didn't belong here, but she didn't know where else to go.

Trapp saw her first, and for the first time since she'd met him, he looked nervous rather than grinning at her. Was it the gunshot wound or her? Did he blame her?

She hadn't meant for him to get hurt.

"We need to talk." Captain Behnam's voice matched the tension in the room, and he seemed in a hurry to get her from the room, actually going so far as to turn her gently and steer her from it, shutting the door firmly behind him.

They blamed her for what happened. There was no other explanation for it.

"I'm really sorry." It wasn't enough. But Trapp was going to be okay, wasn't he?

"For saving our lives?" Captain Behnam's look suggested he thought her crazy, as if he hadn't been the one to all but drag her from the med bay.

"For getting Trapp shot."

"He's fine. He was just grazed, and Ginger'll have him patched up in no time. I just . . . Here . . . " He stepped into the training room and she followed. He shut the door behind her, and it fell into place with a firm *click*.

There was silence between them as he stood there with his brow furrowed, flexing his fingers.

"Did you . . . need something, sir?" El ventured to ask, eyeing him questioningly. There was something about the way he was looking at her, like he had something to say but didn't know how to say it. "Is something . . . Is something the matter?"

"You weren't supposed to come back."

El had been staring at her boots to avoid looking at him, but her head shot up then, her eyes meeting his. "Excuse me, sir?"

He was right, of course, but he didn't know that.

"I told you to make yourself scarce," he said with a sigh, arms at his sides, and he flexed his fingers as if they were bothering him. "You weren't supposed to come back."

Of course he didn't want her around; no one ever did. But why couldn't he come right out and say it? Why was it that everyone always wanted her out of the way, but no one ever had the guts to say it to her face?

Besides, as far as he knew, she was here under orders. So of course she came back. Why would she have left unless ordered otherwise?

"I'm just doing my job, sir," she said.

He let out another sigh. "Listen, Elis, I wanted to respect your secrets, and if you don't want to tell them, it's not my place to pry. And I'm not sorry you saved our lives back there—the stars know, I don't want to die. But when I told you to make yourself scarce, I meant for good. I knew we were coming back here with Gibbs, and I don't know how long I can hold him off from sniffing out your secret."

Her secret?

"What are you talking about, sir?" she asked with a nervous laugh that came out far too fake. "I don't know what you're talking—"

"Your desertion," he said bluntly, the word hanging heavily between them. The silence that followed dragged on for an eternity, El's mind racing, her body rebelling against her as she fought to breathe, fought to think, fought to focus.

"How long have you known?"

She ventured to look at him then, knowing what she would see—the anger at her betrayal written on his face. But she couldn't read his expression.

"I knew when I found you standing outside my ship that day," he said, hands in his pockets as he leaned casually against the training room door. "Ginger says I have an eye for seeing lost things, and I guess you could say that's true. But the biggest tipoff was when I asked if you were assigned to us and you said yes—we didn't have a soldier assigned to us."

It was a trap. He'd tricked her . . . because he'd wanted to help her? She'd thought he'd look at her differently when he found out she was a traitor but here . . . he'd helped her in her treachery. What did that say about him?

"I didn't want to do it," she told him. "I didn't want to betray my country."

He shook his head. "It's not my business."

He was right, it wasn't. But he deserved to know. And, if she were being honest, she needed him to know. That wasn't how she wanted to be remembered; she needed someone to know the truth. "You were right about what you said last night— if you don't believe in the orders you're following, how can you succeed?"

"I told you I was sorry," he said. "I shouldn't have laid it on so thick."

"It's okay," she said, standing up and starting to pace about the little room, unable to keep still all of a sudden. "Because you were right. We're fighting Prince Jarrett's war and none of us even understand what that means. The things that happened in Taras—the things we did—they were . . . " She shook her head as if to keep the images from coming to the forefront of her mind. "There's a reason I don't sleep at night."

"You don't have to justify it," he said. "I can deal with this easier than a government lackey. I was thrown off there when you wanted to go through our messages; thought maybe you were spying on us after all."

"No, sir," she said, then hastened to clarify—they were being honest with each other, after all. "I mean, I was, but not like that. I just needed to be sure you weren't sending or receiving communications about me. And that you . . . well that you weren't involved in . . . in anything too immoral."

"And what exactly did you find?" he asked with a chuckle.

She frowned, shaking her head. "Honestly? The results were inconclusive."

That brought another laugh from him. "Good to know." The mirth disappeared from his face. "I don't want to turn you away, but I don't know how long I can keep Gibbs from finding out. I can distract him while you slip off, though. You can just disappear, and no one will be the wiser."

Just disappear, as simple as that; it was a tempting offer.

It was the right choice to make. Just slip away while no one was looking, disappear into oblivion.

But she'd always wonder. And it wouldn't hurt to ask first.

"What kind of trouble is Gibbs in?" she asked.

"He's not," Captain Behnam said. "But there were some rumors that someone was trying to kill Prince Tov, and he wanted our help investigating that. Though I'd say today proves those rumors are true."

Prince Tov, Crown Prince of Liosa. Someone was trying to assassinate her Prince? But how? Something wasn't adding up.

"It proves someone wants to kill Gibbs," she argued, not understanding. "His Highness wasn't there but Gibbs was. I don't follow how you see that as proof."

Should she have said that? Here he'd done nothing but help her, and she had no business repaying that with judgment.

But he didn't seem too upset with her for asking. "We told them the Prince would be with us and they led us into an ambush, so I'd say that's proof enough."

She was inclined to agree. "Told who? Who exactly are we dealing with here?"

He shook his head. "There's no 'we.' You need to leave."

She looked him straight in the eye. "I'm afraid it might be too late for that. I—I don't know if I can walk away from this."

It was the wrong choice. She should take it back, tell him he was right. She needed to go—take the chance offered her and never look back. They had it under control.

"I'm not going to lie," he said, flexing his fingers. "I feel a lot better having you here. You're good in a fight, and you've a good head on your shoulders."

El wanted to cry as his words sank in, the full meaning of them washing over her. She couldn't remember the last time she'd been seen in that way. Praised and valued and . . . well, needed.

She'd been told her work was adequate before, and she'd known her place on her missions was important, but the Captain's words were something different.

The Captain wanted her help. He wasn't ordering her; he was asking her input.

And most importantly, he trusted her.

She'd be stupid to stay. But if she left? She'd never forgive herself—if something happened to the Prince, she'd blame herself for the rest of her life. If her planet crumbled, it would be her own fault. He was her Prince, not even crowned yet, the late King only just passed and the leadership still in transition until Prince Tov reached his majority.

If someone were trying to assassinate him, the consequences would be dire. And while she had abandoned her vow to the military, that didn't change her allegiance to her planet, to her sovereign, to her heritage.

It was worth the risk of getting caught.

Deep down, she knew the stupidest part wasn't that she might get caught if she stayed. It was that she might get attached. If she stayed, it would be all the harder to make a clean break in the end.

But it wouldn't be a clean break either way. And her planet was at stake. It was the wise choice to stay, to lower the stakes so that all that was left to break was her own heart.

"So who are we dealing with?" she asked again.

"We don't know for sure yet," Captain Behnam said. "But it would seem someone with enough connections to hire Vercentii mercenaries, as we saw today."

"Those weren't Vercentii," she said with a shake of her head.

Captain Behnam frowned at her. "What do you mean? Didn't you see the tattoos?"

"Anyone can get a tattoo, and they can even be faked, but the man I followed had earlobes," she explained. "Which absolutely means they weren't Vercentii."

His frown deepened. "I don't follow . . . "

"He wouldn't have earlobes if he was," she explained as she began to pace, the thin matting squishing underneath her feet. "It's part of the initiation, a sign of true commitment to their cause. The earlobe is a non-essential, but it hurts like fury when it's severed. Only someone truly committed to the group would be willing to go through that kind of pain to join."

"They teach you that in military school?" he asked, and El couldn't tell if he was impressed or deeply concerned.

She ducked her head. "I researched their founding leader for a school assignment about military heroes. I wanted to do someone no one else would."

"Okay . . . " He drew the word out like he didn't quite understand, and she felt the need to explain.

"He fought on every side during the Great War and was a spy for all seven planets involved, if you can imagine that, but somehow everyone loved him. He was decorated in every planet he fought for without ever actually swearing his allegiance to any of them. He remained active in combat until he died in a barroom brawl at age ninety-seven. The great Anara Bellatrix herself trained under him. I just thought it was really impressive. My teacher disagreed though, and it was the only failing grade I ever received."

"The only failing grade you ever received?" He snorted at that. "You were a teacher's pet, weren't you?"

Why was that what he took away from the whole conversation? And why did she find him so easy to talk to? He was capable of making her smile involuntarily as she told the man she'd only met a few days ago things she'd never shared with people she'd known for years.

She wasn't entirely sure her father even knew about that report. She shook her head, chasing the thought away. "So, you haven't a clue as to who wants His Highness dead?"

He bit his lip as he thought, shaking his head. "No idea."

"Whoever they are, they want us to think the Vercentii are involved," she said. "So, someone willing to go to great lengths to keep their identity secret."

"Why not just hire real Vercentii in the first place then?" he asked. "Especially if they're that incredible."

She frowned, thinking a moment. "Impersonators are harder to trace back to the source? If we thought they were the real thing, we'd be looking for someone who had connections or dealings with them. And, of course, they wouldn't lead us to our masterminds because the leads would be false."

"That makes sense," he said, and it was clear that time that he was impressed with her. "So where do we start now?"

She stopped pacing as she considered. "Maybe your contact? The one you were meeting, I mean. Who were they? We find out why they were willing to lead the Prince into an ambush and we'll have a lead."

Captain Behnam shook his head. "The woman's name was Dizara Anali—which, yes, I admit is probably a fake name. But she contacted us, said she could help us with our problem, and against my better judgment, I went because Gibbs insisted. That's the last time I listen to that kid."

Gibbs was probably the same age as the Captain but El had no time to be amused by that, as she was too busy focusing on the larger matter at hand—he had lied to her about the second communication device after all. "Contacted you how? It never came through on the comm."

He waved his hands as if that would clear things up. "No, it was before you came on board."

"But why wasn't it in the log?" she demanded. She wouldn't have cared before but, since they were being honest with each other, she didn't appreciate holes popping up in his story. Either tell her the truth or tell her it wasn't her business. She didn't like liars.

He shrugged like he couldn't quite understand why it was such a big deal to her. "I deleted it, in case a military spy somehow made their way onboard, like if you had been who you actually said you were."

Ouch.

She stood. "I can probably recover the message from the comm. Thing's so outdated, though, so I can't make any promises."

"I deleted it," he said again, but too late. She was already on her way to the control room, ignoring his protests that trailed behind her the whole way.

She got straight to work on the comm, searching through the recovery files to see if she could find the message.

He stood behind her, leaning over her shoulder. She assumed he was frowning as judgment dripped from his voice.

"I told you already, I deleted it."

She sighed, wishing he would just go away. The very fact that he was still letting her sit at the comm after what she had told him meant he trusted her, right? So why didn't he just leave her alone and let her work?

"It still might be on here somewhere," she explained. "Just because you deleted it doesn't mean it's truly gone."

"That doesn't even make sense," he said, and she resisted the urge to turn around and smack him for being such a nuisance. Years of military training came in handy for such situations.

"Even a piece of junk like this is encoded with backups and redundancies," she said, trying to keep her voice level and even. It came across as condescending instead, but she didn't even care. "So it's possible that while you deleted it from part of the comm, there's still another part that has it stored somewhere."

Trapp came over to lean against the console on El's right. Great. She was boxed in on both sides by a judgmental Captain and a giant.

"Can I have a little space please?" she asked, not because she was claustrophobic but because it was just really annoying.

"Oh, sorry," they both said, scrambling back and giving her the requested space.

"Thanks," she said, going back to work. It didn't help that she hadn't removed enough of the backfiles yet and so the machine was still running too slowly, freezing for moments at a time with no warning whenever it felt like it. She swiveled in her chair.

"Hand me that drive, would you?" she requested. She waved her hand in the direction of the device that sat on the edge of the console to her right. Trapp jumped to grab it and placed it in her outstretched hand.

She plugged it into the comm and tried not to scream as she waited for it to come to life in its own good time. After several minutes, the comm began to run louder, indicating that the machine had finally recognized that she had plugged something into it.

The little twirling icon appeared, a soft script dancing across the screen, asking her to please wait. As if she could do anything but wait. Trapp and Captain Behnam had leaned back in once more, watching the comm like it was actually doing something exciting.

"You really need a new comm," she told Captain Behnam. "What happens in an emergency when you need to send out a distress call and this piece of junk decides to take her own sweet time?"

"Did you just call that thing a 'she' while also insulting it at the same time?" Trapp asked like she was crazy.

She let out a frustrated sigh. "That's what you take away from that?" she grumbled as the device's folder opened, the folders within that folder popping up one by one.

Too slowly. They were loading too slowly. She might scream.

"I'm not joking," she persisted. She had nothing else to do while she waited for it to load. "This is a serious hazard here. If this thing decides she doesn't want to work at the wrong time, you'll all be in serious trouble."

"You too, Elis," Captain Behnam said, giving her a grin like it was all a joke or something. She reminded herself again of all the reasons why she wasn't allowed to smack him. "You're one of us now, remember."

"She's one of us now?" Trapp said, and El couldn't tell if it was just surprise or if there were also notes of judgment or disapproval in his voice. "So I'm allowed to talk to her now?"

"You weren't allowed to talk to me?" El demanded, turning to glare at Captain Behnam. She glanced back at the screen to find her folder loaded, and she let out a cry of excitement, any reply she might have made gone. "Finally!"

She clicked on the folder she wanted, holding in a strangled cry of frustration as the waiting began again, the spinning icon appearing and the soft script that read, "Please wait."

But then it loaded and the old recycling bin from the comm appeared, the communication she wanted right on top.

"Why is that folder even on here?" Captain Behnam asked as she clicked on it and the waiting began again.

"I wanted a chance to look through them but wasn't sure if the comm automatically emptied the trash after a period of time," she explained, keeping her focus on the comm, hoping the meaning of her words wouldn't sink in fully.

"So you were spying on us?" Trapp said, but there was a hint of humor in his voice. She only hoped the Captain found it as funny as the pilot did.

"Pretty much?" El admitted, about to peek at Captain Behnam to see if he was upset with her. He was shaking his head, and she couldn't quite read his expression.

"I've got other things to see to," he said. "Let me know if you find anything." And with that, he turned and left El alone with Trapp and the task at hand.

CHAPTER 8

"**WE FOUND IT!**" El said as she dashed through the doorway of the grubbery, pushing Trapp out of the way because he had decided to race her to give Captain Behnam the news. But it was her news to give and she wasn't about to let the pilot steal that from her.

He tried coming through the door, but she gave him another shove, slamming the door behind her and leaning against it in order to keep him out. He pushed, calling for her to let him in, but she held fast, though she knew he was far stronger than her and it wouldn't last.

"What in fury is going on?" Captain Behnam demanded, looking up from the papers he had spread out across the long table. He didn't look too pleased, and she automatically snapped to attention, moving away from the door, straightening her back, holding her head high.

Trapp fell through the doorway as she said, "We found the location, sir."

The pilot straightened, frowning at the Captain. "*Ech*, what'd you do? You made her get all military again."

Captain Behnam ignored him, saying instead to El, "You found the message?"

"Yes, sir," she said. "And where it came from. Or as close as we could get. It's a building. I don't know what exactly the building is for or where the comm is located, as I couldn't find a floor plan."

"That's fine. More than fine. That's—" He shook his head. "That's incredible. How do you even do that?"

"Well it isn't easy," she admitted, seeing her opportunity and taking it. "I mean I did have to reboot the comm three times before it worked long enough for me to—"

"You know what?" he interrupted. "Never mind. Let's just get on with this."

Oh well, it was worth a shot.

"Get on with what?" Gibbs asked as he came through the doorway.

El held back a groan. She'd been so excited for a minute that she'd forgotten about that part. She didn't know the last time she'd really lost herself that way.

She made a fist, putting it to her left shoulder and bowing. When she rose, she found him frowning at her. "Why aren't you in uniform?"

Her jacket had gotten torn somehow in the melee in the alleyway. She had removed it and wore just her standard-issue boots, trousers, and undershirt. It was almost a graver crime than being out of uniform completely. "I—uh . . . "

"Because I gave her permission," Captain Behnam spoke up, in such a tone that just dared the security officer to disagree with him. "And as this is my ship, she's under my authority. I believe we established that earlier?"

Established what earlier? When earlier? Gibbs hadn't been on the ship for more than an hour. What had been said? Unfortunately, it wasn't the best time to demand answers.

"It's required," Gibbs insisted.

"Well you'd better get used to the rules being broken then," Captain Behnam said, crossing to him and resting a hand on his shoulder. Gibbs shrugged under the action and El held back a snort; it was barely even a show of dominance. "Because we're going to break them. A lot. That's what we do."

Gibbs nodded, looking forlorn, almost a little sick. "Very well, Captain, as you say."

"Thank you," Captain Behnam said, in a way that suggested that he wasn't actually thankful; in fact, he seemed quite annoyed with the whole ordeal. "Now I suppose first thing tomorrow we ought to go to the address we recovered and see what we can find out about it. Trapp, you'll stay here with Ginger and Gibbs while Elis and I—"

"Cadet Elis really ought to stay with me," Gibbs objected, his eyes a little wide, perhaps afraid of being left alone. Which made her feel a little bad for him when the Captain protested.

"No offense to Trapp, but I'd rather have a trained soldier by my side," he said.

"Rude," Trapp said with a good-natured grin. "But, also, Ginger wouldn't let me go anyway, not with this arm."

Captain Behnam continued as if he hadn't been interrupted, "And as she's been so helpful up until this point, I don't know that I can do without her. I promise you that you'll be safe enough here without her."

"She was assigned here under me," the security officer insisted, in a tone that suggested he thought the matter closed.

El remained at attention, fighting to not allow herself to feel the disappointment that threatened to course through her. She wanted nothing more than to go with Captain Behnam. But not at the risk of blowing her cover. If she wanted to ensure Gibbs didn't discover her secret she was going to have to comply, to—

"And I'm the Captain," the man replied with a smug grin. "And if you don't like that, you can find someone else to solve your problem."

The jaw of the security officer dropped, imitating the shock El felt. She kept her face emotionless as she had been trained to do, but still, she felt the shock. No one spoke to a member of the Security Forces like that—and the son of a respected general, no less. Even enlistees, who didn't think highly of them as a whole, weren't allowed to speak their mind; no matter their opinion, the armed forces were technically below the security officers in rank and position. The office was considered one of the most important in Liosa.

But Gibbs nodded, not quite meeting Captain Behnam's eyes. "As you say."

El had never met a man who held that kind of power— one who didn't hold the power in the room but commanded it anyway. One who could stand up to a security officer without a twinge of fear and get away with it. Her respect for the man grew. He was certainly someone worth knowing, and she was glad that she and he were on the same side, fighting for the same things, as near as she could tell.

Captain Behnam turned to El. "I guess you'd better get some sleep then. We'll head out first thing in the morning."

"Yes, sir," she replied.

He sighed, sounding a little overdramatic in El's opinion. "And for the last time, could you try not to act so much like a soldier? You'll give us away in a heartbeat and the whole point is to blend in. Got it?"

"Yes-" She cut herself off and swallowed the 'sir' that tried to escape. She frowned, took a deep breath, and said instead, "Sure thing."

He laughed. "See that wasn't so hard, was it?" He waved her off before she could reply. "Actually, never mind, it was completely obvious how hard that was for you. It was painful to watch."

She shook her head. "Good night, sir."

He sighed. "Good night, Elis."

The next morning El and Captain Behnam headed out.

"I thought we were waiting until afternoon?" El asked as she and Captain Behnam left. The ship was closed up behind them, Trapp and Ginger and Gibbs tucked safely inside.

Gibbs suggested that they wait until afternoon because it was a busier time of day and they were, therefore, less likely to arouse suspicion. El agreed—though she'd been eager to get to it—and she thought Captain Behnam had too, but then he'd dragged her off, and she wasn't sure why they were leaving so early.

"We have somewhere to stop first," he told her as he continued to walk with long purposeful strides and didn't look back at her.

He wasn't that much taller than her—a few inches, that was all—but his legs must have been longer because he wasn't running and she had to hurry to keep up with him.

Alvar was less crowded than Cyrene, with fewer people pushing by on the street. Those that were about looked just as ramshackled though. And it was just as cramped—the buildings leaning in on each other as if they might, at any second, give up and collapse.

"Are you going to tell me where we're going? Because I don't do surprises," she told him. "I mean, with all due respect, sir."

"That was implied," he said. "You don't have to say it. And we discussed dropping the 'sir,' remember?"

They had, but she didn't like what that meant. If he wasn't her superior officer, what did that make him? "Yes . . . " she trailed off as the 'sir' tried to force its way out.

"We're going to get you something to wear other than that uniform."

That turned her attention from the hanging 'sir.'

"We're what?"

She didn't particularly like her uniform. It had once been like a second skin but after not wearing it for four months while she recovered, it had felt strange—wrong, even—to put it back on.

But to change out of it had a finality to it. As if as long as she wore it, she could pretend she really was the soldier assigned to the *Aderyn* and not . . .

Who was she without it?

She'd worn one for school and then the military. The person she'd been before she started wearing a uniform had been very young, and she certainly wasn't that girl anymore. She never would be.

"I probably should have said something sooner."

They'd stopped walking, and she didn't know who had stopped first. It must have been her without realizing it. She shook her head. "No, you're right, I'll blend in better out of uniform."

"I could have broken it to you more gently though," he said.

She gave a small shrug as she started to walk again because she didn't like the way he was looking at her. It was probably just concern, but she thought there might be pity in there too, and she didn't want his pity. She didn't even know exactly why he would give it.

It was fine. Of course it was fine. It was just a uniform, after all. Just clothes. It shouldn't matter what she wore.

"I'm not giving up my boots."

Not her boots. Not ever her boots.

They came up to her knees and had little pockets on the inside to hold things like her ID and her knife. And they'd been there for her through everything; her one comfort.

She wasn't giving them up.

"The uniform will sell for more if it's complete," he said as they approached a building, and he pulled the door open. She stepped inside first, her hand going for her gun, but his hand was on hers as he shook his head ever so slightly. It was just habit—walking into a place and assuming it held a threat.

It was a large room full of racks and racks of clothes and shoes and other accessories, crammed together in what was probably some sort of order, but was mostly just too full for the space it occupied.

"Find yourself something you like," Captain Behnam told her before he walked off, and she wasn't sure if she was supposed to follow or go off on her own. She supposed his instructions implied the latter, so she set to work looking through the nearest rack of clothes.

She avoided anything green, though her eyes were instantly drawn to that color; she was trying to avoid detection, and dressing in the color of the uniform she was about to shed hardly seemed practical. She went for more neutral tones instead—a black tee-shirt, a rust-colored jacket, black trousers. She found a pair of boots too, that would come up mid-calve, already broken in with soft, worn leather.

She hated them. They weren't her standard-issue Liosi military boots. They were just some other pair of boots without history and heritage or . . .

It didn't matter. Captain Behnam had told her they were selling them. That was that. It had to be.

She could tell him no. It was a small matter. He wasn't her superior officer. He didn't want to be. He kept telling her that. And he'd said he respected it when Ginger stood up to him and spoke up about her wants and needs.

But she had spoken up and he'd shot her down. And that was that.

CHAPTER 9

ITEMS PILED IN her arms, El went in search of Captain Behnam and found him standing at the counter in the middle of the room, talking with the woman who sat behind it. She was an older woman, wrinkled and weathered, dressed in a flowing robe with hair tied up in a colorful scarf, gold and silver and brass jewelry of every kind—earrings, necklaces, bracelets—clinking with her every movement.

His brow pulled, Captain Behnam frowned at the woman, waving his hands exaggeratedly as El approached. As she got closer, she heard him say, "It's still most of it; it's worth more than that."

He must be talking about the rip in her jacket from the fight yesterday. But he was right, it was just a small tear. She'd meant to mend it last night but hadn't gotten to ask Ginger for a needle and thread.

The woman shook her head, her jewelry jingling with the action. "No, it's the whole thing or nothing."

Whole thing? Was he trying to only sell part of it? Or was he selling something else entirely?

She reached the counter then and set the clothes down. He looked at the pile and then at her. "You found something?"

Obviously, but she didn't say that, just nodded.

"Good." He reached down and took the boots, setting them on the other side of him, away from her. "Not the boots. You can keep yours."

"What?"

She could keep them? But he'd said . . .

"We can get more for the whole uniform."

"We're coming to an agreement." He frowned at the women behind the counter, giving her a pointed look. "The uniform—even without the boots—is worth more than what you've got here. So I'm going to be generous and let us make an even trade instead of asking for the difference back."

The woman threw up her hand, waving it dismissively. "Fine. Take the clothes. Rob an old woman and her orphaned grandchildren of their bread. All for a few dollars."

"You can change in the back," Captain Behnam told El, pointing in that direction as he ignored the woman's show of dramatics.

She went in that direction, finding a little closet with a curtain over the entrance that seemed to be a fitting room of sorts. She slipped inside, hurrying out of her uniform and into the new outfit.

The trousers and jacket were stiff and unusual, fitting poorly as she hadn't had time to get comfortable in them yet. The tank top was loose and didn't look right tucked in, so she untucked it, even though she wasn't used to wearing a shirt untucked.

But she wasn't going to go find something else. They were just clothes, after all, and she had more important things to do.

Folding her uniform, she brought it back to the counter, handing it across to the woman who snatched it eagerly, clearly happy to have it. It would be used for no good, and El pushed back the twinge that weighed on her conscience.

"Are you sure about the boots?" she asked Captain Behnam as he started for the door.

They stepped outside and he looked at her with a curious expression. "Do you want the other boots?"

No. She wanted her standard-issue Liosi military boots. But it wasn't a question of what she wanted; it was a matter of practicality. And besides, he'd been the one to say they were selling them in the first place.

"They're worth a lot of money," she said.

He gave an easy shrug. "They aren't mine to sell. You want to sell them, go ahead."

"But you were the one who said we'd make more if we had a complete uniform," she reminded him, giving him a pointed look. Why had he said that if he hadn't meant it? Why had he made her think he was going to sell them only to act like it wasn't the case at all?

Another shrug. "You said no."

"I did not. I didn't say anything."

Why was he putting it on her? Why was he acting like she'd been the one to decide when he'd been the one who'd made a choice and then changed his mind? She'd do what she was told, it was as simple as that; why was he playing games?

"Exactly. You said you weren't giving them up, I mentioned the money in case it mattered to you, and you didn't say yes.

I'm not taking your boots from you, Elis. You clearly don't want to give them up. If I'm wrong, you're more than welcome to correct me and we'll sell them. But I don't want you under the impression it's anyone's choice but your own."

He looked at her expectantly, like he was waiting for an answer, but she didn't know what to say. He was right, she didn't want to give her boots up, but she wasn't used to people caring about what she wanted. Her needs weren't important, not when there was a greater good involved.

It was like the other night, when he'd said Ginger learning to say no, to voice her own wants, was important, and she realized he was doing the same thing to her.

Like she was one of the—

No. She wasn't going to go there. She couldn't. Because when it was all over, she'd still be running. She was a fugitive, and her choice meant she'd be looking over her shoulder for the rest of her life. She couldn't—wouldn't—ask the *Aderyn* to be a part of that life. It wasn't fair to them.

"Right, so we're going this way," Captain Behnam said, and she realized she'd done it again. Instead of answering, she'd opted to say nothing. Because it was easier, even when she'd been given permission to say it.

She really was hopeless.

The building where the message had been sent from was a hotel as it turned out; a dingy little two-story building with crudely painted birds on the sign along with the name.

El and Captain Behnam crouched in the alleyway across the street, huddled together as they assessed the scene and made a plan.

It was hard to believe he'd been so understanding and perceptive about her boots just a short while ago. They were qualities she wished he would afford her as they stood across from the hotel, arguing about the best course of action.

"I'm just saying that walking in and asking questions seems like a pretty good way to arouse suspicion," she said with an exasperated sigh. He had brought it up several times and she was getting sick of hearing it. When an idea was shot down, that meant you presented a new one, not that you repeated the same one in a more persistent voice.

"And I'm just saying you can't really get answers if you don't ask for them," Captain Behnam countered.

That was the stupidest thing she had ever heard but she had the foresight to hold that back. It was a struggle though—being out of her uniform made her feel like she could just say what she was thinking, and she was still a little shaken about almost losing her boots.

If Captain Behnam realized just how much went on inside her head, he'd regret making her his second on the mission, and she liked her job; she would hate to lose it.

Which she would if he did something stupid and got them both killed.

"You haven't exactly offered any other solutions," he pointed out. "So at the moment, it's the best we've got."

"You can't have something that's the best if it's the only thing." The words just slipped out and El regretted them instantly.

He put up his hands as if warding her off. "You know what? If you don't come up with something better, and fast, I'm going in there and asking questions, got it?"

She sucked in a sharp breath. Why did she always have to be the one to come up with the ideas? She'd been the one who figured out that the mercenaries were impostors and who figured out that the hotel was where the message originated from. Why did she have to come up with more than that? Why couldn't someone else come up with something for once?

Oh *victory*, it was a good thing she had a filter. There was no way she could say all that out loud.

"You might as well just say what's in your head." He spoke through gritted teeth. "It's annoying, you clearly thinking something and not saying it. This isn't really a conversation."

She shook her head. "I already told you what I thought."

"And you haven't presented a better idea," he countered. "So good or bad, it's all we have. So I'm just going to talk to them. It's the best we've got and—"

"No, wait!" she said, an idea starting to form. "What if one of us created a diversion? Then the other one could look for information without anyone else even knowing what was going on."

He frowned, but he was listening. "What kind of diversion were you thinking?"

She bit back her comment about how it still seemed unfair she had to do all the work.

"Well, it depends on how many people we need to distract," she said, thinking it through as she spoke. She didn't like doing it that way—she liked thinking first then discussing after—but Captain Behnam wanted answers, and she didn't think he was going to wait to get them. "If it's just one person, simply engaging them in a conversation, asking some questions, maybe getting them to step outside will be enough. If there are more people, it will require something . . . bigger."

"Bigger?" There was a twinkle in the Captain's eye, suggesting he liked the sound of that. "What were you thinking?"

She wasn't sure if she should be flattered or annoyed that he seemed to think she always had some sort of master plan in her head. She usually did, if she was being honest, but they took work to come up with, and the assumption made her feel a little taken for granted.

"A fight," she said. "One of us could pick a fight outside the hotel; if it gets big enough, enough people start to crowd around to get a look, and whoever's inside will likely come out to see what's going on. The other one slips inside, pokes around, slips out. No one's the wiser."

Captain Behnam grinned at her, and it reminded her that she really shouldn't feel taken for granted whenever he asked for a plan or idea. Because he really was impressed and appreciated them in the end.

"I suppose you want to be the one to slip into the hotel while I create the diversion," he said.

She gave a little shrug. "I wouldn't put it that way exactly. But I do think that would be the most strategic course of action, yes."

"So you want to be the spy," he said, looking annoyed, like he didn't know why she didn't just say so.

"No," she said, because he wasn't going to stop pushing until she told the truth. "I'd rather be the one pulling the punches while you look for the information, but it's more strategic if we reverse the roles. I'm slighter and people tend to be less suspicious of women. And as I'm the one who came up with the idea to look for the information, it's not a stretch to say I have a better idea of what sort of information to look for. Plus, while it's not a given on a planet like this, there is a chance that someone is more likely to step in and stop a fight if a woman's involved, whereas people are more likely to let it go if it's between two men."

He looked even more impressed and she tried not to love it as much as she did. "Hard to argue with logic like that. So what? I just find someone and pick a fight with them outside the hotel?"

"Unless you've got a better idea . . . "

"Nope," he said. "This one's all yours. Okay, okay, fine, I admit that they've all been yours. Just—you're in charge this time."

"Yes, sir," she said with a laugh. "Now go find someone to punch."

CHAPTER 10

E L SLIPPED INTO the hotel lobby, which wasn't much more than a dirty room with a counter in the back.

The man behind the counter looked up as she entered and frowned. "We're booked up. Get out."

He was a middle-aged man, around sixty, his face wrinkled and weathered. His head was bald on top, but along the sides, stringy gray hair fell past his ears. And he was scowling at her, which wasn't a good sign.

"Oh!" she said, her eyes wide, hoping it made her look frightened. "I—I just needed somewhere . . . If I could just wait here a minute, please, I promise I won't be a problem. Just until the man outside goes away? Please? I could just wait in the corner and you'll never even know I was there, *rook di goo*, I won't make a sound—"

"Take a breath already," the man interrupted, looking a bit overwhelmed by all her talking. "Go ahead and sit in the corner. Just be quiet about it, you hear?"

"Yes, sir," she said, bobbing her head. "Thank you so much! I promise—" She cut herself off, pulling in her lip and giving him a sheepish smile as she scurried off to the corner. At this point, there should have been noise outside, but it seemed Captain Behnam was having trouble starting a fight. How? All you had to do was make a snide comment about someone's girlfriend and fists would fly. It was as simple as that.

She took her seat in the one chair in the corner by the window and peeked outside.

She fiddled with her hands on her lap, like she couldn't quite get them comfortable, trying her best to look nervous. She shifted in her seat, sitting up to look out the window better. Captain Behnam was out there all right, but he wasn't even talking to anyone. How did he expect to start a fight if he didn't talk to anyone?

Then he did the simplest thing in the world—as another man walked past, he stuck out his foot and tripped him.

The man jumped and yelled at Captain Behnam about watching where he was going and demanding an apology. The Captain yelled right back about it being the man's fault, giving the man a shove when he got a little too close. El shrank back, listening to the voices growing louder and angrier, hoping that in the confusion she would be forgotten.

The man moved from behind the counter and crossed to look out the window. "Which one are you hiding from?"

"The tall one," she whispered, shrinking down further, trying to look as small and as vulnerable as possible. The tall one was Captain Behnam, as the man he had picked the fight with, while sturdily built, was a good several inches shorter than him.

The man's frown deepened. "Husband?"

She hesitated, weighing her options. Either answer was a gamble. It all depended on whether the man was sympathetic or not. If he was, a plea that Captain Behnam was her abusive husband would go a long way with him. If he wasn't, it would probably end with her getting dragged into the streets in the hopes that her husband wanted her back enough to offer a reward.

But if she denied it, there were too many explanations to offer as to who Captain Behnam was, and each one depended, again, on what kind of a man was here before her.

He was eyeing her then, and she realized she had hesitated for too long. She scrambled for an answer, coming up completely blank. The man nodded once, a disappointed frown on his face.

"Husband." It was a statement, a resignation. "Why don't you go wait in the back until he's gone, in case he decides to come looking in here once he's finished with his . . . business . . ."

He nodded toward the counter, and it was only then that she realized the wall behind it wasn't, in fact, just worn and uneven. There was a dirty piece of fabric hanging from the ceiling, creating a makeshift door that led presumably to the back room the man spoke of.

Her eyes went wide. "Oh! Thank you, sir. Thank you so much. I—"

"Thank me later," he said. "Just get on back there before he sees you."

She knew for a fact that a man in the middle of a fight wasn't going to recognize anyone through a filthy window. But perhaps the back room held secrets the man had forgotten about in his desire to help her—secrets that might lead to the answers she was looking for.

She scurried behind the counter. She waited until she was out of sight to put her hands to her gun, to be sure the man wouldn't see she had a weapon. She wanted to hope he was being nice, but on such a lawless planet, to make such assumptions was a good way to get yourself killed. Or worse. Slavery was still a flourishing business in places, and she wasn't about to be caught off guard.

She threw the man a grateful smile, keeping in character, before slipping behind the curtain and into the back room. As soon as the curtain fell into place behind her, she took out her gun, drawn and at the ready.

The room seemed abandoned, though it was littered with so many crates and barrels that it would be easy for one to hide behind. The floor was covered in sawdust scattered about with no real pattern, as if it had been there for a while and trampled over time. It didn't indicate any signs of recent activity.

There was no sign of a comm anywhere.

A shelving unit covered the entire back wall and contained a variety of boxes in different shapes and sizes, along with books that looked very much like ones records were typically kept in. That seemed like her best bet at the moment.

She crossed to the back, gun still in hand, looking out for anything unusual. Most of the boxes and crates had lids so she couldn't see inside them, though she intended to look if she had the time, once she was done looking at the record books.

She pulled a book from the shelf, balancing it on her arm as she still held her gun. She wasn't an idiot; just because there were no signs of life didn't mean danger couldn't come at any given moment.

Flipping through the book, she found carefully kept records of some sort of transaction. It didn't seem suspicious. It appeared to be for an exchange of goods—not services; some sort of smuggling ring, she would guess, from the prices listed. Which meant her slavery ring theory was still a viable one.

She flipped through the other books quickly, finding much of the same. She returned the books to the spot on the shelf and moved to the crates and barrels that scattered the room. It was hard prying the crates open with one hand—her gun still in the other—but they had already been opened, and while the lids had been replaced, they hadn't been completely nailed back down again.

There was sawdust inside, which explained the debris on the floor. She reached cautiously inside, pushing the sawdust around but finding nothing. That made sense, she supposed, given that the crates had obviously already been opened before. Whatever was in here had already been removed.

She replaced the lid and moved to another crate. It, too, was filled with sawdust and, upon inspection, nothing else. So it was with the next two crates she inspected. There was no trace of what had been stored in them, nor where the contents had gone.

At least she could be certain the smuggling ring was not one of slavery because it wasn't exactly a good idea to pack a live body in sawdust for shipment.

No, it was something else altogether. But what, she didn't know. And she had no way of knowing if it had anything to do with the woman who sent the Captain that message or if she was merely a guest at the sketchy hotel.

She might have been staying there because she depended on the owner's discretion. After all, why would he turn her in to the authorities if he himself were mixed up in something illegal?

No, El had to assume whatever went on there wasn't connected to the assassination attempt. Which meant she was back at square one. Which meant she needed a new starting place.

Replacing her gun into its hiding place, she slipped back into the front room, which was deserted. The sounds of the fight drifted in from outside. From the sound of it, it was quite the fight too; she was sorry to miss it.

She crouched behind the counter, where more record books were kept. They would hopefully tell if the woman was a guest there—assuming she used the same name she had given to Captain Behnam in their communications—and whether or not she had received any visitors. If she had used the same name, El would even know what room the woman had stayed in. And if she found a way upstairs to that room, she might even be able to search it for clues.

It was a stretch—the room had no doubt been cleaned between guests. No, that was a wrong assumption. The place looked as if it hadn't been cleaned in ages; it was actually quite possible that the room hadn't been cleaned and there were still all sorts of clues up there for the finding.

"Looking for something?"

El's hand instinctively went to her gun but she stopped herself just short of pulling it out. She knew she looked guilty—crouching behind the counter, record book in hand, the expression on her face doing nothing to prove her innocence. But there was no need to make him even more suspicious by bringing a weapon into the situation. She could talk her way out of it. She knew she could.

She bit her lip, looking down, keeping her façade of the frightened, abused wife. "I'm looking for—for a woman. Dizara Anali?"

There was an old Liosi saying that if one wished to be believed, then one must tell the truth, even in a lie. And she saw no reason to hide that part of her true purpose. But if she truly wanted him to believe her, then she was going to have to stick to the lie she had already told him.

"I—I was told that—that she could help me? With my . . . my . . . problem." She trailed off, hoping beyond hope that he took her meaning.

He seemed to as his eyes lit with understanding. "What makes you think she can help you?"

"I was told—" She broke off, considering her wording. "I was told she was good at making problems go away."

"And what makes you think she would want to help you?" he pressed.

She looked up then, her eyes meeting his and pleading with him. "I have money. I can pay. It's not much but . . . " She looked away, her gaze downcast, hoping the action would gain her some sympathy. "I don't have the skills she does. I can't—I can't make this go away on my own. I don't have much, but I'll give her everything I have if she can make this go away before . . . "

An idea popped into her head and she ran with it before she could second-guess it. She trailed off, her hand going to her midsection, running her fingers over it gently, carefully, lovingly.

The man sucked in a sharp breath, and she peeked up at him. From his expression, she guessed he took the meaning of her actions quite clearly. There was concern and anger both in his expression, though she guessed only the former was directed at her, with the latter being for Captain Behnam and the man she had falsely painted him to be.

"Does he hurt you?" The words were sharp, harsh, stern. But she knew he didn't mean them to hurt her.

She didn't look at him, didn't look up, didn't meet his eyes. She kept her gaze downcast as she gave the smallest nod.

He let out a small frustrated sound. "Dizara isn't here right now but she should be back soon. She'll take care of this for you. We can make it so he never touches you again. If that's what you want."

"Yes, sir?" She said it like a question, like she wasn't sure. Then she swallowed hard, nodding resolutely, looking up to meet his eyes. "Yes, sir. I do. I need this to go away. I can't let this go on, not with . . . " Her hand was on her stomach again.

He nodded too, his lips pressed into a thin, unhappy line. "All right then."

It was only then, as the agreement was made, that she fully realized what she had done—she had just taken out a hit on her Captain. She had told terrible lies about the kind of man that he was and then she had asked a man to kill him for her.

He was never going to let her be a part of his crew.

The street had grown quiet, and the man looked to El. "You should wait in the back in case he comes in here."

She slipped from the room as bidden, standing by the edge of the curtain, back to the wall, listening.

She still wasn't sure that the proprietor wasn't playing an angle. He had, after all, offered to help her fairly quickly. He could, of course, just have a soft heart; it was stereotypical to assume that just because one lived in a sketchy town that they were also corrupt. Even if he was involved in a smuggling ring, that didn't mean he wanted to see her harmed or dead. Living conditions or occupations—no matter how sketchy—did not determine the state of a man's heart.

But all the same, she couldn't ignore the fact that he had offered to help her so readily. He had either seen through her lies and was, therefore, acting out of suspicion, or she had played the role of an abused wife a little too well. But even if the latter were true, she had no way of knowing if he hoped to gain something or if he truly just desired to help a woman in need.

She had offered to pay, true, but she had made it clear that she didn't have much. And the clothes Captain Behnam had bought her were secondhand, worn. She did not give off the air of affluence or wealth so being held for ransom was out of the question. She had not given him any reason to think Captain Behnam—her "husband"—was anyone of importance and be worth anyone's while to knock off.

No, by all rights there was no reason for him to offer her any sort of assistance. She needed to stay on her guard and not fall prey to his appearance of niceness.

Her fingers tightened around her gun, and she glanced about the back room, looking for any signs that someone had come in since she had been there last. The sawdust that was scattered was in a pattern that suggested her movements and nothing more, so it looked as if she were still alone in the back.

She turned her attention to the front room again. She heard nothing; maybe the man had gone away. If he had, it would be time to leave. She could confer with the Captain and come back later if needed. All she would have to do is apologize to the man and tell him she had gotten scared and run but was back and ready for his help.

She listened a moment more, just making up her mind that the place was, in fact, deserted and that was her chance when she heard the front door open. She pressed herself flat against the wall and listened.

"I'm looking for a woman." It was Captain Behnam's voice, though a bit breathless. "She's about so high, small-boned, hair in a ponytail. She's got on—uh . . . She's wearing, uh, mostly black with a rust-colored jacket, tall boots. Pretty little thing."

He had called her pretty. Which made up for the fact that he had called her little. She was only a few inches shorter than him.

"Haven't seen her," the man said. His voice was on edge, but it was anger or annoyance—or both—that laced it, not fear. It was obvious that he was a man who was comfortable with telling lies.

"I know she came in here," Captain Behnam insisted, his voice urgent, almost afraid.

She felt bad and wanted nothing more than to offer him some assurance that she was, in fact, all right. But there was no way for her to do that without blowing her cover with the man, so Captain Behnam was just going to have to deal with it.

"Listen, mister," the man said, anger not just lacing but defining his tone. "I don't know who you are, but no woman matching that description has come into this hotel today. So I suggest you look elsewhere, otherwise I'll have to call the authorities."

That was a bluff. Given the obvious smuggling that went on in the hotel—they weren't even trying to hide it, really—there was no way the man was going to ask officers of any law enforcement agency to come here for any reason.

Unless he had some sort of deal with them. She wasn't familiar with the law on Alvar, and it was possible that they were willing to look the other way if a portion of the profits found their way into the right pockets.

"Go ahead," Captain Behnam said, though he had no idea of the evidence of smuggling there in the back. He could probably tell that the man was bluffing just by the state of the front room; the whole thing screamed of shady dealings.

But he was banking heavily on it being a bluff, given that if the man did call the authorities—even if he didn't have a deal with them—they were sure to take the side of their countryman over that of an outsider. And even if that weren't the case, the Captain had been involved in a gunfight the day before in which at least seven people were killed. The last thing he needed was the law in his business. So he was taking quite the risk, assuming the man wasn't going to bring down more trouble than he was prepared to deal with.

"You asked for it," the man said, and El heard the cocking of a gun. A Calso-ASQ from the sounds of it. She pressed herself against the wall, straining to hear more.

Captain Behnam drew in an apprehensive breath. He spoke slowly, deliberately. "You can just go ahead and put that thing away."

"You said you wanted the authorities," the man replied, much too relaxed for someone holding a gun. "This is the only real authority around here. So you just head right on out of here and we'll forget any of this ever happened."

El's fingers traced the handle of her gun, ready, waiting.

"That's not going to work for me," Captain Behnam said, slowly, calmly. That was good, neither of them sounded nervous or fidgety; people accidentally got killed when those sorts of emotions ran high. "She's under my authority and so it's my job to see her safe. You hurt her, and I'll see you live just long enough to regret it."

The man snorted at that, his words laced with anger and bitterness as he spoke. "Is that so? So what, you can treat her wrong and it's fine, but anyone else who touches her has to pay? You going to treat the baby the same way or do different rules apply to your blood?"

"What?" There was obvious confusion in Captain Behnam's voice, and confusion and anger were deadly in situations like that.

She drew her gun, holding it steady in case the Captain needed her to back him up. But there was a stone in her stomach, knowing that if guns were fired, she wouldn't be able to get into the room fast enough to be of any use. It would all happen too fast; it always did.

And if anything happened to him, it would be her fault, since he had only come in here looking for her. He'd be back on his ship already if he wasn't looking for her.

"Listen, I have no idea what you're talking about," Captain Behnam said. "But I know my girl came in here. So you can tell me where she is or where she went and then we can get to the part where we forget any of this happened."

"Nothing doing," the man argued. "If you wanted to keep her, you should have treated her right. She came here looking to pay to see you gone. Now I'm going to do the decent thing and give you the chance to walk out of here, but if you push just one more inch, I will end you here and now, do you understand? The authorities won't think twice about it either, not after that fight you just so kindly held. All I have to do it tell them you came in here looking for trouble, and not a single one of them will question whether I was within my rights to end you or not."

"She said she would pay to end me?" El couldn't tell if the emotion in Captain Behnam's voice was confusion or betrayal. She hoped beyond hope that he trusted her long enough that she got a chance to explain everything to him.

"You've got five seconds to get as far away from here as possible," the man said. "I suggest you take advantage of it."

The man sounded serious. There wasn't a hint of emotion in his voice, and she didn't doubt he was going to fire if the Captain didn't leave on the count of five.

"I'm not going anywhere until I get my answers," Captain Behnam said.

"One."

El knew she ought to step out and end it. But if she did, they might not find out the information they needed. She had a cover that was too valuable to just throw away. If only Captain Behnam would just give up and go; if only he would trust her.

"Two."

"You can stop counting now," Captain Behnam said, sounding annoyed. "Just tell me where the girl is. Elis?" he called. "Are you here? Elis?"

She wanted to scream at him, wishing there was some way to communicate to him that the man was serious, that she had the situation under control. She didn't need him looking out for her.

"Three."

"Where's my girl?"

He wasn't going to leave. The idiot was going to just stay here and get shot over her. And she ought to let him. She was here, after all, to save the Prince, not him. If she let him get shot, she might still be able to find out the information she needed.

"Four."

"Where. Is. She."

But then he wasn't doing any of it for the Prince, not really. He was doing it for her—risking his life, willing to get shot and killed, over her. When was the last time she had been on a team because someone wanted her there? When was the last time someone had put their life on the line for her, hadn't taken the chance when it was given to walk out on her, to leave her and save themselves?

"Five."

Time was up.

CHAPTER 11

E
L SHOVED THE curtain aside, stepping into the front room. Her gun was trained on the proprietor, whose own gun was trained on Captain Behnam. To his credit, the Captain was standing rather easily, not looking at all like someone about to be murdered in some sketchy hotel on a lawless planet in the middle of nowhere.

"All right, mister, you can drop the gun," she ordered.

Captain Behnam let out a sigh of relief when he saw her, but it quickly turned to confusion as his brow furrowed. "What is going on here? He said you took a hit out on me? And you're pregnant?"

"I was trying to get information," she said. "Seriously, mister, drop it."

"You don't have to do this," the man said. "I can take care of him here and now, and no one will be the wiser. You don't have to stay loyal to him, not after the kind of husband he's been."

Captain Behnam's eyebrows raised. "Husband? I don't remember us getting married. What is going on?"

"I told him you were my abusive husband," she explained. "And I might have inferred that maybe I was pregnant."

"But you're not?" he clarified.

"No!"

"And the part about you paying money to end me?" he pressed.

She didn't look at him. "I said I was looking for someone to . . . to take . . . care of you . . . "

"You seriously did take out a hit on me." Disbelief was plainly written in both his voice and expression.

"It was the fastest way," she defended herself.

"You took a hit out on me!" Incredulity filled his voice and expression. He looked hurt and maybe even a little angry.

El snorted. "I didn't let him shoot you, did I? I had it all under control—you were the one who messed it all up."

"I messed it up?" Captain Behnam's eyebrows rose so high they disappeared under the hair that fell across his forehead. "You mean when I was looking out for you and making sure you weren't bleeding to death in the back room here or worse? Do you have any idea what could have happened to you in a place like this?"

She pursed her lips, frowning at him. "Do you have any idea how capable I am of taking care of these sorts of things? It's only what I was trained to do. I had it under control."

"I'm sure you did." But he said it in a tone that suggested that maybe he wasn't so sure.

She drew in a breath, reminding herself that he was still her Captain and they had more important matters at hand. "He said he knew Dizara Anali. And he said she or her associates might be able to help me. It was a lead—the only one we have at the moment, I might remind you—and I went with it. So, yes, I had it under control."

"I knew something was wrong with your story," the man said, and El jumped at his input. She had been so lost in her argument with Captain Behnam that she had forgotten he was there. That was what he did to her—he made her forget everything she was trained to do.

The man's eyes were narrowed into little slits as he glared at her like she had betrayed him. And she supposed she had, but he offered to kill a man for her, so she only felt a little bit bad about it.

"Would you stay out of this?" Captain Behnam demanded. "And just drop your gun already, would you? She's not joking. She will shoot you if she has to. The girl's crazy."

"Excuse me?" she demanded. "I am a lot of things, but crazy isn't one of them. I'm just doing my job, all right? If you don't like that, you should have left me on the ship and brought Trapp instead. So this is all on you."

"I meant that in the nicest way possible," Captain Behnam said, frowning at her like she was supposed to know that. "But you would try and blame me for this." He turned to the man, who still had his gun trained on him, watching the scene before him unfold in dazed confusion. "If you don't drop that gun in the next two seconds, I swear on the stars I'm going to lose it."

"Just drop the gun," El told him. "Now. And then how about we all have a little chat?"

The man didn't lower his gun, shaking his head. "I've got nothing to talk to you about. And he's right—you're crazy."

"Hey!" she exclaimed. Then to Captain Behnam, she said, "You see what you started?"

"Me?" Captain Behnam demanded, putting up his hands in defense. "I'm not on his side. We—" He waved his finger between him and the man to indicate the two of them. "—are not on a team. We—" He waved a finger between himself and El. "—we are on a team. You and me. I'm on your side all the way."

"Did you hear that?" El said to the man. "It's two against one. Now drop the gun."

The man lowered it to the counter, eyeing her with bitter suspicion. He raised both his hands in the air and Captain Behnam jumped for the gun, sweeping it off the counter in one swift movement.

"All right," El said to the man as Captain Behnam stepped back. "Now start talking—what do you know about Dizara Anali?"

"Surrender is not the same as compliance," the man said, crossing his arms and looking sullen. "I have nothing to say to the likes of you."

El rolled her eyes. "You aren't going to make me feel guilty about any of that. And I'm not going anywhere until you talk. So tell me what you know."

"No," the man said, his words definitive, assertive, final.

She let out a frustrated sigh. "Captain, please make the man talk."

"What makes you think I can make him talk?" Captain Behnam said, looking at her like she might be out of her mind. He was thinking she was crazy again; she knew that's what he was thinking. "I thought you said you had this under control!"

"I did until you came and messed up my plans," she reminded him yet again.

"Why should I tell you anything?" the man demanded, giving her a look of defiance. "Why should I tell you the truth when you give me nothing but lies?"

He had a point. A good one. El couldn't deny that. She was asking the man to talk to her when she had spewed nothing but lies in his direction. "I'm El and this is Captain Behnam. We're part of the crew of the *Aderyn*."

Captain Behnam didn't look too pleased with her, like she had done something wrong by giving the man their names. But she didn't much care. She knew what she was doing. She hoped she did anyway.

The man squinted and studied her. His jaw set in a firm line. "The *Aderyn*. You were supposed to meet Dizara yesterday."

"You know about that?" Captain Behnam asked, perking up. El sighed with relief. The man was talking; she did know what she was doing after all.

The man glared at Captain Behnam, turning his attention to El instead. "Did you meet her?"

El and Captain Behnam exchanged a look, a weight settling into El's stomach. She had hoped to be away from here before that came up, had hoped that she would not have to be the one to tell the man the truth.

The man's frown deepened, marked with concern. "What's happened? What happened to Dizara? Did you not meet her?"

"She led us into an ambush," El said, swallowing hard, forcing the words out. "She—she was killed in the fight."

A fire of rage was lit in the man's eyes. "Which one of you killed her?"

He flung himself at El, not waiting for an answer, a guttural cry escaping him as if he were being strangled.

The man was strong, but he was much older than El, and she had been trained hard; he was no match for her. She had him on the ground in an instant, his arms pinned behind his back and face pressed against the floor.

"Why did Dizara lead us into that trap?" she demanded. "Who was she working for?"

"I don't talk to murderers," the man said, and El noticed the moisture in his eyes; surely she had not hurt him so badly? She eased her grip in the slightest.

"You were willing to carry out a hit on my husband for a price, and Dizara was about to kill a friend of mine when I shot her. I'm pretty sure that puts us all in the same category."

"Don't lump me in with him," Captain Behnam objected. She shot him a look to tell him he was certainly not helping matters.

She addressed the man. "All we want to know is who hired her. Give us a name and you'll never have to see us again."

"Tempting," the man said, frowning. He said no more, and El guessed he wasn't about to budge any time soon. She rose slowly, cautiously, taking a step back and keeping her gun trained on the man. He rose to his feet, rubbing his wrists and giving her a cross and sullen look.

She needed answers and she couldn't wait for them. They could stand and argue all day and get nowhere, and there was no guarantee that his friends weren't going to show up at any second and turn the situation into something far more dangerous.

"What was your relationship with Dizara?" El asked, deciding to approach it from a different angle. It was clear there was something personal between the two, and if she could get to the heart of it, she might be able to use it to her advantage.

"Who cares?" Captain Behnam demanded, looking none too patient about how it was all playing out.

"I do," she snapped, shooting him a look that caused him to shut his mouth. He nodded, taking a step back, indicating that he was deferring to her. A sign of trust, and one that would not go unnoticed.

"Was there something between you two?" she asked the man, keeping her voice soft, gentle, calm. Demanding answers were obviously not going to get them anywhere. "Something more than business?"

He frowned at her, a frown so deep it was clear that he was not pleased with her current line of questioning. But he had just lost someone, someone more than a colleague, someone he cared for. And when that happened, didn't you want to talk about them? Didn't you want to talk it all through to make it all make sense? You wanted to hold onto them, and if you couldn't, if people shut you down, you went crazy. You needed to keep them alive, even if it was only with the power of your voice.

"You loved her, didn't you?" El pressed, unsure at the moment what kind of love exactly was between them. But there were so many kinds that it wasn't a stretch to think they shared one. "Was that it?"

The man drew in a breath, letting it out unhappily. For a moment, El thought he intended to stay silent, but then he said, "Not like that. I'm too old for a girl like her. She was made for someone younger, someone with more life ahead of them."

"But you were close then?" El said, pleased she had been right. Of course, it wasn't a far leap given the way he spoke of her, the way his face softened and his voice wavered, the way he fought to hold back the tears he so clearly wanted to shed for her.

"As close as someone can get to someone like her," he said. "She was too wild and free. There was no holding that girl down, no keeping her back."

"You didn't want her to go yesterday, did you?" Captain Behnam piped up, studying the man.

The man glared at him but said, "She never did like being told what she should or shouldn't do."

"Then why don't you tell us who sent her there?" El said. "We want the same thing—to see that person pay. It was them who sent her into that alley; it was their fault that she died."

The man snorted, fixing her with an ugly glare. "It was you who fired the bullet that killed her; don't think I didn't pick up on that."

"Which I did to save a friend," El defended herself, knowing as she said the words that she was making a confession, confirming his accusation. "A friend that whoever sent us all into the alleyway wanted dead. Your friend died for someone else's fight, and I would be willing to bet whoever that was doesn't care. She's expendable, collateral damage to them. And it's not fair. Not even close to fair. If you give us a name—just a name is all I'm asking—we can see that the person pays for what they did. We will see that her death is avenged, *rook di goo*."

She'd been in that woman's shoes—a stranger in an alleyway fighting someone else's war. It wouldn't make amends, but it would be something.

"You wouldn't be doing it for her," he said, cold, sullen.

"We would," she promised him. "For her and for every other person who shouldn't have died. Because people shouldn't be allowed to get away with that. Innocent people shouldn't die just because someone isn't willing to do their own dirty work. All we need is a name," she said again. "Can you give us a name?"

There was a pause, a silence between them all. And then, ever so slightly, the man nodded.

The man from the hotel hadn't been willing to give them his own name but he gave them the name of the man who had hired Dizara Anali. The man who wanted Prince Tov dead.

As El and Captain Behnam made their way back to the ship, El clutched the paper with the name written on it tightly in her hand, too afraid she might lose it if she put it in her pocket. Captain Behnam grinned at her as they walked, and she found she liked the expression very much; she almost wasn't even mad at him anymore.

"You took out a hit on me," he said. How long was it going to be until he stopped bringing that up? The thought surprised her because she realized it meant she was assuming she was going to be around for at least a little while.

She shook that thought away because she couldn't afford to think like that.

"I also got the name we needed," she pointed out.

The grin widened. "That too. You did a good job. A really good job. I'm—I'm impressed, to say the least."

Impressed. She tried to think of the last time someone had said that to her, and she came up empty. Had anyone ever?

"Thanks." She ducked her head and looked away, trying to keep back the smile that came to her lips unbidden.

"How did you know?" he asked. She looked up at him, her expression a question. "That if you asked about their relationship, he would talk. How did you know that was the right question to ask?"

She shrugged. "Wasn't it obvious? He was clearly taking her loss personally; it stood to reason that the wisest thing to ask was what you'd want someone to ask if you were in that situation."

"I've never actually been in that position," he admitted sheepishly as he offered her an apologetic smile; what was he apologizing for? It's not as if it were his fault that he had never lost anyone close to him; it was just nearly impossible to imagine.

"Never?" she said, studying him to see if maybe she had misunderstood his words. "What about your parents? Grandparents? Friends?"

"Still alive, all dead long before I was born, and Trapp and Ginger," he said, ticking them off on his fingers as he spoke, eyes rolled up as he thought, considering.

"Really?" she said with a laugh. As soon as it was out, she felt bad about that laugh. "Just—Trapp and Ginger are your only friends?"

He shrugged. "I mean, no, they're just . . . they're the closest. But there are other people whose loss would affect me; it just hasn't happened before."

She couldn't fathom someone who hadn't been hurt by the loss of a loved one. "I would have thought someone as grumpy as you would have a reason."

"Never said I haven't been hurt before," he said, his expression none too happy; maybe she should have kept the comment about him being grumpy to herself. "I just haven't lost anyone close to me through death. But you have. You've had that happen to you."

She gave a small shrug, not looking at him, but instead keeping her gaze on the dusty street. She really ought to be on her guard, but she couldn't bring herself to look up just then. "Until a moment ago, I assumed everyone had. So yes, I've definitely lost someone close to me."

"Your mother," he said.

It was a statement, not a question. She looked up then, meeting his eyes, her own wide with question. "How . . . ?"

He shrugged. "Not a huge leap. You said your father joined the military after your mother died, that he enrolled you into the military academy then. I just figured if there was anywhere you didn't get asked the questions you wanted to be asked to grieve properly, it would be the military."

"Oh. Yeah."

She forgot she had told him all of that. And she was surprised that he remembered. True, she had remembered what he had told her about his own family—vague and undetailed as it was—but then, she just had a brain for those things.

But she wasn't used to other people remembering things about her. Or caring when they did. She wasn't quite sure how to deal with that. How was she supposed to react?

"Right," Captain Behnam said, not quite meeting her eyes. Though she felt bad, she was glad that he seemed to find the whole situation as awkward as she did. "So, uh—yeah. Do you have any ideas, then, about how we go about finding this . . . What was his name again?"

"Radian Darius," she supplied. She opened her hand and uncrumpled the paper, checking to be sure she was right. "Yeah, Radian Darius."

"Right, him," Captain Behnam said. "What are your ideas on how to find him?"

There he went again, assuming she had a master plan.

"The comm connects to the info database," she said. "That would be a start, though I don't know exactly how much we'll find out there unless he's done anything newsworthy. I'm going to guess a man like this works discreetly, too discreetly for that to be of much help, unfortunately. But it's worth a shot starting there. After that . . . " She paused, thinking. "After that, I have no idea. I'll need to think about it."

He nodded. "Yeah, okay. I'll see if I can come up with anything too. And maybe we'll get lucky, maybe Gibbs knows the name."

There was a chance, but she wasn't going to hold her breath. He had, after all, been assigned the mission back when it had been considered a fool's game.

Captain Behnam stopped, and El felt the hairs on the back of her neck standing up. "What's the matter?"

He shook his head. "I don't know . . . I just . . . Do you get the feeling we're being followed?"

She looked about them but didn't see anything unusual. Still, she kept her guard up and her hand on her gun as they started walking again.

They made it to the ship without an incident, however, and the gangplank started to descend as they approached. El felt herself shaking as she waited, glancing about, her breath coming in small, sharp bursts. "We need to get out of here."

The gangplank settled into place as El caught a flash of something out of the corner of her eyes. Liosi soldiers, coming toward them.

Even if they ran up the gangplank, it wouldn't close before the soldiers reached them. Like everything else on the ship, the gangplank moved much, much, much too slowly.

She knew what being caught meant. In a place like Alvar, she might not even get a proper execution—just dragged off to who knew where and never seen again. She wouldn't even go down in history as a traitor—she'd just be gone, wiped from existence.

And while she knew someday her past would catch up with her, that she'd have nowhere left to run, she didn't want to die.

"I need to hide."

She didn't wait for a response, running off then, not stopping to wait for a reply. All she knew was that she couldn't get caught.

She didn't have room for the thoughts that started filling her mind. She was running because it was the right thing, not just because she was scared to die.

At least, that's what she kept telling herself.

CHAPTER 12

EL SHUT THE door to her bunk and went straight
for the bed.

She felt along the floor underneath, searching for
the panel she knew was there. Her fingers found the small hole
and she cracked it open. She eased her way inside the hidden
compartment beneath the bed and pulled the panel back in
place, shutting herself in.

There were footsteps coming closer, voices speaking clipped
words. The door to the room opened and the footsteps sounded
above her.

"Whose room is this?" a voice demanded, cold and
commanding.

It was Captain Behnam who replied, sharp and annoyed, "I
told you, we had a passenger, but we haven't seen him since yesterday when we docked. We were just about to take off without

him. And with all due respect, you have no right to search this ship—Alvar isn't under Liosi occupation."

"We're in the midst of a war, Captain," the man replied. "And Alvar has been wise enough to choose to partner with the winning side. That gives us the right to conduct any military business we need to."

"And just what kind of military business are you conducting?" Gibbs demanded.

No. No, no, no, no, no.

If Captain Behnam had asked, the soldier would have told him that it was military business and none of his. But the man who asked was a military official, ranking higher than the one to whom the question had been asked. And so he got an answer. "We're looking for a deserter. A cadet by the name of Elis."

Captain Behnam knew her secret. He was okay with her secret. But Gibbs wasn't Captain Behnam. And she was going to have to face the consequences of that as soon as these soldiers left.

Assuming they left. They had to leave. She couldn't stay locked in that little hold forever. She suddenly realized just how small it was. Was there actually any way for air to get in?

The walls were closing in on her faster and faster as she looked about. The space was barely big enough for her to scrunch up, lying crouched there in the dark, the metal above her, beneath her, all around her.

She would die down here, suffocating in her own cowardice because she was too afraid of standing up for what was right and facing the consequences.

And the worst part was she wasn't sure which fate was worse.

The man spoke again. "I want this entire ship torn apart, every inch searched. Pull the walls off if you have to."

"Now see here!" Captain Behnam began, El's breath catching at the command; they were going to destroy the ship. And the Captain would give her up before he let that happen. Torn between the two alternatives—a razed ship or a razed life—she lay there, frozen in indecision.

"Silence, you," the man said, his words sharp and stern. "Or I'll have you arrested for hindering us in our business and therefore siding with the enemy."

Captain Behnam didn't respond, and El could only imagine the expression that graced his face just then.

The ship meant so much to him, and it would be her fault if it were destroyed. When it was destroyed. She knew what Liosi soldiers were capable of. She'd been a part of it in Taras, and if they could do that to an entire planet, she could only imagine what short work they would make of a ship that was already falling apart at the seams.

Her breath caught in her throat, the space growing smaller still.

It was all her fault. The *Aderyn* wasn't exactly the pinnacle of beauty but it held a special place in Captain Behnam's heart. It was his home, and when it was destroyed, it would be her fault once more.

How many homes had she destroyed in the last year? How many people had she displaced or decimated? How many times had she told herself it was for a good cause, that she was on the side of right? How many times had she pushed back the questions, swallowed her insubordination because that was what a good soldier did?

But lying there in the belly of the ship, she saw herself for what she really was.

But to face them would be admitting those meting out the punishment were right. If she were in the wrong, they couldn't be as well. And she had been in the right. That was the only thing she'd been sure of in a very, very long time.

She loved her country. She loved it more than she loved the very breath in her lungs. But she could not and would not allow herself to believe for a second that what they were mixed up in was right. It couldn't be. And she refused to die for something so very wrong.

And yet at the sound of the first crash of metal on metal, horrible and hollow, a sound that rang throughout the little space in which she was hiding, her resolve wavered. She could feel the sound as it clawed at her, deep within her bones, bitter and painful. The grotesque song of metal scraping against metal, harsh and ugly.

She drew in a breath, slowly, carefully, willing herself to do the right thing.

While she might not be willing to die for what was wrong, she was Liosi, and that meant she had to die for what was right; it was in her blood. And in that moment, what was right happened to be not letting a group of destructive soldiers destroy the home of people who had been nothing but kind to her.

Captain Behnam hadn't looked at her the way she'd expected when her secret had been revealed. He should have seen her as a traitor but instead, he had listened to the horrible things she had done, had taken her words in stride, and then he had made her part of his crew.

He'd almost let that man at the hotel shoot him today over her. Sure, she hadn't needed his help, but he hadn't known that. He had been willing to take a bullet for her, needing to know that she was safe.

And most of all, he hadn't given her up yet. They were destroying the thing he loved most in the galaxy and he was allowing it.

For her.

Her mind was made up then, her resolve set.

The ship grew eerily silent.

It put El all the more on edge, the quiet less a comfort and more a threat she didn't quite know how to deal with. If you couldn't hear something coming how could you deal with it? How could you prepare for it?

And then there were footsteps.

They made a beeline straight for her room, straight for the cot. The panel opened and without even thinking about it, she had her gun out, cocked and ready.

"*Ech*, El, it's me."

Trapp. There was a shakiness to his voice underneath the usual merriment, though she supposed she couldn't blame him. She felt exhausted herself, even more so than she usually did, and she hadn't actually been above to see the destruction that had taken place.

He reached out and offered her a hand, and she took it as she slipped her gun into her holster. She scrambled from her hiding place and gulped in the fresh air, savoring each breath with new delight. Ginger was there and El let the girl wrap her in a hug as she tried not to look at the state of disarray that her room was in.

"I thought you were a goner for sure," Ginger said, her voice soft and soothing but laced with tears; but then of course Ginger was crying, she always cried.

"They didn't even bother to look under the beds," Trapp said. "Because they're bolted down, they must have just assumed there was no way to have a hiding place under there. How'd you even know they were there?"

She offered him a weak smile. "I found the ship's schematics on the comm."

He looked as if he wanted to say something in response, but Gibbs entered just then, crowding the already cramped little room. He locked eyes with her, and she knew what was coming.

She pushed it all aside, forcing herself into action. Her hand made a fist and she put it to her shoulder, bowing low, saying nothing; there wasn't anything to say.

He swallowed hard, so loud she could hear it, as she remained doubled up in a bow. Or maybe the room was just that silent. His words were unsure, not certain, as he spoke. "You're a disgrace to your Liosi blood."

"I'm not proud of the fact that I ran from my duties," she said, truthfully. He was right, she was a disgrace. But so was every person who had made her do the things she'd been forced to do, and that was something a security officer could never understand. "But I don't regret my decision. I'm still a proud Liosi and nothing can change that."

She hoped beyond hope that her last statement was, in fact, true.

He shook his head, and she feared he would drag her off to the nearest Liosi soldier to have her executed there and then.

But it was Trapp who spoke, his brow wrinkled into a scowl directed at Gibbs. "Are you seriously doing this now? That's what you think is important?"

"What do you mean?" She looked from Trapp to Ginger to Gibbs and then realized something—one very important person was missing. "Where's Captain Behnam?"

Trapp, Ginger, and Gibbs all exchanged a look, and El's chest grew tight. Something was wrong. Where was Captain Behnam?

"What happened?" Her words came out more clipped and harsh than she intended, and yet she had no inclination to offer an apology as she felt little, if any, remorse. If they didn't start giving her answers, she might even start yelling.

It was Gibbs who spoke, drawing in a sharp breath and setting his shoulders with resolve. "Captain Behnam has been arrested."

El felt as if the breath had been knocked out of her.

She had expected the ship to get torn apart. But arrested? She hadn't dreamed her actions would come back on Captain Behnam like that.

"Why?" she said, because while there were a thousand thoughts spinning in her head, that was the one that made it to the surface first.

Gibbs and Ginger looked to Trapp, and in that moment El came to a weird realization—with the Captain gone, Trapp was in charge. At least so far. El doubted it would take long for Gibbs to get over his shock and start trying to assert his dominance, as he continually did, even with Captain Behnam.

"He wasn't actually arrested," Trapp clarified. "Just detained for questioning."

El knew a little something of the legal system on planets like Alvar and even more about how the military operated in these kinds of situations. So she knew exactly what detaining someone for questioning looked like.

"Where'd they take him?"

Trapp shook his head. "They weren't inclined to answer any of our questions."

She frowned, nodding. That made sense. "We'll obviously have to figure that out before we can make any sort of plan."

"Excuse me, but who put the traitor in charge?" Gibbs demanded. Then to El, he said, "You should be grateful you're not in handcuffs right now."

"We both need to do this—me because I own him a debt, you because without him, this mission of yours is back to the beginning. So might I suggest we set our differences aside for now until this is over? Once Captain Behnam is safely returned to us, we can revisit this. And you have my word that I'll be here and ready to submit to your authority when such a time comes, *rook di goo*."

His frown deepened. "Your word means little in light of your crime; how do I know I can trust you?"

"*Ech*!" Trapp exclaimed. "El's been nothing but loyal and trustworthy since she stepped foot on this ship. Might I remind you that she has had ample opportunity to run in the last two days and instead she's put her life on the line for you and your purpose on three separate occasions in that time? I suggest you take her deal, Officer, unless you'd like to find yourself a different crew to help you."

El nearly took a step back in her shock—had that speech been made about her?

Gibbs narrowed his eyes. "I don't have to answer to you, pilot, and I am frankly getting a little tired of you thinking you call all the shots now. This isn't your ship."

"I've more right to a say in the matter than you," Trapp replied levelly, not even batting an eye at the security officer's tone. "So take her deal or pack your bags; it's just rust off my hull as far as I'm concerned."

They both stared at each other; how long would it be before one of them backed down? Men.

"This is ridiculous," Ginger said with a shake of her head as she stepped closer to them, putting one hand on each of their chests and not quite pushing them apart, though that was clearly the idea. "This is how this is going to go—we're going to forget that we have any differences between us until we take care of Leiv. If the situation were different and he was here, he wouldn't let anything stand in his way to get us back here safely. So we're going to do the same for him. And until then, I don't want to hear another word about any of this. Am I clear?"

There was silence again, the two men still glaring at each other.

"Am I clear?" Ginger said again, her voice as soft as it ever was, but there was no mistaking the deep emotions lying beneath the surface.

Neither man said anything, but they stepped apart, breaking the deep glare that passed between them. Ginger accepted that, nodding once in affirmation. "All right then." She turned to El. "What now?"

"I still have issues with her being in charge," Gibbs said. It made sense that he would question Ginger's taking command since Trapp was technically the second-in-command, as there was no first mate on the ship.

But then Ginger spoke. "In the absence of a captain, it's the first mate's job to assume command."

They were all looking at El. Gibbs was questioning El being consulted, which was fair in light of what El had done. Still, she did tend to be the one coming up with the plans these days, so it did make sense.

137

But wait, had Ginger called her—

"I'm not the first mate."

El had barely been on the ship for any time at all and most of it had been under false pretenses.

Ginger offered her the softest of smiles. "Perhaps not officially."

El looked from Trapp to Gibbs and then back at Ginger. No one was arguing the point; Gibbs didn't look too pleased about it, but his mouth was also closed, which wasn't exactly an easy task to pull off. And Trapp looked downright pleased with himself as if he'd something to do with the whole thing.

But still, El shook her head. "I can't—"

She couldn't stay. Captain Behanm had made it clear the lengths he would go for her, and she couldn't allow that. She wouldn't let destruction like that happen on the ship again, not because of her.

"You can," Ginger said. "And this isn't your fault."

El shook her head. "I wasn't thinking that."

"You were," Ginger insisted gently; for a medic who considered herself useless, she somehow knew everything. "And it isn't true. If you had come out of there sooner and confronted them, all that would have happened is this situation would be the same, except we'd be rescuing you instead of Leiv. Or worse, if you'd been killed, who knows what Leiv would have done."

She was right, but all it did was confirm what El already knew—her being on the ship brought nothing but trouble.

"So what do we do?" Trapp asked.

She took a deep breath. Captain Behnam needed their help and that was what she was going to focus on. "Right. We start by greasing some palms, getting as much information as we can. Trapp and I can do that and—"

"I'll go as well." The tone in Gibbs' voice made it clear he did not consider the matter up for debate, but since she had been put in charge, El didn't much like the idea of immediately being told what to do.

"Given what just happened, I'd rather not leave Ginger alone," El said firmly.

Gibbs shrugged. "Then you stay here. I'm going, though, and that's that."

"You aren't exactly the model of inconspicuousness," Trapp said with a snort. "But if you want to be steel-headed about this, I'll stay here with Ginger."

Gibbs nodded once in affirmation as if Trapp hadn't just insulted him. He turned to El. "Shall we get to it then?"

CHAPTER 13

EL MADE GIBBS change out of his uniform. Even in his displeasure, he complied though because, as Trapp had said, they were trying to blend in, not stick out.

A little later when they entered the Rusty Mushroom—a back-alley bar in the heart of the city's sketchiest district—she was more than glad she'd made that call.

The room was small, with tables and chairs packed onto the floor so that there was barely room to weave among them. Shady looking characters dotted the room in small clusters, some nursing drinks quietly, some talking loudly, others deep in conversations or hardcore games of chance.

El moved among the crowd to the bar, taking a seat at a stool and slamming a coin down on the battered metal.

"What can I do you for?" the girl behind the bar asked. She was Tarisian. Had El been part of the girl's displacement? Had she been the one to obliterate her home so she was forced to move to the back-alley planet and scrape out a living serving drinks to characters of ill-repute?

She was only fourteen or fifteen, and El wondered if her parents were still alive or if they'd been killed. Worse, was El in some way responsible for their death?

Gibbs cleared his throat harshly and El zoned back in, shaking her head to shake away the thoughts that were creeping in. The last thing she needed was more guilt. That wouldn't do anything to save Captain Behnam.

The girl frowned at her, lips pursed into a thin line as she tucked a stray strand of dark hair behind her ear. "You gonna order or just sit there wasting my time?"

"We need information," Gibbs said curtly from behind El before she could say anything.

She let out a sigh as she shot a death glare over her shoulder at him. She turned back to the girl behind the bar, who had taken a step away from them and crossed her arms defensively.

"I don't know anything."

"You don't even know what sort of information we're looking for," Gibbs protested. He stood with his arms crossed and a scowl gracing his face. Was he trying to be intimidating? And did he know he wasn't actually pulling it off?

The girl raised an eyebrow at him, her lip twitching upward in what was almost a smirk but not quite, as if she were too cool and collected to actually complete the action. "Whatever it is, I don't know anything about it. Now if you're not going to order, would you excuse me while I go serve the paying customers?"

She turned before they could say anything, which El was grateful for because there was no way to know what would have come out of Gibbs' mouth given half a chance.

"What was that about?" she demanded once the girl was gone.

Gibbs took a seat on the stool next to her. "What're you talking about? I was just asking her for the information we needed."

"In the wrong way," El snapped. "We'll be lucky if she even comes close enough for us to talk to her again."

Gibbs was saying something else but El assumed it was just grumpy comments and not worth her time, so she ignored him, turning her attention instead to the rest of the bar.

A couple in the corner were arguing passionately, heads bowed together. The girl kept looking up and glancing around as if she were embarrassed to be having such a heated conversation in a public setting. The guy's focus, however, was solely on her, though it seemed more as if he were pleading with her than threatening her, so El didn't feel the need to intervene.

There was a rowdy game of Kitask dice going on right in the center of the room, taking up three tables, all pushed together, though it made for an awkward playing space given that the tables were round. A dozen or more men crowded around and El wasn't sure who was playing and who was a spectator.

There were several tables occupied by lone drinkers, all working-class people, who'd no doubt had a hard day and were drowning their sorrows in alcohol to wash the dust and the stress away. How many were going home to family members and how many would sleep alone?

And on the far side of the bar was the Tarisian girl who had come to take their order.

She was talking to an older man in his fifties or sixties, El guessed, who had an air of affluence and authority about him. His posture was straight, his shoulders squared, his eyes darting about the room as he spoke to her, as if whatever she was saying wasn't important enough to warrant his full attention.

The girl, however, looked fully engaged in the conversation, speaking earnestly. El couldn't hear what was being said but it was clear the conversation was an important one.

Finally, the man turned to her, and El had to stop herself from jumping up to put herself between the man and the girl. She wasn't there to cause trouble. But then if he laid one finger on that girl, she wasn't sure if she'd be able to stop herself.

But he didn't touch her—or hit her, as El expected he would. Instead, he merely leaned in close and said something in her ear. The girl stiffened at his words and a shiver ran down El's spine. After a moment, he straightened and walked away, stalking about as if he owned the place, and El realized that he probably did.

He wasn't Tarisian so he wasn't the girl's father—not that his threatening or intimidating her would be acceptable either way—so he was probably her employer, and one she clearly wasn't happy with.

She stalked back over to the bar, her shoulders sagging, her demeanor much less confident than before.

"You going to order something?" she snapped at them. "Because if you aren't, leave and make room for paying customers, would you?"

"I don't think so," Gibbs said, leaning on the bar easily. "Here's what's actually going to happen—you're going to give us the information we need or we're going to go talk to your boss over there and tell him just how displeased we are with your service. It looked to me like you were already on his bad side, and I'm guessing you don't want to get in any more trouble than you already are."

The girl stared at them for a long minute, silent, eyes wide, and El scrambled for something to say. The girl probably did have the information they needed but El also wasn't exactly impressed with Gibbs' tactics. If it did somehow come out that she had given them the information, she'd be in a lot of trouble.

El really didn't need yet another thing like that on her conscience.

The girl finally nodded, once, firmly, definitively. "Okay but not here. Meet me out back in five minutes."

"We're not meeting you in a secluded alley," Gibbs said with a snort.

"And I'm not telling you anything out here in the open," she replied, firm, her mind clearly made up. "So you can either take what I'm offering or do your worst."

It was a bluff and El knew it. The girl didn't want them to talk to her boss, to get her into trouble, and El had no intention of letting Gibbs do that.

"Just take the deal, Gibbs."

He shot her a look but immediately turned his attention back to the girl. He nodded. "All right, fine. Alleyway, five minutes. But we see even a hint of trouble and you will pay for it, are we clear?"

She nodded and something in her eyes—the raw fear that threatened to brim over as her confident mask shattered—made El trust her. "You have my word, sir."

El and Gibbs slipped outside, moving around to the place in question.

Meetings in back alleys weren't something El normally agreed to. And she was warier than ever after that last debacle in an alleyway.

But part of being a soldier was learning to trust your instincts, and her instincts said she could trust the girl. She seemed innocent, and while El didn't approve of Gibbs' methods, the girl seemed genuine in her fear and not at all as if she were plotting something against them.

Still, El was on her guard as they slipped behind the building, Gibbs keeping an eye on one side and her the other. He might be a complete idiot most of the time, but as a security officer, he had completed much of the same training that she had, and she was grateful to have someone with those skills at her back.

At the very least, if it did come down to trouble, she'd have someone she could trust here with her.

"You shouldn't have been so aggressive," El told him as she leaned against the wall of the bar. "You came down on her too hard."

"I was doing what was needed to get the job done," he said plainly.

She wanted to fight with him, but the sound of footsteps caught her attention—not those of one girl light on her feet but several grown men in boots.

She caught Gibbs' eyes and he nodded to her as they focused on the direction the footsteps were coming from. They were too close to a crowded public place to use gunfire as a first resort, but she also wasn't above shooting anyone who tried to stand in her way.

The alleyway was dark, made darker still by the three men who stopped in the opening. El couldn't see their expressions but she guessed they were smirking based on the tone of voice of the one who spoke.

"Pretty little thing like you shouldn't be back here all alone."

It took El a moment to process before she realized he must not see Gibbs—unless he was talking to Gibbs and didn't see her, but she doubted that from his words. She decided to use their lack of knowledge at their numbers to her advantage.

"I just needed a breath of fresh air," she said, trying to keep her voice light and innocent. "I was just about to head back inside."

"No, I don't think you were," the man said, and all three of them stepped into the alley, coming closer toward her.

It was over in a matter of seconds, not even really starting before it ended—El got several good hits in and managed to avoid being pummeled too seriously.

Once they realized she was stronger than the innocent maid they had taken her for and that she wasn't, in fact, alone, they made their way out of there as fast as their ignorant legs would carry them.

"You all right?" she asked Gibbs once they were alone again. She rolled her shoulder, not much liking the ache that was settling there but also grateful that was all the pain she was really in. A sore shoulder was a small price to pay for what she'd just gotten into.

He grunted, and she realized he was holding his jaw.

"They get any teeth?" she asked.

"Naw," he said. "Just grazed it but it's still sore."

That was all right then. Ginger would be able to fix him up when they got back to the ship and he'd be fine before the sun rose tomorrow.

There were footsteps again, and the girl appeared at the edge of the alleyway. She took a few steps toward them cautiously.

"I wasn't sure you'd be here."

Gibbs snorted, and before El even had time to process any of it, his hands were on the girl as he shoved her against the wall of the bar. She hit the wood with a thud and let out a little squeak as the breath was knocked out of her.

"What are you doing?" El demanded.

"She led us into this," Gibbs said, a cold, hard edge to his voice.

"You've got to be kidding," she said since surely he wasn't serious. "They thought I was alone, they weren't sent here by anyone, especially not her. Get your hands off of her."

"I didn't, I swear," the girl said, her voice soft and pleading. It shook as she spoke, coming out in small, panting breaths.

"Shut it," Gibbs said. "The next thing I want to hear out of your mouth are answers and nothing else, is that clear?"

"Yes, sir." Her voice cracked and the last word was almost a sob.

"Gibbs, let her go."

It took all of her strength for El to get the words out, and her chest was tight as she said them.

It was the pleading and the sobs that did it to her, sounding too familiar, bringing back too many memories, the smell of smoke filling her senses as shadowy images filled her mind. Too many Tarisians had been harmed at her hands. Too many times had she stood by and said nothing.

Because she was too afraid. She was always too afraid.

But not anymore.

She was too tired and too done with it all. The girl was innocent, and if Gibbs didn't take his hands off her in two seconds, *rook di goo,* she was going to kill him.

He eased his hold on the girl, but his angry, violent hands were still on her, and it wasn't good enough for El.

"Hands. Off."

There must have been a warning in her voice because he did let her go, holding his hands up defensively as he took a step back.

"Are you all right?" she asked the girl.

The girl didn't say anything for a moment before she sniffled and replied, "I've been worse."

Her words cut a little too deep, and El had to force herself to speak. "I'd like to apologize for my associate. We don't stand for this sort of thing, and I don't know what came over him. You don't owe us anything, but if you could find it in your heart to tell us what we need to know, we'll be forever in your debt."

"Sure, whatever," she said, but there were still tears in her voice and it shook just a little bit under all the confidence.

"There's a group of Liosi soldiers operating in an official capacity somewhere around here. We need to know where their base of operation is."

The girl shook her head, and even in the dim electrical glow coming from the street, El could see her eyes widening. "I'm not getting mixed up in that. I won't—not with Philosanthrians."

"They're Liosi," El said again. How could the girl mistake the two? True, they were allies, but they were vastly different.

"They might be Liosi, but they aren't soldiers and they pay with Philosanthrian money," the girl stated firmly. "There are enough people that come and go here, I know the difference between a soldier and something even worse than that. Please, don't ask me to get mixed up with them. I—I just can't."

El nodded even as she heard Gibbs opening his mouth to speak. "We understand," she said before he could say something to the contrary. "You've no reason to risk your life for us, especially after how we've treated you."

She was more concerned about the bit of information she had just given them. If they were working with the Philosanthrians, that meant—

"Thank you," the girl said, and it stung. She was thanking them after the way they'd treated her, for not treating her worse, and it wasn't okay.

"Listen," she said before she lost her nerve, "I think I know someone who can help you if you want out of here."

The girl snorted. "Like I'm going to trust you not to send me straight to a den of slavers."

Okay, that was fair. Of course she wouldn't trust them.

"You're right," El said. "You don't have any reason to trust us. Especially after the complete mess we've made of this whole situation. But you do deserve better than this. You shouldn't be thanking strangers in an alleyway for not hurting you more than they already have, and no one should be allowed to push you around ever again. You're worth more than that, and if you'll let me, I might be able to help you, for no other reason than I'm sorry and you deserve so much better."

"You should go," the girl said, but her voice wavered. "Please."

It was fair and El had no intention of pushing her any further.

"If you change your mind, the hotel on Diameter Street, the one with the birds painted on the sign," she said. "There's a man there who helps people like you. Just tell him you're in trouble and looking for a way out."

She knew the girl likely wouldn't take it. It was easier to stay in a situation she was in than to risk walking into a slaver's den. At least her pain was known; whatever evil might be found elsewhere had the potential to be even worse. But still, she had to try.

She nodded to Gibbs, indicating it was time for them to go, and they both took several steps to leave before the girl said, "Wait!"

El turned, not sure what to expect, telling herself not to hope for anything. "Yeah?"

There was a pause, and El thought for a moment the girl wouldn't say anything at all. And then, "The soldiers you're looking for, they're over on Prejudice, in the old Foxworthy building."

The past was the past, and El knew that, in situations like the one in the alley, it made the most sense to just move on, to go forward and not look back. What had happened in the alleyway was over and done with.

She also knew that Gibbs had not only been doing what he felt the situation warranted, but he also held her very fate in her hands.

And yet as soon as the girl was gone, as soon as they stepped out of the alley and onto the street once more, El punched him.

He staggered backward, holding his jaw, and it was only then that El remembered that it had already been hit once before that night.

Even so, she didn't feel even a little bit sorry.

"What in the void?" he demanded, glaring up at her as he cradled his jaw in his hands.

El rolled her eyes as she flexed her burning hand. "Please, I barely tapped you. It's nothing near what you deserve."

"Excuse me?"

She ought to apologize. She wanted to live—didn't want to be executed for treason. And yet, she didn't want to kiss up to a bully just to preserve her own life. Not anymore.

She was done standing by and saying nothing.

"You had no right to treat her that way," she said. "You were too aggressive, and if you want to keep working together, you need to understand that your actions were not acceptable."

She started walking back in the direction of the *Aderyn*, beginning to process the information they'd gotten and formulating a plan.

"If you want Captain Behnam back, you're going to have to ruffle a few feathers," he said.

She whirled around to face him, and he almost crashed right into her, she stopped so fast. He barely managed to skid to a stop just in the nick of time. "That was not ruffling a few feathers. That was coming on too aggressive to a girl who is probably only here because of a war we waged on her planet. Just because we need information doesn't make it okay to treat her that way. She's a bystander in all this, and I'm not interested in making innocents our casualties."

"This is about what happened on Taras, isn't it?"

She turned and started walking again, saying nothing.

"Just because you can't stomach war—"

She turned again and that time he did run into her. He stumbled backward and nearly lost his footing while she remained upright and indignant. "Are you calling me a coward? Because I'm pretty sure we both know that's not true."

It was a little bit true, but Gibbs didn't know that. He had no right to call her bravery into question.

"You're not the golden child Security Head Elis made me think I had to live up to."

Golden child? She'd never been anything close to that in her father's eyes. "It was probably just another game of his." She couldn't believe they were having the conversation on a street in Alvar, but here they were. "I was never anything to him, no matter what I did. Anything he said to the contrary was a lie."

"I just wanted him to be proud of me," Gibbs told her, "to speak of me the way he spoke of you. And it turns out, you're nothing like the person he made you out to be."

She had no idea what her father had said about her and she maintained it was a lie, plain and simple. Her father had never cared, absent in his praise and distant in his role as a father. She'd never been anything to him, and she'd stopped hoping for his approval a long time ago.

But Gibbs' words were so honest, his tone soft and more confused than accusatory, and it was only because of that that El considered that perhaps she did owe him an explanation after all.

"I'll tell you about what happened," she said, her voice soft to match his own. He ought to know before he could truly pass sentence on her. "About why I ran. But now isn't the time. Right now, we're talking about you and the way you treated that girl."

"We got the answers we needed."

She shook her head. "The end doesn't justify the means. You act like that again and you're done. I can do this on my own; I'd rather not, but I'd prefer it to having someone by my side who thinks such actions are appropriate."

"All right, fine," he said. "We do it your way. What do we do first?"

She let out a sigh. "First we have to get my uniform back."

CHAPTER 14

EL WASN'T SURPRISED that the shop she and Captain Behnam had sold her uniform to was still open when they arrived, even though it was well into the night. There was a man working, and El also wasn't surprised that he didn't want to sell the uniform back to her.

But El was not in the mood to play games.

"Listen," she said, calmly. "I'm offering you a fair price—twice it's worth—and so this is how it's going to go—you're going to let us buy the uniform back at the price we're offering, or this gentleman behind me is going to pull out his officer's badge and arrest all of you for being in possession of a stolen army uniform. If you're lucky, that's the only charge that will stick." She glanced over her shoulder at Gibbs. "Is it just me or does it seem like maybe they've got some other things to hide too?"

"They've got some other things to hide," Gibbs agreed.

The man frowned at her, and for a minute El thought he might be stupid enough to reject the deal. But then he nodded. "Whatever, fine. Just take it and go—and I don't want to see the likes of you in here again."

"*Rook di goo*, I have no intention of coming back," El told him as she took the familiar green outfit from him. "Thank you."

They headed back to the *Aderyn*, and Gibbs hurried to keep up with her so he could say, "How come you could be aggressive in there but my tactics—"

"She was just a kid," El told him before he could finish the question. "That man was clearly mixed up in all manner of shady business, and I can only imagine the sort of character he'd feel comfortable selling this to. It's different."

He didn't look convinced, but he also didn't argue, which was enough for El.

They made it back to the ship and Trapp and Ginger met them in the entryway.

"What happened?" Trapp demanded when he saw them, taking in their disheveled appearance and the uniform in El's hand. "Did you find him?"

"Ginger, Gibbs needs you to look at his jaw," El said as she moved to make her way to the control room.

"What happened to him?" Ginger asked.

El spoke under her breath as she kept walking so there was no way Ginger heard her, but Trapp was right behind her, so he did. "I punched him."

"You did what now?"

She was booking it to the control room then and didn't stop as she replied. "He was out of line."

Tossing her uniform aside, she took a seat at the comm, swearing under her breath as she powered it to life. The stupid thing took too long to boot up.

When it finally did, she punched in the information the girl had given them. Then, after what felt like an eternity, she pulled up an overhead view of the neighborhood and then floor plans for the building itself.

"So what's the plan?" Trapp asked, looking over her shoulder at the screen.

She frowned. "I don't like any of this. I can't put my finger on it but something about this just isn't sitting right with me; it's as if . . . "

She trailed off, her mind almost settling on something but not quite. It was there, she just needed to work through it, needed to process, needed to—

"El?"

She looked up then, meeting Trapp's eyes. "I know how to get him out of there."

It would have felt weird putting her uniform back on, even though El had taken it off less than a day ago. Could a person really change so much in one day?

But weirder still was putting Gibbs' uniform on and letting him wear hers.

Neither fit the other well, but they were passable. The real miracle of the situation was that Gibbs even allowed her to convince him to swap without putting up too much of a fight.

He stood beside her outside the Foxworthy Building on Prejudice Street, looking a little sick.

"Are you sure about this plan?"

"Honestly?"

That made him look even more worried. "Yes?"

"Pretty sure."

He didn't look too reassured, and she didn't blame him. But then, the task ahead wasn't to make Gibbs feel better—it was to rescue Captain Behnam, and that was all that filled her mind.

She stood a little straighter, squaring her shoulders and lifting her head. Then, taking a deep breath, she opened the door and stepped inside, alone.

The room was small, cramped, and dark. A set of long lightbulbs ran across the ceiling, washing the room in an orangey-yellow glow.

There was only one soldier—positioned behind a high, dented metal table—when she stepped through the door, but two more came through the door on the right when she entered. They all had their weapons out and trained on them, but their body language was casual as if things weren't as tense for them as they were for El.

"You're not allowed to be here."

She recognized his voice as that of the man who ordered the destruction of the *Aderyn* and who had, no doubt, been the one to have Captain Behnam arrested. He was clearly the leader of the group.

"Are you sure about that?" El asked with a smirk.

Not a single one of them had made a move to salute her, not a single one. She had been right.

"We're going to have to ask you to leave," the soldier said again, his voice cold, hard, stern. There was a mark of authority to it, and it brought El great pleasure that she was going to take him down several pegs.

"You can do that, but I don't think Radian Darius will be too happy about it."

It was the name the man at the hotel had given them, a name she had searched the information database long and hard for last night and came up with few details. What she had gotten had been rather telling though.

It was also the name of the man she believed these sol-diers—or rather, imposters—were taking orders from.

At least, she hoped that were the case because her entire plan hinged on that fact.

"I beg your pardon?" the man stuttered, and she could see she had him flustered. That was good; it was right where she wanted him.

"You heard me, Officer," she replied easily, more than a little pleased with the power shift that had clearly overtaken the room. "I assume you aren't looking to get on Mr. Darius' bad side. I personally wouldn't recommend it, but then we all have to make our own life choices, don't we?"

"What can I do for you, Miss . . . ?"

"Mr. Darius wants you to transfer possession of your pris-oner to me—the one you took into custody this afternoon. He'd like to question him himself."

She was hoping beyond hope that Radian Darius wasn't there himself, but then since his record was so elusive, it was clear he wasn't one to do his own dirty work. He was a man who stayed behind the scenes—a fact that she was very grateful for.

"I'll have to check—"

"Will you?" she interrupted. "Will you be the one to interrupt Mr. Darius in the middle of his very important meet—ah, of course, but then you wouldn't be privileged to such information, now would you, being as low on the chain of command as you are?"

She smirked and saw the way her words and the action grated on the leader. He took a moment to regain his composure before saying, "Still, I must check, Miss . . . "

He was trying so hard to get her name and she knew it frustrated him that she sidestepped every time. She could just make up a fake name to feed him, but it was a power play to withhold it; and besides, it was just so much fun to annoy him that way.

"Go ahead, soldier," she replied with a humorless laugh. "Do you have a widow I should send flowers to?"

He hesitated, clearly weighing his choices. "Mr. Darius gave me express orders, and I haven't been informed otherwise so I think—"

"Ah, yes, because Mr. Darius' main concern is keeping you apprised of his every whim," she said, aware that she was interrupting him yet again and also aware of just how much it annoyed him. "I don't have all day to waste—unlike you, I actually have important tasks to see to. So if you're not going to comply, I'll be happy to convey to Mr. Darius just how uncomfortable you are with plans changing. I'm sure he'll be more than willing to replace you with someone who is a little more flexible."

She could tell that got to him, and yet still he didn't give in.

She turned then, moving toward the door, slowly but confidently, giving the air that she wasn't in a hurry.

"Wait."

She turned back to him, an eyebrow raised, her lips pursed.

"Mr. Darius gave you his express orders?" he clarified.

El pushed back the twinge of her conscience. The man would lose his life when he complied with her and his blood would be on her hands. But then, she couldn't bring herself to feel too guilty about it, given that the man had been the one to tear the *Aderyn* apart and then arrest Captain Behnam.

Who knew what he was doing to Captain Behnam that very moment or what he had done prior to her arrival. And besides, that was what he got for getting himself mixed up with a man like Radian Darius.

His blood wasn't innocent, and she'd not feel guilty if it was shed after she was gone.

"I don't have all day to stand around repeating this," she snapped. "So I'll only say this once more—Mr. Darius' orders were for you to hand your prisoner over to me. Today. As in, right now."

The man hesitated a moment more, and El thought she might have to go through another song and dance of her pretending she was going to leave. But then he nodded, turning to the soldier—imposter—who had been behind the desk when she had entered. "You heard her: prisoner, now."

The young man hopped up and skittered away, and the leader turned his attention back to El. "Is there anything else I can do for you, Miss . . . ?"

She was about to tell him that would be all, but then she had come that far, so why stop? "I also require your data files."

"Excuse me?"

"Data files," she demanded coldly. "Now"

The young man returned a minute later with Captain Behnam just as the leader handed over a drive with the ordered data files.

Captain Behnam's clothes were dirty and tattered, his face a mess of cuts and bruises; it had only been a few hours since he'd been taken, but they had clearly gotten right to work on him.

Her heart leaped, her breath catching in her throat, and it was only then that she realized a part of her hadn't expected to see him alive again. His eyes lit up when he saw her, and El realized she had to shut him up before he opened his mouth and ruined everything.

"Silence," she ordered him before he could even say anything. Her tone was harsh and clipped, and the shift in his expression, from delight to solemnity, told her that he got the message.

He dropped his gaze and slumped his shoulders, all but falling on her when the young man passed him to her. His arm landed heavily around her shoulder and his hand gripped her arm so tightly she knew it would bruise later. A shock ran through her, and an image of them torturing him flashed through her mind.

She tried not to think about what they had done to him, or the way his feet dragged, or the smell of sweat and iron and blood that surrounded him. His breathing was labored as they moved toward the door.

They left the building and the door shut firmly behind them. Gibbs was waiting outside where El had left him. He moved to take some of the Captain's weight off El, supporting him from the other side.

Captain Behnam had the good sense to wait until they were away from the building before he spoke, his voice a low, angry hiss. "What in the void was that?"

"I can't believe that worked," Gibbs said.

"That's not an answer," Captain Behnam growled as they moved, but there was a wince in his voice underneath it that showed how clearly in pain he was.

"We did what it took to get you back," El said as another tingle of shock ran through her. "You'd've done the same for us."

"Maybe not quite the same way," Captain Behnam said.

She furrowed her brow. "Are you sure? Because as I recall yesterday, you wanted to march into the hotel and demand answers so that seems like it's the same level of reckless to me."

"Nowhere close," Captain Behnam said and stopped. The others stopped along with him and gave him a second to catch his breath. "Near as I can tell, you marched into a Liosi base and demanded they release me to you while dressed as a security officer? Are you insane or just plain stupid?"

He wasn't going to like her answer, and she had a feeling he was about to start yelling at her. But she'd made up her mind to only tell him the truth and that's what she had to do. "They aren't Liosi soldiers—they're being paid by the Philosanthrians to impersonate Liosi soldiers. I assumed they were working for Radian Darius, so I bluffed my way in and told them he had ordered that they release you to me. They did, here we are, and the day is won."

The Captain had taken a few steps while she spoke, but he stopped, and she could feel the anger seething through him—or maybe that was just the electricity, but either way, it was stronger. He was going to kill her.

"I'm sorry, you did what?"

She took a deep breath. "I told you, I did what it took to get you back. Just like you would have done for any one of us."

"More one of you than one of us," Gibbs cut in.

"Not helping," El hissed.

"Is he talking about . . . ?" Captain Behnam trailed off.

"Yup."

"He knows about that?" Captain Behnam clearly wasn't happy about that either, but then he couldn't blame her for that one.

"You were there when the leader told him—on the *Aderyn*, yesterday, before you were arrested."

"Oh . . . yeah . . . that . . . that sounds right?" He shook his head. "Just a lot to remember."

"I have every intention of allowing her to explain herself before I make a decision about what's to be done with her," Gibbs said, still trying to help and still making things worse.

"What's to be done with her?"

Victory, Captain Behnam didn't know about their deal. "I promised Gibbs that if he let me save you then I'd submit to whatever action he felt appropriate to deal with my . . . you know . . . " She couldn't quite force the word out.

"Desertion," Gibbs supplied.

"Yeah . . . "

"And you're just going to let him hold your fate in his hands?" Captain Behnam demanded as if Gibbs wasn't there.

She snorted, also forgetting that they were discussing someone who by all rights should also be part of the conversation. At that moment, all that mattered was Captain Behnam and making him understand. "What choice do I have? That's all part of being a soldier, submitting to your superior—whether you agree with them or not."

"But you're not a soldier," he said, giving her a look like he had made some incredible point. "That's all part of being a deserter."

She drew in another breath, reminding herself of all that he had been through in the last day, and that a rational answer was the only appropriate response here.

"I don't know that you can understand it since you don't have a planet to which you swear your allegiance. But I do, and it's a planet I'm deeply proud of. So yes, I'd like a chance to explain my case before he makes a decision, because I had my reasons and I won't apologize for them. But if he arrests me for treason after that, I'll submit to my King and his laws, because that's what you do when you believe in something."

He pulled away from her as if he couldn't even stand to touch her, leaning all his weight on Gibbs, who winced hard. "I don't get you. How do you believe in a cause when you refuse to continue fighting for it? I don't see the difference between the two."

Of course he didn't. Because he was like a Vercentii—no allegiance to anyone but willing to help anyone. How could she explain it to someone like him?

"I didn't run from my country, I ran from a pointless war," she said, the smoke and flames and lifeless bodies filling her mind and her senses. She pushed them back as she struggled to breathe. "The things I did—I—" She shook her head, swallowing hard, forcing out the words. "I don't sleep at night because of them."

"So you said," he said, looking at her with concern like he did whenever she said anything remotely honest. "You do know

Ginger's trained to help with that sort of thing, right? If you need help . . . " He broke off then, letting out a wheezing cough. He drew a deep breath after a moment and started walking again.

"That's not the point," she said. "Even good people do horrible things in war. They lose sight of what they believe, and it gets messier than they intend it to. But just because I finally took a stand against it, that doesn't change what all the rest of it means."

"And what does it mean?" He asked it so naturally, as if he hadn't just been through the void and nearly not come out on the other side of it. As if they weren't in a fight and he wasn't on the wrong side of it.

She shook her head, unable to wrap her mind around someone who didn't understand it. How did she explain it to someone like that? "It's . . . " She shook her head again, and her brow wrinkled as she tried to come up with the words. "It's about having pride in who you are, where you're from, and the people who came before you. It's about being a part of something."

She could see it in his eyes that he wasn't getting it. He didn't understand and she couldn't explain it. Not to him, not when he didn't actually want to understand.

"You know what?" she said. "I'm not doing this. Not here, not now. We need to get you back to the ship so Ginger can look over your injuries."

"Oh yeah, she likes giving orders now," Gibbs said.

"Not to me," Captain Behnam muttered. "We're not done talking about this."

"Fine," she snapped. "Once we're done with all this, we'll have a Q&A session and all of you can ask me about my deep dark secrets, and I'll give several more rousing speeches about patriotism and honor and Liosa, and maybe Ginger can even make snacks."

She stalked away then, because Gibbs seemed to have a handle on supporting Captain Behnam, and it was clear he didn't need her. Of course he didn't; why would he?

She had only just walked into a room full of people who were hurting him and demanded his release. She had only just bluffed her way through it, risking her life to save him. She had only bargained away her life—instead of turning tail and running—so that Gibbs would give her the chance to rescue him. She had only given up everything to return him safely to his ship.

And so as much as she hated to admit it, even to herself, it hurt that he'd done nothing but bicker with her, berate her, question her, in light of all she'd done. All she wanted was one simple thing; she didn't think that was too much to ask.

After all she had risked, he hadn't even bothered to say thank you.

CHAPTER 15

CAPTAIN BEHNAM WAS taken to the med bay as soon as they returned to the ship. El went to take a shower to hopefully wash away her bad mood.

When she got out several minutes later, she did feel a little better, though not much. Still, she had a plan, which was good.

She'd slipped from Gibbs' uniform into the tee-shirt and lounge pants Ginger had given her and hadn't bothered putting on her shoes—as much as she loved them, she didn't need to wear them all the time. It felt good as she stepped out of the shower room into the grubbery, the cool metal beneath her feet.

Everyone was crowded around the grubbery table, and Captain Behnam had a scowl on his face, clearly none too pleased with all the attention the others were giving him. His eyes lit up when he saw El, and she remembered how pleased he'd been to see her earlier when she'd come to rescue him; if only that could have lasted.

"Hey." He grinned, focusing in on her as if the others weren't even there.

She ignored the warmth that fluttered through her at the grin as she turned her attention to Gibbs, tossing him his uniform. He wasn't wearing hers anymore either; what had he done with it?

"Thanks for the loan," she said because gratitude was polite. "And the backup today."

He nodded in acknowledgment. "Of course."

Only then did she turn her attention back to Captain Behnam. "I need another comm."

He rolled his eyes. "Seriously? We're doing that? Right now?"

"It has nothing to do with that." She held up the drive the leader had given her. "I'm not about to stick this into our own comm because I've no way of knowing if they rigged it or anything. It could give us the information we need, or it could fry our system."

His eyes lit up at that, and she loved that he didn't question her, that he trusted her without a second thought, and she hated herself for the way she got warm all over and the smile that came to her lips unbidden at the look. "Let's find you another comm then."

He moved to stand as if he were going to go and find her one right then.

"Not here," she said with a shake of her head. "We need to get off this planet before they realize we're not actually connected to Radian Darius. That comm's going to have to be somewhere else."

He frowned a moment and then nodded. "I think I know just the place."

El didn't talk to Captain Behnam any more than she needed to for the next two days—it helped that a good bit of that time was spent with her catching up on some of her lost sleep and him resting under Ginger's orders. They barely saw each other at all, which suited her just fine.

But then they landed, and she, unfortunately, couldn't avoid him any longer.

Still, she didn't have to talk to him any more than necessary, and she didn't as they set out again.

They left behind an annoyed Trapp, an angry Gibbs, and a sympathetic Ginger. Trapp made a couple of jokes about getting left behind to babysit that El thought might not have just been jokes. The security officer and the Captain argued heatedly because Gibbs wanted to go along, and Captain Behnam refused. And Ginger took her aside right before they left and told her to be careful–and also to keep an eye on Captain Behnam to make sure he wasn't overexerting himself.

So in the end, it was El who was the babysitter.

Resna was less cramped than Cyrene and Alvar, with wider, cleaner streets. There weren't as many people about and those that were carried themselves with a dignity, as if it hadn't been sucked from them as those from the other planets had.

Even the buildings stood straighter as if they had something worth standing for; though in actuality, it was no doubt that those who had built them had actually taken pride in the construction, seeking to do more than slap the buildings up and call it a day.

The sun beat down and El basked in its warmth. The wider streets meant the sun had more room to spread, not blocked out by the buildings. Even the air smelled cleaner. Not as clean as the air of Liosa, but better than where she'd spent the last four months. And better certainly than—

No. Not today. She wasn't going to think about Taras today.

She almost wished she wasn't angry with Captain Behnam. If things were good between them, she could almost imagine they were out for some sightseeing or a leisurely walk instead of on a mission of grave importance.

He was walking all right, so perhaps his weakness had been fatigue, something cured by a good night's sleep and a little more. Or perhaps Ginger truly was just that good at what she did.

They stopped outside a two-story building made of smooth stone, strong and sturdy, which made El ache for Liosa and the stone structures of her homeland.

Captain Behnam pulled open the door and then stood aside so she could go in first. The action put her on edge, and her hand went to her gun. She went to take a step inside when his hand on her arm stopped her. He shook his head. "There's no danger. I was just—" He shook his head again. "I was just trying to be a gentleman."

"Oh." She felt her face growing red. She had thought he was deferring to her as the soldier, was relying on her to keep them out of trouble. And how was she supposed to respond to him? Was she supposed to act like a lady then? How did one exactly do that?

Something her mother had told her years ago sprang to her mind, about being both gentle and strong. It was her mother's idea of what being a lady looked like. She had always told El she could be anything she set her mind to, but El always knew her mother wanted her to set her mind to those things; that if she could see her little girl be anything, it would be both gentle and strong.

And like everyone else in her life, El had done nothing but fail her mother and her expectations.

"You okay?"

She shook her head, to clear it, not in response to Captain Behnam's question. There she went zoning out again. Not a good habit for her to be getting into. It wasn't safe to clock out of your surroundings, to lose that connection. That was how people got the drop on you. That was how people wound up dead.

"I'm fine," she said. "And thank you," she added as she slipped through the door he held open for her because it was what one normally said in such situations.

The inside of the building was dim, with worn carpet underfoot and the cool smell of stone and books filling the air. The ache in her heart grew stronger as the realization hit her that there was a good chance she wouldn't see her home again. Or even if she did, it wouldn't be for a very long time—or just the once before they executed her.

At least if she was going to die for treason, she would get to die on her own soil.

There were books lining all the walls and several rows of shelves as well, along with four comm consoles dotting here and there.

El turned to Captain Behnam, giving him an amusingly confused look. "Did you bring me to some sort of a shady library?"

"You said you needed a comm," he said, which wasn't really a response. "Well, there's your comm."

She rolled her eyes as a figure slipped through the door to the far right. Her hand went to her gun in an instant, and she would have drawn it except that Captain Behnam's hand was on her hand then, stopping her.

In that moment, she realized that the figure was a light-haired girl, maybe fourteen or fifteen at the oldest, young and gangly and awkward. Her pale face was covered in a mess of freckles and pimples, all mixed together so it was hard to distinguish one from the other.

She smiled when she saw Captain Behnam, her pale eyes lighting up. "Well hello there, stranger."

"Hey, Channing," he said, offering her a smile that was sweet and kind and made El forget he was a jerk. "We came to use the comms. Is your dad here?"

The girl shook her head, frowning. "He left this morning but wouldn't tell me where he was going so I don't know when he'll be back. You're welcome to use the comms though."

He frowned, his brow wrinkled with thought and indecision as he looked from the girl called Channing to the comms to El to the door they had come through. He nodded, slowly, hesitantly, after a moment. "Yeah, okay. Just, maybe . . . maybe go for a walk or something, get out of here for a few minutes? And if anyone asks, you weren't here and have no idea that anyone came in?"

"You going to bring trouble on us, Captain Behnam?" she asked, giving him a look.

He got that look of indecision again. Then he said, "I'm not rightly sure. But if something goes down, I'll not have you on my conscience."

"You know, I was thinking today would be a good day to take a walk," she said as if the whole thing had been her idea.

He nodded his appreciation. "Thank you."

So he could say those words apparently.

"And hey, if something does happen, tell your dad we're even now, would you?"

She raised an eyebrow. "You must be mixed up in a powerful lot of trouble for you to be even, Captain Behnam."

"Which is why I suggest you get out of here and pretend we walked through those doors about two minutes after you left."

She grinned at him. "Aye, aye, Captain."

El looked at Captain Behnam, stern and serious, as the girl disappeared back through the door she had initially come through. "She isn't going to get hurt, is she?"

He shook his head. "I don't think so."

"I kind of need you to be sure," she said pointedly.

"She's a smart girl," he said. "She'll heed my warning and stay out of the way."

She nodded. "Okay then, I guess we're doing this."

She crossed to one of the consoles, all of which were deserted. Aside from Channing, there didn't appear to be another living soul.

Slipping into a chair, she booted up the comm, noting that it ran faster than the one on the ship. She decided against mentioning it. She didn't need Captain Behnam grumpy with her, not when things were going well.

She plugged in the drive and the screen flashed to life.

"Anything there?" Captain Behnam asked, leaning down to look over her shoulder. He was too close; she could feel his breath on her cheek and neck, and it sent shivers down her spine. But she didn't exactly want him to move away.

Victory, what was she thinking?

"Do you mind?" she snapped.

He stepped back, hands up defensively. "Sorry."

His tone suggested otherwise.

"Are you?" she asked, turning away from the console to face him. The chair spun, which El appreciated as it made it so she could better face Captain Behnam.

His brow furrowed, and his tone showed he was clearly confused by whatever was happening. "Is there something between us, Elis? You've been on edge ever since . . . "

"Ever since you yelled at me?" she snapped back, realizing her voice was raised and she was in a library; but there was no one else there so it didn't matter, right? It wasn't like the books minded.

"What?"

He didn't get it. She could see it in his eyes that the stupid idiot had no idea what she was talking about.

"You yelled at me," she said, not caring that she was coming across as irrational and unhinged. She was angry, and she wanted him to know that. "Do you know what I risked for you? I bargained away my life to make sure you made it back to your ship safely and you just yelled at me!"

She was going to cry. *Victory*, how she hated herself in that moment. She was going to let something that stupid make her cry. She had fought in a war, and she couldn't even handle something as trivial as that?

"What did you expect me to do?" He was yelling again. Actually yelling—not just venting or reprimanding; he was actually yelling at her. And she didn't care.

"You could have said thank you!"

"Are you serious right now?" His words were accompanied by a humorless laugh; he flexed his fingers absentmindedly as if they were hurting him. "You're actually serious right now. In case you missed it, they were torturing me! So forgive me if I forgot the minor details of polite society. Especially when you're the one who pulled a foolhardy stunt like you did."

"I saved your life."

"That's just it, Elis," he said. "You bargained away your life for mine, and I'm not entirely sure what I'm supposed to do about that."

"Say thank you?" she suggested.

He sighed, his jaw a firm line, his expression and demeanor suggesting it wasn't going to be that simple. "This all happened because I was trying to avoid you getting arrested and killed. So to find out you promised your life into Gibbs' hands? I'm not going to say thank you for it because, at the moment, I'm not exactly feeling any gratitude."

"Fine then," she snapped, swirling in her chair to look back at comm screen. She ought to focus on the task at hand. "Next time someone is trying to kill you I'll just let them."

"Thanks," he said bitterly. "I'd appreciate that."

She was going to kill him.

Swirling back in her chair, she fixed him with the darkest glare. His expression said he realized exactly what he had done, his eyes wide with horror, his hands up in defense. "I didn't mean it like that."

"Sure," she said as she turned back to the console once more. "Whatever."

She turned all her attention to the screen, grateful to find it wasn't a mess of bugs and traps. There was a chance it had sent up a signal to Radian Darius or his minions as to their location, but the chance that they had people on Resna who would be there at any moment was slim.

So there was plenty of time to sit and search each file one by one.

Radian Darius was a careful man, and so there wasn't too much information, but then she hadn't expected there to be a detailed brief of his entire master plan.

Still, there was enough if you knew what to look for, and El had some sort of an idea. She just wasn't sure what it all meant.

"The Philosanthrians' fingerprints are all over this," she said because she needed to say it out loud, to work it out that way and have someone else's perspective on it. "Shipping records, payouts, orders, all Philosanthrian. Radian Darius is working with the Philosanthrians."

"We already knew that, didn't we?" Captain Behnam asked, leaning in close, and she hated that she wanted him there. "Are you okay?"

El turned, though she didn't have to see his face to know it had that concerned look on it. "You really don't need to ask that every five seconds."

As soon as the words were out, she realized she didn't mean them. Well, maybe she did mean them—he was always asking her if she was okay, and it was annoying; if she wasn't okay, she'd tell him. Maybe.

But she didn't mean her tone. Not really. The squabble between them was foolish. He wasn't her enemy. He was the person who always had her back, the person who'd been worried about her, who was angry with her because she'd risked her life.

"Sorry," she said, shaking her head. "I just . . . I think the Philosanthrians are plotting to assassinate the Prince."

CHAPTER 16

APTAIN BEHNAM TOOK her words in stride, looking not at all surprised, as if she had just said she wanted to take a shower or would like a cup of tea. As if she hadn't just announced news of an assassination attempt seeped in conspiracy and lies.

"So what does that mean?" he asked in a level voice.

She took a breath as she thought. "It means we have to tread delicately. We can't just march in and accuse them of plotting to kill the Prince—we're too closely tied to them."

"You're sure about this?"

"No, I have no idea. But it makes the most sense, honestly. It'll weaken us politically, especially given how we just lost our King. On the cusp of an exchange of power, losing the Prince when there is only one heir . . . " She trailed off, shaking her head.

"How does this benefit the Philosanthrians?"

It was a valid question with a straightforward answer, but still not one El much liked. "They want us next. Prince Jarrett pretends to be our ally, pretends he is not his father, the usurper—our oppressor—but if this war in Taras proves anything, it's how brutal he is in pursuit of power."

She was still mad at Captain Behnam, but it melted a little at his level look, unquestioning. "So what do we do about it?"

She closed her eyes, putting her fingers to her temples as she took a deep breath, clearing her head and her heart, quieting all the noise. It was a trick she had picked up from a Tarisian turncoat. She hadn't much liked the woman—given that she was willing to betray her planet and bring it to complete ruin for money—but the meditation trick had been a good one and, though El hated it, she still used it from time to time when faced with particularly difficult problems.

"Prince Tov's headed to Philosanthron now; they're throwing a ball to commemorate the anniversary of our liberation as a way to celebrate the newfound peace between our counties. We need to find real ties between the two—Radian Darius and the Philosanthrians."

"And how do we do that?" Captain Behnam pressed.

Another deep breath. "Gibbs gets us into the ball, we use their comms, search through them, find what we need to know."

"That's dangerous." Captain Behnam's voice was hard.

"No more dangerous than anything else we've done," she replied easily.

"There'll be Liosi there," he said. "Someone is sure to recognize you. And if you get caught—"

"A little makeup and the right hairstyle and I don't think anyone would recognize me," she said. "They're used to seeing me in my uniform. And I'm just a cadet; it's not like I'm that well known in any higher circles."

"Elis, I won't ask you to—"

"You didn't," she interrupted. "And I appreciate you wanting to look out for me—it's what makes you such a good captain, the way you look after those on your crew. But you've trusted me thus far and I'm asking you to trust me again."

He cringed. "No."

That cut. After all they'd been through, she deserved something more; she'd been a fool to think whatever was between them was different. Of course it wasn't.

"It's not like that," he said with a sigh, and El looked up to meet his eyes. He flexed his fingers at his side. "I'm not going to let you gamble with your life that way."

"Not going to let me?" she demanded.

"You can do whatever you want with your life," he amended, the edge back in his voice. "I'm just not going to help you make reckless, foolhardy decisions. You want to do that, you can do it all on your own."

"Fine," she said, removing the storage device from the comm. She tucked it into her pocket as she stood, moving toward the door.

She heard his footsteps behind her as he followed after her. "Where are you going?"

"To find someone to take me to Philosanthron so I can stop this."

"Elis, wait."

There was something in his tone—tired and heavy—that made her stop, though she didn't turn to look at him.

"Why does it always have to be you?" he asked. "Why can't someone else put their life on the line for once?"

She'd asked herself that same question plenty of times. Why did it always have to be her? Why was it that she gave and gave and she just kept having to give?

When was it someone else's turn?

"If someone else was here right now, I'd gladly turn the job over to them," she said, stuffing her hands into her pockets, not sure what to do with herself all of a sudden. "I didn't want to march in there to rescue you if we're being honest. I'd have gladly given that job to someone else. But what was I going to do, send Ginger in there? Or Trapp?"

"You think you're more expendable than them," he said, understanding lighting his face. "It's not that you think you're better than them, you think you're the better one to die."

He wasn't wrong, but she hated him for getting it right. "I gave up my life a long time ago. And now, with my desertion hanging over my head, it's just a matter of time. And if I'm going to die, I want it to be for a reason."

"What does it matter?" he said. "You'll still be dead. How does having a reason change anything?"

He couldn't understand. And she didn't know if she could explain it to him.

But if she walked away from the conversation, she might never find the courage to talk to him about it later. And she found she needed him to understand. She needed to at least try, because, for the first time in a very long time, she cared what someone thought of her.

He was waiting for her to respond, a look of concern mixing with the annoyance on his face. The concern almost made her lose her nerve. He was always giving her that look, and she assumed it was because she had given him some reason to think she needed the concern. And she didn't know that sharing her idealism with him would do anything to help her face in that department.

But she wanted him to understand. So she had to at least try to explain it.

She started pacing because she thought better when she walked. "In five days Liosa celebrates its forty-fifth Liberation Day.

He shook his head. "What does this have to do with . . . ?"

"It's important," she told him, because it was. To understand her, he had to understand her heritage. "I don't know if you're familiar with the history of that or not . . . "

He crossed his arms, leaning back against the console that sat beside him, getting comfortable. "I've heard stories, but I'd like to hear your side."

She drew in a breath, nodded. "Okay. Um . . . Well, the Liosi are a fierce and proud people who conquered the wilds of our jungles with tenacity and determination. When you have a planet full of plants and creatures that are constantly trying to kill you, you either learn to fight back or you die. And we . . . "

"Learned to fight back." Captain Behnam was giving her a small smile, and she felt a swell of hope like maybe he could understand after all, even just a little.

"Yeah, but when the Philosanthrians came with their science and their ships, we didn't stand a chance. And so, for almost twenty-five years, we were under their rule." She paused because she hated that part of the story, the part where they lost. The part where her people weren't strong enough. But it made way for the best part, she reminded herself.

"But if you're about to celebrate Liberty Day it obviously didn't last," Captain Behnam said.

"Liberation Day," she corrected. She stopped pacing but it felt weird to just stand there so she started it up again, moving a few steps before she turned and walked in the other direction another few steps before beginning again. "And no, it didn't, because we refused to be tamed. They tried and we let them think they won. But we were too clever for them, biding our time, waiting, passing our pride and traditions onto our children in secret. And we learned everything we could."

He smirked at her. "You talk like you were there."

"My ancestors were," she replied. "So in a way, I was."

"So how'd they do it?" he asked, crossing his arms, his demeanor almost a challenge, saying 'impress me.'

"They waited for their chance and the right leader. Surely you've heard of him—Alaric, the Pendragon?"

He nodded. "Yeah, I've heard the stories."

She shook her head. "They're more than stories. He was just a teenager—no training, nothing special about him—but he was the chosen one, the one who rose up and took the Philosanthrians by the scruffs of their necks and threw them off of our planet. He refused to give in to the oppression, refused to let anyone tell him to give up on who he was, and the people responded to that. They rallied with him until he had an army, a revolution."

"But then he died, right? All that work and then he died before he even got to reap the benefits. Why does it matter if there was some reason for it or not?"

She let out a frustrated sigh because maybe he wasn't getting it after all. "That wasn't the point. He died, yes, but he gave his life for a cause he firmly believed in. And that's the incredible part—it didn't die with him, that cause. His second-in-command took it up; despite all their problems with each other, they had one very important thing in common, and so the cause went on, even after Alaric died."

She stopped there because she couldn't go on; she was too choked up by the idea, by her story and what it meant, and the fact she had come from people who fought and never gave up.

She looked up and found Captain Behnam looking a little uncomfortable.

"What's wrong?"

He shook his head. "I was—I was going to ask if you were okay, but I figured you might not like that. You just looked a little . . . emotional."

"I am," she admitted. "I just—I love that story so much. And to think . . . I get to be a part of that legacy. I came from those people, the ones who rallied, the ones who followed their leader to victory so that their children could be raised on a planet free of oppression. So maybe I don't know how to explain it right—maybe you'll never be able to understand what it all means to me—but . . . I had to try. Because it means something to me. It means so incredibly much. And I wanted you to understand that, to know that I'm not just following something blindly or doing things I don't understand. I do. I know what I'm doing, and I know the consequences of it. But for me, it doesn't change anything. If anything, it makes me bolder, stronger."

He nodded slowly, not saying anything. There was a silence between them for much too long, and El knew that was that. He'd never understand, he couldn't.

She turned to leave then because she'd meant what she'd said. She needed to stop Radian Darius and she would, with or without his help.

"Elis, wait."

She sighed, stopping again. "You can't change my mind."

"You're right," he said. "I don't understand it. But I don't have to because it's not my heritage—well, it is, but not like—"

"Wait, what?" she interrupted, whirling to face him, her eyes wide. "I thought you were Mahsirian. Your surname, it's—"

"Yeah, but I have two parents," he said. "One Mahsirian, one Liosi." Her jaw dropped, but before she could say anything, he continued. "But while I don't understand that loyalty to a planet, to a heritage, I understand wanting to help people. And I'm loyal to my friends. So if we're what's standing between Radian Darius and thousands of innocent lives, and you're going to do this with or without my help anyway, well, then I guess our next course of action is we plot a course for the Philosanthrian capital."

"So you're in?"

He looked her straight in the eyes and it warmed her to her toes in a way that made her wonder for the first time since they'd met about Mahsirian magic; there was no other explanation for what she felt just then.

"I'm in," he said. "For you."

They left the library then, walking back the way they came. It was a gorgeous day and not even the threat of an assassination attempt could shake El's mood.

Captain Behnam had agreed to help her save her—their—people. She was going to do something important; dangerous, but important. That was what she'd dreamed of when she'd joined the military or spent all that time poring over history books and writing reports her instructors never understood.

But even more than that, Captain Behnam had called her his friend? She didn't know the last time someone had called her that and meant it. But somehow, in her heart of hearts, she knew he meant it.

He offered her a grin as they walked, holding out his hand to her. She took it, not sure why they needed to hold hands. But still, it felt nice, so she didn't pull away when it proved to serve no purpose.

They were going to Philosanthron, to save her people, to die as heroes.

And more than ever El found she didn't care about that last part.

So what if she died? She was putting her life on the line for a cause she believed in, but even more importantly, she would do so with a friend at her back.

PART II

Quiver and shake, brave one
But do not waver or throw down your gun
Though you shake in your boots
Hold fast to your roots
Quiver and shake
But never break
Quiver and shake
But never break

-From a Traditional Liosi Lullaby

CHAPTER 17

WHEN EL AND Captain Behnam got back to the ship, the Captain called a meeting in the grubbery to explain everything. After some debating, arguing, and general name-calling, they all reached an agreement.

They were setting off for Philosanthron.

Trapp went to set a course and El contacted the right people to make sure they had clearance to land. But after it was all taken care of, there was little for her to do until they actually reached their destination. A full week of flying with nothing to do.

Well, almost nothing.

She wandered down to the grubbery and found she was a little disappointed Captain Behnam wasn't there doing the dishes.

But Ginger was, and it seemed rude to walk away just because it wasn't the Captain working.

"Need some help?" she asked, moving to stand beside the medic.

Ginger offered her a soft smile. "I can manage, you don't have to do that."

El had already picked up a towel and was drying the clean dishes. They worked in silence for a few minutes.

"I actually wanted to talk to you."

El said the words before she could keep them back, hurrying to get them said before she lost her courage.

Ginger immediately stopped what she was doing, turning to give her attention to El. "As a friend or in a professional capacity?"

El knew the answer to the question, but it took her time to gather her courage to admit it. She wanted to say she needed a friend because it was so much easier to say that than the truth.

The truth was an admission of something dark and scary, and she didn't know if she was ready for that.

But she also knew she couldn't live with her demons any longer; she needed to learn to sleep again.

"Professional," El confirmed. Ginger nodded, wiping her hands on a towel and stepping away from the sink.

"Oh, it doesn't have to be right now . . . " El said as Ginger went to the intercom and said, "Trapp, you're on dish-duty. I'm working tonight."

"Do I have to?" came Trapp's groan of a reply.

"I'm working," Ginger said again. "And it's your turn anyway. If I come out and see there are dishes in this sink, I'm going to be disappointed."

"*Ech*," Trapp replied. "I'll get them done."

"Disappointed?" El said as they moved toward the med bay. "Really?"

Ginger shrugged. "I've learned to do what I have to." They reached the med bay and Ginger closed the door behind them, offering El a seat. "Now then, what exactly did you want to talk about?"

It took some time—and courage—but El finally got it out. She told Ginger about the nightmares and the anxiety. And somehow along the way, Ginger became the first person El told about what happened on Taras, telling her things she'd never told anyone, things she'd held back for far too long.

But even though she ended up sobbing there in the med bay, she felt better at the end, being able to get it all out and talking it through with Ginger. The medic gave her some exercises to try when she felt the anxiety coming on, as well as pointed out some errors in El's way of framing the narrative.

It was late by the time they were done—so late everyone else had gone to bed. El made an excuse about needing a drink of water before she went up, waiting for Ginger to disappear before she settled on the bench she'd claimed as her bed.

Small steps. Ginger was good, but she wasn't able to fix everything yet.

El woke the next morning more exhausted than she did on nights when she fell asleep after a workout. The one upside was her body didn't ache quite as much as usual, but then, there was another kind of ache, and she wasn't sure she liked it any better.

Ginger had said El'd probably want to talk more in the days to come and she'd been right. She already wanted to talk more.

"You know the bunks are more comfortable?"

El sat up, reaching for her gun only to realize she didn't have it with her, and the threat was only Gibbs.

He stood in grubbery, looking over the sink at her, a mug in his hands and a neutral expression on his face.

195

She scrubbed a hand over her face, ignoring his words. He wouldn't understand. He probably didn't even care.

Except she needed to explain. She'd promised him she would. Even if she couldn't, she had to.

She had no idea what time it was, but she knew it was too early for any of it. But then, it didn't matter what time it was; she'd always have an excuse to avoid it. If she could, she'd avoid it until they shot her down for her desertion, but Gibbs would ask, and she'd rather answer then instead of being ambushed by the question later.

But then, maybe he wouldn't ask.

"We should talk."

Or maybe he would.

Gibbs stepped around into the dining area, stopping at the end of the bench, looking down at her levelly.

She couldn't do it. It was a bad idea. It had been bad enough doing it with Ginger the night before—sweet, kindhearted Ginger who she could tell anything.

But she was talking to Gibbs.

"You promised to tell me about what happened," he said. "About Taras."

The memories came then. The smell of smoke—always the smell of smoke—came first, followed by the flames and the screams. No matter how many sessions she had with Ginger, she didn't think she'd ever forget the screams.

"I thought you were a coward."

El winced at his words but she didn't refute them. Of course he thought that. She'd betrayed her planet. "But you aren't and that makes it all the more confusing."

That wasn't the direction she'd expected the conversation to take.

"You saved my life in that alleyway, you marched into a warehouse and stared down those men for the Captain, you're willing to throw your life away now, I don't understand. It made sense when you were a coward who was too weak to stomach war and too disloyal to honor a vow, but . . . " He scrubbed a hand over his face and sighed. "That's not you. And I don't . . . I just don't understand."

Of course he didn't. Because he was at the palace, because he worked fighting domestic threats, because he hadn't been to Taras. She wanted him to understand but she didn't want to tell him. She couldn't tell him.

She rose and moved around him to the grubbery, filling a mug with water as she tried to get the breath to fill her lungs again. Her chest tightened, and the room felt smaller than usual.

He moved to look at her through the opening in the wall over the sink, not letting it go, not giving her the space to retreat that she sought.

"We're not fighting a war; we're razing a planet." The words came out far calmer than she felt; she wasn't even sure how she managed to force them out.

The mug had a dent in the side, which she ran her thumb over. Why hadn't she noticed that before? The ship only had six mugs, she must have used that one at some point; she ought to have noticed the dent.

"Destruction is part of—"

"No."

The word came out as strangled as she felt. Her legs shook beneath her; she should have stayed on the bench. She was afraid if she tried walking back, her legs would give out on her completely.

"I know what war is, I've spent my whole life studying it. I know its horrors and I know what it does to a person. But this . . . " She shook her head as she remembered. "This isn't war."

He didn't believe her, didn't understand, she could see it in the way he looked at her, the way his body remained hunched and defensive. It had been enough for Captain Behnam, but the Captain hadn't felt so betrayed by her actions. Gibbs needed a deeper explanation, whether she wanted to give it or not.

"Do you even know what we're fighting for?" she asked but didn't wait for a response. "Because I don't. I don't think a single Liosi soldier does. We're fighting a Philosanthrian war to make peace with them, but in the process . . . "

Why was it always so hard to breathe? Why was that always the first thing to betray her?

"We didn't fight soldiers." She could picture it so clearly; she'd relived it often enough in her dreams. She sucked in a breath, putting her hands on the counter, thinking about the cold metal beneath her hands. The room smelled like hash and beans and lemon dish soap, the combination strange but comforting. The lighting overhead cast a weird glow about the room, flickering in a rhythmic pattern, two deep breaths apart.

Gibbs stood across from her, illuminated by that light, watching her intently, saying nothing, letting her breathe. *In. Out. In. Out.*

"I told myself they were rebels, insurgents. We were just doing what we were told, and it was easier to not question why they didn't fight back." She could still hear their cries for mercy as their homes and families burned. "We burned everything. There'll be no more of Taras left by the time we're done."

She could still smell the smoke, still see the flames lapping at everything when she closed her eyes.

"The night I was shot . . . "

Victory, she had to tell him. He would understand if she told him. He had to. But she had to be able to breathe to get the words out.

Tears formed in her eyes and she didn't even try to hold them back. There was too much else to focus on.

"They were children." She could still see their tiny frames lying dead in the dark, littering the landscape, lifeless. They must have been so scared. "We were told it was a rebel hideout, but it wasn't. It was just a hospital. They were operating to assist the victims of our crimes—they'd taken in so many children with nowhere else to go—and we burned it to the ground."

Too many had died, far, far too many. It shouldn't have happened.

"One of them got hold of a gun somehow—I don't know how," she went on, forcing out the words. "They just fired, I don't even think they were aiming or even really knew how to use it. They just fired and it hit me and one of my squad killed them for it."

She pictured the tiny frame as it fell, one second full of life, shooting in a blind panic, the next lying on the ground, gasping for breath before it went still. So still. She'd fought the urge to run to it because she knew what she would find.

The same lifeless forms that always came after a mission. Except she couldn't lie to herself that time. She couldn't tell herself it was the price that had to be paid. Cadet Rumen had vomited afterward—El heard the sound of him retching as she was carried away on a stretcher; she knew it wasn't the smoke that had caused it.

Gibbs looked at her with horror written plainly on his face. Of course he did. She was a monster, and she hadn't even told him the worst of it. She'd done so many things.

"The truth is, I don't even know what I signed up for," she told him. "I don't think any of us do. We're just following orders in a war we don't understand. We look to our ancestors, proud of them for fighting back, for standing up against oppression, and here we're participating in it."

She didn't deserve the blood pumping through her veins.

The sobs came then as she completely lost control. The tears streamed down her face as the shook. Her legs gave out and she dropped to the floor, curling up in a ball, no longer able to muster even the strength to sit up.

Her whole body was weak as she cried, remembering everything she'd done. She didn't know how long she cried; time was surreal enough in space and when one broke down, so the two together made time almost obsolete.

After a while, she started to breathe again, able to regain some semblance of control. She took hold of it, sitting up, not quite ready to stand, grounding herself to the grubbery, inhaling and exhaling as she reminded herself of the things she could see—Gibbs sitting next to her, though when it had happened she didn't know; the rough wood of the cupboards; the light switch on the wall; the frame around the doorway, the doorway itself shrouded in shadows; the metal of the sink unit. She thought of what she could feel—the warm, wet tears on her face; the smooth, cool metal beneath her body; the soles of her shoes under her feet. She could smell Gibbs' tea;

the lemon dish soap scent that always filled the air; the stew they'd eaten for dinner last night.

Her breathing returned to something close to normal—or, whatever normal was for her—and she looked over at Gibbs who sat cross-legged beside her as if it were all a perfectly normal occurrence. She sniffed, breathing through her mouth as her nose was completely stuffed up.

"I know running betrayed everything we stand for as Liosi, but *rook di goo*, what I did on Taras, it betrayed our heritage far, far more."

Gibbs nodded once, dropping his gaze to look at the mug in his hands. "It's really . . . You really . . . did all that?"

There wasn't the judgment in his eyes that she'd expected to see. He looked sad and maybe even a little scared. She hoped he wasn't scared of her.

"I did."

The silence that followed was maddening. She understood he was processing, that he needed time to think, but she wished he'd say something—anything.

"You shouldn't be held accountable for that."

No, she shouldn't. But still, it was somehow left to her to pay the price. It always was.

Gibbs raised his cup to his lips, taking a long, slow sip. He swallowed. "How can you keep fighting to save a planet that did this to you—that is doing this to another planet?"

It was the same question Captain Behnam asked but it was different because, well, Gibbs knew more than Captain Behnam did.

"Prince Tov is young—I don't think . . . " She shook her head. "This was his father's war and now that King Rowen is dead, His

201

Highness still isn't even king—not until he reaches his majority." Gibbs knew all this—he probably understood the finer points better than she did—but she needed to spell it out for him, needed him to see it as she did.

"I doubt he even has any say in the matter. This war is being fought by generals and regents and Prince Jarrett—it's always been his war."

Gibbs nodded, which surprised her; she'd come to expect Gibbs to contradict the things she said. "His Highness is . . . very inexperienced. Though, his inexperience is far better than no one on the throne."

They agreed on that. Liosa couldn't survive such a loss of power. Any number of planets would waste no time in taking advantage of that, and Liosa would be back under foreign rule once more.

"And I don't think . . . " She shook her head. "This isn't us. This isn't Liosa. It's a mistake, but this isn't what we stand for. They'll see that. They have to. This will forever be a black spot in our history, but it shouldn't end this way. It can't end this way."

"I don't . . . " He frowned. "There's not . . . " He stopped again and shook his head. "I don't have the influence to help you—I can't change things on Taras, and I can't even promise you that my word would hold any weight should you stand trial."

She'd never ask him for that. "I'm too far gone, I know that. There's no reason to sink your own career tying yourself to me."

She didn't want anything more from him than understanding. Or, rather, an admittance that he didn't understand, that he couldn't. She'd never ask him to sacrifice anything, not for her.

"I can let you go," he said.

She looked at him, questioning.

He looked down. "I can't offer you anything else, but *rook di goo,* when this is over, I'll turn a blind eye and you can leave. I won't turn you in. I'm relieving you of your promise."

It was more than she'd expected him to give. Maybe there was more to him than she thought.

"Thank you."

There was silence then. Ought El to leave? Was there anything left to discuss?

"It's funny," he said, and she guessed there was more to say. "Your father speaks so highly of you; I never liked you just on that alone. But you're . . . you're not what I expected."

She snorted. "I wouldn't take anything my father says about me too seriously. How could he know anything about me when we've barely spoken since . . . well, since I was a child?" Gibbs didn't need to know about her mother; they weren't that close. "You've probably spoken to him more since you've known him than I have in the same space of time. I don't doubt he was using his tales of me simply to push you harder; you're far more his golden child than I could ever hope to be."

"No." There was humor in his voice. "He sent me on this mission because he thought it was a fool's errand. We can't even call for backup because we have no proof. Unless we have definite proof, no one would even think to listen to me. If we fail . . . " He shook his head. "We'll die heroes and everyone will call us fools."

She'd already expected to die a traitor. To die a fool might actually be a step above that.

"So we die as fools," she said with a shrug. "Better that than to live as cowards."

She didn't want to die, but she could see why people thought she did when she said things like that.

"How do you not care what people think of you?" Gibbs' words were soft as he avoided her gaze, as if he were embarrassed by the question.

She did care. She cared far too much. "I've found that no matter how hard I try, I'll never live up to everyone's expectations so I stopped trying." She just wanted to make her ancestors proud. "I already live with the crushing obligation to make my ancestors proud. I don't think I can handle caring about what anyone else thinks to."

Gibbs had lifted his cup to take another sip of his tea and spit it back into the cup as he snorted at her words. "That's fair."

Was that almost a smile playing at his lips?

Were she and Gibbs . . . bonding?

She didn't have time to dwell on it though as footsteps sounded, coming from the cargo bay, and she jumped to her feet as Gibbs scrambled up as well. They were light, unlike Captain Behnam's deliberate steps and Trapp's definitive tromping. So El wasn't surprised when Ginger appeared in the doorway.

The medic took in the two before her. "Am I interrupting anything?"

"We were just talking," Gibbs said at the same time that El said, "We're done now."

"Good." Ginger stood on the other side of the sink and peered into the grubbery at them. "I hope it was good. And if either of you needs to talk anything through, you know that's what I'm here for."

"I will," El told her. She still felt shaky from everything she'd told Gibbs—more than she'd told anyone, except Ginger. Not even Captain Behnam knew that much. "But . . . later?"

"That's fine. Does anyone want to help me with breakfast?"

El moved away from the sink. "I can."

The day passed with an easy comfort—meals, working on transferring files, a session with Ginger that involved more crying, and no longer having to avoid anyone because they all knew her secrets. She didn't have to hide anymore. She didn't have to run.

It felt good.

CHAPTER 18

SEVEN DAYS AFTER leaving Resna, the *Aderyn* landed on Philosanthron.

The ship was abuzz with energy. Not just the usual landing energy that came with the difference in the schedule—of dealing with air control and a sophisticated one at that—but there was a shift in everyone's moods. They were all on edge, as they knew what they'd come to Philosanthron to do was important, but none of them wanted to discuss the gravity of it. So it hung there in the air between them all, unspoken, but a clear, defined presence.

"We're boarded in five," Captain Behnam when they'd landed, poking his head into the cockpit.

El jumped up, making a dash for her bunk, slipping into the panel underneath it. She closed her eyes and breathed deeply, picturing the cockpit, putting the details into place one by one— her sitting at the boxy comm console, Trapp at the controls, the clicking as she typed and he . . . did whatever it was he did, the smell of musk mixed with whatever those snacks Trapp was always munching on here, salty and sweaty—until she was there in her mind and no longer trapped in some stuffy metal coffin about to be arrested.

It wasn't a full inspection, thankfully. Even if Gibbs wasn't acting in any official capacity right then, he did still have some sort of political immunity afforded him. So there would be no inspection of the ship, no reason for El to worry that she'd be found out.

But then footsteps approached and El had to remember how to breathe again. It didn't mean anything that she didn't recognize the footsteps. It didn't mean anything at all.

Maybe one of the soldiers just needed to see the control room. Or maybe one of the crew was wearing a different pair of shoes. Maybe she just didn't recognize the footsteps when she was locked in a metal box.

Maybe the room wasn't getting smaller and smaller. Maybe the walls weren't closing in on her. Maybe her lungs weren't being squeezed by a vice and maybe her heart wasn't going to explode in her chest from beating so hard.

Deep breaths, she reminded herself, Ginger's voice in her head. Picture the cockpit, picture each detail one by one, putting it into its place—sights, sounds, smells, to make it as real and detailed as she could. She'd never been good with her imagination but even just trying helped her breathing to steady, her heart to not feel quite so sure to explode.

"Elis?"

It was Captain Behnam's voice, followed by the sound of the panel being moved. Light flooded the little space.

"It's all clear."

She breathed a sigh of relief.

"It's all good?" she asked as she took the Captain's offered outstretched hand, allowing him to support her as she wiggled out of the space and into the room. He helped her to her feet before releasing her once she was stable.

"All good," he confirmed. "We're—uh—meeting in the grubbery in five."

She nodded, brushing the dust off her clothes and trying not to think about how small the room was with two people in it. Any two people, she told herself. It had nothing to do with the fact that she was standing that close to Captain Behnam.

Had she gotten that dusty when she'd been down there the other day? How exactly did one dust a secret compartment intended for smuggling and other nefarious purposes? That was probably something no one worried about.

"Meeting in the grubbery?" she said then, because she needed to say something or else they'd just keep standing there thinking about dust and how small the room was and Captain Behnam awkwardly looking anywhere but at her as she brushed her clothes off.

"Huh? Oh, yeah," he said, looking at her then as he offered her a nervous smile. "Right, we should get to that."

They left her bunk and strode down the hall, through the cargo bay, and to the grubbery, where everyone else was waiting.

Ginger sat the end of the table to the left and Gibbs sat on the other end opposite her. Trapp was on the far side, in between the two, and Captain Behnam went to sit beside his pilot and friend. El stood there a moment, knowing she ought to sit across from the Captain and Trapp but trying instead to figure out how to make everyone move so they could sit evenly.

"You okay, Elis?" Captain Behnam asked, a look of concern wrinkled into his brown. Ginger, too, was looking at her with marked regard, as if the medic thought El was having another anxiety attack.

She shook her head, realizing there was no way to make it work out for five people to sit evenly around a rectangular table. Perhaps they ought to consider changing to a circular one. But then, it wouldn't fit as well in the space and it wasn't as if redoing the grubbery was her responsibility.

Pulling herself away from her thought, she walked to the table to take her seat when she realized by doing so, she'd be putting her back to the door. She stood frozen again, looking from Trapp to Captain Behnam and back again. "Could we . . . trade?"

The Captain looked at her like she'd lost her mind, maybe even a little annoyed that she was being so particular, but Trapp jumped up, grinning at her. "Sure thing."

As they circled around the table to trade spots, El realized what the switch meant. She dropped into her place beside Captain Behnam, knowing it was the better option but not entirely sure it was the safer one; not with the way it made her heart beat faster, her breath catch in her chest.

Ginger squeezed her hand reassuringly. Could she have possibly heard the hitch in El's breath? Had they all heard it? Did they think she was on the verge of another attack or did they know the real reason for her difficulties?

She wasn't sure which she preferred.

"Right," Captain Behnam said after a minute. "Let's get this meeting to order."

"Why are we even meeting? Did we not already discuss all there was to discuss?" Gibbs asked, his brow furrowed, and El was grateful the expression was directed at someone other than her for once.

Trapp drummed his fingers on the tabletop absentmindedly. "*Ech*, if I miss my appointment with Hallah she's not going to be happy, and we might not get a dress. And if we don't get a dress, the whole plan is done before we even get started."

Why Trapp had been so eager to volunteer to be responsible for getting El a dress, El didn't know. And she didn't understand why everyone else was unfazed by the pilot's insistence.

"I just need to hear it again," Captain Behnam said, ignoring his friend's impatient tapping. "We start this, there's no going back. So I need to hear it from you all that it's what you really want."

He looked at each of the people sitting around the table, one by one, but El would have sworn his gaze rested on her longer than it had the others. She sat up straighter, refusing to shrink under his questioning frown.

"Nothing's changed for me. I understand if any of you want to back out—I know what I'm asking and Liosa isn't your country." She gave Captain Behnam a pointed look.

Trapp's drumming became all the more persistent as he sighed. "Really, Leiv? Yeah, I'm in, can I go now? Because we're not doing anything if Hallah gets stood up."

"Go," Captain Behnam said, and El realized it had all been for her benefit; if she'd said the word, he'd have told Trapp to get them off the ground and they'd be out of here. It was probably the choice he was hoping she'd make. She wasn't sure if she should be grateful for the opportunity or annoyed that he'd yet again felt the need to give it; did he not understand that she was serious?

She pushed herself up from the table, not looking at him as she said, "I'm going to take a shower."

"We'll have to blow-dry your hair then," Ginger called after her, and El waved in acknowledgment, not looking back at her as she left. El had never actually blow-dried her hair before, but she assumed Ginger knew what she was doing; it was a Ginger problem, not an El problem.

El's problem was getting her mind off the way she felt, getting the nervous agitation out, and somehow setting aside her frustration with Captain Behnam. Usually a good workout helped with that, but she didn't want to tire herself out. And if she did work out, she'd have to shower afterward anyway. So the shower would have to suffice.

CHAPTER 19

"**I** STILL SAY THIS is an insane idea," Gibbs mumbled under his breath even as he and El approached the gates of the palace in the vehicle he'd acquired somewhere. El had been too busy being painted and poked to ask.

El rolled her eyes. "Are you still going on about me wearing my boots? Because I told you, it's wiser than trying to do anything in heels." She tugged at the bodice of her dress, not liking how low is dipped. "That's one thing the military neglected to teach me how to do. Besides, these are ridiculously comfortable, and I'm not going to risk anything happening to them by leaving them on that heap of scrap."

"I'm right here," the Captain said from the front seat, where he was behind the wheel, driving. He'd insisted on taking that role with far more determination than El had expected. "And everyone had their chance to back out. It's too late now."

"You know you love that ship," Gibbs said to El as their vehicle slowed, and the Captain rolled down his window to speak to the guards. Gibbs handed up his ID before he was waved inside. She looked down at her lap and she smoothed the skirt of her ball gown, the garnet fabric rustling under her touch.

Not that she had ever come into contact with Philosanthrian palace guards before; her connections more with their foot soldiers than anything else.

"Where did Trapp even find this dress?" she asked, pulling at the bodice again and adjusting her sleeves. If you could call the little scraps of lace that hung off her shoulders 'sleeves.' The skirt was layers upon layers of shining tulle—which made the boots less of a dangerous choice as no one was going to see anything under her skirt. She hoped.

Except when she climbed out of the vehicle—which she thought of the moment the door was opened and a hand appeared, presumably attached to a uniformed footman, eager to assist her. She flashed the Captain a concerned look in the mirror, hating herself for being tied up by a mere dress. She could face-off a group of mercenaries in an alleyway, but that confounded dress would be the end of her.

She took a deep breath and started to rise but Captain Behnam was already springing into action, jumping from the vehicle and gently inserting himself between it and the footman.

"My lady," he said as he held out a hand to her, offering her a mischievous grin. She accepted his hand, grateful for him as he angled his body to shield any flash of her boots from the suspicious eyes of the footman.

A rush of cold air hit her neck and shoulders as her feet planted firmly on the ground, the dress lacking in real covering of any kind.

Her head itched, stick with far more bobby pins than she had ever worn before. She always used elastic bands, but Ginger had said pins would work better for the sweeping up-do she'd done—after they'd managed to blow-dry El's wet hair into something that wasn't a complete disaster. The medic promised her it looked amazing, and Gibbs and Trapp had both backed her up on that fact, but El was still skeptical on the matter.

"You can do this," Captain Behnam said, hand still in hers as he drew her a little closer than was strictly proper for a footman. His breath was warm on her ear and she leaned into it, craving the relief from the chilly air. At least, that's what she told herself. "For Liosa."

"For Liosa," she replied, not wanting to admit how his words warmed her more than anything else possibly could; he had no allegiance to their planet, but he knew what those two small words meant to her.

A little shock ran through her, that tingle of electricity, and Captain Behnam pulled his hand away, muttering, "Sorry."

It was the same tingle she'd felt when they'd rescued him, but he should be recovered from whatever they'd done. But then, she'd felt it before then, always with the Captain. She'd thought it was other things but . . .

She didn't have time to think about it, not as he stepped back, and Gibbs exited the vehicle and took her arm; she had a job to do. She cast a wistful look over her shoulder at the Captain as she walked away from him, wishing more than anything to be going into battle with him rather than the security officer.

She turned her attention to Gibbs, who offered her a half-smile. It was almost sad, and El thought she understood what he was feeling. He was in his element, what he knew, and it was hard when you found out that something that held so much comfort had turned on you, betrayed you. If you couldn't feel at home where you always had, then where was home supposed to be?

But that wasn't her concern, she reminded herself. Her job was to protect Prince Tov, to find out who was trying to kill him while also avoiding capture and execution. She didn't have time to babysit Gibbs' emotions as well, and that was okay. He hadn't even asked her to, so it was foolish to feel the need to take on yet another task.

She had to remind herself to breathe.

They started up the stairs, white marble, so sleek and classic. There were so many of them too, several dozen or more, low and long. Then they were at the doors, white and thin and glass. The footman leaned in to ask Gibbs what name to announce her by, and her heart caught as she realized they hadn't discussed that.

They hadn't discussed much of anything, everyone hurrying about making plans for her, finding her a dress and doing her hair and trying to steal her boots from her when she wasn't looking but not giving her the time or space to think these things through. She was going in blind and that wasn't okay.

Her hand went to where her gun was tucked into her dress—in a secret pocket that fit the weapon so perfectly. She breathed a sigh of relief.

"Officer Carrigan Gibbs of Liosa and his guest," the footman announced, sweeping his arm to the side, inviting the two of them into the ballroom.

His guest. That worked. No name, no lies to remember. He had worked things out without her having a plan after all. But one lucky bout of quick thinking did not make up for having a real, solid plan.

They stepped inside, the sights, smells, and sounds of the room surrounding her, engulfing her. She took a deep breath, dizzy as she was bombarded with it all.

The tinkling of glasses. Something sugary sweet. Pale tones, all from the same palette blending together in a pastel rainbow. People chattering. Sweat, though the ball had just begun, brought on from the heat and so many bodies in one room. Tulle and lace, wrapping every woman in the room up like a package. Laughter. Low, twinkling lights strung by the hundreds, reflecting off everything. So many different perfumes mingling together—retten and paintbrush and musky colognes.

Gibbs whispered something low in her ear and she tried to focus on his words, but they were a blur, moving past her before she could puzzle them out.

And then he was gone, slipping away from her, moving across the room with a confidence she wished she had at that moment. She wanted to chase after him but found her legs held her rooted in place and yet felt like jelly at the same time. If she tried to step, she wasn't sure if she would find herself stuck or if she'd fall flat on her face; either was a viable option at the moment.

Her hand went to her gun once more, but the weapon would do her little good. She had nothing to shoot at. It was all moving too fast, like trying to use bullets to stop the mighty river that flowed through the Liosa capital—a foolish and futile attempt.

Besides, she couldn't just draw her weapon in the middle of a crowded ballroom without drawing attention, and attention was the last thing she wanted.

She looked about the room, scanning for anyone she knew, but all she saw was a blur of faces, her mind swirling dizzyingly as the scents and sounds and movements danced around her.

Her heart beat so fast it shot pain through her chest as she struggled to draw in a breath. A shiver ran up her back as the cold sweats came. She'd forgotten how much she hated those.

Wiping her damp palms on the skirt of her dress, she drew in another shaky breath, trying to remember what Ginger had said, but afraid if she closed her eyes and did her breathing exercise, she'd miss something vital.

But as it was, she was useless—somewhere in between eyes closed and wide open, flitting between being too aware of everything around her and unaware of it completely.

She jumped as she realized someone had come up beside her, but try as she might, she couldn't focus on them beyond a few basic details—Liosi, well dressed, not quite as tall as her.

And blond. He was blond.

It wasn't a common hair color for Liosi, and it didn't look particularly good on him. Was it natural or had he dyed it to make it that color?

And then he was asking her a question, taking her hand and propelling her forward before the request sunk in and she formed an answer. It turned out her legs could move after all, but for how long, she wasn't sure.

"I don't think . . . " she protested as the man slipped an arm around her waist. It wasn't that he was disrespectful—his touch was light, and he clearly didn't seek to take advantage.

But she wasn't sure that was a good idea, not with the way her head was spinning.

"Just one dance," he said, offering her a smile so wide and earnest she couldn't muster up the energy to refuse.

She stumbled as they took the first step, finding his arms strong and secure, his movements sure even as hers were halting and hesitant.

"I'm sorry," she murmured as she took a deep breath.

"I can only imagine how hard dancing in heels must be," he said, his words smooth and gracious.

She didn't correct him, though she supposed her silence would be taken for affirmation. But she had lied about far more serious things in her life and wasn't deeply concerned about the impression the man had about her footwear.

Instead, she focused on what her feet were doing, finding it made the breathing easier to think about; that and nothing else. Her partner was a skilled dancer, moving easily, gliding among the crowd. She wasn't the best of dancers, as she'd had little chance for practice, but she found herself moving with him, discovering that if she let him lead and focused on simply keeping herself from falling on her face, then his dancing was enough to carry her own. And she knew beyond a shadow of a doubt that they were indeed making a scene.

Her skin might have stood out among a group of Philosanthrians but there were enough of her own people here to keep her from being too concerned about that.

Her dress, however, was a deep garnet color, and even her own countrymen were dressed in the pale tones of their host. Trapp must not have known there was a color scheme to match or else he'd not had much of a choice when asking his favor.

Her object had been to blend in. If she'd wanted to stand out, she could have worn her uniform.

But as she looked up at her partner, her head a whole lot clearer, she realized they weren't just staring at her because of her dress.

As she looked up into her partner's eyes, she found she was staring up at Prince Tov, crown prince of Liosa. Her sovereign, whom she had sworn allegiance to, who she was here to save, though she'd broken that vow of fidelity.

She stumbled again, tripping over her own feet and grateful once more that she had opted for boots rather than heels, just as the music ended.

He caught her and she looked up at him again, realizing he was younger than she'd first imagined him to be—she knew for a fact that he was eighteen, a good several years younger than her—and she found, upon inspection, that his wide, bright smile didn't actually meet his eyes. The dark orbs instead held an immeasurable weight of sadness and fatigue.

She understood those all too well.

"Forgive me, Your Highness," she said, having to stop herself short of balling her hand to a fist and bowing over it, fist to her shoulder. It was instinct and she fought it, for the action would surely give her away.

He gave a light laugh. How long had he been playing the role of the dutiful prince? Surely his whole life, for he played it with such ease. "Whatever are you apologizing for? For dancing with the ease of an Elassi? Because I assure you, the offense of perfection is one I will readily forgive."

She started to laugh because that seemed the appropriate response to someone casually flirting with her, but then she caught his eyes and saw they were serious, his expression earnest.

She looked away and she was glad she did, because it was then that she saw them—Gibbs' father, Commander Ector Gibbs, and the man himself: her own father, Security Head Urian Elis.

CHAPTER 20

SECURITY HEAD ELIS and Commander Gibbs had
their backs to El and Prince Tov, so she didn't think they
had seen her yet. Or if they had, it had been mere flashes
of her as she'd danced, and they hadn't recognized her.

As she watched, they started to turn around just as the
music began again. Prince Tov slipped his arm about her waist
once more. She didn't protest, though she wished nothing more
than to break from his hold and run from the room as fast as
she could.

"Are you unwell?" the Prince said, eyeing her with concern.

She shook her head, watching as her father and the commander started toward them. "It's just a little crowded in here.
I—I should go."

He pulled her closer to him. She didn't pull back because
Commander Gibbs and Security Head Elis were moving past
them, and she needed somewhere to hide.

"Let me take you to get some air," Prince Tov requested. "These formal affairs can be a bit overwhelming for me too."

Before she could protest, he was moving toward the doors with El in tow, arm securely about her waist, steps sure and confident.

They slipped through the doors and out onto the balcony, which had a few scattered ball-goers all engaged in their own conversations, not one giving El and the Prince a single glance. He led her down the stairs into the actual gardens.

El kept glancing over her shoulder, hand close to her gun, ready to draw it at any second. "We shouldn't go too far."

Had Gibbs noticed she was gone or was he preoccupied with something else? She had to get back; they had a job to do.

"Just here," Prince Tov said, nodding to a bench a few feet off. With a resigned sigh, she let him lead her to it and took a seat.

"I really do need to get back, Your Highness," she told him, feeling bad as she looked at his earnest expression. But his life was far more important than whatever flirtatious conversation he wished to have.

It wasn't as if anything would come of it. Not only was El a traitor—having broken a vow to the young man sitting before her—but she would make a lousy princess—queen. She hardly knew how to deal with such an event for an evening.

He opened his mouth to speak but something else caught her ear. The sounds of the ball drifted to them, but she heard something else.

Wrestling with the folds of her dress, she found her gun, withdrawing it. The Prince's eyes grew wide as he let out a little gasp. "You're an assassin."

If only her mission were that simple.

She needed to get them out of here. There was no way whoever that was had good intentions; if they did, they wouldn't be creeping about.

"I'm here to help you, *rook di goo*," she told Prince Tov, knowing her words did little to ease the fear written clearly on his face. "I need you to come with me."

He looked at her gun, eyes wide; he thought she was threatening him, and she didn't have time to correct him. Whatever got him to come; it wasn't the first act of treason she'd committed.

He didn't struggle or protest in the least as she took hold of his arm, dragging him along with her into the maze of hedges that rested not too far away.

It was a risky move tactically, but the best El had. Her other options were to stay where she was or to go back to the ballroom—both options that were sure to end in her meeting whoever it was who was sneaking up on them. And El would rather have the advantage of being just as lost as the person approaching them.

That would also give her time to try and figure out just who she was dealing with.

The last thing she needed was the added trouble of whatever it was he would try.

"I'm not an assassin, I'm a soldier," El explained to Prince Tov. "Former soldier." No need to get into the specifics about her being a deserter and the like. "But there is someone who wants you dead, and I'm here to warn you about them."

He shook his head, looking lost and forlorn, so unlike the flirtatious, confident man she had danced with not fifteen minutes ago. "I should have known you were too good to be true."

"I'm true," she told him. "No matter what else, you can be sure of that. I'm a true Liosi, Your Highness, and I will give my life protecting you if it comes to that. *Rook di goo.*"

He didn't say anything, which El hoped was a good sign. He wasn't arguing so she counted it as a win.

Her gun drawn, she turned her attention then to the threat—whoever it was creeping up on them. She listened for sounds of their approach and found them a little ways off to her right. She backed up, taking Prince Tov farther into the maze. Ducking around a corner, she pressed herself against the hedge wall, breathing slowly so it wouldn't be heard over the sound of the approaching footsteps.

The footsteps stopped and El all but stopped breathing, hoping beyond hope that they started again. Then they did, and she had to keep herself from letting out a sigh of relief; she wasn't about to risk even that small sound being heard.

The person came closer, and she was sure then that it was just one person. That was good. That made the odds even, made things easier.

She waited as they came closer. And closer. She waited. And waited. Her timing needed to be perfect. A second too soon and they'd have a chance to get away from her; a second too late and she'd no longer have the advantage of surprise.

She breathed ever so slowly as she heard the footsteps came closer. And closer. And closer.

They paused again, and it took all she had not to curse aloud. Instead, she drew in a breath ever so slowly, letting it out again even slower. The footsteps resumed and she marked off how far away they were based on the sound.

Six yards.

Five yards.

Four yards.

Three.

Two.

One.

She sprang into action then, coming around the corner of the maze, and was on top of the person in an instant. He was on the ground as she knocked his gun from his hand, pinning him to the gravel in the path.

He put up a fight and, after a moment, he managed to break free of her hold, reaching for the discarded gun. She wasn't about to let that happen so she, too, lunged for it, managing to knock it away before he could.

Unfortunately, she wasn't able to also keep him from knocking her from her feet at the same time, and so next thing she knew, her legs were knocked out from under her, and she fell to the ground.

She landed hard and the wind was knocked out of her, but she didn't let that keep her down. Pushing herself up, she jumped on her assailant, wrapping her arms around his neck as she pulled him away from the gun.

She tightened her grip around his neck, and he stopped struggling as he started to lose consciousness. Easing him from her grasp, she knew she had just enough time to grab his gun and stand over him, pointing it at him.

"Who do you work for?" she asked, able to get a good look at him. It was pretty obvious that he worked for Radian Darius, but she wanted him to say the words.

The man was groggy, confused. "I—I'm a Vercentii."

She snorted at that. "Nice try, but no."

Like the other imposters, he had his earlobes; she would have thought someone as thorough as Radian Darius would pay attention to a detail like that.

She glanced up at Prince Tov and found him looking at her with wide eyes. Shoot. He was falling deeper into infatuation with her, she could see it. But she couldn't get distracted by that. She looked back to the man before her, asking again, "Who do you work for?"

"I told you," the man maintained, growing more confident in his words. He was glaring at her, which wasn't a good sign. "I'm a Vercentii mercenary and if you try to stand in my way—"

"No," she interrupted. They didn't have the time for games. The man had answers, but she didn't have time to get them. What they needed was a guard, but she couldn't just walk up to one and turn the man over to them without turning herself in as well.

She pondered a moment, stuck in indecision. The sound of footsteps filled the air, and the man before her grinned. "Those are my friends. You're not getting out of here alive."

That was stupid on his part, El thought, giving the enemy tactical information. But it worked in her favor, so she didn't bother to correct him.

She didn't even hesitate, lowering the gun to point it at his leg and firing. It wouldn't kill him, but he also wouldn't be able to get far if he tried giving chase to them.

Taking Prince Tov's hand, she pulled him further into the maze, further away from the man's screamed curses.

"Do you have any idea how to navigate here?" she asked, knowing she ought to have asked the question sooner before they were well into the place.

But it didn't matter anyway. Prince Tov shook his head, looking a little lost.

She kept moving, telling herself not to panic, one hand wrapped around the handle of her gun, the other around the Prince's arm. She needed to get out of here, to the other side of the maze, and then go back to the ballroom. Deserter or not, it seemed the most logical way to protect the Prince.

Once they were in the ballroom, they'd be safe; no one—especially someone as careful as Radian Darius—would try to assassinate the Prince in such a crowded place.

All she had to do was get him to the ballroom and then her job was done.

She could do that.

El continued making turns or going straight based on instinct, though she had a bad feeling that it wasn't the best method to use. They didn't come to any dead ends though, and she took the win and stuck with the method.

After a while, she paused and listened.

There were footsteps behind them.

How had someone kept pace with her? *Victory.* They needed to move faster.

If only she knew the way. If only she didn't have a prince in tow. If only she were more prepared. She should have been prepared.

Of course someone would take advantage of the deserter whisking Prince Tov off to some secluded place alone. They could even blame her for the assassination. It would be messy politically, yes, but it would make things awkward more than anything else. No wars would be started over it. In fact, everyone would be so afraid of getting the blame placed on them that they would be willing to take something as serious as a prince's assassination and try to sweep it under the rug.

She was an idiot, and if Radian Darius didn't stand against everything she believed in, she'd have almost been impressed.

"Wait," the Prince hissed, stopping. She gave his arm a tug, trying to drag him again but he was holding firm, shaking his head. "I think we need to go that way to get out of here. This looks familiar."

He was pointing in the opposite direction of where she'd been headed but the footsteps were approaching fast, and at least Prince Tov had been here before, unlike her.

Gunshots.

Shoving the Prince in the direction he'd indicated, she fired off several shots of her own in the direction the others had come from. She couldn't see anyone, but it would hold back anyone coming their way.

She took off after Prince Tov, catching him in an instant but allowing him to lead since he seemed to know where he was going, and he didn't seem inclined to hand the leadership back to her. She could live with that.

Sure enough, she saw an exit just ahead of them.

But it wasn't over yet. Not until they were back in the ballroom. Someone could easily be waiting to pick them off when they came through it.

That's what she would do.

But the footsteps approached, and she had to do something.

She took a deep breath and barreled through the opening, both her own gun and the one she'd taken off the fake Vercentii drawn. She fired on either side of her, the shots coming off fast and missing everything. But she wasn't trying to hit anything.

Prince Tov was behind her, keeping pace as he ran hunched over with his head ducked.

To her surprise, no one fired back. She'd been wrong about someone waiting for her after all.

But they were still being chased, and she wasn't about to stand there and get caught. So she started moving, putting Prince Tov in front of her again.

They moved around the outside of the maze, circling back around to the garden where Prince Tov had first whisked her away.

There were guards everywhere, people El had every reason to avoid.

"Trust your guards," she told the Prince. "Keep them close."

"Where are you going?" he demanded, reaching for her, no doubt to drag her into the garden with him.

She stepped away from him, shaking her head. "I can't be seen."

"You really are an Elassi, aren't you?" he said with a look of wonder.

If he wanted to believe she was a glowing being from outer space, so be it. Fist to her shoulder, she bowed. "Goodbye, Your Highness."

Then she darted away as the guards came and surrounded their Prince, calling for her to stop—but of course, she didn't listen.

CHAPTER 21

EL MADE IT back to the vehicle where Captain Behnam was waiting. She slipped into the backseat and let out a relieved sigh, a weight falling off of her as she sank against the seat.

"Trapp's going to kill you," the Captain said with a grin. "What where you doing? Climbing a tree?"

Her dress truly was a mess of tatters and rags; the skirt was all but shredded, and part of the bodice was torn away from the collar. "It was actually a maze of hedges."

He raised his eyebrows at her, an expression she saw as he turned to climb over the seat. "Do tell."

He settled beside her, the seat wide enough for at least three people—maybe four if they squished—but he'd sat closer than that, just at the edge of her mess of skirts, so close their arms were almost touching. Her breath hitched and she told herself it was because she'd been running, because she hadn't yet caught the breath she'd lost. And her heart, she knew, was racing because she hadn't yet recovered from what had happened.

What had happened. Captain Behnam had asked about that. So she told him, to get her mind off what was happening just then—not that anything was happening—starting with when they'd left the vehicle and what ensued in the ballroom.

"You danced with a prince?" he asked when she got to that part, disbelief in his voice. Which was fair. "And he really fell in love with you?"

Was that jealousy she heard? *Victory*, it wasn't a good color on him.

She skipped over that, moving on to the gardens. She'd just gotten to the part where she'd drawn her gun when he shifted, clearly having heard something, his attention no longer on her.

Her gun came out. "What's the matter?"

He twisted around in his seat, pulling down the back of the seat to reveal a passage to the trunk. "Guards."

That was all he had to say and El was twisting herself to slip into the hole he'd opened, doing her best to pull her dress with her. Captain Behnam helped with the stuffing, offering her a sheepish grin as he wrangled her skirts.

"Sorry," he mouthed as he lifted the seat back into place, plunging El into darkness. She reflected on how many times she'd been holed up in a small, dark space in the last several weeks; was it an indication of how the rest of her life would go?

But then, of course, it was. She'd spend the rest of her life running. The moment she stopped was the moment she got caught and from there . . .

There was no good ending. There never would be. For her to think she could get away, go someplace and start a new life, to think she could ever belong somewhere, it was foolish.

The vehicle door opened, and El's hand went to her gun. The door closed again and then the seat started to come down, Captain Behnam's voice accompanying it. "Please don't shoot me, Elis."

It was too dark for him to have seen her gun, which meant he knew her well enough to know she'd have it out. She smiled at that as she tucked her gun away, saying, "Is it all clear?"

"I told them I saw someone run off down the driveway," he replied. "You should probably stay back there just to be safe though. Sorry."

It was a fair point, so he had nothing to be sorry about. Goosebumps ran all along her skin and a shiver shook her body. "*Rook di goo*, it's even colder back here than out there. Why is it as cold as the void? Isn't this supposed to be Philosanthron's warm season?"

She heard the Captain shift and then next thing she knew, his jacket was smacking her in the face. She gave him the benefit of the doubt and assumed it was because it was too dark for him to actually see where her face was.

"Now you'll be cold," she protested.

She heard him shift once more, settling back just beside the entrance, so when he spoke his voice was soft, but she could still hear it clearly. "I've got Mahsirian blood. I don't get as cold as you Liosi."

He was Liosi too, but she decided not to press that point. "Thank you."

She shrugged into the jacket, finding it still warm. She told herself the shiver that came was from the warm fabric against her cool skin and not the intimacy of finding warmth from the jacket the Captain had just been wearing. It was long, so it wrapped around her like a blanket.

"So then what happened?" he asked, and her thoughts were pulled from the jacket to what he was saying. "You were in the garden with the Prince, and you drew your gun, and then what?"

She continued her story, her soft voice tickling the cool air as she spoke. She told him about the hedges and the man pretending to be a Vercentii and how she'd shot him.

"So that's where the blood was from," he said simply, and she cringed, not even having realized she'd gotten blood on her.

"Trapp's going to be so mad," she said with a sigh.

"Trapp'll get over it," Captain Behnam replied easily. Was he saying it because it was true or because the two were friends and allowed to say things like that about each other? "So then what?"

She knew why he was asking, but she still liked to think he was actually interested in what she had to say. But she shook the thought away as soon as it entered her head. There wasn't anything but business between them; there couldn't be, no matter how warm his jacket or his personality was.

She continued with her story until she ended with getting back to the vehicle. "I didn't get the information we needed."

"You saved the Prince's life," Captain Behnam pointed out.

"Temporarily," she argued. "And that means nothing if we can't keep him alive."

"Has anyone ever told you that you're too hard on yourself?"

His words were easy, nonchalant, almost as if he were teasing. But they struck El because she suddenly realized that no, no one had ever told her that before. They'd always told her to be harder on herself or to be easier on other people. Work hard, her father had said, while her mother told her to be compassionate.

But never had anyone ever told her to be easier on herself.

"Actually, no," she said honestly. "I don't think they have."

"Well that sucks," he said, and somehow it was exactly what she needed him to say. She liked that about him, that he didn't always have to say something profound or flowery. Most times he was direct and straight to the point, and even if she didn't always like what he said, she liked that he was saying it.

And then, sometimes, he said the exact right thing and it made her feel a little better about something she hadn't even realized was hurting.

There was silence between them until she finally said, "I wonder where Gibbs is."

"Flirting with a girl, maybe?" Captain Behnam suggested and then gave a little chuckle. El tried to picture it, Gibbs flirting with a girl, and she couldn't quite. He seemed too . . . harsh? cold? awkward? for such a pursuit.

"Maybe he went and got the information without me," she suggested, not much liking the idea, but shaking off the feeling; all that mattered was that they succeeded.

"Someone's coming." Captain Behnam shifted again, his voice low as he shut the seat once more.

It opened again almost immediately as she heard Gibbs say, "Nice of you to invite me to the party."

"Where have you been?" Captain Behnam demanded, his tone harsh. Why was he upset?

"There was an assassination attempt," Gibbs said, slipping into the car. "Where's El?"

She started to climb out of the trunk. "I'm right here."

"And should probably stay there," Captain Behnam said as he slipped from the backseat and into the front. "At least until we're clear of the palace."

He was right, of course, so she slipped back into the darkness.

"Why are we smuggling El out of the palace?" Gibbs asked in a low, urgent hiss, as if he were afraid someone might be there to overhear them in the moving vehicle.

"Where have you been?" Captain Behnam demanded again, and that time El heard the annoyance in his voice. "Elis stopped the assassination attempt. How do you know about the attempt but not that she stopped it?"

"Did no one see me?" El asked, hope swelling in her. If she hadn't been seen, there was a chance . . .

"Seat up," the Captain said as he slowed the vehicle, and Gibbs closed the seat, nothing but darkness surrounding her once more. Would they insist on searching the vehicle? And if they did, would it be ethical to shoot them? And even if she did, would it do any good? She didn't want to shoot people if it still ended with her being caught. She wasn't interested in wasting lives.

There were voices, though she couldn't make out what they were saying, no matter how hard she strained to hear. Then Gibbs spoke, his voice steady and sure. "I am a Liosi security officer. The vehicle has already been searched and I won't waste my time having it searched again. I assure you, if there was an assassin—a threat to my own Prince, I might add—in this car, I would know."

The other voice came again, low and indistinct.

"Thank you for your good sense," Gibbs said. "I'll see that your good work is commended."

The vehicle lurched forward, and, after a few minutes, the seat came down again.

"All clear?" she asked.

"All clear," Gibbs and Captain Behnam both confirmed in unison.

"So did no one see me?" she asked, wriggling out of the trunk, paying close attention to her dress to make sure she avoided wriggling out of that too. The seat was settled into place once more and she sank back against it, grateful to be out with the others rather than closed in the darkness.

Gibbs, who sat beside her, gave a shake of his head. "They know there was a woman involved, but the rumor is His Highness claims she was an Elassi."

Captain Behnam gave a low whistle. "Mistaken for an Elassi, huh? That's impressive."

"So it was you, then," Gibbs said, not a question. "What happened?"

El told him, starting with when they separated—but leaving out the part about her panic that time—and ending with when she made it back to the vehicle.

"So now what?" he asked when she'd finished.

El gave a shrug. "We go back tomorrow and try again?"

"No, we absolutely don't do that," Captain Behnam said, giving her a stern look in the rearview mirror. "You barely made it out this time; I'm not sending you back in there to do it again."

"Excuse me?" El demanded, bristling at his words and tone. "You didn't send me anywhere, I volunteered. And I'll go anywhere I please. The only question is whether or not you'll be at my back when I do."

The vehicle filled with a heavy silence. Had El pushed too far? She forgot herself sometimes and spoke to Captain Behnam in ways she never had with anyone else. When she spoke to him, she said what was in her head instead of holding it back like she did with everyone else.

"I'm sorry," she said, her voice softer as she broke the silence. "I just don't know why it matters so much to you."

What she really meant was she didn't know why she mattered. He was so quick to jump in and defend or protect her like she was Ginger or Trapp. But he'd known them for a while; he'd only known her for such a short amount of time. He shouldn't care what happened to her.

And he shouldn't be willing to risk as much as he was for her.

"I'll have your back," he said by way of a reply. "But you'll also have to take my opinion with it—that's just the price you'll have to pay. I don't like it, Elis, the way you carelessly gamble with your life. You'd almost think it wasn't worth anything, the way you're always trying to throw it away."

It wasn't worth anything. She'd always known that—it was part of her Liosi heritage.

"No one is worth more than the fate of the galaxy," she said. "And if I have to give my life for the good of everyone else, it's the price I'm willing to pay."

"There's a difference between being willing to sacrifice your life as a last resort and constantly trying to throw it away," he said, his voice soft, making eye contact with her via the rearview mirror. "I hope you live long enough to learn the difference."

And with that said, the rest of the drive was made in heavy, uncomfortable silence.

El headed straight for her bunk, walking right past Trapp and ignoring his questions and demands. She could explain it later.

Or better yet, let someone else explain it.

It took her less time than she thought it would wrangling the dress off and slipping into her lounge pants and tee-shirt and pulling all the pins from her hair, shaking it out with her fingers. She even left her boots in her room, hurrying barefoot to the grubbery where the others were waiting.

They were seated around the table, steaming mugs in front of them, when she arrived. She slipped into a seat just as Ginger came out with another cup, a grin lighting her face when she saw El. "Just in time—this one's for you."

She set the mug in front of El and then took her seat at the far end of the table. El picked up the mug and inhaled—warm and sweet and minty. She let out a contented sigh; it had been a long day.

"Right then," she said, drinking in the tea's scent again, the liquid still too hot to actually drink. She set the cup on the table before her and looked at the group sitting around the table. She'd only known them a short time, but she found there was no one else she'd rather be sitting with.

Especially Captain Behnam, who she sat down next to without thinking. She could have sat in the empty seat at the end of the table, but she'd chosen the one next to the Captain instead.

She wasn't going to think about that, she couldn't.

"What we know is someone tried to assassinate Prince Tov tonight," she said, focusing on the task at hand. "They were posing as Vercentii again, just like they did when they tried to kill Gibbs. So it would be safe to assume they're working for Radian Darius because that kind of a coincidence is too big to ignore. We still have no concrete proof, but it still seems likely that Prince Jarett is somehow involved."

"I still don't understand that," Ginger said, looking concerned. She was at the far end of the table and she looked so small. The sleeves of her oversized sweater covered her hands, which she cupped around the steaming cup, holding it but not actually drinking from it. "Won't that start a war, for a Liosi head to be killed on Philosanthrian soil? In their own garden, no less . . . "

"Most likely," El said. "But he also knows most of our soldiers are stationed on Taras, under Philosanthrian command. If he wanted to, one word and he could destroy them."

"He wouldn't do that," Gibbs argued. "Why would he do that?"

He hadn't been on Taras. He hadn't seen the things she had. Hadn't done the things—

She rose, started pacing because the pacing kept the shaking at bay.

"Remember to breathe," she heard Ginger tell her, the soft, sweet voice cutting through the panic.

She turned and met the medic's eyes, gentle and kind. The young woman smiled at her and all their conversations came back to her. El closed her eyes, breathing deeply. In her mind she pictured the ship's control room, putting every detail into place, until she felt her heart rate slowing, her breathing coming naturally again.

She opened her eyes again and saw them all looking at her.

"I'm fine," she said, sitting down again and taking a long swig of her tea. "But he would do that. Trust me. Prince Jarett wouldn't think twice about doing that. We're at his mercy and he knows it. If Prince Tov dies, we're left weak and without a leader. It would be easier than anyone would care to admit for them to overthrow us."

"*Ech,*" Trapp said. "So what do we do? How do we stop it?"

"Same plan as tonight," she said. "We go back tomorrow, and we get proof."

Trapp frowned, looking to Captain Behnam. "You're okay with this?"

"No," he said with a shrug. "But Elis'll go with or without us, we know that, and when she dies, I'd rather it not be on my conscience that she did because I wasn't there for her."

"Excuse me?" she said, turning to him. Surely she heard him wrong.

He shook his head. "Sorry, 'if' you die, I didn't mean 'when.'"

"I think you did," she countered.

He let out a sigh. "You know how I feel about this plan."

"So offer a counter plan," she challenged. "If you think there's a better way, I'm open to ideas."

He paused, looking a bit caught off guard, before he shook his head. "I didn't—I mean, I don't . . . " He flexed his fingers as he admitted, "I don't have a better plan."

"Exactly," she said, pushing down the smug feeling that rose within her at having won the argument. "I'm not trying to throw my life away, *rook di goo*. I just can't stand by and watch it all come crashing down, and I don't have any other ideas. We need our proof. So Gibbs and I go back tomorrow and we get it."

Captain Behnam glared at her, but she wasn't about to take it. She was done with him acting like he wasn't going to take her suggestions—of course he was; he knew they were the right things to do.

She took a long swig of her tea—which was still too hot, but she'd already put it in her mouth, so she let it burn all the way down—and then returned the Captain's glare. He didn't say anything for a long while, and El let him stew, also saying nothing. No one else dared to speak and break the silence, and so the room was quiet for a long time.

Finally, the Captain drew in a long breath and let it out in a sigh. "Why do you always have to be right?"

"I don't know what you mean," she said, even though she did, unable to keep the smug smile from dancing across her face.

His glare deepened. "Yes, you do. And smugness doesn't suit you. All right, we do it your way. But when it all goes into the void, I'm blaming you."

"I don't doubt you will," she said as his glared deepened, and the easiness that existed between them returned.

Trapp frowned. "That means you'll need another dress."

She offered him an appreciative smile. "I'll try not to ruin this one."

"I doubt that," he said with a grin. "Is that it then? Same plan as tonight?"

"Same plan as tonight," El confirmed.

"And in the meantime," Captain Behnam said, "everyone should get some sleep. Since we're doing this we might as well stack the deck in our favor by being well-rested and on top of our game."

CHAPTER 22

EVEN AFTER EVERYTHING that had happened—the ball, the ambush in the gardens, the heated discussion in the grubbery—El still found herself not quite tired enough for sleep.

The comm still needed files moved, and so while she wasn't looking through the files anymore for information, she decided to move some more of them to the external drive.

It was short work since she wasn't going through and reading the files anymore, just moving them from the comm and into the file on the drive. She wasn't sure why Captain Behnam was so insistent that the files were saved, but she respected his wishes—no matter how stupid she thought those wishes to be.

In no time at all, she came to the first message Captain Behnam sent—which was nothing more than a test to ensure the comm actually worked. Then there was a message from twenty years before, granting permission to land on Elialech. There were no messages in between the two.

Captain Behnam had said his parents flew the ship before he had—she hadn't realized it had stayed dormant for so long. No wonder it was falling apart; it had been neglected for so many years.

But if these messages were from his parents, then what might she learn about him from them? She knew so little—he'd said his parents were Mahsirian and Liosi, and, given his last name, she assumed his father was Mahsirian, leaving the Liosi parentage to his mother.

She began skimming the files, finding them quite a bit more interesting than the current ones. They came from a time before the Information Database's existence when, if you wanted information, you had to ask the right people for it, and whoever ran the comm certainly knew all the right people.

It gave her no information about the crew though, aside from how many people were aboard the ship when they filed docking registrations. There seemed to be a captain and four other crew members. But no names, no positions. Nothing about what they did on the ship or who they were. It seemed the crew recovered items for people, as there were a lot of communications about having found the article or people requesting these services—but there were no receipts to indicate whether they'd received money for those services.

But it didn't explain why Captain Behnam—her Captain Behnam—no! the current Captain Behnam—wanted these files saved. It didn't explain why they hadn't been wiped out when he first began captaining the ship, why he insisted on saving them years later. They might hold sentimental value since they were his parents, but it wasn't as if they were interesting or anything.

It was early, no longer late into the night but having crossed the threshold into the wee hours of the morning. But El was in too deep; much too deep. She needed answers and she wasn't going to sleep until she had gone through every file on that comm. Captain Behnam had all but told her the comm held secrets, and she was going to find them.

The time ticked by, and while she learned quite a bit about the items the crew had recovered, she found nothing until an hour later when she discovered a folder tucked away in a hidden corner of the comm, marked quite simply "Journal Entries."

Journals meant one thing—information. No one wrote a journal that wasn't personal; they kept ship's logs or record books for the business or impersonal stuff. Journals were about personal accounts, and it didn't matter that she hadn't slept in almost a full day. She was going to look through those files.

They were in the folder with the newest entry at the top and the oldest buried down at the bottom. She reversed the order, thinking that while she could read shipping manifests and docking requests backward in terms of when they were sent, it seemed irrational to read someone's journal entries that way.

Except the first one was long. Super long. She scrolled through it before she started reading to see exactly how long it was, and it just kept going. Whoever the writer was, they had a lot to say. And suddenly sleep was starting to look like a good idea. There was no way she could concentrate on something that long.

But then she got to the end and saw who had signed it. A name she knew well, a name she had heard since she was a girl but had never identified with. Her mother had told the stories until El began to wish the woman had never existed at all.

"You're up early."

She jumped at the Captain's voice, whirling around to find him coming through the doorway. He wore lounge pants and a tee-shirt, his brown hair messy, sticking up in different directions. There was sleep in his eyes, and El assumed he had just woken up.

"I never went to bed," she admitted, biting her lip.

"I can see that now," he told her, crossing to her. "You look a mess." His gaze fell on the comm and he frowned at her. "What are you doing?"

It was a demand, the sleep disappearing from his eyes, replaced with anger, coldness, sternness.

"I was just putting the old files onto the external drive," she said.

"And reading through them?" he demanded, though his voice remained even. "You just decided to stay up all night and go through private files? What happened to getting sleep so we could be on top of our game? What happened to nothing being more important than Liosa?"

"They're on a public comm," she told him, ignoring the jabs he'd tacked on at the end; she didn't have the time to address those. "It's not like the files were even encrypted, and you did give me control of the machine."

His eyes flashed, and she knew he wasn't buying her defense. "That doesn't make it okay. You should have gone to bed." He stepped away from the comm, pacing a few feet away from her.

"I didn't read them," she said.

He turned back to look at her, a question in his eyes.

"The journal entries. I was going to read them, but I opened the first one and it was so long. I didn't actually read it. And I won't if it means that much to you."

He nodded, not exactly looking at her. "Good. Thank you."

"I don't understand though," she said. "Why does it matter? These were written almost thirty years ago. Why does it matter to you if I read them now? Why even bother keeping them?"

"You wouldn't understand," he said with a sigh and a shake of his head.

"Because you won't explain it to me," she said. He looked up then, met her eyes, his own flashing with pain. "Which is fine," she hurried to tell him. "But don't act like I'm stupid. Just tell me the truth—you don't want to talk about it."

"Okay, I don't."

"Okay," she said, turning back to the comm. "Then we're clear. I'll just put the files onto the drive, and we'll be done."

She closed the file, aware that he was watching her. Not that she wasn't going to do exactly as she had said she would. But still, it felt weird to have him there, looking over her shoulder but not saying anything.

"Her name was Elisandra," she said, partially to fill the silence, partially because she wanted to talk about it. She was tired, her determination to keep things impersonal all but forgotten. "Like the legend. I assume she was your mother?"

He nodded slowly, as if he were reluctant to confirm it, as he stared at her with that questioning frown, urging her to get to the point of whatever it was she was saying.

The very sight of the name had brought back so many memories. And since she had started talking, she found she couldn't stop. And besides, she was too tired to hold herself back.

"She was one of my mother's favorite people," she continued. "The legendary one, not your mother. Not that they had met or anything, but she had heard the stories—who hadn't?—and she always loved her."

"I never really knew much about what happened to her, to be honest," he admitted, crossing to the comm, leaning against the console next to it, facing her, fully engaged in their conversation; it was too late to end it.

"She was a Mahsirian princess, loved by an Elassi—a prince of the stars." El had never made up her mind whether she believed in the Elassi or whether they were simply tales of wonder and magic, made up to explain the unknown and to pass the time. "He gifted her with the Sight—the ability to see into a person's entire life. In exchange he wanted her to give herself to him, but she refused. He cursed her by scrambling the Sight so that she couldn't tell if she was looking at a person's past or their future."

Captain Behnam pulled his hand from the console of the comm as if he'd been burned. El hadn't felt anything though. But before she could ask about it, he said, "The Elassi prince sounds like a real jerk."

"He was," El confirmed. "But Elisandra was unwavering and she used her Sight during the Great War to help save a lot of people. That's why my mother loved her so much—'If you can be like anyone in this galaxy,' she would say, 'be like her. Because she's proof that you can be kind and good and still change the world.' It was the last story I remember her telling me before she died."

There was a long silence in which neither of them said anything. And then she said, "I was named after her, you know—Elisandra Elis. I hated her for that—Elisandra, that is. Because

I will never be like her. Kindness and goodness aren't how I operate. If I can shoot a problem, I will. I never understood how anyone could solve anything simply by talking about it."

"She knew how to shoot a gun." The words were level, matter-of-fact. "Crack shot, actually. She just also knew how to get herself out of situations she couldn't shoot her way out of. Which isn't that different from you, is it? I've watched you use your head so many times since we met—the girl who faked a pregnancy and took out a hit on me to get information, who walked into a warehouse full of brigands and demanded my release, who danced with a prince and got mistaken for an Elassi to save a galaxy. That's more than just the girl who shoots her way out of things. You're a lot more than you give yourself credit for."

She hadn't thought any of those things were all that noteworthy, but with the way the Captain looked at her, perhaps they were. At the very least, she liked the way he looked at her when he said them.

"You have a way of connecting with people," he continued. "True, you're doing it to get something from them, but I think, deep down, you care a lot more than you admit. And I think your mother would be proud of you for it."

She ducked her head at his words, because she felt tears welling in her eyes, and she didn't want him to see her cry. She needed to go to bed. If she didn't get some sleep, there was no way she was going to be able to do her job tonight.

But then a thought occurred to her. She looked up, meeting his eyes, frowning. "How do you know she could shoot a gun?"

His eyes went wide for half a second, flashing with something ill—fear maybe? Panic? He ducked his head, refusing to look at her. "Uh—eh—yeah . . . I must have read it somewhere."

"*Victory*, she was real," she said, a thought hitting her. It should have hit her long before that, but she blamed it on the lack of sleep. "The stories—she disappeared, and no one knows what happened to her. Those journal entries were written by the real Elisandra, weren't they? That's why you don't want them deleted."

And then a new thought occurred to her—if that were true, it meant she was his mother. Oh, *victory*, she had just told him she hated his mother.

That was why normal people went to sleep and didn't stay up all night having weird conversations with their captain. That was why people shouldn't open up and be honest with each other.

"I am so sorry," El said, her hands going to her mouth in horror and embarrassment. "I never meant to insult your mother—I'm sure she's an incredible woman who—"

She cut off then because what was she supposed to say?

He was grinning at her, which seemed like the strangest response, and only served to fluster her even more. "She'd find it funny. She—she has the best sense of humor. And like I said, any of your resentment is really just misunderstanding. If you knew her, you wouldn't be able to dislike her. She's—" He shook his head. "Well, never mind."

He clearly didn't want to talk about it, though she did note that he spoke of his mother as if she were still alive. She tried not to think about what that meant—that the legend was alive and well, living somewhere—Elialech, she would assume, given that's where the last message came from.

And then another thought occurred to her.

"*Victory*!" she said. "Can you imagine the history contained in those entries?"

"Which you promised not to read," he reminded her.

"Oh . . . " she said. "Right. No, of course. A promise is a promise. I won't read them. But . . . " She trailed off, pausing, then found the courage to say, "I still don't understand. Why would you want to keep something like this a secret?"

"You really should get some sleep," he said, which was not a reply at all.

But he was not wrong. She needed sleep. Desperately. If she was going to be of any use tonight, she needed to be well-rested. Plus, she wasn't about to argue with her Captain.

"You're right," she said, pushing herself up, standing. "I really do need to get some sleep. Good night, Captain."

"Good night, Elis," he said, offering her a half of a smile.

She left then, padding back to her room in her bare feet, the ship empty and silent. Everyone was still asleep so there was no electricity filling the air, no voices carrying in either heated or friendly conversation. It had an eerie, surreal quality to it, and it was then that she realized how used to life on the ship she had become. She was used to the voices and the sounds and the family they all seemed to be. The family they were inviting her to be a part of.

She shook her head as she reached her room as if to shake away the thought. No matter how many times Captain Behnam told her he was impressed with her or Trapp teased her or Ginger offered her one of her warm encouraging smiles or Gibbs gave her that look like maybe they were friends, she couldn't get involved.

Not when the rest of her life—no matter how long that was—would be spent looking over her shoulder. She couldn't ask them to do that too. She wouldn't.

Because deep down she knew if she asked them to, they would say yes. And she'd never be able to forgive herself for the consequences of that.

CHAPTER 23

EL SLEPT ALL day, not waking until late afternoon. She'd been so tired she'd fallen asleep in her bunk for the first time since coming aboard the ship, and it felt weird waking up there rather than on the bench.

She did not feel at all like nine hours of sleep ought to have made her feel. But she rose anyway, rolling out of bed and giving her teeth a quick brush before leaving her room. She had fallen asleep in the lounge pants and tee-shirt she had put on after the ball. She hadn't even bothered to wash the makeup off, and it was still streaked on her face in some places. She knew she ought to take care of that, but she was just too hungry.

She found the ship pleasantly empty as she moved toward the grubbery in search of food. Voices carried from somewhere, but she didn't encounter anyone, which made things easier for her. She was on a mission, and distractions were not something she was looking for. Reaching the grubbery, she fixed herself something quick and then moved to the control room to eat.

She found Trapp there, midnight beanie covering his dark curls, feet up on the control panel, one ankle resting on the other.

"Hey, sleepyhead." He greeted her with his usual grin. "Sleep well?"

There was something so familiar about it that made her heart ache. She offered him a one-shouldered shrug as she took a seat at the comm, setting her plate on her lap and beginning to eat. "It was sleep. I can't complain."

He snorted at that. "*Ech*, you don't get excited about much of anything, do you?"

"Not sleep," she said with a little shrug. She paused, deciding if she ought to say anything or not. Last time they had that conversation, it hadn't gone well. But she wanted to know. "Probably because I didn't get enough of it. I was up working on the comm most of the night. I found the entries from when the Captain's parents piloted it."

"Did you now?" He looked a bit wary, like he didn't want to say too much. But she didn't let the matter rest because she wanted to know. Besides, she already knew the hidden parts.

"He already told his secret," she said, getting that out of the way.

"He told you?" Trapp questioned, eyebrows raised, tone suggesting he more than didn't believe what she said.

She nodded. "But then he told me to leave it be, and I don't understand why."

"I kind of get it," he said with an easy shrug. "His parents are wonderful—they took me in and made me part of the family when I had no one—but for Leiv, he just wants to make his own name without the added pressure of having to live up to their legacy. When your parents are Elisandra the Prophet and King Alaric the Pendragon, you feel a little insecure."

"What was that about King Alaric?" she demanded, barely able to keep herself from squealing. King Alaric had literally shaped Liosi history, and she owed everything to him—her very being was because of what he had accomplished.

And Trapp had said he was Captain Behnam's father?

He was supposed to have died—he'd been injured during the revolution, gravely, and then his death was what spurred on so many others to take up the fight and win the war. But it was rumored that he'd recovered, that he'd survived. El had never paid much mind to the rumors—there was no evidence to support it, after all—but could it be true? He was alive. And married to another legend and father to a child. Father to someone she knew.

"Wait, you didn't know?" Trapp said, looking a little panicked. "I thought you said—"

She shook her head. "I knew Elisandra was his mother, he never said anything about his dad being—" She shook her head again, almost unable to say the words. But then that didn't make sense. "Why didn't he say anything when I gave him that entire Liosi history lesson? He told me he'd 'heard the stories' or something like that. And he said he died."

But Trapp wasn't listening. He leaned back his head, looking at the ceiling, his hand on his forehead. "*Ech,* he's going to kill me."

He cut off at the sound of footfalls coming toward the room. Both kept their eyes on the door, exchanging a glance only when the Captain appeared in the doorway.

Captain Behnam frowned at them as his frame filled the doorway. He narrowed his eyes at them. "What's going on here?"

"Nothing!" Trapp said just a bit too quickly. "Nothing's going on. We were just chatting."

"About what?" the Captain said, studying them like maybe he could tell just by looking at them.

Trapp mumbled the words, as if saying them quickly would spare him the Captain's wrath. "I accidentally told El who your dad is."

"You. Did. What?" Each word was drawn out with rage and displeasure. His mouth set in a firm line as he fixed Trapp with such a glare that El was almost afraid of what might happen next.

"Why didn't you tell me?" she asked, hoping to turn the attention away from Trapp. "You acted like you didn't know about our Liberation, but your father defined it."

He fixed her with a hard look, unlike any he'd given her before, and she swallowed whatever else she might have squealed about next. When he'd said he didn't want to talk about it, he'd meant it.

"Not everyone's lives revolve around Liosa, Elis." He flexed his fingers. "It certainly wasn't how I was raised. Trapp had no business telling you any of that."

There was a hard set to his jaw and a hardened glare on his face. She'd never seen him that upset; she hadn't realized the gravity of his words when he'd said he didn't want to talk about it.

"It was an accident," she defended. "And it was my fault. I never should have asked, and I won't ever again. From now on, your business is your business, and I will stay out of it."

It hurt to say those words as he was standing right before her with all the answers she wanted. She was fairly bursting with the desire to let all the questions spill forth. But she knew better than to ask; she wasn't getting answers.

"Which you should have done from the start," he said, which she felt was a little unfair. She had, after all, said just exactly that.

"Yes, sir," she replied, remembering—finally—to keep herself in check when she spoke to him and not say exactly what was on her mind. "It won't happen again."

He let out a huff, his mouth still firm, his shoulders rigid. "What exactly did he tell you?"

"Just that he was your father," she replied. "And that you don't want to talk about it."

Because he felt like his parents' legacy was too much to live up to. She resented Elisandra because she had heard stories of the woman—she couldn't imagine what it was like to be raised by two such incredible people who had accomplished so much.

But also, she would give her right arm—maybe even both of her arms—to meet King Alaric, and here Captain Behnam had been raised by the man. She was standing before King Alaric's son. How could he not want to talk about that? If her father were someone worth talking about, she'd be shouting it over the comm for all the galaxy to hear.

"And?"

"That's all."

"There's clearly more. You've got that look on your face," he said. "You get it when you're judging someone but don't want to say anything."

How in the galaxy did he know what look she got? "I don't know what you mean."

"You're thinking something that you don't want to say," he said. "But I want you to say it. What were you thinking?"

She shook her head. "It isn't my place."

He raised an eyebrow, giving her a pointed look. "Isn't it a little late for that?"

There was no getting around it. So she needed to figure out the right way to say it so that it would make him the least mad at her. "I was just thinking about how I was standing in front of the son of one of my greatest heroes and how I don't understand why you don't want to talk about it. Also, I have about a thousand and seven questions. But mostly I was thinking about what you said to me last night, about my mother being proud of me."

His eyebrows furrowed like he was trying to figure out where her words were going before she said them.

"Well," she said slowly, "Trapp said you don't like talking about your parents because you feel like their legacy is a lot to live up to." She hurried to get the rest out because he shot Trapp a look like he was about to bite the pilot's head clean off. "But from reading the manifests on the comm—which you never told me not to read—haven't you done exactly that? You made a name for yourself helping others, and that was exactly what they did on this ship all those years ago. And what are your parents even famous for but doing everything in their power to do the right thing, no matter the cost? You can't tell me that isn't exactly what you do here."

She bit her lip, looking up at him, waiting to see if he was going to explode on either her or Trapp. He was frowning, not looking all that happy. She wanted to remind him that she hadn't wanted to say any of that, but he had insisted. But it didn't seem like the right thing to do. It seemed like saying anything at all might set him over the edge, so she just sat silently and waited.

Finally, after a silence that seemed to stretch on forever, he simply said, "I know they're proud of me—I've never doubted that—I just don't need the galaxy watching me; expecting something from me. You're looking at me differently now but we both know I haven't changed at all. I'm still the person you fought with a few days ago because you think I'm stubborn and pigheaded."

"I never—" she started to protest but cut herself off because of the look he shot her. It dared her to continue, to contradict him, because they both knew what he'd said was true; she'd absolutely thought that about him, even if she hadn't said as much outright.

And besides, what he'd said made sense. Of course he didn't want to have to live with that hanging over his head every second. There was a reason she hated telling people her name, having grown sick of always having to explain to people that no, just because they shared a name, that didn't mean she had the Sight. It was exhausting. The best part of joining the military was losing that part of herself as Cadet Elis became her name, her identity, killing the expectations of a legacy she never could—and didn't necessarily want to—live up to.

"You two ought to be getting ready for tonight," Captain Behnam said, changing the subject, much to her relief. "The dress from last night isn't in any shape to be worn again. And I think Ginger was waiting to do your hair and makeup again."

"Yes, sir," El said. Apparently that was good enough for him because he turned then and left, leaving Trapp and El alone together.

"Do you think he's really mad?" she said.

"Probably," Trapp said. "But he'll also get over it, he always does. I just—I wouldn't recommend bringing it up ever again."

She nodded. "Okay."

"But he was right," he continued. "You need a new dress. And I have just the thing."

He was grinning gleefully, like a small child with a mischievous plan, and she could only hope he wasn't up to something crazy.

Trapp left and returned to the ship a little while later with a dress of orange. Its shade was somewhere in between bright and pale, and the subtle vibrancy reminded her of home.

It had a higher neckline than the one from the night before, with a collar that sat high on her throat, encircling it. The skirt was more flowy than poofy, and that made El happy. She rather liked the way it hung about her, swishing and twirling as she moved.

Of course, she never would have let Trapp know that. Besides, it was incredibly impractical for her job, so she refused to enjoy it too much.

Ginger did her hair up again, sweeping it into something elegant. The girl's own hair was so short; where had she learned to do hair so well, and when had she had the occasion to stay in practice?

Of course, it was hardly the time to ask since they were putting makeup on her face, so much of it she probably wouldn't be able to talk when they were done. But then she'd been able to talk last night so surely she'd be able to again.

Gibbs came into the med bay—which had been turned into her changing room—just as they were finishing. He was adjusting his cufflinks as he entered, looking at them instead of at her. Which made her happy since she'd be stared at enough later that evening; she saw no reason for it to start.

After a moment, he did look up, and when he saw her, he gave a satisfied nod. "Not bad."

"Excuse me?" Ginger demanded. But El caught the twinkle in Gibbs' eyes as he said it and she realized he was teasing. Apparently they had that kind of a relationship.

She was going to have to remember that for future reference; one could only hope he could take as much as he dished out.

Captain Behnam poked his head in next, not looking all that pleased. Was he still mad at her about earlier? Trapp said he would get over it but how long would that take? She didn't know why the idea that he might still be upset with her bothered her, but she pushed the thought aside. She's apologized, after all, had admitted her error, and she had a job to do. She didn't have time to nurse his hurting.

"Are we just going to stand here ogling Elis or are we going to get this over with?"

"Depends," Ginger said. "Does she look ready?"

"What?" Captain Behnam's glance flickered to El before he turned his attention to his medic with a haste that would have offended El had she put stock in such stuff; but she didn't, so it didn't hurt, she told herself.

"How does El look?" Ginger pressed, giving him a pointed look. What was it that everyone seemed to know about her and the Captain that El, herself, didn't know?

Captain Behnam flexed his fingers, finally looking up and taking her in. She suddenly felt very ridiculous and wished nothing more than to sink into the floor, to become one with the ship and never be seen again.

No one said anything.

"We should go," El said, because she didn't like standing here while everyone stared at her—everyone, that was, except Captain Behnam. He was right, she wasn't dressed like that to be ogled; she was dressed like that for a job. And she couldn't do that job in the med bay.

She went through the grubbery, not caring if anyone was following her. They'd catch up eventually.

"Elis!"

She had made it all the way to the cargo bay before the Captain's voice stopped her. She turned, whirling around, her skirt swishing out around her as she moved.

He had jogged to catch up with her and he took a moment to catch his breath before he said, "I'm sorry if I . . . I didn't mean to make you feel . . . " He trailed off, flexing his fingers. "I'm not good at this."

"Neither am I," she said. "You were right, I don't want to be ogled. This isn't me and I just want to get this over with."

He nodded like he understood, and she liked that feeling, of being understood. "We should get to the vehicle. Gibbs'll catch up."

El banked on one important fact—she hadn't been seen by anyone but Prince Tov the night before, not really, and so anyone on the lookout for her again would be looking for a girl in a garnet dress.

She didn't love the dress Trapp had acquired for her, but it was better than the one from the night before. It didn't feel like it was about to fall off her at any second, and it offered her back and neck some covering from the chill.

She loved her Liosi blood, but it was inconvenient at times, demanding much, much warmer conditions. Unfortunately, while it would be warm inside the ballroom, she didn't plan to stay there long. And the rest of the palace was drafty.

Gibbs got them through the gates without a problem, and once again, Captain Behnam jumped out to assist El. After she was out, her skirts situated around her, he still didn't release her hand, his warm fingers encircled around hers. She ought to have pulled away, to get inside, but she found that for all her urgency, she wasn't in a hurry to pull away.

"You look . . . " He trailed off but it broke the spell.

"Please don't," she said, shaking her head. She didn't want that, didn't want a compliment from him that he didn't mean, that he felt forced to give.

"I was just going to say you looked ridiculous," he said, offering her a grin that suggested he had only just changed what he was going to say.

She felt herself relax as he grinned at her, and she offered him a smile in return. "Thanks, I appreciate it."

His words shouldn't have warmed her, but they did. The compliment he'd wanted to give was there underneath the teasing, unstated but more honest than if he'd said the words. She hated how much it meant to her.

"For Liosa?" he said, just as he had the night before. The tingle ran through her again and she remembered she wanted to ask him about that. But as he started to recoil his hand, she held it firmly; she wasn't ready to give it up, not yet.

"For the galaxy," she replied.

Gibbs offered her his arm then, and she had to take it, had to break away from whatever that was, and do her job; that was why she was here, after all. Whatever had just happened, it meant nothing, she reminded herself. It couldn't. Not if she didn't want things to get out of her control.

She was announced as Gibbs' guest, and she didn't like the look the footman gave her—a sneer as he looked down on her, like he was somehow better than her. He thought she was Gibbs' fling and thought less of her for it, like he didn't have better things to occupy his mind with.

They stepped into the ballroom, and El's breath was taken away once more. But she was prepared for it that time and tried to remember to breathe. "There's Prince Jarett," the security officer said in her ear, discreetly waving his hand to the opposite side of the room. His other hand was still on her arm, firmly cradling her elbow.

The crown prince of Philosanthron was indeed standing tall and proud by the far wall. His father was still alive and therefore the ruling monarch, but the old King's mind had grown feeble in the last years, according to the rumors, and Prince Jarett had all but taken over reigning duties. It was his war the Liosi fought on Taras, and it was he who was to blame for all she'd done that kept her up at night.

And it was he who was working with Radian Darius to assassinate her Prince and take over the galaxy. He looked so innocent—handsome and confident and not like a power-hungry mastermind.

"Oh, and there's Lord Callinger. I really ought to go say hello," Gibbs continued, keeping his voice low, so close she could feel his breath tickling the inside of her ear. "He's got powerful connections, after all, and it would be rude to ignore him."

"Don't you dare drag me over there," El hissed, giving him a pointed look. She was here to find a comm and protect the Prince, not to socialize with people who might be good connections for Gibbs.

"Relax, I'll just tell him you're a friend. He won't ask." The security officer led her in that direction. "You have nothing to worry about."

"I'll be the judge of that," she hissed.

They made their way across the ballroom floor, weaving around people, some of whom were polite enough to step out of the way, others who remained in place for them to walk around. A few offered a greeting, which Gibbs returned cordially but kept moving as he did. His hand remained firmly on her arm as he led the way, and she trusted him, allowing him to guide her as she looked around the room, keeping an eye out for any signs of trouble.

"Our fathers are talking on the far side of the room," Gibbs said in her ear. "They aren't looking our way, and even if they did, I doubt they'd give either of us a second glance."

Commander Gibbs had never been an easy man, and El remembered something Gibbs had said about wanting her father's respect. She wished he could see that it was something he'd never obtain, no matter how hard he tried; he might as well set out to capture an Elassi—the pursuit was just as likely to produce results.

The thought didn't have much time to stew though, because they reached Lord Callinger, and Gibbs greeted the man, introducing El simply as a friend.

The conversation made El want to gag at the amount of polite nothingness being exchanged. Neither of them meant the nice things they were saying, but Gibbs couldn't tell Lord Callinger he was only here because he wanted something from the man, and the man could hardly tell Gibbs he knew that's why he was there.

She took a step away, having to remove herself from the conversation before she went crazy. As she did, she looked about the room, and that's when she saw him, too late. He had seen her.

Prince Tov stood across the ballroom with a boyish grin on his face as their eyes met across the ballroom.

She looked about for somewhere to run to but knew that booking it across the crowded ballroom would draw exactly the kind of attention she wished to avoid. So she let him approach.

She gave a curtsy as he reached her and took her hands in his own. His voice was breathy with excitement. "I didn't know if you'd come back."

"I wouldn't have missed it, Your Highness."

"I haven't stopped thinking about you since you left last night. I sent my guards after you, but they couldn't find you.

I—I thought perhaps you might be a phantom or maybe even an Elassi."

He blushed at his words, and he was just so adorable, like a little boy. El shook off the thought, unable to believe she was thinking it about her crown prince.

"I assure you, Your Highness, I am neither of those things."

He ducked his head. "I know, I know. It was a foolish thought. And please, call me Tov."

Victory, that couldn't continue. "Your Highness—"

"Please?" he said, his face earnest and pleading. "Just one dance, that's all I ask."

Gibbs was still talking, and Prince Tov was looking at her with earnest eyes so that she didn't have the heart to refuse him. So she allowed him to take her in his arms and lead her to the dance floor.

"Just one dance," she said.

CHAPTER 24

"JUST ONE DANCE" turned into an hour or more of dancing and several attempts by other partners to steal El away from Prince Tov. He always declined, though that was against the rules of polite society.

"One last dance," he begged at the end of that final 'one more dance.' And as she opened her mouth to protest, he added, "I promise this will be it."

The clock was chiming then, the sound faintly drifting above the livelier din of the ball-goers. Twelve strikes. Though the ball would no doubt go on for hours more, it was late, and El knew if she wanted information, she needed to get to work finding it.

"I really should go," she said, though she felt bad as that pained look returned to his eyes.

She pulled away and he released her, after drawing her hand to his lips and kissing it delicately. "I hope to see you again tomorrow night, my lady."

"And I you," she replied, even though she was nearly certain she would find what she needed and be done with the whole ordeal before the morning. All she needed to do was find out who hired Radian Darius and then stop them both before they did any permanent damage to the Prince. Surely she could accomplish that in the little time she had left.

She moved to walk away, then turned back to him, not quite able to just leave it at that. "Your Highness?"

He looked at her questioning, hopeful. "Yes?"

"Stay safe, please?"

He offered her a small smile. "*Rook di goo.*"

"Thank you," she said and left him then.

Gibbs was on the other side of the room, in the middle of a conversation with a very pretty girl, and not looking El's way. If he looked at her, she could let him know they needed to go. But he was deep in conversation.

El crossed the ballroom in sure steps, keeping a lookout for her father and Commander Gibbs, but they had disappeared. Stalking up beside Gibbs, she slipped his left arm about her, leaning her head on his shoulder, smiling at the young woman he'd been talking to.

"Who's this, love?" she asked easily, entwining her fingers through his left hand. The young woman was Philosanthrian—petite and blonde, with soft curls and a little turned-up nose. Her dress was a pale blue, hugging her curves, and she wore it with a confidence El wished she could muster.

Gibbs tried pulling away from El but her other arm was about his waist and she wasn't letting go; maybe he'd think twice next time before brushing her off. "Oh, uh . . . This is Lady Lovelace. Lady Lovelace, this is . . . uh . . . "

"Oh, don't tell me you're embarrassed of me," El said, a careful balance of tease and whine in her voice. She pulled her face into a pout before smoothing it back into a smile as she turned her attention back to the young woman. "Lavinia Salova, milady. It's a pleasure to meet you. Thank you so much for occupying my Carrigan while I was dancing." She turned to pout at him again. "Though I should have been dancing with you. Why do you never ask me to dance?"

The young woman—Lady Lovelace—frowned at her and then turned her attention to Gibbs. "I was unaware your affections lay elsewhere, Officer." She looked at El, her expression softening. "With looks and personality like yours, you can do far better than him, Miss Salova."

Gibbs opened his mouth to no doubt protest, but Lady Lovelace moved off with a huff before he could say anything. El let out a laugh. He glared at her. "You could have just said you were ready. I had to do something while you danced with His Highness."

That cut but it wasn't unjust.

El kept a smile on her face, tossing flirtatious smiles back his way, giggling for the sake of the people who littered the hall; she wanted people to think they were sneaking away for something more acceptably illicit than comm hacking.

Not that she was good at hacking. They would have to find a comm she could get into without having to do anything fancy because she had never been one for that sort of thing.

He jogged a step to catch up to her, wrapping his arm around her, drawing him to her as they moved, playing along with her ruse. Pressing his mouth to her ear, his words tickling her ear as they came out breathless, "As much as I hate to admit it, your legs are longer than mine."

She started to ask what his point was when she realized—she was all but dragging him down the hall, her quick, confident steps a workout to keep up with. She slowed her pace a bit.

"Was she important to you?" she asked, thinking about what he'd said; she might have messed something important up for him. They slipped into a more secluded hallway.

He shook his head. "I've never met her before tonight; I'm sure I'll recover."

She nodded and there was a pause between them. They were away from all the people, and they had a job to do.

"So I looked up floor plans of this place." Even though they were a safe distance away to be sure they wouldn't be overheard, she still spoke low so as not to be overheard by a passing servant or guard. "They were obviously hard to find, given the security protocols in place for this sort of thing, but I managed to find some on some in the sketchiest recesses of the information database. So I'm not entirely certain where we need to be, but the labs seem to be located in the Elmerick wing, below ground. If we find stairs and go down, hopefully we'll find our way there?"

"I thought you were the girl who always had a plan," he said, his tone suggesting he might be teasing. But then why would Gibbs be teasing her? Was he trying to get back at her for her flirting?

"It's easier to make a plan when I have all the information," she told him. "And I don't."

But there had to be someone who did. And if she could convince them that they needed to share that information with her, it would be so much better than aimlessly wandering the halls of the palace, hoping to find their destination.

She needed to find a guard. Alone. Because her plan wouldn't work if Gibbs was with her.

"Wait here," she told him, shoving him into an empty alcove. He seemed to be protesting but a glance over her shoulder told her that while his mouth was protesting, his body was obeying, and that was all that mattered.

She stumbled down the halls, putting on her act in case she accidentally happened upon someone who might be able to help her.

And then she rounded a corner and found exactly who she was looking for. Two guards, looking bored, not even paying attention or looking in her direction. They were Liosi, something about them familiar. El pushed back the homesickness; it wasn't the time.

"Excuse me," she called, tripping as she approached them, giggling as she steadied herself, keeping her voice light and airy. They turned to her, straightening at the sight of her. "Could you give me directions?"

She gave another giggle as she stumbled and tripped over her feet again, nearly falling on her face. She caught herself, offering them an embarrassed smile. "I'm so sorry, just a little clumsy tonight. They had something to drink in there that was all bubbly, and it's making my head a bit fuzzy. I think the bubbles went to my head." She let out a laugh like she had made a joke that was actually funny. "The bubbles went to my head. That's funny. I'm so funny."

She reached them then, stumbling once more for good measure. One reached out and took her elbow steadying her. "I think you need to find somewhere to rest."

"No, I need to find the labs," she told him, wrinkling her nose up in what she hoped was a cute smile. "There was a cute guy I danced with in there who told me to meet him in the labs, except I don't know where that is." She gave an exaggerated shrug. "I can't meet him there if I don't know where that is." She giggled again. "How could I? How could I go somewhere if I don't know where that is? That's impossible isn't it?" She frowned like she was thinking about that. "That is impossible isn't it?"

"I really think you've had enough excitement for tonight," the guard told her. "Perhaps I can call someone to take you home?"

"No, I'm fine!" she told him, panicking a moment, her drunk act perhaps too convincing. What if he insisted on seeing her home and refused to give her the directions she needed? "A cute guy wants to kiss me," she told him, pleading with him, forcing tears to her eyes. They came with effort, and for the first time ever, she cursed herself for not being the kind of girl who could cry at will. "If a cute guy wanted to kiss you, you wouldn't just go home because someone told you to, would you?"

He chuckled at that. "I would pass on that opportunity," he said, offering her a kind smile. Almost condescending, like he was talking to someone much simpler than himself. "But I do take your meaning. I'm just concerned you're not in the right frame of mind for that sort of excitement."

"I am, sir," she pleaded with him. "*Rook di goo,* I am. Please, don't ruin my chances at happiness. Don't I deserve a chance at happiness? Don't we all deserve a chance at happiness?"

She felt like maybe she was laying it on too thick, but he offered her directions, which she pretended to mix up at first so that she didn't appear suddenly too clearheaded. And then, when she was sure he wasn't suspicious, she repeated them back to him, stood up on her tiptoes to kiss his cheek as she told him what a perfectly lovely man he was, offered him a giggled

"Thank you," and stumbled back down the hall in the direction she had come.

Once she had rounded the corner and was certain he could no longer see or hear her, she hiked up the skirt of her ball gown with some effort and took off down the hall, running to where she had left the security officer.

She found Gibbs sulking in the alcove where she had left him, leaning against the wall, arms crossed, and a sullen expression on his face. When he saw her, his frown deepened.

"It's about time you came back."

She used every ounce of willpower to keep herself from rolling her eyes. "I was just down the hall and around the corner," she told him. "I was gone a moment."

"But how was I supposed to know that?" he argued. "What if something had happened to you? How long was I supposed to wait here? If you have a plan, you're supposed to share it with your team; that's how it works."

She appreciated that he called himself her teammate rather than her superior. But she didn't have time to pat him and his bruised ego on the back. "Do you want to stand here and argue about this or do you want to go to the labs? Using the directions that I got, I might add."

He was still frowning at her, and she thought for sure that he was going to press the point further. But then the frown softened, and he nodded. "All right, fine. Just, don't leave me alone next time."

She couldn't make that promise and so she didn't. Instead, she started down the hall in the direction the guard had told her to go and assumed Gibbs would follow her. He did, jogging a couple steps to catch up with her.

"You got directions? How? From whom?"

"A guard," she said, still walking. The security officer slowed down when he started talking, much to El's dismay. She would have liked to be down in the labs and looking for her information already.

"A guard told you?" Gibbs said, obviously not content to just let it go. He hurried to catch up with her, matching her strides and keeping pace. "Did you just go up and ask him?"

"Actually, yes," she said.

"And he just gave you directions?" She didn't have to turn to look to know there was an expression of disbelief on his face; it was written all over his voice.

She gave a small shrug. "I mean, I think it helped that I pretended to be drunk and told him I was meeting a boy there for a late-night rendezvous. But yes, I asked, and he told me."

"The Captain's right, you really are incredible."

Captain Behnam said what?

No. She didn't have time. She had things to do and places to be and asking Gibbs when—and why—he and Captain Behnam had been discussing her just didn't fit into that right then.

But she needed to remember she had that information so she could circle back to it later when she had time.

Provided they weren't caught and arrested and convicted for treason.

He didn't say anything more, which she was grateful for. They walked in silence, him keeping the pace with her but allowing her to lead. And then they finally finished winding through the palace corridors and came to a flight of stairs.

"Here we are," she said, moving toward the stairs. Her hand went to her gun, since they were, after all, about to descend into a dark hole in which just about anything could be waiting for them.

Gibbs reached out and put his hand on hers. "How about you just take it slowly," he suggested. "And don't go assuming you'll have to shoot someone."

"It's my job to assume I'll have to shoot someone," she told him.

It was his job too, as a security officer, but she wasn't going to press that point; if he couldn't do his job, she'd still do hers.

"And there's an assassin on the loose," she continued. "So chances are that at some point soon, I will have to shoot someone. And when that point comes, you are going to be very grateful for the fact that I am so ready and willing."

"Point taken," he said. "But just, don't shoot anyone unless you have to?"

She rolled her eyes. "I wasn't planning on it."

She pulled away from him, drawing her gun and slowly moving down the stairs. She motioned for him to follow her, waving him on as she moved down a few more steps.

A faint blue light glowed overhead, leaving much of the labs little more than shadows and mystery. The stairs led to a long corridor with the different lab rooms on either side, each with a door and glass walls, offering little to no privacy. And all the doors were closed with little keypads by the handles and tiny blinking red lights.

El assumed that meant the doors were locked. Which meant even just touching them could set off an alarm, depending on what type of security measures were in place. Hacking was required after all, and that wasn't something she was prepared—or even equipped—to do.

"Now what?" Gibbs asked behind her, whispering into the dark stillness. His breath hit her bare neck and shoulders, sending a shiver down her spine.

"I don't know," she said, waving him off, shaking her head. "Give me a minute to think."

"We could just hack the lock," he said, brow furrowed. "Can't we? Or is there a reason we shouldn't?"

"I can't hack those types of locks," she told him, not looking at him, though she realized as soon as she said it that her words implied that there were other types of locks she could hack. There weren't, but she was too busy trying to come up with a solution to their problem to correct herself.

"Yeah, but I can," he said, which got her attention.

She looked at him then, really looked at him, afraid it was some sort of terrible joke. "You can?"

He looked almost offended at how surprised she looked. "I'm a man of many talents."

He moved to the door, crouching down by the lock. His back was to El, and she couldn't quite see what he was doing, so all she could do was hold her breath and hope beyond hope that he didn't do anything to alert security to their presence.

There was a faint click, which seemed louder than it probably was in the still silence. The little light on the lock turned blue and Gibbs grinned up at her, then turned the handle on the door and gave the door a push. He rose to his feet, pushing the door all the way open and stepping aside, holding out his arms to indicate he intended for her to proceed him.

"After you, my lady." He bowed then, accompanying his words with the animated gesture. He righted himself as she walked through the door.

She waited for an alarm to go off, and even when one didn't, she still didn't relax, sure that with one wrong move, they'd set one off.

She swept to the comm, taking a seat in the desk chair, cursing that poofy skirt of hers which made sitting down much harder than it really ought to be. It was much like she imagined sitting on a cloud much feel like—soft, cushioned, and entirely unstable.

A click of a button and the screen sprang to life. In an instant, the logo for the comm's manufacturer appeared, and then it disappeared as a box for a password took its place. She looked at Gibbs, who waved her aside. She slid the chair to the left, grateful it was on wheels because she didn't trust herself to stand right that second.

Gibbs positioned himself before the comm in such a way that he blocked her view of the screen, so she had no idea what he was doing. But then after a minute, he stepped away as the main page settled on the screen.

He looked to her, clearly seeking some sort of validation, but she was too busy being impressed with something else entirely.

"Did you see how fast that loaded?" she breathed, staring at the screen in wonder for a moment before shaking it off and getting back to the task at hand. She didn't know how much time she had, so she needed to work fast. "Okay, here goes nothing."

"I thought . . . "

She turned to Gibbs, even though she didn't have the time.

"I believe the plan was for me to do that?"

What was he talking about? Had he not been paying attention to their meetings? Captain Behnam had clearly . . .

. . . not been talking about her hacking the comms.

But she'd assumed he was because she'd assumed the entire plan hinged on her.

She scooted aside, looking down at her lap—the orange fabric of her dress, at her calloused hands, at anything but Gibbs. "Sorry."

He didn't respond as he set to work, his finger moving rapidly across the keyboard as he worked.

"Are you finding anything?"

"Hm."

That wasn't a reply.

But then, if she were the one working, she'd be just as annoyed at him for interrupting her. She'd snapped at Trapp and Captain Behnam multiple times for the exact same offense.

The sound of the *clack*ing keys was deafening in the otherwise silent labs, El's mind having nothing else to focus on. She bit back the questions as they arose, swallowing them before they had a chance to escape.

"If you've got nothing better to do than grind your teeth, you could stand guard at the door," Gibbs suggested without looking up.

"Are you finding anything?"

He sighed and turned to look at her then. "No, they don't just have a file marked 'Radian Darius' with all the proof we need neatly compiled and labeled."

"But are you finding anything?" He hadn't actually answered the question.

Another sigh. "It's like someone erased him from the database, like he doesn't exist."

But he did exist. They knew he did.

Didn't they?

"Someone's coming," Gibbs said in an urgent whisper, looking over at her with panic in his eyes.

She jumped up from the comm, gun out, looking around frantically for a way out of there. Except the only way out was through the door and up the stairs. They were trapped.

El had two ideas as for how she could maintain control of the situation. Her first was treason, and so she scrambled for a second and remembered her cover story that she had told the helpful guard just a few minutes before.

The most logical course of action would be to kiss Gibbs. That was, after all, what she had said she was doing in the labs, and so it just made sense to stick with that. Except she didn't want to kiss him. The very thought made her a little sick, and then there was always the chance that he would think she meant it.

Her mind went back to her original idea and she hesitated for just a second before she made up her mind.

Because when it came to a choice between kissing Gibbs and committing treason, treason seemed like a better option.

The footsteps were just outside the lab so she only a second to act. Gun in hand, she grabbed the security officer.

"Please trust me," she requested.

Gibbs frowned at her. "I'm going to hate this, aren't I?"

CHAPTER 25

BY WAY OF an answer, El pushed Gibbs behind her, cocking her gun just as the intruder stepped into the lab.

"Keep your hands where I can see them," she ordered the man who stepped into the room, gun trained on him. She took him in fast—the livery of a palace servant, sharp and crisp, the dark blue fabric blending into the darkness surrounding him. All that was left was a pale face with a lopsided smile formed around perfect teeth and a head of hair, soft and thick.

"You're not supposed to be here," he said, but he said it casually, like he didn't actually intend to do anything about it. He leaned on the doorframe, putting his hands in his pockets and eyeing her easily, the action such a sharp contrast against his perfect uniform. His accent was almost Philosanthrian but there was something else underneath it. Was he Veronian?

He didn't belong there either.

"Also, if you shoot that off in here, the bullets will ricochet."

She glanced around to see that, indeed, the room was made of metal and glass. Any bullet fired would either ricochet as the man suggested or shatter the glass, either of which would put them all into a very dangerous position.

"It doesn't matter. I won't miss. Hands where I can see them. Now."

He started to pull his hands from his pockets.

"Slowly."

He moved with ease, raising his hands to the air. "Now what?"

"You can keep working," El told Gibbs as she released him. Then to the man, "And you can tell me what you're doing down here."

Gibbs returned to his seat at the comm, the sound of the keys as he typed filling the air once more.

"And why would I do that?"

Upon further inspection, El found the man was younger than she'd originally thought—he was probably twenty or twenty-one, he couldn't be any more than that.

"Because it's been a long . . . " She trailed off. Was it a long day? Week? Month? The last decade or more had been long. "I'm at the end of my patience." Gibbs snorted at that, and she refused to become distracted by it. "So I'm only going to ask once—what are you doing down here?"

"Same thing you are?"

Not an answer. "Which is?"

"Taking advantage of a very busy night to look for proof before someone tries to kill Prince Tov again."

She shook her head. "Why would you care?"

The grin wavered. "Prince Jarett has designs on the entire galaxy. I can't stomach oppression, especially not on this scale."

"Then we're on the same side," she told him. Not that she believed his words to be anything more than him saying exactly what she wanted to hear.

"No." The word was cold, harsh. "I'm not on the same side as Philosanthrian lackeys."

"We're not—"

"Save your breath," he cut her off. "You're Liosi—I'll save your Prince because it's better him than Prince Jarrett on the Liosi throne, but not by much."

She bit back the rage that filled her; his words were not untrue, and she needed to respond to them with rationality and logic. "Liosa will see her errors, I'm sure of it. We can't continue like this, we won't. What we're doing on Taras goes against everything we've ever stood for, and, given time, our leaders will see that."

Okay, so maybe she didn't know how to be rational or logical when it came to her planet.

He shook his head. "You don't understand what they're doing—"

"She does," Gibbs said before she could say anything, to her amazement; he'd been at her throat the whole time, and she hadn't expected him to have her back, not in that. "She understands."

"It doesn't matter, either way," the man replied, the edge still in his voice. "I'll help you."

The air conditioner kicked on then, flooding the room with cool air. A shiver ran down El's spine as goosebumps crawled up her skin.

"Why should we trust you? You're just a nameless stranger—how do we know you aren't going to lie through your teeth? How do we know you aren't working for the enemy?"

He gave a small shrug. "You don't. I'd swear it on my life if it would make a difference to you—or what is it you Liosi say? *Rook di goo?*"

"For our children's children and the good of our people," El finished for him, because while the expression was thrown around a lot, an actual vow—like the one he spoke—ought to be finished. Not that it made any difference.

"But you wouldn't believe me even if I said that," he said with another shrug. "So you take the proof, you look it over, and you decide if it looks like something someone carefully fabricated or if it's the truth. But I think, deep down, even without any of it here before you, you know. That's why you're here at all. You know Prince Jarett needs to be stopped, for the good of the galaxy."

He was right—she did know. She knew deep down that the war on Taras was bigger even than the atrocity it was. She knew it was Philosanthron's war, not Liosa's, and that that meant it was Prince Jarett's war. The War of the Usurper. And no matter how many ways he spun it, no matter how many people he fooled onto his side, it was still the same thing—a big show to cover up something far more sinister.

He was going to destroy the galaxy, and he'd see to it that every planet willingly followed him.

"So what do you know about Radian Darius?" Gibbs asked, turning in his chair. El shot him a look but he just gave a resigned shrug. "I can't find anything. So we either take his help or we leave empty-handed. I'd rather risk leaving here with lies than going with nothing."

"If you so much as breathe wrong," El told the man, "I will shoot you."

His grin returned as he stepped toward the comms. "I don't doubt it."

Gibbs jumped up, letting the man have his seat as El leaned in closer so she could keep an eye on every move he made.

The man's fingers moved at a dizzying speed, flying over the keys as he worked, pointing out various documents and information of interest as they appeared on the screen. With every word he spoke, El felt a little bit sicker, realizing the extent of Prince Jarett's tyranny. It was all there, everything they needed to prove Radian Darius had been hired by the Philosanthrians to assassinate Prince Tov.

And proof of a lot of other things El wished she could unlearn.

After several minutes, the man turned, handing El a sleek external storage drive. "Here's everything you need."

"Thank you," she said.

"Use it well. If the galaxy is destroyed, I'm blaming you." That easy grin had spread across his face once more. How could he tease her at a time like that?

"It won't," she promised, though she knew it was a promise she had no business making. "I don't suppose you're going to give us your name?"

There was that grin again as he held out his hand to introduce himself. "They call me Zephyr, though we both know that isn't my real name—for security reasons."

She wasn't sure if he was teasing her or not, but she still shook his hand. "El," she said. "And thank you. The galaxy owes you."

"Unfortunately, it'll never know," he returned with another small shrug. "But then, that's one less debt they'll have to worry about paying. I look forward to meeting you again, El. Perhaps we might work together again someday."

She shouldn't trust him, but still . . .

Before she could finish the thought, the blue light of the labs turned red, flashing as the piercing shriek of an alarm filled the air.

She turned to Zephyr, gun raised, but saw the fear that flashed in his eyes, and she hesitated from pulling the trigger. He was just as surprised at the alarms as she was.

Keeping her gun trained on him, she said, "Gibbs, let's go."

Gibbs was already out the door and El followed, moving backward so she could keep an eye on Zephyr, her gun still at the ready. To his credit, he didn't move.

She stepped through the doorway, closing the door behind her as she said, "I'm sorry."

He had helped them, after all. And she didn't think he'd set off the alarms. But still, she had to be safe.

"Thanks for not shooting me," he said with a resigned shrug. She shut the door and heard the lock click into place.

The storage device was still there in her hand, her fingers wrapped around it, and she tucked it securely into her dress as she and Gibbs hurried up the stairs.

"How could you leave him back there?" Gibbs demanded as he followed her up the stairs.

"Just being cautious," she said, moving to the doorway at the top of the stairs, looking out, and motioning for Gibbs to follow her.

The security officer followed her up the stairs, demanding, "Are you serious? After the help he just gave us?"

The wisest course of action would be to go back the way they had come because that was familiar, and one always had an advantage on familiar ground. But Commander Gibbs and Security Head Elis were that way.

"Which we can't even be sure is true," she said, assessing their options. "What was he even doing down here? He came down, helped us, and then the alarms went off. I don't think he betrayed us, but you can't tell me that isn't at least a little bit suspicious."

The wall to the left of the top of the stairs was made entirely of glass, and right beside where they were standing was a glass door that led into what looked like a garden. That was their other option—to go that way and hope that they were able to find their way from there.

"I can't believe we're having this conversation," he said. "Do you not trust anyone?"

"No," she said in response to Gibbs' question as she moved to go in the direction they had come from. She would rather take the advantage of knowing where she was going than getting lost. Either way could produce problems, and she'd rather have some sort of a clue about where she was going. Especially since finding floor plans to that level of the palace was a rather simple matter, if you knew the right corners of the Information Database to hunt.

"You really should try it sometime," Gibbs suggested, following her as if they weren't walking through the halls of a palace possibly containing a galaxy-renowned assassin.

Was Gibbs—a security officer—really lecturing her about the importance of trusting people? No wonder the Prince was in danger if those were the people protecting him.

El kept her gun hidden in the folds of her skirt, taking Gibbs' advice to heart about not shooting anyone unless necessary.

After all, if she wound up in a prison cell, she'd never be able to warn the Prince.

"Now's really not the time for this conversation."

If she was being honest, never was the right time for that conversation. The last thing she wanted was to talk about it—especially with Gibbs. It had been bad enough baring her soul to him about her desertion; she had no desire to continue their relationship by also discussing her paranoia and trust issues.

They rounded the corner to find Philosanthrian soldiers in their formal, pale blue uniforms. They yelled for her and Gibbs to stop.

She kicked into survival mode as she drew her gun. She glanced about for a good place to make her stand when she felt Gibbs' hand on her own.

"Remember?" Gibbs hissed in her ear. "We aren't going to shoot anyone unless we have to."

"What do you suggest?" she hissed back urgently.

"We run."

She let him drag her in the other direction, veering off after a moment and pulling her through a door that led into a garden. She was impressed; had he noticed that before when they passed? Perhaps he wasn't completely useless as a security officer after all.

There were footsteps behind them as the two made their way down the garden path. El didn't much like the idea of going somewhere she wasn't familiar with, but she'd rather go somewhere unfamiliar than back into what could be a trap.

Gibbs was still leading, and after a minute, when they had gotten far enough ahead, she found herself pulled into a dark little building that stood rather out of place beside the garden path.

She noticed the smell almost before she heard the sound. It was the musky, sweet scent of animals. But once she heard the noise, it was all she could hear and really all she could think of, so loud it filled her ears until the noise was deafening.

They were birds. She didn't know why there were birds there in the little building by the garden, but it sounded like there were many of them who lived there. They cooed, the noise ringing in her ears. She swore sharply under her breath.

"They're just birds," Gibbs said.

"I hate birds."

She didn't actually hate birds. They just reminded her of her mother, and she didn't want to think about her mother right then. She wanted to focus on their mission and the moment in front of her, not something that happened too many years ago.

Thankfully Gibbs didn't say anything in return to her words, letting the matter end there. They stood in silence—or rather, neither of them said anything; the birds certainly made enough noise—for what felt like an eternity.

Voices. Shouts and footsteps coming closer and closer. She held her breath. The sound of the birds filled her ears. She pushed past that sound, focusing her attention on the voices and whoever approached.

The footsteps stopped outside the little house, several soldiers from the sounds of them. One of them suggested looking inside. El's breath caught as her chest grew tight, and her hand instinctively went to her gun. Gibbs put his hand on hers, the action clearly meant as a reminder not to shoot anyone.

"I've got this," he said in a low voice. Maybe the birds weren't really as loud as they seemed after all. "Give me the drive."

She was reluctant to hand it over, but she reminded herself that Gibbs was there not just out of necessity but because she trusted him. It was a strange realization to come to, an unexpected one, considering how she'd felt about the young man, but true all the same. She handed over the drive.

"Once I get them to leave, go to the Captain. I'll meet you there." He slipped from the little house, squeezing around the poof of her skirts. She crushed herself against the back wall to avoid being seen when he opened the door a crack to leave.

"There's no one in there," he said to the soldiers with a voice of authority, as if he knew exactly what was going on, as if he were part of the search that he didn't even know existed until a few minutes ago.

"I want her found." It was her father's voice, and El's breath caught in her throat. "We have reason to believe that she's the deserter."

Had he seen her then? Or had the encounter with Zephyr been a trap after all?

"What makes you say that?" Gibbs asked, his tone light, as if he was more curious than anything else. She had never appreciated Gibbs so much as in that moment.

There was a pause and El could picture the expression on her father's face. He was thinking, contemplating, probably determining whether Gibbs was worthy of an answer or not. He finally said, "His Highness said the girl wore odd footwear, and from his description, they could very well be standard issue military boots."

"I see . . . " Gibbs said, drawing the words out. He was going to give her a hard time about that later, she knew it. She still didn't regret wearing them. "And of course there's no chance it was someone else?"

"Why would anyone else come to a ball in military boots?"

"Why would she?" Gibbs demanded as if the whole thing were ludicrous. He was definitely going to give her a hard time about it later.

"We have reason to believe the girl is mentally unstable," her father said. "So nothing she does will necessarily fall within rational parameters."

El bit her tongue to keep from scoffing. She couldn't make a sound because she doubted even the infuriating cooing of the birds would cover the noise.

"Then we had better find her," Gibbs stated. "Did your soldiers look over there?"

They had a brief discussion about where they ought to look and where they had already looked, and then they were off. El waited a good several minutes before she poked her head out. The coast was clear. But she couldn't stay there—no, she needed to get out of that place.

There would be guards by the vehicles. Philosanthrian guards, no doubt, but still. She needed to get past them without them asking her a lot of awkward questions. And without them taking her to the Prince. Because if she was taken to Prince Tov she was sure to run into her father.

Good thing she had a plan.

CHAPTER 26

EL HOPED BEYOND hope that Trapp would not kill her for it, but she pulled her knife from her boot and set to work slashing the bodice, making little rips in the fabric until it was a mess of shreds and frayed fabric. She rumpled up her hair, making a mess of the gorgeous up-do that Ginger had worked so tirelessly on. Then she reached down and gathered a little dirt from a flowerbed, rubbing it over her bodice, smudging her face, then wiping her hands off on her hair.

She was ready.

She hurried in the direction she and Gibbs had originally been going, toward the front gate where the vehicles were parked. Where the Captain was waiting. The path was deserted, and she met no one until she heard the noise of the party and vehicles and the general sounds of life.

There was a group of guards coming around the corner ahead of her, heading in her direction. She let them see her, let them call out for her to stop. But she didn't stop, she ran straight toward them, letting out a dry sob as she did.

"Oh, thank the stars!" She ran straight for the scrawniest one, falling into his arms. He was only a kid of perhaps sixteen, and while he was several inches taller than her, he had a skinniness about him that was almost unhealthy.

He put his arms about her, returning the hug, though his stiffness made it clear that he found the encounter uncomfortable.

"What is the meaning of this?" another guard snapped. She turned to face him, though she stayed close to the scrawny guard. He seemed reluctant to let her go, keeping an arm about her shoulder, which she leaned into, shrinking to make herself seem even smaller as she addressed the head guard.

"I'm sorry, sir. I—" A dry sob escaped her. "I—I was just—" An exaggerated sniffle. "I was just running. From the woman. I was just out in the gardens getting some air—because it's so warm in there, you see, and I was feeling lightheaded, and so I went for a walk and there was this woman. She looked crazy. She had a gun. So I hid and then I got stuck in a bush and I'm just a mess and then I got so lost-"

She broke off here, letting out a wail as she turned and buried her face against the scrawny guard's shoulder. He held her, patting her back and making soothing noises while the head guard scoffed and sputtered a moment. Then he said, "Would you let go of my guard please?"

She sniffled as she pushed herself back, her mouth and eyes wide. "Oh! I do beg your pardon. I—I don't know what's gotten into me. I didn't mean to—that is, I was just so scared . . . "

The head guard held up his hand, though it was his stern expression that silenced her more than the gesture. He was a good deal older, perhaps her father's age, though he had wrinkles around his eyes that told El he smiled a good deal more than her father ever had.

"Tell me who you came with, and I'll see to it you're returned to them, safely."

She widened her eyes, horror on her face. "Oh, please, you mustn't! If Mama finds out I snuck in, she'll have my hide. And if Mama's employer finds out—she might fire Mama! Oh, I should have stayed home . . . " She buried her face in her hands, letting out a few exaggerated sobs.

She took a moment to compose herself, then looked up, meeting the eyes of the head guard, putting on a brave face. "If you please, sir. I just need to get on home. If you could let me through the gates, I promise I won't cause anyone any more trouble ever again. *Rook di goo*—"

"What is going on here?"

Everyone turned at the sound of the voice. El almost couldn't believe what she saw—Gibbs, standing there, strong and proud, arms crossed across his chest, a deep frown on his face. He spoke with such authority, his voice ringing as he spoke, dripping with confidence.

The head guard turned his attention to the security officer, nodding respectfully. "This girl says she snuck into the party and went for a stroll in the gardens where she was frightened by a crazy woman with a gun."

El turned her attention to Gibbs then, crying out, "I promise I'm a good girl, sir. I know I shouldn't have snuck in and if Mama finds out . . . If she gets into trouble over me . . . " She broke off, shaking her head as she bit her lip and drew in a sob. "I just want to go home."

"Then you shall," Gibbs promised her, nodding definitely.

The head guard looked a bit concerned. "But—"

Gibbs gave the man a pointed look. "As an officer in the Liosi Security Force, I assure you I'll see to this myself. You are dismissed."

The guard opened his mouth to protest but must have thought better of it because his mouth snapped shut then, and he nodded. "As you say."

He directed his guards away and left El and Gibbs alone. The security officer rushed over to her, taking her arm to guide her away. "We'd better get out of here; I'm pretty sure he's going straight to your father."

"You were pretty brilliant," she admitted, impressed someone else had taken initiative and she hadn't been forced to come up with a plan all on her own again. "That was really impressive."

He looked a bit flustered, giving her a shy little shrug as he ducked his head, back to the Gibbs she knew well. "I just did what I thought Captain Behnam would do. The situation seemed to call for a man of his authority."

Victory, that was who he had reminded her of. His voice and air had been exactly like the Captain's when he'd told the security officer that the *Aderyn* was his ship and therefore El would do what he wanted, not what Gibbs deemed best.

"Well you played the role rather well," she told with him a grin.

"You were rather good at your part," the security officer admitted. "But Trapp is going to kill you for ruining another dress."

"Yeah, well, I'll deal with that wire when it shorts."

They were approaching the vehicles, and when El saw the Captain, she gave a little wave in case he didn't see them. As soon as she did, she felt stupid and tucked her hand behind her back.

She didn't have to feel embarrassed though, as the Captain's mind wasn't on the wave but instead the rest of her appearance. He looked her up and down with his eyebrows raised and his mouth set in a thin, firm line.

They were a good several yards away when he spoke. "What in fury happened?"

She scurried to close the distance between them as his attention remained on her as if Gibbs wasn't even there.

"I'm fine," she told him, because there he went with that concerned look again. "We just had a little trouble getting out of the palace. I can tell you about it on the way back to the ship."

So she and Gibbs did, telling him everything.

"You got the drive to the Prince?" she asked Gibbs when they got to the end.

He nodded. "Your father, but he'll use the information well."

He would, it was true; he might have been a terrible father, but he was good at his job.

"So now what?" she asked, feeling a little empty. She really ought to feel happier, but what did it mean for her? They'd succeeded, but if she was done with the job, did that mean she was done with the *Aderyn* too? Captain Behnam had been generous in opening his ship to her, but she knew realistically it wasn't a permanent solution. Asking him to harbor a fugitive wasn't fair to him or the others.

"I don't know," Gibbs said.

301

"What is wrong with you two?" Captain Behnam demanded. "Do soldiers never win or something? It seems like you would grasp the concept of celebration a little easier. Take the win."

"You're right," Gibbs said. "This is a start for me, a chance I never would've had without you two. I know I'm not the easiest person to work with, so I . . . well, I really appreciate it."

There as an awkward silence, like maybe neither El nor the Captain knew what to do with his words. Then Gibbs spoke again. "I'll make sure those in charge know you helped us, El. I'll put in as many good words as they'll let me."

"No!" El said.

Gibbs's eyes widened, and she saw the Captain giving her a puzzled look in the rearview mirror.

She let out a breath. "If you tell them you worked with me, you're all but admitting to knowingly working with a deserter. You haven't saved Liosa yet, and they're not bound to give you the chance if you tell them about this. You'd be ruining your career and it wouldn't even do me that much good. Maybe they wouldn't execute me, but I'd still be exiled and disgraced—is that really worth ruining your own life for?"

"Back up," the Captain said. "Can we go back to the part about them executing you? Why did no one tell me about this before I let you go in there? Twice. I sent you in there twice."

"You didn't send me, I volunteered," El said. "It was my choice. And I assumed you knew that's what they do to deserters. How did you not know that? You said you didn't want me throwing my life away . . . what else would you have meant?"

"I thought we were talking about prison, or exile or something. Not . . . not execution."

"Then what did you mean when you said I was going to die, and you wanted to be there so your conscience was clear?" she demanded.

"That is not what I said, and you know it," he said as he parked the vehicle in front of the *Aderyn*. "There's an assassin running around and you've all but dangled yourself in front of him as bait—of course you getting yourself killed was a pretty likely option. I didn't realize your own people . . . " He turned in his seat to face her, to look her in the eye. "You're honestly willing to die for a planet that would execute you for standing up against tyranny?"

"I didn't stand up against it, I ran from it," she corrected him. "And therein lies the difference between a hero and a coward."

"You're not a coward," Gibbs told her.

Captain Behnam glared at him. "Don't even get me started on you. How could you send her in there, knowing the consequences? Did you really think her that expendable?"

"Of course not!" Gibbs said, looking hurt and even a little angry at the words. "Maybe I just had more faith in her abilities than you did. I knew she could do it and that she could do it without getting caught. I also thought you knew what they'd do to her if she was caught. I thought we were on the same page."

"Same page?" the Captain demanded. "I don't think we were even reading the same book!"

"I thought we were supposed to be celebrating, not fighting," El said. "I, for one, would love to put on something less . . . well, less whatever this is. And a cup of Ginger's tea would taste great right about now. I didn't get caught and I didn't get executed. I chose to do what I did knowing the consequences, and that's all that matters. But there aren't any consequences—so let's take the win, right?"

With that, she opened the door and slipped from the vehicle, glad to be back at the ship, even if she couldn't have a place aboard it since her job was completed.

She took a shower, savoring the warm water as she tried not to think about how it could well be one of her last showers aboard the ship.

She wasn't going to feel nostalgic about the shower. She wasn't. She didn't even like the shower.

Hair still wet, she made her way to the grubbery to make herself a cup of tea. Ginger was already there making her one.

"You all right?" the medic asked with a soft smile. "I heard you had quite the night."

El nodded, leaning against the sink and looking at the cup in her hands instead of the medic before her.

She'd been too busy to think about any of it while it was happening, but it had brought back memories. Memories she didn't want to think about. Memories that were threatening to cut off her breathing and made her heart beat just a little too fast.

Control room. Everything in its place, one by one, each little detail.

Except that might not be her control room anymore. They might not need her anymore.

She pushed that thought back. It didn't matter if it was hers or not anymore. It didn't change what the place meant to her.

"I should be okay," she admitted after all of that cycled through her mind. She wasn't sure if the time that passed was really just a lot shorter than it seemed or if Ginger was just that patient.

"I found a pharmacy yesterday," the medic said. "I know you seemed unsure about medication, but I think it would help, so if that's something you would like to try, I do have it. The choice is yours though; I'd never want you to do anything you're uncomfortable with."

El frowned. "I don't need medication for my brain."

"Did you take medication after you were shot?" Ginger's tone was pointed, but El didn't see the connection.

What kind of a silly question was that? "Of course I did."

"It's the same thing, El." The words were soft and earnest. "Your brain just wants to heal, it's okay to help it along. And we'll get back into our sessions again now that this is over."

Except if it was over, that meant El wasn't going to be around for their sessions. Not for much longer anyway.

But she wasn't going to argue since she didn't know what was next; she still needed to discuss that with the Captain. So she just nodded. "Can I let you know? About the medication."

"Absolutely; take your time to think about it, and I'm happy to walk you through it if you have any questions or concerns." Ginger sat forward, a grin on her freckled face. "And in the meantime, I want to hear about everything that happened. Did you dance with the Prince again?"

"I did."

"Is he terribly smitten with you still?"

El rolled her eyes. "He is."

Trapp poked his head into the grubbery then, giving her an amused frown. "*Ech,* I'm beginning to see that putting you in a dress is a bad idea."

Gibbs and the Captain joined the party not too long after, and it turned into just that—a party. El was able to push back any of her apprehensions and allow herself to become distracted from the little voice in the back of her head that told her it couldn't last, not if she cared about these people.

By the time she went to bed that night—late into the evening, nearly morning—she had all but forgotten the thoughts and feelings swirling inside her since she climbed into the back of the vehicle after the ball.

But still, she slept fitfully.

The room was too hot, and El was unable to fall into a deep sleep. She tossed and turned, dreaming the most vivid dreams. In every one, she was running or fighting. She kept waking up more tired than when she went to bed and falling asleep again hoping beyond hope that she'd truly fall into slumber.

She was in Taras for some of her dreams, but the events were either entirely fabricated or else mixed with the events of the last few weeks. She was in that alleyway again with Captain Behnam and Gibbs and Trapp, but some of her fellow cadets were there too. She was in the maze but those who were chasing her were Tarisian in their blue and scarlet uniforms. She never did understand why they chose those colors for their military when everything was so green.

Taras had been as green as Liosa when El had first been stationed there.

The maze grew brown, dead, just like Taras was when she'd left. Just like she had helped make it. She'd helped kill a planet. An entire planet. She'd taken something so beautiful, so alive, and made it dead and brown and ugly.

And that wasn't even the worst thing she'd done.

She was back in the labs, the red lights flashing around her, gun trained on the figure before her. Except in her dream, it wasn't the man called Zephyr, it was a Tarisian girl, no more than fifteen. The girl from the bar on Alvar. And her finger didn't hesitate on the trigger. It was a kill shot to the forehead.

She ran, through the gardens in that orange dress, like a Liosi bird, her view of the scene outside of herself in the dream. It was green again, the garden landscape shifting to the greens of Liosa, the contrast of the green and the orange the same as the Liosi flag.

It was so beautiful and so heartbreaking. How could something that had been a symbol of hope for so long be a symbol of destruction?

She woke in an unrefreshing sweat and with the intense need to punch something.

Untangling herself from her sheets, she rose and padded down the hall to the training room. It was where she had first told Captain Behnam the truth about herself. Or part of it. There were still so many messy pieces that he didn't know.

The first punch she took at the bag felt amazing. It offered a release she hadn't felt in a long time, and she fell headfirst into it without question, allowing herself to get lost in the feeling as she hit the bag again and again.

Images of all the things she had done flashed through her mind as she punched, the lives she had ruined, the choices she'd made. For every sickening thought, she landed another blow, then another and another. There came a satisfying sound as her wrapped hand hit the fabric of the bag and she savored it as she struck again and again.

The anger built inside of her and released with each punch. Over and over again. She felt it mounting and swirling inside her as it all came rushing to the forefront of her mind. She let it come, feeling as if she could handle it since she had somewhere to direct her emotions. She rained down blows on the bag, striking again. And again. And again.

Tears came, followed by angry sobs. Those rose in her throat, all but choking her before they escaped, filling the air with their mournful sounds.

Again and again, she replayed the events in her mind, the things that led her to that moment—her mother's death, her enlistment, her time in Taras and all the awful things that happened there, getting shot and recovering in that awful little hospital in the middle of nowhere, her desertion. And of course, there was all that happened after that, all that came with her time here on the *Aderyn*. That alleyway. Captain Behnam's arrest. The maze of hedges. Leave Zephyr in the labs.

Zephyr's face as she closed the lab door seared into her mind as it brought back her dream. In her mind, the expression in his eyes morphed into the one the girl wore in her dream. El had seen it in the eyes of so many other people whose lives she had ended.

She'd ended so many innocent lives.

Another sob escaped her as she took a step back from the bag, allowing her knees to buckle under her as she sank to the floor.

As she lay there and sobbed, the events of that night played over and over again in her head—dancing with the Prince, talking with Zephyr in the labs, the alarms, hiding in the bird house. She didn't know why her mind chose those events, but she took the mercy. There were so many other moments she had no interest in reliving.

It played on a loop as she cried, curled up in a ball on the training room floor. She tried to muffle the sobs, to keep quiet so as not to disturb anyone else. They were all trying to sleep; they didn't need to be bothered.

She shouldn't be bothering any of them—Gibbs, who was willing to ruin his career and even his life for her; Ginger, who went to great lengths to try to fix her even though she was broken beyond repair; Trapp, who treated her like she always thought a brother might treat her; and Captain Behnam, who—

Where did she even begin with the Captain? There was no way she could unpack what she felt for him, nor did she have any desire to add any of that to the list of complicated emotions she already felt.

And in the back of it all was the events of the night before, playing in her mind. They rolled over and over again, replaying and replaying, though she didn't know why.

But the more it played, the more she realized something wasn't right.

But what?

Her mood shifted immediately from emotionally broken to focused on the task at hand. She examined each and every detail, putting it into place in her mind with patience and precision. Starting at the very beginning, she went through everything—walking into the ballroom, being approached by the Prince, the dancing, slipping away with Gibbs, the guards she'd asked for directions . . .

The guards.

She'd thought there was something familiar about them when she'd mistaken it for homesickness for Liosa, for her home.

But it was something more than that.

She knew one of the guards.

CHAPTER 27

"**C**APTAIN!" EL CALLED from outside Captain Behnam's room. She pounded her hand on the thin metal. "Captain, are you awake?"

"No," came his groggy response.

"Well, wake up!" she said, hoping the urgency showed in her voice. She also hoped he wasn't too upset with her. It was beyond against her better judgment, but it needed to be done. He would understand once she explained. She hoped. She hoped beyond hope that he would.

Ginger's door opened and the medic poked her head out, blinking sleepily as she ran a hand through her short curls, which shot up in all directions, slept on and untamed "What's going on?"

"Sorry," El said, biting her lip. She hadn't thought about the fact that in waking the Captain up, she was going to wake everyone else up too. "I just really need to talk to Captain Behnam."

"Are you okay?" Ginger asked. "El, have you been crying?"

El wasn't about to lie but she also wasn't about to get into that standing there in the corridor. "I just need to talk to the Captain. It's important."

"It'd better be," Captain Behnam grumbled as he opened his door. His face was marked by a dark scowl.

She bit her lip. "Sorry, it is. I just—"

"Not here," he said crossly. "In the grubbery. Go back to bed, Ging. I'm sure it's fine."

A look of concern crossed Ginger's freckled face, but she nodded slowly before retreating back into her room, shutting the door behind her.

"If this could have waited until morning, I'm going to kill you," Captain Behnam said as he started walking toward the grubbery. El followed behind, questioning herself for a second before she realized that was foolish. She was in the right.

They were far enough out of earshot of the rooms that El felt it safe to speak without disturbing anyone else. "It's very important, *rook di goo*."

They reached the grubbery, and the Captain moved to the counter. His back was to her so she couldn't see what he was doing, but when he turned, he had a mug full of what looked like tea. He'd only been there a moment though, so he must have been drinking some of the leftovers from earlier.

"All right." He leaned up against the wall and eyed her levelly. "Go ahead and give it to me. What was so important that it couldn't wait until the morning?"

If her calculations were correct, it was early morning already, but it didn't seem the appropriate time to mention that. "We're not finished."

"What?" he said, looking confused. He let out a long yawn before taking a swig of tea. "What are you talking about?"

She took a seat on one of the padded benches, tucking her legs up under her. "His Highness isn't safe. I was going over the events of last night—"

"At four in the morning?" he interrupted to ask.

See, she was right. It was morning after all.

"That's not important." She shifted on the bench but couldn't get comfortable. "But as I was going over it in my mind, I remembered one of the guards I asked for directions to the lab—I recognized him."

"Okay . . . ?" He drew the word out, questioning, as he hunched in closer as if to hear her better, even though she wasn't speaking that quietly.

"He was one of the Liosi imposters who arrested you," she explained. "So whoever is trying to kill the Prince is working with at least some of the Liosi guards. I told him to trust his guards. I told him he could trust me. If he dies . . . "

She stood, walking around the table and then back again, pacing. If they failed, her planet would fall apart at the seams, crumble from within and without, and it would be all her fault. And what happened to the galaxy afterward . . .

There were enough awful things to blame her for and she had no desire to add any more to the list. She didn't know if she could live with that.

"You're sure?" He gave her that level look, the one that said he trusted her, no other questions required.

She nodded. "I am—*rook di goo*."

313

He gave a definitive nod as he pushed away from the wall. "All right then. We'll talk about what to do about this in the morning."

"In the morning? With all due respect, that might be too late. We might even already be too late. If we wait—"

"I'm not waking everyone else up for this," the man said, his tone firm. "It can wait until morning."

There was an edge to his voice, a warning that he wasn't in the mood for arguing. She swallowed hard and nodded. "Yes, sir."

"Get some sleep, Elis," he said with a sigh.

"Yes, sir," she said, turning to go back to her room, though she doubted very much she'd be able to fall asleep.

"Oh, and Elis?"

She turned at his words.

He offered her a small smile. "Good work."

Despite her suspicions otherwise, El did, in fact, manage to fall asleep, and she slept hard.

Waking with panic, she jumped from the bed, untangling herself from the sheets and not even bothering to put on her boots or do anything with her hair which fell about her shoulders in an unsightly display.

But who cared about her hair when the Prince's life was at stake?

She found everyone in the grubbery, seated around the table with steaming cups of tea in front of them.

"Nice of you to invite me to the party," she said crossly.

"Good morning to you too," Trapp said with a grin as he adjusted his midnight beanie.

She wasn't in the mood for teasing, not from Trapp or anyone else. So she turned her attention to Captain Behnam instead, to the matter at hand. "Did you fill everyone in?"

Captain Behnam gave a lazy yawn, looking a little bothered that she'd brought the matter up. Too bad. She wasn't going to apologize for trying to keep the Prince from getting assassinated.

"Not yet," he said. "I was getting there."

"'Getting there'?" she demanded. "With all due respect, this is serious."

"Cool it, Elis. I understand what's at stake here."

There was a patronizing tone to his words, and it took every ounce of control to not bite his head off. "Again, with all due respect, but I don't think you do."

"What's going on?" Gibbs asked, his brow furrowed in a concerned expression.

She looked to the Captain, who nodded, giving her permission to explain. "One of the guards who gave me directions to the labs last night, I recognized him—he was one of the Liosi imposters who arrested Captain Behnam."

Gibbs' brow furrowed deeper and there was an edge to his voice as he spoke. "And you didn't think to mention this before?"

"I just realized it this morning," she hastened to defend herself. "Something wasn't sitting right with me about this whole thing, but I just thought it was . . . " Wait, no, she couldn't tell them she was upset because she had to leave since the job was done. "Well, never mind that."

"Now I want to know what you thought," Trapp said before she could say any more.

"It's not important," she maintained, all but snapping at him.

He raised an eyebrow, not looking convinced. "Yeah, I totally believe that. But whatever. So you realized this morning?"

"At four this morning," Captain Behnam added, clearly none too pleased with that bit of information.

She waved him off because that detail was unimportant at the moment.

"Oh, was that what that was about?" Ginger said, looking pleased with having it make sense.

"What *what* was about?" Trapp demanded.

Ginger pulled her brows in. "Didn't you hear her banging on the Captain's door?"

Trapp and Gibbs shook their heads, both looking a bit confused by the whole ordeal.

El rolled her eyes. "I'm not calling on either of you in an emergency. I was making enough noise to raise the Elassi. But anyway! If one of the imposters was at the ball, it means Radian Darius has people on the Prince's guard in his service. Which means our job isn't done. They could be assassinating him right now, as we speak."

"As much as I hate to suggest it, the last ball tonight is probably our best opening," Captain Behnam said with a displeased sigh.

"I'm not waiting that long," El stated. "The Prince could already be dead by then. I'm not giving the assassins hours to work."

"And how do you presume you get into the palace?" the Captain asked. "You've been the one who maintained this whole time that if Gibbs avows himself to you, he'd be ruined. So what do you suggest? That he goes there himself? What does he tell them when they ask for his source? That he's going on the hunch of a known deserter?"

"It isn't a hunch!" she said, but it was a defense mechanism because he was right on all the other accounts.

"I'm sure they're all going to believe that," he said. "Trust me, Elis, I thought this through. Tonight's our best bet—again, as much as I hate to say it."

She looked around the table to the other crewmembers to see if any of them were going to challenge the man. They didn't, of course, since he was right, but that didn't stop her from hoping one of them would come up with some counter-argument that made sense.

After a minute, when they didn't say anything, she sighed and said, "Okay, so what do we do in the meantime?"

"We wait," the Captain said with a shrug.

Trapp let out an exaggerated sigh as he rose. "*Ech,* now I've got to find you another dress. I'm not even going to bother asking you to try to keep from ruining it. Seriously, you're harder on dresses than any other girl I know."

"Sorry." She offered him an apologetic smile.

He was already headed toward the cargo bay, waving her off as he did. "Yeah, yeah."

Gibbs left too, and Ginger gathered up the cups and took them to the grubbery, leaving Captain Behnam and El alone at the table.

"Sorry I'm touchy," she said.

He shrugged. "Sorry I'm not handling it the way you want. I do take it seriously, I promise. What is it you say? *Rook di goo?*"

She nodded, staring dejectedly down at her mug of tea. "Yeah, *rook di goo.*"

"I just don't like the idea of sending you back in there," he said. "You may be willing to gamble, but I don't like the odds. You've defied them twice now, what are the chances you'll manage that again?"

"Slim to none," she admitted. "But if I don't, I'm not willing to gamble it'll all work itself out. I know you might not believe me, but I don't actually want to die."

"You do take chances with your life that would suggest otherwise," he said, and there was a little tease underneath the seriousness in his voice that she liked; it meant things were okay between them, and while that shouldn't matter to her, it did.

She offered him a small smile in return by way of acknowledgment. "I'm afraid of dying, same as everyone else, but what scares me more is it not meaning anything, you know? I'm going to die, it's a fact, and I don't want to spend the rest of my life trying to outrun that."

"You could maybe stand to try and outrun it just a little," he said. "But I get it. My mother always said to always help in any situation because your only other option is to hinder—'there is nowhere in the middle to rest.'" He smiled that far off smile he got sometimes, as if he was remembering when his mother had said it. He looked over at her and offered her an apologetic grin. "Sorry, I know that's not what you want to hear."

She was about to ask why he would think that when she remembered their conversation the other night—yesterday morning?—and groaned. "You're never going to let me live that down, are you?"

She realized as she said it that her words implied she'd be around for him to keep bringing it up. And that couldn't happen; for his own sake, it couldn't happen. She started to shake her head, though she didn't know how to tell him to forget about it.

He grinned at her, his words a teasing promise as he said, "Nope, never."

Her heart skipped a beat as she realized how much of a promise she took from those words. She shouldn't. She couldn't. It wasn't fair to even ask it of him.

"And just so we're clear," he said, unaware of the thoughts swirling through her head, of the frantic beating of her heart. "Trapp runs headfirst into danger all the time too—maybe a little different than the kind you do, but reckless and ill-advised all the same—and I say the exact same thing to him. I'm not coming against you, Elis. It's not personal."

It wasn't personal.

It couldn't be. Not with her. She thought of the way he'd let the imposter soldiers destroy the *Aderyn*, how he'd let himself be arrested, how he willingly put himself into danger for her again and again.

He blamed her for her rashness, for how willing she was to throw her life away for Liosa, when he was willing—always—to do the same for her.

Sitting there next to the man who she'd only known a short while but whose opinion meant more to her than anyone she had ever known, she knew it could never be personal.

"I should go talk to Ginger," she said, standing, taking her cup of tea with her.

"Are you okay?" he asked, standing too, looking concerned.

She offered him a smile meant to reassure him even though she wasn't sure herself. "I'm fine."

He frowned at her, still looking concerned, and she reached to squeeze his hand because that was something people did sometimes in these situations—or so she thought.

But he pulled away as she reached to touch him.

"Oh . . . " she said, pulling back. "Right, I'm sorry." He didn't want her to touch him. That was fine. She was fine. She turned.

"Elis, wait."

She turned back, shaking. She was always shaking. She should've just gone to talk to Ginger, she shouldn't have stayed there. "It's fine, I should talk to Ginger. I—I'm sorry."

"It's the Mahsirian," he said by way of a reply. She furrowed her brow at him, and he waved his hand at her, flexing his fingers as he did. "I didn't want you to get shocked."

It took a moment for his words to sink in. "You mean Mahsirian magic? That's actually real?"

"I guess you could call it that?" He gave a little shrug, his expression sheepish. "It's just an inconvenient tick, really. Sometimes, when I'm upset usually, I just get these little bursts. It's not dangerous but I can't control it. I just . . . I didn't want . . . I'd never want . . . " He shook his head, flexing his fingers. "Never mind."

"It doesn't hurt," she told him because she was pretty sure that's what he was trying to say. "It feels a little weird, but I got used to it."

Victory, did she just say that?

And did he notice?

Of course he noticed. What must he think of her? She should have just gone and talked to Ginger. She should have remembered that it wasn't personal. It couldn't be.

320

Instead, they stood there in silence until he finally said, "You were going to go talk to Ginger?"

"Right," she said. She reached for her tea as she turned, and he caught her hand, giving it a squeeze, as she had intended to do with him. There was no shock that time, no tingle, but the warmth of his fingers on hers spread through her.

"Thanks, Elis," he said, releasing it, taking a step back and looking everywhere but her all of a sudden. "I should, uh, go . . . "

He trailed off and she spared him any further discomfort. "I'm going to go find Ginger."

Taking her tea, she walked across the grubbery and poked her head into the med bay, happy to find Ginger there. "Are you busy?"

The medic looked up from the port screen she was bent over and set it aside. "Not with anything important. Did you need something?"

"Can we talk?" El asked, biting her lip, pushing out the words before she lost her nerve.

"Absolutely," Ginger said as El stepped all the way into the room and shut the door behind her. "As friends or in a professional capacity?"

El took a seat across from her. "Professional."

"Were you crying?" Trapp asked as he swept into the med bay with a garment bag, frowning at her as he surveyed her up and down.

Ginger had left a while ago, giving El her requested time alone after their session together. El had let the medic talk her through the medication she thought would help, and El had accepted the little bottle of pills. She'd left them up in her room, not quite ready to take them, but finding comfort in knowing she could if she wanted.

"Yeah, I was just talking to Ginger," she said simply, brushing away a tear. It had been helpful, necessary, but it'd also hurt like all fury. And not just because El wasn't sure if that was the last time she'd get a chance to do so. There was still so much El had left to work through, she and Ginger having only barely scratched the surface, but there just wasn't the time; it would all end soon, one way or another.

"Ah," Trapp said with an understanding nod. "Professional talk?"

El nodded.

"Yeah, she'll do that to you."

What could Trapp possibly have to talk to Ginger about? El tried to picture him crying but he was too self-assured, too easy-going, for the picture to be an easy one to conjure. But she supposed it just went to show how everyone, in their own way, really was a little messed up.

"Is that my dress?" she asked because she needed to talk about something else. She needed to think about the night ahead and not about everything else clouding her mind.

Ginger returned, and Trapp left to give them the privacy needed to get El into her dress. Then he came back after she'd changed so he could commentate unhelpfully on how she looked while Ginger did her makeup and hair.

It was a pale pink dress, soft and delicate. The strapless bodice hugged her torso with its draped fabric and extensive delicate beading. She couldn't help feeling as if it might fall off at any second. Ginger assured her it wouldn't but El didn't believe her, even if the medic wasn't one to lie. The skirt poofed out around her in layers upon layers of fabric.

She felt more vulnerable than she had on the other nights and even less like herself than usual. But it was the dress Trapp had gotten for her, and she'd been so hard on the others she could hardly complain about the wardrobe choice. Though she did have a suspicion that Trapp had chosen it specifically to get back at her for her treatment of the other two.

Ginger swept her hair up into an intricate up-do of twists and braids, a few tendrils framing her face, and then did her makeup once more.

"You look amazing," Ginger said when she was finished. "Every man who sees you will fall madly in love with you."

El laughed at the words. "Not really a selling point."

The Captain drove again and he, Gibbs, and El arrived at the palace. They were let through the gates, which made El respect Gibbs a little more—somehow there had been an assassination attempt and a break-in, and he'd managed to completely avoid suspicion.

Maybe he was better at his job than she gave him credit for.

Captain Behnam helped her out of the vehicle once more. "For Liosa."

"For the galaxy," she replied, trying not to think about how it was the last time they had that exchange. That didn't bother her as much as the implication behind it—that it would be the last time they worked together. It had to be.

She wished there were more, that they'd actually be working side by side like they had at the hotel or the library. She wished she could walk in there with him by her side and not Gibbs—no offense to the security officer.

She was getting used to the sights and sounds and smells of the ballroom, so it was easier to keep from getting distracted by them.

She saw Prince Tov almost as soon as she entered the room, and she was actually grateful when he crossed the room to her. She had, after all, come to talk to him.

"I was hoping you would come tonight," he said, taking her hand in his and bringing it to his lips, kissing it ever so gently. "But I didn't think you actually would."

"I wasn't going to, but I had more information I needed to discuss with you," she told him honestly.

"Do you just work all the time?" he said, not releasing her hand, but holding it close to his face instead. It was intimate and highly inappropriate for her to be standing in that manner with the crown prince. "Surely it wouldn't hurt you to have a little fun sometimes."

"But it might hurt you, what with all the threats on your life recently," she said bluntly, keeping her voice low. But still, she glanced about her, knowing any one of the many people around them could prove to be more than an innocent bystander.

"And if I'm willing to risk it?" he said, grinning at her, flirtatious.

"I'm not," she replied, not having any part of his games.

He looked offended, but there was something else in his eyes that put her on edge. Something wasn't right, but unlike last night, she wasn't going to ignore her intuition. It had turned out to be right last night, and she wasn't going to just push it aside.

"Perhaps we can go somewhere to talk?" she asked, glancing about, looking for whatever it was that was putting the Prince on edge. "Somewhere more private?"

"The gardens?" he suggested.

She shook her head. "I'd rather not have a repeat of the first night. Perhaps we might find a quiet alcove? There's sure to be an abandoned one somewhere."

She and Gibbs had passed a good number of them on their quest to the labs, but she couldn't exactly tell him that without admitting she'd been the one to break in last night.

He glanced about, looking nervous, and she honestly couldn't blame him. But it still put her all the more on edge. It took every ounce of willpower for her to not draw her gun then and there in the middle of the crowded ballroom. This was neither the time nor the place for her to draw a weapon, and it would be the surest way to ensure trouble if she did draw it.

And then she wouldn't be able to protect the Prince at all, not from a jail cell.

"Are you sure you wouldn't rather go outside?" Prince Tov pressed. "Surely an assassin wouldn't try the same thing twice."

"Only because we wouldn't be foolish enough to underestimate them like that," she said. "Please, Your Highness, I ask you to trust me."

He drew in a breath, looking about quickly before he exhaled, looking her as he nodded. "All right. If that's what you think is best."

She slipped her arm in his, shooting a glance at Gibbs who was on the other side of the room, talking to Lord Callinger. Next, she scanned for her father and Commander Gibbs and found she didn't see them anywhere.

The Prince was moving then, and she allowed herself to be led down the corridor. She pulled herself from her paranoid thoughts and focused instead on the matter at hand.

They moved down the hall, passing servants and guards and guests alike. Most noticed them as they passed but ignored them. El supposed it looked much like the Prince leading her off to some sort of illicit rendezvous. Oh well, she couldn't stop them thinking what they wished.

Shaking the thought off, she continued to keep an eye on her surroundings, looking out for signs that something wasn't right, that any one of the people they passed intended to do them harm, that even the slightest detail was amiss.

She saw nothing though, and it was with relief that she sank into the little alcove she chose, pulling the Prince in behind her.

Her dress poofed out enough that she was able to tuck him into a corner and all but block the opening with her form.

"I'm so sorry to do things this way, Your Highness," she began. "I assure you if there was some other way, I would have taken it, but I had no way of knowing who I could trust. And . . . there are other complications that I can't get into. Not right now."

"I understand," Prince Tov said. "And I also don't. I don't understand how someone can pretend to love her country so much when she betrays it so brutally."

"What . . . ?" What had she done? Why would he think her a betrayer of her country? When had she given him any cause to think that she was anything but a loyal servant to the crown?

Unless he meant—

"I know who you are, Miss Elis," he said. "I know I might come across as such, but I'm no fool."

326

He knew. He knew who she was, what she'd done. That was why Prince Tov had been so nervous. That was why he'd wanted to go to the garden. That was why her father and the other guards were nowhere to be seen.

They'd set a trap for her. And she had walked right into it.

CHAPTER 28

EL NEEDED TO think fast.

She needed out of the palace, but she doubted she could get out through the front gate. But she could hardly stay in the little alcove with the Prince and no protection.

Wait, she had the Prince.

Holding him hostage was treason, but she knew she was too far gone. And for all she knew, the trap was an elaborate ruse to cover the assassination plot. If they took down a deserter and the Prince got killed too, who was to say whether one of the guards shot him or the traitor did?

So she could either commit treason to save the man's life or she could let him go and be responsible for his death.

Treason it was.

Pulling out her gun she said, "Let's go."

"Where are we going?" the Prince asked, his eyes growing wide with fear. There was a wildness to his expression that she recognized as pure terror. He was out of his mind with fear, and there wasn't anything she could do to put him at ease.

Still, she had to try, though her words were sure to fall on deaf ears. "I'm no traitor, Your Highness. I said I was here to save your life, and I have every intention of doing just that."

It would be smart for her to get Captain Behnam and Gibbs to help her, but she had no way of contacting them without marching the Prince into a very crowded place at gunpoint. Not exactly a move she wanted to play out.

So going solo it was.

They moved in the direction of the labs because she remembered there was a glass wall of windows at the top of the stairs with a door leading outside. They hadn't gone out it because El had thought it better to go the route she knew than the unknown that night. But what she needed was a way out, and she'd take the unknown if she had to.

They made it to the door, and mercy of mercy, it was unlocked. She went through it first, her gun leading the way, as she dragged the Prince behind her.

"This is treason," he told her. "If you stop now, I can help you. I have authority, I can make this go away. I can give you what you want."

As far as Prince Tov knew, she was an assassin and a terrorist; he really shouldn't be offering to make deals with her that included giving her whatever she wanted.

"What I want is to keep you safe," she told him, realizing how crazy she sounded.

She had a choice to go down the path to the left—which she guessed connected to the path with the bird house that led to where the vehicles were parked—and the path to the right which seemed to lead to some trees and what seemed to be a forest of sorts.

The path to the left was sure to lead her to people and guards and all sorts of obstacles. And she doubted they could just hide in the bird house until it all blew over again.

The other way seemed safer, though there were more unknown variables. At least that way she was less likely to meet people, less likely to be swarmed with the complications the other path promised.

She headed in that direction, reaching the tree line and finding a little set of stairs as the terrain dipped. She moved down them, stepping on the first step only to find her boots stuck to it, unable to move.

She turned to the Prince, her eyes wide, questioning. Her hand was still about his arm, holding him fast as she held her gun in the other hand. She tried to lift her foot again but found it unable to lift.

"It's the material in your boots," he told her. "It's reacting to the material in the steps. At least, that's what I was told when I signed off on doing it. Prince Jarett recommended it when he heard about my dilemma. He said one of his advisors recommended it."

How did they know she would go that way? And how did they know what her shoes were made of?

The Prince. He had told everyone he'd seen her boots, and her father had figured out right away that they were military boots.

Her precious boots. She had to give up her precious boots.

"Down the stairs," she commanded him. She still had every intention of going that way. It might be a trap, but it was better to go ahead toward the possibility of danger than to go back to where she knew trouble was sure to be.

The Prince did as he was told, keeping his eyes on her gun even though she hadn't even pointed it at him or used it in any other way. It was simply in her hand, drawn, ready for danger.

When he reached the bottom of the stairs, she hastened to slip off her boots, keeping her eyes on Prince Tov as she did in case he decided to try anything.

She gave the bodice of her dress a tug before moving again, still uncomfortable with how it hung. She was in a strapless dress with no shoes while she tried to protect a Prince who thought her a traitor who was going to assassinate him.

She wanted to say the night couldn't get any worse but, sadly, she knew it could.

They moved down the path that wasn't really a path—it was the only way through the trees, but it was also covered in grass, as if it weren't traversed very often, which made no sense given the set of stairs. She doubted they installed those just for her.

How had they known she would come back?

They walked for several minutes; who had decided that building a palace next to an endless forest was a good idea? Then they came to a little clearing and a wall.

A very tall wall.

A dead end.

El took a deep breath, unwilling to give up hope just yet. She had come that far and had no intention of giving up just because she'd run into a wall. Literally.

It was just another roadblock. She'd overcome so many thus far, and there was no reason to think she couldn't keep going.

Except that she was wearing that ridiculous dress and she had no shoes. Soldiers had a uniform when they went into battle, and there was a reason why it was never a poofy ball gown. It was beyond impractical to go into combat like that; saying the dress was unconducive was more than an understatement.

But even that was no reason to quit. Just because something was improbable or even impossible didn't mean you shouldn't try—especially when it was your only option.

"Would you like a little help, Miss Elis?"

She turned at the sound of the voice coming from the direction she had just come from. She pointed her gun in that direction first as she put herself between the speaker and the Prince.

The speaker was a Philosanthrian man, perhaps in his early thirties, well-dressed and clean-shaven, with dark hair and a little taller than El—perhaps the same height as the Captain, though definitely shorter than Trapp.

She was distracted by the man that she didn't notice until it was too late that Prince Tov had moved from behind her to break away and run.

In an instant, the man's hand raised, and he fired his gun before she could act.

As soon as she realized what was happening, she jumped to try and intercept the shot, firing off a shot of her own.

Her shot landed on its target, hitting the man in the arm and causing him to drop the gun. Unfortunately, his shot landed as well, and all she could do was look down in horror at the Prince's still body.

"Don't worry, it was just a knock-out dart," the man said in a pained voice as she dropped to her knees to put two fingers to his neck. She exhaled in relief as she found a faint but steady pulse.

"He'll be fine, though a little groggy on the events of tonight when he finally wakes up. I really should have seen your shot coming though. I can't believe after all this I somehow managed to underestimate you."

She rose, gun trained on the man, even though she knew he wasn't armed, which made it murder to shoot him. She didn't care; she needed answers.

"Who are you?" she demanded.

He smirked at her, though the expression was made through gritted teeth as he gripped his bleeding arm. "I think you know who I am. You've been thwarting every one of my plans the last few weeks."

El all but forced the name out, nearly choking on the words as she said them. "Radian Darius."

"In the flesh," the man said with a grin and a dip of his head. "And may I say, it's a pleasure to finally meet you. Though I admit I wish it could have been under better circumstances. I'm sorry I had to go to such drastic measures to arrange this, but I wanted to make sure that my suspicions about you were indeed warranted."

"What do you mean?" He hadn't arranged anything. She'd worked hard the last few weeks to stay one step ahead of him, and she was there because of choices she had made; not because of arrangements he or anyone else had made.

He frowned. "Please, Elisandra, this has been your grand audition, and I'm pleased to say you've more than impressed me."

The events of the several weeks before tumbled through her mind as it all fell into place. He'd meant her to find his men in Alvar, meant her to end up with the drive that led her to the balls. He'd meant her to stop his assassination attempts.

"Zephyr was your man." Of course he'd been planted, his presence far too convenient to have any other explanation.

The man's brows wrinkled in. "Who?"

Was Zephyr not his man? But then who . . . ?

She didn't have time to dwell on that.

"I'm not interested in an audition," she said, because that was the important matter at hand. "I'm here to stop you—I know what you and Prince Jarett are up to, and if I have to give my life to keep that from happening, I will, *rook di goo*."

He shook his head, a pained look on his face, though whether it was from the gunshot wound or her announcement was unclear. "There was just so much wrong with that sentence, I don't even know where to begin. Do you honestly think this was all masterminded by a fool like Prince Jarett? He knows nothing. He's not smart enough to think higher than the base desires of power and revenge. He seeks admiration and thinks having control will get him that."

"That doesn't change anything," she said. "Whether you're behind it or someone else, this is wrong."

"No, you're wrong," he said, firmly but gently, like he understood why she was amiss in her thinking and he had every intention of patiently explaining it to her. "You're willing to give your life for a cause that's broken. And you're much too clever to live a life of running, always looking over your shoulder. It's been heartbreaking to see all that potential go to waste like that. You were born for great things, Elisandra, and I can give you that."

"I'm not going to work for you." Her words were accompanied by a mirthless laugh.

He shook his head. "It's not funny. It's not funny what Liosa has done to you—the way she stole your father, the things she made you do in Taras, the nightmares, so much heartache, and for what? What has she ever given you in return? You give and you give to her, you all but break yourself for her, willing to give her your very life. And what has she done but continue to ask you to give more? What has Liosa ever given you in return?"

He was making valid points, and she didn't want to listen to them. She didn't want his words to make sense. They couldn't make sense. Because if they made sense, it meant he was right, didn't it?

"I can offer you so much more than that," he continued. "And I won't even ask as much in return. I don't expect you to give everything to me, I don't need to break you beyond repair."

Was she broken beyond repair? Ginger didn't seem to think so, but then Ginger saw the best in everyone. Of course she'd tell her she could be fixed. Of course she'd say the pills and the exercises and the conversations would help. Of course she'd tell her she wasn't broken, just bruised, that she just needed to reset her mind, to learn to think of things differently, to process them and let them go.

But Ginger didn't know. What had Ginger ever been through that could make her even begin to understand just how far gone El was? The medic saw the world through a rosy lens, so of course she saw El the same way. But that didn't make it the truth.

"You're considering it," Radian Darius said. "That's good. You should consider it. You should consider what you deserve and who can give it to you."

"You?" she said because she was stalling, hoping to come up with some sort of a refute for his words. But nothing came to mind. His words made too much sense; she hated how much sense they made.

"I would appreciate you," he said. "Tell me, who else has appreciated you as much as you deserve? Who else has given you the credit you earn again and again?"

Captain Behnam appreciated her. So did Gibbs. And Trapp and Ginger had made her feel like family from the moment she'd stepped onto their ship. But it was dangerous to let them care. For their own sake, she couldn't let them.

"I knew you'd come back tonight," he continued. "I knew you'd recognize my man though you didn't even speak to him. He was my only man on the inside, by the way, one who turned out to be completely useless. I had to end him, to spare the rest of the galaxy his complete incompetence."

That was it. That was why she couldn't work with him.

"I'm not a killer."

He gave her a sympathetic smile. "Aren't you? Isn't that what Liosa made you into? You signed up to be a hero, and they had you wiping out an entire nation."

"That was under Philosanthrian orders," she argued.

"But who gave permission for those ordered to be given?" he pressed. "Who signed off on them without a second thought? Who blamed you when those orders were too much to follow and they broke you? You are a killer, Elisandra, and that's what your country has given you. That's what Liosa has made you into."

337

El didn't have anything to say to that because all that filled her mind right then were images of what he spoke of. Images of Taras and the people she had killed there, the beautiful planet she had helped bring to ruin—the smoke and the flames and death and destruction she left in her wake.

Maybe she deserved to serve a person like the man who stood before her. Evil deserved evil companions; how could she hope for anything more?

"We only have a few minutes before they find us," he said. "They're on their way here even as we speak, I'm sure. And when they do get here, they're going to shoot you. You know that. They're going to put you down like a rabid dog, like a traitor. Are you truly willing to give your life for that? Is that really worth dying for?"

Was it? Was she willing to die for what she'd done in Taras? She deserved it, she didn't doubt that. But she didn't deserve to be executed for her crimes by those who had given her the orders to carry them out. She didn't deserve to be executed for what she'd done—she wasn't a soldier anymore; she had become an executioner that snuffed out innocent lives. Was she really willing to let them kill her after what they'd made her?

"This is Liosa," he said. "This is the country you love so much. This is what she really is."

"No." It came out in a whisper, a plea for him to stop. She felt tears threatening to fall, and an anger rose at him for pushing her so close to that.

"Then explain it to me so I can understand."

What was the truth? Was Liosa really what he said she was? Was El truly so blind that she was wrong to think her country wasn't evil, that she was just misguided?

El didn't want to believe Liosa was what happened in Taras. Liosa was something more, something better.

She was a people who endured years of oppression without giving up hope because they knew, someday, they would be free. They knew tyranny couldn't reign forever, and they were willing to hold on until the day justice arrived.

She was a people who rallied around a boy, who raised him up as a hero even though he didn't look like one.

They were a people, fierce and proud, who had carved out lives for themselves on a planet that man surely wasn't meant to inhabit.

They were survivors. They were a people who fought back no matter the odds, who stood up for what was right no matter how easy it was to give up, to give in.

Today was Liberation Day. She'd forgotten that—she'd been so caught up in everything else. She'd forgotten to celebrate. Forgotten to remember just what that meant.

Had El's ancestors ever been faced with that situation—the chance to look evil in the face and be seduced by his lies? Had they, too, been tempted with the path that seemed right, even though they knew in their hearts that it was wrong?

They hadn't given up. And neither would she.

"You're right that Liosa has taken a lot from me," she admitted. "And I'm not saying that's right. But you're wrong that she hasn't given me anything—she has. She's given me everything."

"Is that so?" he said. He sounded displeased and unconvinced. That was okay; he didn't have to be convinced. It was enough that she was.

"She's given me my identity," she explained. "She's made me who I am. You want the girl before you, but the joke's on you because that girl is only here because of the Liosi blood pumping through her veins. So thank you for your offer, but I'm going to have to decline. If they want to kill me, they can kill me. Because I would rather die at their hands—even if those hands are misguided right now—than live to become like you."

"That's a very pretty speech, Elisandra," he said. "But unfortunately, that's all it is. Just words. I thought you were a woman of action, and I'm sorry to find myself so mislead."

"You don't know me," she said.

"Oh, but I do," he said with a smirk. "I knew you'd come back, and I knew you wouldn't go to the garden like they were planning—of course you'd be smart enough to not take the Prince's suggestion. I knew you'd go back to the one place in the palace you knew there was an unguarded exit, and I knew you wouldn't take the path back to a crowded area of people. I knew you wouldn't turn back even after you lost your shoes, those precious boots of yours, and I knew you'd end up right here. But you're right that I don't know you entirely. As I mentioned, I should have expected the shot, but I'm sorry to say I didn't anticipate that. I really ought to have, though. You always have been one to shoot your way out of a situation."

There was a time when those words would have cut her, would have come as an insult, but in that moment, they just reminded her of the conversation she'd had with the Captain about her namesake—about his mother.

He'd told El that she was enough, that her own mother would be proud of her. It shouldn't have meant so much coming from someone who didn't even know her mother. But she realized then that it had been his way of telling her he was proud of her, and that meant more to her than it should.

"I really hoped this would end differently," Radian Darius said, with a sad shake of his head. With his left hand—the one that hadn't been shot—he reached into his jacket and withdrew a gun. "And yes, this one shoots real bullets."

El hesitated for just a second, all that talk about being a killer getting to her head and filling it. Images of Taras and all that had happened there filled her mind until it was almost too much to bear.

But it was just for a second. Because then she realized he wasn't pointing the gun at her; he was pointing it at the still unconscious Prince. And she knew what she had to do.

The man hardly even had time to aim before El's gun was up and she fired.

And in the next instant, Radian Darius was dead.

CHAPTER 29

EL FELT A little hollow for a moment after the shot was fired, and she stood looking at the result of what she had done.

He was dead.

Radian Darius was dead, and, with him, the threats she'd been running from.

Kneeling beside Prince Tov, she found him barely awake, and he let out a groan in lieu of words when he saw her.

She put a hand to his wrist, feeling for a pulse, finding it was strong and steady; Radian Darius had told the truth and really just stunned him. "It's going to be all right."

"Was he going to shoot me?"

She nodded, not having time for a conversation.

What she needed was a plan, but she didn't have one.

Even if she ran, she wouldn't be able to make it to Captain Behnam before the guards caught her. And even if she did make it, she'd just be bringing trouble straight to him. Captain Behnam would die for her, and she refused to give him that chance.

She could make a stand, build herself a good defense and hold off as long as she could. Except she didn't want to wage a war. Not here. Not ever again.

She'd be shooting at innocent guards. Men who had signed up to keep Prince Tov safe—who were trying to accomplish the same goal as her.

Innocent lives would be lost that night and at her hand.

Again.

Those hands of hers were stained beyond cleansing with blood that didn't deserve to be shed. That was why her mother would be ashamed of her. It wasn't just that she shot her way out of things—it was that she never stopped to think who would get caught in the crossfire.

In all of it, she'd defended herself by saying that she was doing the right thing—she was working to save the Prince and for that, she had to survive. But it wasn't true.

She was scared, scared of the things she'd done and the people who had made her do them.

She thought about her conversation the other night when Captain Behnam had told her she was in the right because she'd stood up against tyranny. She thought about how she had admitted the truth to him—that she hadn't stood up for anything, she'd only run from it.

All she did was run. Her whole life was one long string of running and hiding. Sucking it up and putting on a brave face. She'd told the Captain she liked to face a problem head-on, but that wasn't true. Not always. Not when it truly mattered.

She could shoot her way out of an alleyway, could talk her way around getting some shady hotel owner to give her the name she needed. But she couldn't face the horrors she'd endured, that she'd carried out on Taras. She couldn't face the people who'd ordered them.

Instead, she'd run from it. Just like she always did. Because it was her father and because there was an understanding between them that they didn't talk about things. They never had, not since her mother died.

No, instead they ran from things, and she had been foolish enough to think that, too, was something she could get away from if she only ran fast enough.

But she couldn't run anymore. Things would never change if she did. And if it meant she had to die for it, she realized in that instant that she was willing.

Hadn't her ancestors been willing to die for what was right? Hadn't they thought fighting oppression more important than preserving their own lives? Hadn't they laid down their lives for truth and justice to prevail?

Revolutions weren't fought by people who played it safe. Her life would be forfeited, but it was better than running any longer. She could speak up, take a stand. And if she saved her people and the innocent lives that were left, who cared if she lost her own life in the process?

Drawing in a breath, she turned to face the guards that were running toward her. It would take them a minute to reach her but when they did, they were going to find her compliant, her hands raised in the air, non-threatening in her surrender.

"Get down on the ground," they ordered when they reached her, waving their guns at her to emphasize their point. She did as they said, getting down on her knees and then laying all the way down, face to the ground.

The last thing she saw before her face pressed against the dirt was her father standing over her, his expression blank and emotionless.

Radian Darius was right—Liosa had done nothing but take. El had given of herself, again and again, and in the end, Liosa only demanded more.

She might have had a father, a normal upbringing, real childhood memories. But instead, all she had was the man standing over her, more dutiful soldier than doting father. Her own father had been taken from her.

And that night, she'd give Liosa the one last thing she had to offer. That night, Liosa would claim her life.

El was handcuffed and taken to a dark cell deep underground the palace.

She had no idea how long they left her for. It felt like an eternity, but it was too dark to judge the passage of time.

The room was cold. Not so cold that she worried about freezing to death or anything, but cold enough that it was impossible for her to properly get comfortable enough to sit still, her Liosi blood sobbing in protest. She paced to keep herself warm.

The temperature also made her all the more aware of just how much of her skin was exposed. The strapless dress left her neck and shoulders and back and arms uncovered; the skirt had been shredded, and running without her boots tore her socks, leaving her legs without protection.

The boning of the bodice dug into her ribs, bruising her. Her hairpins had started to make her head throb, and she ached to take them out, unable to with the range of motion the handcuffs allowed her.

She continued to pace, moving just enough to keep her blood flowing. The thoughts were creeping in; maybe she should have taken the pills from Ginger after all. Maybe that would have helped.

She knew it was all in her mind, but that was kind of the point. There was something wrong with her brain and those pills were supposed to help.

The thoughts filled her mind, spilling into the room and filling that too. Her chest grew tight, all but cutting off her breath. She needed out of the room, away from the thoughts.

She sucked in a breath, forcing the air into her lungs as her world spun. Closing her eyes—though it was so dark she almost didn't even need to—she pictured the control room on the *Aderyn*. She put each detail into place, one by one, slowly, carefully.

They'd hopefully made the smart choice and left without her. Captain Behnam had all but said he'd expected it to end that way with her. He'd supported her so his conscience was clear, but surely he'd be wise enough to let her go when things had fallen into place exactly the way he'd expected.

She wasn't worth risking his life for.

Her mind continued to swirl around, over and over again, going in circles, never making any progress, just rehashing the same things again and again.

She knew what they were doing. It was the oldest trick in the book—keep your prisoner isolated long enough that when you do finally go talk to them, they've already worn themselves down.

It was just a matter of them waiting it out, waiting for her to lose it completely before they let her out of there and took her somewhere to actually interrogate her.

They'd probably want to know all about her involvement with the assassination attempts on the Prince. And, she supposed, the death of Radian Darius. She had killed a man.

But then, it didn't matter what crime she went down for, not really. Not as long as she got to speak her mind first, to say her piece. After that, they could do whatever they wanted to her.

The one thing she regretted, though, was the loss of her boots. And the fact that she wasn't wearing something more . . . well, something more. She felt too exposed in the dress, too uncomfortable.

Too vulnerable.

She had no way of knowing how long her thoughts ran in these circles before the door opened. Light flooded the room, creating a silhouette of the figure who stood in the doorway.

"Cadet Elis, you're to come with me," the woman said, her voice monotone, emotionless. Dressed in a green Liosi uniform, like the one El had worn for so long. The one she'd betrayed by taking off. The woman was the same age as El, and the thought crossed El's mind that they might have gone to the same school, could have fought in some of the same battles. Their paths might have crossed any number of times.

The soldier standing before her was a perfect stranger but looking at her, El found she knew her well. Because if she hadn't run, that could have been her standing there.

"Where are you taking me?" El asked as she followed the soldier from the cell, even though she knew the women was no doubt under orders not to tell her anything.

"You'll see," she said, confirming the suspicion. Either that or she just didn't want to talk to El.

Not that El blamed her. No doubt, in her eyes, El was a traitor. El had, after all, turned her back on her planet, betraying a blood vow. No matter what she had done after, that act was unforgivable.

"I'm sorry." El knew the words weren't nearly enough, they couldn't be. "About all of this. I'm true Liosi. I never meant to betray my people."

The woman stopped walking and turned to face her, eyes narrowed into tiny slits. "I never said this, and if you say I did, I'll deny it and it'll make you look even crazier, got it?"

El nodded. What in the galaxy could she be about to say?

The woman leaned in closer, speaking softly so just El could hear. "You made the right choice. And, it's one I wish I had the guts to make, too. What we're doing is wrong and you had the right idea getting out while you could." She straightened then, looking El dead in the eyes through her narrowed eyelids. "But I never said that."

She started walking again and El followed, unsure what exactly she was supposed to say to that. She supposed nothing since the woman didn't give her a chance, but still, it felt weird not to even acknowledge it.

But she had already turned her attention back to the corridor before her, rounding a corner and saying no more. Still, the words rang in El's mind. Who knew she'd find such comfort in words from a stranger? They gave her a boost of courage, the confirmation that she'd done the right thing.

What had happened in Taras was wrong. She wasn't the only one who knew it.

They went down several corridors, turning corners until El was all but lost as to where they were. Should her survival depend on it, she didn't think she would be able to get back to the cell.

Finally, they came to a door, which the women opened and motioned for El to go through first. A burst of scalding air enveloped her, and El sighed with relief as it hit her frozen skin.

The room was fitted with an outdated light sourced that washed everything in a harsh, bitter glow, including all the people packed into it. Her father was there, along with Gibbs' father, Commander Gibbs. And she was surprised to see both Prince Tov and Gibbs himself, the latter of whom gave her a concerned smile when she entered. What had he told them? And how badly would she have to wring his neck for it? If he ruined his career for her, she might kill him.

The soldier slipped into the room and shut the door behind her, standing at the door, rigid, at attention, so unlike the woman El had spoken with just moments before.

"If I'd known this was a party, I'd have changed into a nicer dress," she said, looking down at the shredded pink piece of fluff she wore. Prince Tov snickered at her words, and Gibbs shot her a look of horrified humiliation, as if he couldn't believe she'd just said that. The expressions of Commander Gibbs and Security Head Elis remained the same, emotionless.

They were off to a good start.

CHAPTER 30

"**Y**OU CAN START by removing her handcuffs," Prince Tov commanded, looking at Security Head Elis and Commander Gibbs. Then he turned his attention to El. "And I can start by thanking you for your service last night. I doubt I would be here if not for your bravery." He glared at the two men. "Despite some people's efforts to cover it up."

El narrowed her eyes, questioning, as the woman stepped forward to remove the cuffs.

"They tried pinning it on two other cadets," Gibbs explained.

"And two fine soldiers would have gotten well-deserved attention if someone hadn't insisted on bringing up some unimportant details," the Commander said, giving his son a death glare.

"It's not deserved if they didn't earn it," Gibbs argued.

"And what exactly do you know about earning honor?" the man argued back. "Don't think there won't be consequences for your involvement with all of this."

Yup, she was going to have to kill him. He'd gone and told them everything.

"Does someone want to fill me in on what's going on here?" El asked.

"We brought you here to discuss the terms of your pardon," Security Head Elis stated. He was all business, his face stern and expressionless, as if he was standing before someone else in her position and not his only daughter.

El couldn't believe her ears. "My what now?"

Had he really just said pardon? He couldn't have. It was a dream. It had to be a dream. There was no way he was really talking about pardoning her.

"His Highness was most insistent on it," Security Head Elis explained. "Against strong council otherwise."

She couldn't help thinking how nice it was that her father was making it clear where he stood in all of that. How wonderful to know he was on the side that wanted her executed.

"But Officer Gibbs brought it to our attention that there are other forces at work here, which we wouldn't have learned of if not for your involvement," Commander Gibbs admitted.

How much had it hurt for him to have to admit that—that the head of national security and the Commander of their armed forces had only learned of a huge political plot against their sovereign and their galaxy because of a deserter?

"Unfortunately, Cadet Elisandra Elis has to die," Security Head Elis said. "A Liosi soldier killed a Philosanthrian noble, and it could start a war if Prince Jarrett thinks we didn't sufficiently handle the matter."

Her father declared she would be executed in a cold, emotionless voice, and it was then that it finally hit her—Liosa had never taken her father from her. He had given himself away and willingly, so lost in his own grief over the loss of his wife that he was also willing to sacrifice his daughter along with her.

"So do I die or don't I?" El asked. How did her pardon fit in? Or did they just bring that up to tease her?

"You do," Gibbs said. "But you don't. Cadet Elisandra Elis dies, and you get to become someone else. As far as the galaxy's concerned, you're dead, but for those of us in this room, you're a hero."

"I see," she said. "So that's it then?"

"Unfortunately, yes," Security Head Elis said.

"Unfortunately?" Gibbs questioned. El had seen him stand up to Captain Behnam and push back at her constantly. But to see him speak that way to his commanding officer was another matter entirely. She'd never imagined him to be so bold before. But then, if there was one thing she had learned working with him, it was that Carrigan Gibbs wasn't to be underestimated. "So you don't think she deserves to be rewarded for saving the life of our Prince? For unraveling a plot to utterly destroy us?"

Her father's reply didn't surprise her. "I never thought I'd see the day when we took the assistance of a traitor."

She wanted to fight him, but she bit her tongue. She was safe, pardoned. She'd be free to go, though it pained her that she would never see Liosa again. But she wouldn't have to look over her shoulder every second for people chasing her.

Gibbs, however, must have felt he had less to lose. "Deserter, not traitor. There's a difference."

"Not on Liosa."

Her father had a point, surely Gibbs could see that.

Gibbs looked to her then, seeking something—back up? affirmation? or perhaps he needed one of those plans he was always looking to her for?

She shook her head, hoping he got the message to just let it go. It wasn't worth it. She was free. She was escaping with her life, and that was enough, right?

Right?

She'd come in here with resolve, to speak her mind and make her voice heard. But that was before they had offered her a pardon. If she spoke up, they might take that away from her. They might not let her live after she'd said her piece.

But then, was that not just another act of cowardice? Of running away instead of facing her problems? She had missed Liberation Day, but she could honor those who came before her by earning the blood that pumped through her veins.

"Just because I deserted doesn't mean I wish harm upon my country. I'm loyal to Liosa, even if I can no longer stomach the practices of their military."

"Oh, so now you're an expert in military tactics?" Security Head Elis snorted. "Perhaps you'd like to enlighten us about what exactly it is we're doing wrong."

"That won't be necessary," Commander Gibbs said with a thin smile and shake of his head. "We're bigger than this—there's no need to pick meaningless fights."

"Actually, I would love to," El said, though she knew that wasn't the answer he was wanting.

"Elis," he said, looking her straight in the eyes, his voice a warning.

No.

It was a threat.

And it all made sense then.

El had blamed regents and inexperience for Liosa's involvement in what happened on Taras. But El wasn't the only person in the room who had been there. Her orders had come from someone—Prince Jarett wasn't in charge of Liosi forces, not like that.

A Liosi had to sign off on them.

She'd been so busy looking for the source of the orders, she'd never considered who had given them to her.

No wonder he wanted her pardoned and out of here—because Commander Gibbs wasn't just a coward, he was a traitor.

She was going to regret not shutting her mouth. But she'd run for too long, she was too tired of keeping silent.

"Wiping out an entire planet isn't a military tactic," she said. "It's genocide."

"You should be careful about throwing around words like genocide," the Commander said, his words a growl. She almost laughed at the realization. Her words alone were making him powerless. Commander Gibbs, powerless by the words of a deserter and a fugitive.

"What else would you call it?" she demanded, no longer able to remind calm. He was really standing there trying to silence her after all they'd done; he really felt no remorse. "What else do you call the systematic destruction of an entire planet? The Philosanthrians won't stop until the planet is razed to the ground, and who are we if we've tied ourselves to them?"

The room was silent, the only sound the buzzing of the electric lights overhead. She didn't want to talk about it, but since she'd started, she couldn't stop. The memories bubbled out of her, her anger breaking the dam that had held it all back for so long.

She shouldn't go on, but it was too late.

"You lied to us." She spoke straight to Commander Gibbs because all the times she had blamed Prince Jarett and Radian Darius, she'd never once thought to look a little closer to home.

Liosa hadn't made her a killer, but the man standing before her had.

Oh *victory*, how many lives had she ended? There was blood on her hands she could never make up for, blood she could never be free or redeemed from.

"She's mad," Commander Gibbs said. "Perhaps we were wrong—"

"We were," Gibbs ground out, his expression strangled as he stared at his father, the horror written on his face. Had he come to the same realization as El? And how much harder had it hit him than it had her?

"Perhaps we were," Security Head Elis agreed, looking at Commander Gibbs in a way that said maybe he thought they'd been wrong about the Commander and not El.

"Surely we can't stand here and listen to her."

"I don't think we have any choice but to listen," Prince Tov said. "Did you know about this, Commander?"

"She's mad," the man said again.

"Officer Maren, please escort Commander Gibbs from the room so he can have a chance to settle down and we can get to the bottom of this," Prince Tov ordered.

"You've no right," the man ground out.

"Officer Maren?" Prince Tov simply said, and the Commander was led protesting from the room. Gibbs stared at the door even after it had closed, his jaw squarely set, his expression unreadable. But El knew enough of learning your father wasn't worthy of your respect to know the thoughts that swirled through his mind.

But she didn't have time to dwell on it because Prince Tov turned his attention back to her and said, "I believe you were saying something important."

She told them everything in rushed, breathy sentences as she let it flow from her. As she remembered in vivid detail each and every life she had taken.

She didn't deserve her sessions with Ginger or those little pills that were supposed to fix her brain because she didn't deserve to be fixed. She didn't know how Ginger could sit and listen to her talk without being repulsed beyond belief. How could she not see anything but a monster? How could she still look on her with understanding and compassion, knowing all that she was capable of?

"I don't regret deserting," she said, her voice a whisper because if she spoke any louder, she was scared she might start crying. "I only regret not doing it sooner. I thought I was doing the right thing, that surely if I was fighting for my country, it couldn't be wrong because Liosa couldn't be wrong.

"I know war isn't black and white, and sometimes you make decisions you regret for the greater good. I know it's morally gray, and sometimes it's just plain black. But this? This is wrong. And there's no way to justify it. Nor will I try to. I made a pledge to the Liosi crown and to the flag to defend all those who would seek to destroy what they stand for. No one told me those people would be the very people I made that pledge beside.

"I know what my flag stands for and this isn't it."

They were all silent once more, no one breaking the spell that El had put over the room. Had she shocked them all too much with her words? Perhaps they were simply unable to process or handle what she'd said. Or perhaps they were trying to think up ways to refute it.

Let them if they wanted to; she'd said her piece, and it was up to them what they did with it.

"I had no idea," Prince Tov finally said, his voice low. He looked sad, and El regretted that she'd had to expose someone so innocent to the horrors she'd just admitted. But then, there were people younger than him living it every day. And that, unfortunately, was the weight of the crown he wore. He turned to Security Head Elis. "Why was I never apprised of this situation before now? Why did my advisors never bring it to my attention?"

Her father didn't meet the young man's eyes, and his words were cautious and slow as he said, "It would be easy to pass the blame and say it was not my job to bring the matter to your attention, but in truth, it was simply easier to stay silent. I'm humbled that my own daughter and one of my officers had the courage I lacked."

He was right, it wasn't his job. He protected the Prince, and the wars they fought were not something that concerned him. He was good at that, closing himself off and only focusing on what was right in front of him, ignoring the things that needed his attention but weren't in his job description—like his daughter and his duty as a Liosi.

Prince Tov probably didn't realize it, but for him to admit his guilt—and to give El and Gibbs credit—was no small feat.

The Prince simply nodded and said, "We will discuss this later, in-depth, perhaps over a court-martial." To El, he said, "This will not go unchecked. We will put an end to this, *rook di goo.*"

And then before she knew what was happening, Prince Tov, crown prince of Liosa, was on one knee before her, looking up at her earnestly. "Miss Elis, will you do me the honor of marrying me and becoming the greatest queen Liosa has ever had? You are our savior, and with you by my side, I know we could put an end to all the injustice in the world."

She took a step back, looking to Gibbs, to her father, to see if they were seeing the same thing she was.

It was a dream. It was the only explanation for it. There was no way it was happening, not in real life.

"Your Highness!" both Gibbs and her father exclaimed at the same time. Both looked equally horrified.

The Prince turned to them, his tone level. "I know your position on this, but I can't agree. Liosa was built on strong women who stood up for what they believed in, no matter the consequences. And I'd be a fool to let this one slip through my fingers."

El wanted to laugh. She was standing here, a complete mess—dress in shreds, arms streaked with dirt, face streaked with makeup, barefoot, hair spilling about her shoulders. That was who he was offering his planet to. That was who he wanted to make queen.

"With all due respect," she said, because she couldn't think of anything else to say, "I'm supposed to be dead."

The Prince shook his head, looking a little disappointed that she'd chosen that direction to take the conversation. "None of the Philosanthrians have actually seen your face. With a new name, a fabricated backstory, we could make it work. You saved Liosa from ruin, like a true warrior. That is what our planet needs, someone to keep it on track, to hold it to what is right and true, to remind us of what it truly means to be Liosi."

It was all she had ever wanted to be—someone who lived to make her ancestors proud—a true Liosi. But she had done that, she didn't need more. She didn't want more.

"Thank you, Your Majesty." She hadn't even considered it, not really, but that didn't mean she wasn't a little bit flattered. "But I'm afraid I can't accept."

There was a collective sigh from her father and Gibbs. She understood the sketchiness of the situation, but she was also a little offended that they were all that relieved. She didn't think she'd be that horrible at the job, had she chosen to take it. Surely it wouldn't have been the end of the world.

"Why?" Prince Tov asked. The word came out softly, and as she looked down at him, still on one knee before her, she saw the sorrow in his eyes. He was trying not to show it, but he had been rather brave, putting himself out there as he had, and of course the rejection would hurt.

And so she had to be honest with him, even if it meant being honest with herself about something she had never dared to admit before. "Quite simply, because I think there might be someone else."

Even if she never saw him again. Even if he never felt the same way. She wasn't fully ready to admit the feelings she felt, but she wasn't ready to completely deny them either.

The Prince nodded slowly, looking a little lost and embarrassed by the whole ordeal. "I see." He rose then, getting up from the ground to stand in front of her. "So how can I repay you then, for everything you've done for me and for Liosa?"

"I don't need repayment," she told him. "I am proud of my country and it's my pleasure to serve it. And you're doing enough in pardoning me, for listening and for seeing the truth. I don't need any other form of repayment."

He shook his head, and the confidence returned, his next words firmer, more definitive. "It's not enough. Surely there is something I can do for you—anything. Name it and it's yours—*rook di goo.*"

She looked over to Security Head Elis as he tugged at the collar of his jacket, his eyes wide. The Prince had forgotten to include the customary 'up to half my kingdom' which meant, technically, she could ask for his throne, and he had promised to give it to her. "Your Highness, surely . . . "

But it had already been established that she didn't want his throne, so there was no danger there. "I want it known that Gibbs was sent on a mission, and he not only completed that mission but also helped uncover a plot against the throne bigger than anything we've ever seen before in Liosa. He didn't sign off on anything that happened last night, nor would he have if I had run it by him before acting. So I don't want any of my actions to reflect poorly on him, not when he has done nothing but a spectacular job."

"He harbored a known deserter," her father pointed out.

"Who was arrested at the end of the mission and properly dealt with," El reminded him. "He did his job, and I want him rewarded for it."

"Done," Prince Tov said without a moment's hesitation. "What else?"

Oh *victory*, he wasn't going to let it go, was he?

"I would like a pair of boots." If that was her chance to ask for a pair, she wasn't going to turn it down.

"Boots?" His brow furrowed, confused.

She nodded, finding her courage. "Yes, Your Highness, a pair of standard-issue military boots. Mine mean the galaxy to me, and the worst part of last night was losing them. If I could have them replaced, I'd be forever in your debt."

"Of course," the Prince agreed. "You shall have the boots, and also an open understanding that should anything happen to them, a replacement pair shall be provided. What else? Surely that can't be all you want in exchange for the debt we owe you."

"You owe me nothing," she said. But an idea popped into her head and since he was offering . . . "But perhaps I would accept a new comm and the services of a mechanic to fix the engine on the *Aderyn*—the crew was a large part of our success, and they deserve to be rewarded."

Even if she never saw them again.

The Prince nodded. "Of course, the best there is to be had. But even that isn't enough."

"It is for me," she told him. "I don't need anything else."

"Surely there is more," he said. "I can make you rich or offer you some sort of employment if you'd rather earn the wages yourself. I can open doors for you if you want; just say the word, and I will."

"With all due respect, Your Highness," Gibbs said, stepping forward, "I think she already has a job." He grinned at her questioning look. "He never left; he's waiting for you."

Of course he was. Because Captain Behnam had an eye for lost things, and when he found them, he didn't give them up easily.

"Then I guess I have a job," El said, a wave of emotions crashing over her. She wouldn't cry. She wouldn't. Not in front of all these people. "But I thank you for your generous offer. For everything. Your wife is going to be a very lucky woman someday."

AFTER

EL WAS GIVEN a change of clothes—a comfortable pair of pants, a tee-shirt, and a sweater. And while her boots had been destroyed on the steps that night, she was given a new pair, as promised. They were stiff and new but El looked forward to breaking them in.

Once she had changed, they moved her to the ship that was said to be transporting her back to Liosa. They were actually stopping off on Aliseth for her to be picked up by the *Aderyn*. From there, they would part ways—her to start her new life, the others to return to Liosa to fake her execution.

She was given a packet of papers with her new identity all neatly tucked inside, including a birth certificate that declared she was a Liosi born on Taras—a truth in its own way—and an ID card that proudly displayed her new name.

She had chosen 'El Cynders.' She'd grown rather attached to her nickname the last few weeks and couldn't imagine being called anything else. And the 'Cynders' came from the Liosi national flower, to her a symbol of who she was, where she had come from, and where she was going. She could only imagine how Captain Behnam would react, though, to her taking such a sentimentally patriotic name.

The trip only lasted a few days, which she spent cooped up in her room—not by orders but more because, as much as she appreciated all he had done, she was trying to avoid Prince Tov.

She made friends with Officer Maren—the soldier she'd spoken with after her arrest—and they were able to talk about what had happened on Taras; it felt good to have someone who understood. Gibbs spent a good deal of time with her, too, and she laughed to herself, thinking of how far they had come; she had actually come to enjoy his company.

She left her room only to speak with the medic on board—for sessions not quite as good as Ginger's, but helpful all the same, and for the medication she'd finally worked up the courage to take.

She didn't see her father once and, strangely enough, she found she was okay with that. He'd stood up for her in the end, but it didn't erase all the years he hadn't. He could admire her actions, perhaps even be proud of them, but he could do it from afar and without her.

And then, finally, the ship landed.

The *Aderyn* was waiting for them, and El stepped off the ship, a little embarrassed as she saw Captain Behnam waiting with that inviting grin of his as he leaned against the ship, as if he hadn't a care in the world. So unlike the first time she had met him. She found she really liked that grin. Maybe even a little too much.

Maybe taking a job with him was a dangerous idea.

But even if it was, she wasn't going to run away from it. Not anymore. She was done being a runner.

She felt a hand on her shoulder, and she turned to find Gibbs standing behind her with a sheepish grin on his face. He held his hands on either side of him, his eyes a question, and, even though she'd never been big on physical touch, she drew her friend into a hug.

"Don't get into too much trouble without me," she said as she embraced him; she couldn't believe it, but she was actually going to miss Gibbs.

He laughed. "I think trouble will be far easier to avoid without you around. And I'm going to miss it—you—dearly."

He returned to the ship, leaving El standing in the middle of a sandy desert on Aliseth with nothing to her name but some "borrowed" clothes, a packet of papers, a whole lot of emotional baggage she wasn't sure she was ready to unpack yet, and Captain Behnam.

"Hey," he said. He worried his lip a moment and then pulled something out of his pocket. She recognized the bit of orange and green ribbon immediately. "You—ah—you missed Liberation Day, and I thought you'd want . . . "

It was a Liberation Day cockade, just a bit of ribbon meant to look like their national flower; everyone wore them to commemorate their victory, their independence, their freedom. And even though he claimed he didn't understand, Captain Behnam had gotten her one and made a point of giving it to her.

She blinked back the tears. "Thank you."

They stood there, looking at each other, as the Liosi ship took off behind her, making too much noise for either of them to say anything else. But they didn't go inside the *Aderyn* either, both standing there, just waiting.

She didn't want to go in just yet, where Trapp and Ginger waited; she wanted a moment alone with the Captain first.

Not that she knew what she was going to say once it was quiet enough.

But then she didn't have to, because it was the Captain who spoke first. "So, I heard the Prince offered you anything in the galaxy, and you walked away with a pair of boots and a new comm."

He set the tone for the conversation, easy and light, and it felt good to know things hadn't changed between them. In everything else that was uncertain in her life, at least that was solid. "What else do I need? I have my boots, I have my job—thank you for that, by the way—and I have . . . " She trailed off, unsure if she should say it. But she found she needed to, needed to put it out into the world so that it was said and known. "I have a family."

A lopsided grin broke out across his perfect face. "Yeah, well, I didn't get a chance to discuss it with you before, but I was thinking about making you my first mate. If that was okay with you."

First mate. *Victory*, she liked the sound of that. "When you got arrested, Ginger said I ought to be in charge because you'd get around to making me first mate eventually."

He laughed at that, and she couldn't help thinking it was one of the greatest sounds in the world. "She's rarely wrong. If you want it, the job's yours."

If she wanted it. As if there was any doubt. "I do. I do want it. Thank you."

"I was thinking too, maybe it's time you started calling me Leiv? Like the others do?"

Leiv. It was personal, though whether like a friend or something more, she didn't know. But the good thing was, she didn't have to figure it out right away. "I think I can do that. Leiv."

He nodded, ducking his head, opening his mouth and then closing it again, nothing coming out. There was a pause before he looked up at her with an earnest expression on his face. "Gibbs told me about everything that went down—you know, with the Prince and everything."

"Did he . . . ?" she asked. Was he going to reprimand her once more for being foolish, or was that jealousy she heard creeping into his voice?

There was a pause again as he looked down at the ground then looked back up at her. "He said you told His Highness that you thought there might be someone else?"

"Yeah . . . " She hadn't meant for that to get back to him. If only Gibbs were there for her to tell him just exactly what she thought of him for tattling on her. Except Gibbs wasn't going to be around for her to want to tease and argue with anymore.

"Is he someone I know . . . ?" the Captain asked.

There was something about the way he said it, the way he was looking at her, the hope and the question in his eyes; they all made her bold, and so she didn't even think about it when she blurted out, "I would hope you know him because he's you."

He froze, looking at her with wide eyes, and El knew she had said the wrong thing. She'd had a chance at an amazing new life, and she'd botched the whole thing. That was why she ran—because it was easier than facing things like that. She was about to get shot down, rejected, and then she was going to have to either work with him or stay on a desert planet that was already too dry for her liking.

"And I understand if you don't feel the same way," she hurried to say, because it needed to be said. "I—I'm not even sure what it is I feel. But if you're open to figuring it out, together, I—well, I wouldn't be opposed to that."

"Would you just let me get a word in?" he said, but he was grinning, grinning at her so easily that she knew everything was going to be all right. It was going to be more right than it had been in such a long time, maybe being righter than it had ever been.

She stopped talking, pulling in her lips and looking at him expectantly. He let her wait too, for a long moment, just standing there, silent. Then when she was just about to say something because she couldn't take it any longer, he finally spoke.

"I think I'd like to figure this out too, yeah," he said, offering her that easy smile, telling her nothing had changed between them with her words. And yet, at the same time, everything had changed.

Trapp's head appeared in the opening of the ship. "Are you two coming aboard or not?"

Leiv held out his hand to her, his expression a question, and she took it, finding no tingle, no shock, just a warmth that spread through her.

She laughed then, because if she didn't laugh, she would have cried. She had never felt so happy in her entire life, and she couldn't believe that it got to be the rest of her life. It welled inside of her until she thought she might burst with the feeling.

For the first time since her mother had died, she wanted to run, not away from something but *to* something—to happiness, to life, to fulfillment, even to love. So she let herself laugh as she responded with the only thing that made sense.

"Yes."

Rook di goo, rook di goo
There will be blood within this coup
We know what's right
So we'll stand and fight
Hey, ho, rook di goo, we'll live free forever after

-From a Traditional Liosi War Song

BONUS MATERIAL

ROOK DI GOO PLAYLIST

The Story of Tonight by We the Kings—a song for the Liosi

High Hopes by Panic! At The Disco

Something Just Like This by The Chainsmokers—El and Leiv's song

Luck by American Authors

You'll Always Be My Best Friend by Relient K—El and Leiv's song

Unpack Your Heart by Philip Philips—a song for the Aderyn crew

Think About It by American Authors

Walk Me Home by P!nk—El and Leiv's song

Getaway by Saint Motel—the "you took out a hit on me!" scene

Home by American Authors

Gravity by Sara Bareilles—El's song for Liosa

Worn by Tenth Avenue North

I so Hate Consequences by Relient K—El's workout song

Nine by Sleeping at Last—El is a very definite Enneagram 9

Eight by Sleeping at Last—with a strong Wing 8

Be Kind to Yourself by Andrew Peterson

Noble Blood by Tommee Profitt—a song for Liosi soldiers

She Said by Jon Foreman

Gone, Gone, Gone by Philip Philips—a song for the Aderyn crew

Mars by Sleeping at Last—a song for the Liosi fighting on Taras

Home by Philip Philips—a song for the Aderyn crew

Haunted by Taylor Swift—El's song for Liosa

Home from Bright: The Album

Up All Night by Owl City—Prince Tov's song

Fine By Me by Andy Grammer—for the end scene

The Outsiders by NEEDTOBREATHE—first end credits song

Invincible by David Archuleta—second end credits song

CHARACTER LOVE LETTERS

Somewhere in the midst of working on this book I wrote love letters to the main characters that detailed how they came into being, why I love them, and my hopes for them. It is one of my favorite writing exercises I've ever done and I wanted to share them—and a piece of my heart—with you.

Dear El,

You were born because of a typewriter. It was gray and electronic and had a cover that was nearly impossible to open; it hurt my fingers every time I tried. It used to work but by the time it got exiled to the basement it didn't anymore.

Maybe I'd read a sci-fi book recently or maybe it was just the mood I was in, but as it sat there looking all cool and spacey, I knew I needed to create a character who it belonged to.

I never shared that game with anyone—by the time you came along, everyone else had outgrown imagination games—and so it was just you and me. You had black hair then and the name "Simrey" because I thought that was cool.

You were smart—you spoke twenty different languages and had attended an elite college on a full-ride scholarship. Your major was "communications" and operating a comm was your forte.

There was hardly any plot, though what it did have was always tied to your father. He was controlling and decided about your life and you were a duty-filler. You were always determined to please him, letting him choose your career path even though you wanted to be a teacher. But nothing you did was ever enough.

Your story, at its core, has always been about your healing. It's always been about you finding yourself, about growing into who you are as you seek to discover who exactly that even is.

When I played your game, I mostly just ran around pretending to be you, yelling things in frenzied panic into the comm and meeting new people and creatures on strange and wonderful planets. You had never been far from your planet before and while you knew all about these planets' languages and customs, you were fascinated with actually getting to know them in person.

You're more jaded and cynical now than that girl who experienced the worlds with wide-eyed wonder but I still see her in you. It comes out when you're solving problems, that little bit of unbridled delight, and I can see the joy that shines in your eyes whenever it happens. The others see it and it brings them joy too.

The captain feeds off that energy when you work together, your enthusiasm giving way to his own. That's part of why he loves you—because you bring that out in him in ways no one else ever has. There are so many other reasons, which you are too self-deprecating to acknowledge, but that is a major one.

I added the prince years later, after it had grown from a game into an actual story idea. The typewriter was long gone and I had all but stopped playing in the basement anymore. But you were still there.

The story never went anywhere. I set it aside and all but forgot about it, save a Pinterest board I would pull out once in a while and look at longingly. But it was never the right time and I knew it.

Then I started writing the other books in this galaxy and I knew. I loved you and the crew of your ship so much and I knew you would fit perfectly into this world. Except your story wasn't a fairy tale retelling.

I started puzzling and pondering and trying to make it into a retelling. I don't remember if Cinderella was the first I thought of or if I considered others first. But Cinderella just stuck. I knew the moment I thought of it that I could make it work, the details I'd already had in mind for the story fitting so well with the details of the original fairy tales.

You grew then. You were always practical and pragmatic, always reasonable, always smart. But now you have an extra layer of depth, your pain more real and more traumatic. Your brain has leveled out too, going from almost inhuman level of smarts to a more realistic version of that, a more nuanced level of brainpower.

I put you through more pain too, no longer just tired of being part of something you never wanted to be, but now trapped in the memory of horrible, horrible things. I was struggling when I wrote this version of your story and I gave you some of the darkest, ugliest parts of myself.

I'm sorry for that. The pain gives way to even brighter things though and that's why I did it. I allowed you to break and heal as a promise to myself that the breaking wasn't the end. That learning to sleep through the night wasn't just a dream, that finding your people was something attainable.

You're an incredible young woman and one I almost can't believe I get to call mine. You've let me into your heart and mind and I appreciate you entrusting me with your story. I promise to do my best to tell it and to tell it well. I promise to try to do it justice and show the world the pieces of you I've been given to share.

I want the world to know how special you are. To see how special your story is. I hope your journey—your searching and longing and questioning—will help others with their own journey. I hope that they too can find a place to call home and to understand the meaning of that. I hope they can learn to love the broken pieces of their lives and see the flaws in the things they love while still holding it dear.

I hope they can grow and learn and change as you have, to discover who they are and the incredible wealth of strength they have within them. Your story is for fighters. For searchers. For longers.

Thank you for trusting me. I promise to take care of you in the same way you've taken care of me. I'll be there for you, the same way you've been for me and I hope you'll be for countless others.

You are strong and you are able, El. You are a fighter and a survivor.

Don't ever stop being you.

Humbly your author,

Jenni

Dear Leiv,

You are my most frustrating character.

When I wrote my first draft of these letters years ago, you never got one. Because I didn't know what to say to you. What was there to say to the man I hardly knew?

You've had at least three different names and while your personality has stayed much the same I never knew why you were the way you were. It was like pulling teeth trying to unlock your backstory. You hate talking to me, the same way you hate talking to everyone else.

But you slowly have. You keep showing me more and more and it all makes sense. This final draft really showed your loyal side, the way you'll do anything for your friends and how easily friends become family.

I've always known you struggled with the pressure of trying to live up to the expectations. I always thought they were expectations placed on you by your parents and it wasn't even until draft 5 that I really realized that didn't make sense. You are the only person in this book that has good parents. It made no sense for you to struggle with that pressure.

It was then that I realized the pressure came from everyone else. Being Mr. and Mrs. Behnam's son is amazing. I know you wouldn't trade it for the world. But sometimes it's hard. You don't get seen as Leiv, you're just one of the Behnam kids.

I've been there—loving the legacy your parents give you but also struggling to live up to it. You know you make them proud by just existing but you also want to be worthy of your name—of their name.

You know what it means to have a good family and you want to share that with people. You're the only one on the *Aderyn* who isn't part of this found family because of tragedy. You open your heart to those who don't have family because it breaks you to think that these people—these wonderful, amazing people you love with your whole heart—don't have the family they deserve.

It started with Trapp, when he showed up on your family's doorstep and somewhere along the way he went from being your best friend to being your brother. You didn't even think about it, it just happened.

Ginger came into your life much the same way. You thought one little sister was enough but then there was Ginger and everything changed.

El, well she's a different kind of family, but you've always known that. From the moment she stepped onto your ship she was different. She wormed her way into your heart and you were a willing victim. You would follow that girl to the end of the galaxy and back again with only mild protesting.

She needs you. Ginger needs you. Trapp needs you. Even Gibbs needs you, though he'd be the last to admit that. But they don't need you to be anything more than yourself. Leiv Behnam is enough for them. You don't have to prove yourself or perform for them. You have and always will be enough.

This may surprise you, but people love you. And I know more and more people are going to love you as they are given the opportunity to meet you. From that first moment you appear, scowl on your face, grumpily saving El's life as only you can, you are someone worth loving.

Thank you for being a constant in this story. As so much else changed, thank you for always being there, steady and stable.

Thank you for being a constant in my life—as El broke alongside me, you were the stable parts of me. In my darkest times, you reminded me of who I was at my core. You reminded me of the good times, of the happy childhood I did have, of the parents who love me. You remind me what it is to be healthy and that sometimes even the healthy struggle and that's okay.

I wish I could tell more of your story, wish the world could see more of you. But in true Leiv fashion, you're just going to be a steady constant in the background of the future books.

I'm glad you'll be there though. Because at their heart, so many books set in this world are about the people Leiv Behnam saved, in one way or another. And that's a really special role to fill. I don't think there's anyone else who could fill it.

Keep flying, keeping being you, don't be afraid to push back when El gets a little too bossy. Life is good, it's okay to enjoy it.

Loyally Yours,

Jenni

Dear Trapp,

You used to be a mechanic. You were hipster and even a little emo and just all around a downer who people still seemed to like. You and Leiv were friends, even before his name was changed.

And El . . . you were actually engaged to her. You two were once young and in love but you let her dad pay you off to leave. You had your reasons; I don't remember what all they were, I just remember how angry you were at El, for being angry with you. As much as she felt you were at fault, as much as she felt abandoned by you, so too you felt justified in your anger, so too you blamed her.

I almost kept that subplot when I started writing but I didn't because a later book in the series includes a relationship with the same anger and heartbreak yours was supposed to.

I also didn't want anything to get in the way of El and Leiv's relationship.

Plus you were someone different at that point. I had stolen the emo mechanic for another story and I didn't want the *Aderyn* to have a permanent mechanic at this point. You became the pilot in this stage of development and also Leiv's best friend. You became snark and good-natured teasing, the easygoing crewman with a lopsided smile and ears that are just a little too big.

You also became the only one who knew all of Leiv's secrets, his childhood friend who always stands by him, though you don't always agree with him, nor do you have any issue calling him on his crap. You were the person I never realized he needed in his life.

You mean the world to him. When people talk about friends you're the person who pops into his head. You're his best friend, his brother, his partner-in-crime (literally and metaphorically). You're important to the *Aderyn*—you keep the others grounded, which is ironic since your job is literally to keep them flying.

You bring something special to life—not quite a cynic but also not entirely an optimist. You're a realist who sees the world as it is—beautiful and terrifying and light and dark and complex. It isn't all good or all bad, nor does it lean one way or the other. It's full of pockets of goodness and pockets of evil but neither keeps you from seeing the other. I want to see the world through your eyes more often.

You're good at hiding it, but I know how hard it is for you to show up as much as you do. I know how much you doubt and how much the fear creeps in. You wrestle with the questions and the terribly inconvenient thing known as human nature. But you also push through. You're the epitome of "scared but did it anyway."

I want you to be nothing but happy. I want you to find the joy in life that you bring to others. I want you to live life to the fullest, to get the most joy and excitement out of it. Nothing holds you back, nothing stops you from living and doing and experiencing.

I want you to have all the adventures. And then I want you to annoy the heck out of some amazing woman until she falls madly in love with you. I want you to fall in love with her and get married and raise incredible kids. I want you to live to be ridiculously old and still stay young at heart until the day you die.

I am so grateful you're who you are now instead of that angsty mechanic you originally were. I'm grateful to have you in my life. Thank you for sharing yourself with me and with the world. You have so much to give; thank you for choosing to give it in this way.

With Love,

Jenni

Dear Ginger,

You came into creation when I created the first Pinterest board for El's story. You were a nurse whose tech was a lot more advanced than it is now, you were blonde, and your name was Aida.

You became a medic rather than a nurse way too far into my second draft. I'm ashamed to say it took me far too long to realize you didn't have to be a nurse and it just made more sense for you to be a medic. I think I've just been conditioned by media—sci-fi medics tend to either be male or tougher, harder. I'm sorry it took me so long to give you the credit you deserved.

Your bond with the captain was the same, the friendship that runs so deep it's basically blood. I never knew why, didn't know your past or what brought you to that place but I knew how you felt about him. He was always your brother, always your friend. He has always thought the galaxy of you and I knew that couldn't change in this version of the story.

You were Rapunzel first and your personality was born out of hers. It was tricky though, as I tried to write a spunky, rebellious girl and you kept quietly informing me that you'd much rather follow the rules, please and thank you. How do you make your Rapunzel a rebel if she's a good girl?

That's why your past is so messed up, so complicated. It made sense, shaping out of the rule follower who was traversing the galaxy looking for the man she loved.

Monti didn't have a name yet but I knew he was going to be your downfall from the start. I named him Raiden after a while but that never really fit his goofy personality, I just liked the name. He wasn't like the prince in the original tale because you didn't fall for him after your first meeting. He was your childhood friend, the guy who was always there, a bestie who annoyed you to no end. I loved the two of you from the moment I created you.

I don't remember when you became Juliet—probably somewhere in the midst of developing your backstory. Or maybe I was reading about Romeo and Juliet and decided I wanted to retell it and you were a good way. I'm sorry I don't remember. But I'm not sorry I made the choice.

The more tragic your backstory became, the more I broke you, the sweeter you became. You became a survivor, a fighter, a believer. I'm sorry I put you through so much. Sometimes I can't believe the things that happened in your past and then I'm blown away when I remember that it's my doing.

You don't deserve any of it. You should have nothing but goodness, happiness, joy. That's what you bring to everyone around you, even though by all rights you should be bitter, cynical, and closed. But no. Not you. You build people up even though life has done nothing but tear you down. You bring light even though you're surrounded by darkness. You see goodness in a world that has done its best to show you nothing but evil.

You have my heart, dear one. You inspire me more than words can say. I want to see the world the way you do, to look at people through your eyes. I want to face adversity with that same courage and strength. I want to be able to come out on the other side of trouble with the same softness you have.

I know it isn't always sunshine for you though. I know it's hard for you. Some days every second is a fight not to give up, not to break down. You cry far too often. I know you take care of others because you can't take care of yourself. You cling to Leiv and his friendship because he's one of the very few people who hasn't hurt you in all of this.

I know you wonder if it's all worth it. You wonder if maybe you should just give up. Maybe everyone else it right—maybe you don't get to have a happily ever after, maybe your love does end in tragedy.

Look to the stars, dear one. Always look upward and don't look back, except to see just how far you've come. And never forget who you are and how hard you fought to be that person. You have every reason to be proud of what you've accomplished; stop beating yourself up for the things you haven't.

Thank you for sharing your heart with me. Thank you for being your sweet, beautiful self. Thank you for letting me tell your story.

I promise I'll try to tell it well. I promise I'll share you with others so they can know it's going to be okay. So they can see that hardship doesn't have to break you. So they can see good in a world of darkness.

Thank you for being patient with me while I figured out who you are. Thank you for trusting me even as I hurt you more and more. I promise it will be worth it. And I promise your story will inspire others.

I wish I could give you the hug you so desperately deserve, but since I can't I'll say instead—go hug someone today. Hug them hard and tight. I'd recommend Leiv, but the choice is yours.

Chin up, dear one. It will get better and it will be worth it. I promise.

With All My Heart,

Jenni

Dear Gibbs,

I'm sorry to say you were almost never created.

I was well into the second draft of my story, feeling like I was close to finishing it, but something was just . . . missing. I didn't know what though.

You came into being in Minnesota, at a High Kings concert. My brain likes to solve story problems at the strangest times and for some reason at the concert—which I enjoyed very much, by the way—my brain decided you needed to come into being.

I liked the idea as soon as I got it. Before this it was Prince Tov on the *Aderyn* running around with El at the balls, trying to save Liosa. Except I kept feeling like Tov was acting out of character and didn't know why. But then I created you and it all made sense.

All the times the prince was acting out of character it turned out that was actually your character. Your sweet, stubborn character.

I love you. You bring something to the story Tov never did when he was in your place. Unlike him, you just fit. It all make sense. You're just right for this role.

Since the story is from El's perspective it also means the world will never get to know you any better than she does. They won't get to see all the things you've suffered, the things you've overcome, the things you've fought to get as far ahead as you are.

But I see it, the demons you suffer from. I see how hard you fight each and every day. And I see that you aren't nearly as arrogant or as confident as you pretend to be.

You're a good man, Carrigan Gibbs, a very good man. You make my story so much better.

I hope others see that. That they all go from "I wanted to smack him" to "I love him" because, while sometimes you deserve to be smacked, you also most definitely deserve the love.

Thank you for being part of my story. Thank you for adding to it. Thank you for being you.

You're going to go far. I can promise you that. You have a good head on your shoulders and a very good mind inside that head. I see nothing but good in your future if you just keep holding on. You're a fighter, you are, and that's going to take you far.

I'm excited to explore all that but, in the meantime, know that you'll always hold a special place in my heart. Don't ever forget how much you're worth and know that the people who matter do notice. Don't ever think they don't.

You've got this, Gibbs.

Respectfully Yours,

Jenni

ACKNOWLEDGEMENTS

My favorite part of a book is that section at the end where the author gives us a glimpse of all the love and support they received through their book's process. But I find they're a lot less fun to write because how can I even begin to express the gratitude overflowing within me? And no one told me how emotional I'd get, reliving all that nostalgia. The people mentioned here deserve more than a paragraph, but unfortunately, that's all I have the space for:

Mama and Vati—your overwhelming support of me and my writing is too great to list out here. You go above and beyond for me, always, and I don't thank you enough for it—I never could. You've give me every opportunity to pursue my writing, to grow in my craft, and didn't complain, even when it seemed like I was just sitting at my computer all day. You talk me through every doubt, share every excitement, listen to me ramble as I talk things through, and have believed in me since before I even understood what that concept was.

Great Aunt Yentl—for your support, wisdom, and feedback. Seriously, love, this book wouldn't be a thing without you. You believed in it long before others knew to and it was only because of you that this book isn't tucked safely in a folder somewhere, never to be spoken of again. Your passion and support mean so much to me. Whether it's offering feedback, helping me brainstorm, or fangirling, it brought this book to life and I owe you big for it. Also you willingness to answer all my mental health questions and make sure it is both represented well and that my own mental health isn't compromised is invaluable. I hope you know the *Aderyn* would be proud to have you on their crew, even if you would try to steal Leiv from El and we can't have that . . .

Hannah—you've been there, always, for so many stages of this book. Encouraging me and supporting me and just . . . being you. You believe in me and push me forward and always knew I'd get here, even when I doubted it. Thank you for always matching my energy—while you may tease me for being dramatic, you've been there for every valley defeat and mountaintop victory and have always given it the same gravity I have. Thank you for all the million tiny things you do—for being my girl in the chair. You're always down for my random messages and I appreciate that.

Stephie—I always thought I only needed one sister and then God gave me you and proved me so wrong; I never knew what I was missing until you came along. Your unmitigated love and support is more than I will ever deserve. Bribing me to write words, listening to me rant at any given moment about story stuff, encouraging me when I'm down, matching my energy when I'm excited, always proud of me and believing in me. You have no idea how much I appreciate you.

Selina—you are such a constant pillar of support and there are no words for how much I appreciate your friendship. You're a wonderful mix of supportive and rational and I need that. Also your ability to pinpoint my story's weaknesses coupled with your unwavering encouragement is so helpful. Thank you for loving me where I am while never being afraid to push me to meet my potential. Even if we don't remember how it happened, I'm so grateful we became such close friends.

Abby—you are one of the kindest souls God ever created. I love your bright, sassy personality. The love and support you've given this book means so much. It's so pure and raw and genuine and I appreciate it more than I can say.

Jessie—your unbridled enthusiasm and support of me and this book has blown me away. You take every chance to encourage me, to share about this book, and to make me feel well and truly loved. Thank you.

Meredith—you took the time to really dig into Rook Di Goo and the work you put into it really made it a much better book. I felt so much better doing my final edits and going through your comments. I know it's far better than what I had before thanks to you. I especially appreciate you being willing to read it even though it's not your usual genre and I'm so happy you enjoyed it!

Andrea—you are one of the most honest souls I know and even the hard stuff always comes from a place of love. Thank you for digging so deeply into my book and truly pushing me to make it amazing. And thank you for always speaking the truth.

Savanna—you have been such a constant and I appreciate you more than I can say. Your kind heart, your unique creativity, your unwavering support, they mean so much to me. Also thanks for your wonderful proofreading services—really needed those . . . I look forward to working with you in the future and seeing how much better my stories can be with your help.

Elly—your feedback meant so much. Thank you for taking the time to read my story and for giving me such glowing praise. It meant so, so much. And also for pinpointing a problem area I hadn't seen before.

Lina—your positive encouragement makes me feel like I could conquer the (publishing) world. I am grateful for your friendship, your love, and your support, always. I can't wait for our books to sit on a shelf together!

Rosie—thank you for taking the time to read my book, for giving me feedback, for always being excited and encouraging, for being a constant supporter.

Penny, Bekah, and Jessica—for being part of my group chat and for all the little ways you go out of your way to support me. You've always showed up for me, showing enthusiasm and support, going above and beyond for me. I don't know where I'd be without you <3

Gabby—you'll probably laugh when you see this, but you did save me so much time (and sanity) by suggesting I use my phone for edits. Simple, yes, but necessary. Plus, even if it doesn't come into play in this book, you did help me with that Ginger problem. So thanks.

Garrett and Chelsea—for all the character games and prompts and for being part of my little Facebook group. You were a key part of this book's toddler years and developmental stages. It wouldn't be here without you.

The Arantar critique group—such a fun SW, I adored you all, thanks for being such an amazing critique group.

Allie—you aren't in my life anymore and that's okay but you were a huge part of this book coming to be—working through my problem scenes with me, listening to me rant and squeal, helping with little details to add depth—so I'd be remiss for not mentioning you here. You were there for me through this and I can admit that it meant a lot, even if I don't need you here anymore.

The Gragers—Spencer and Susie, you'll probably never even see this but you need to be mentioned because a good portion of the first draft of this was written on your kitchen floor. I know I could have written on the couch or at a table, but the kitchen floor just happened; I was comfy, I promise. This book might not even be a thing if not for those couple hours a day, sneaking in as many words as I could while your son napped. So thank you, for so many things, but specifically here for the unknowing role you played in bringing this book into the world.

Isabel Luke—you'll probably never see this, but I once promised I'd put you in all my acknowledgements so here we are. I miss getting to talk stories with you and see all your creative endeavors. And if you do see this, I hope you know you're worth keeping promises to.

And the members of the Bookstagram and Writers of Instagram communities—you have all made it such a welcoming space that gave me so much confidence when I made the choice to publish this book. You've invested in me in so many ways both big and small. If your name isn't on the list here, don't think it means I don't see you or appreciate you. There isn't enough space for me to list you all, but I do see all you do—the likes, the comments, the messages, the encouragement, the enthusiasm—and your support is invaluable. You make me feel like I can do anything and you wouldn't be holding this book right now if it wasn't for all the support you've poured into me.

ABOUT THE AUTHOR

Jenni Sauer is a 20-something city girl from New York (but no, not The City). A pragmatic optimist, she writes fairy tale retellings woven with realism and laced with hope, striving to offer light that shines in, rather than denies the darkness. She's been telling stories since before she could even hold a pencil and hasn't slowed down since.

When not writing she spends her time nannying, overanalyzing stories, buying too many candles, and investing in her friends and the #bookstagram and writing communities on Instagram. You can find her there @ivorypalaceprincess or on her website:

www.ivorypalacepress.com

Made in the USA
Middletown, DE
18 August 2023

36954454R00250